## DATE DUE

BN 6/17

# To Follow Her Heart

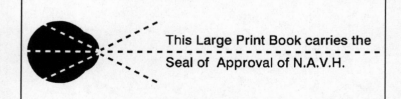

This Large Print Book carries the
Seal of Approval of N.A.V.H.

THE SOUTHOLD CHRONICLES, BOOK 3

# To Follow Her Heart

## Rebecca DeMarino

**THORNDIKE PRESS**
*A part of Gale, Cengage Learning*

GALE
CENGAGE Learning®

Farmington Hills, Mich • San Francisco • New York • Waterville, Maine
Meriden, Conn • Mason, Ohio • Chicago

GALE
CENGAGE Learning®

LIBRARY OF CONGRESS CATALOGING-IN-PUBLICATION DATA

Names: DeMarino, Rebecca, author.
Title: To follow her heart / by Rebecca Demarino.
Description: Waterville, Maine : Thorndike Press, 2016. | Series: The Southold chronicles ; #3 | Series: Thorndike Press large print Christian romance
Identifiers: LCCN 2016040625| ISBN 9781410495754 (hardcover) | ISBN 1410495752 (hardcover)
Subjects: LCSH: Large type books. | GSAFD: Love stories. | Christian fiction.
Classification: LCC PS3604.E4544 T63 2016b | DDC 813/.6—dc23
LC record available at https://lccn.loc.gov/2016040625

Published in 2017 by arrangement with Revell Books, a division of Baker Publishing Group

Printed in Mexico
1 2 3 4 5 6 7 21 20 19 18 17

Dedicated to
Tom DeMarino,
my husband and my true North Star

In loving memory of
Lory DeMarino,
my mother-in-law,
who left a legacy of faith and love —
1925 to 2015

# 1

*July 16, 1664*
*Southold, Long Island*

"Did you hear me?"

Patience Terry stood silent, her mind awhirl. Had she not guarded her heart against this day? Against this pain that ripped through her like a thunderbolt? She looked into Mary Horton's teary hazel-blue eyes. *The Swallow* had shipwrecked off the coast of Barbados, tattered and abandoned. No survivors. Captain Jeremy Horton and his crew lost at sea. Some bodies recovered, but no survivors.

Her mouth opened, but no words came out. Her lungs ached, so bereft were they of any air, she of any hope. As her legs gave way, she fell to the pillowed bench in front of the hat display and buried her face in the folds of her blue silk skirt. Her shoulders heaved with each silent sob.

Her friend knelt and drew her into her

arms. "That's good, dear. Cry. Let the tears fall."

Patience could no longer hold back as torrents of tears soaked Mary's shoulder. Her friend's gentle hands patted her back to comfort, but her temples pulsed with each new thought. Would she never be able to look up and see Jeremy's form framed in the doorway again? Or could he lie hurt somewhere? She'd begged him at his last visit to give up the sailing, to make a home here in Southold. One she dreamt would include her.

"What if he's not dead? What if he needs me?" She'd always prayed he would come to know he needed her in his life, but Lord, this was not how she'd envisioned it.

"You mustn't think like that. The ship has sunk. There was such a storm. And if survivors were able to make land at all, they would have landed on the shores of Barbados. Nathaniel Sylvester brought the news himself. He's just returned from his meetings there. 'Tis such a shock to know both of Barney's brothers are gone. It was so difficult when Thomas died. And now Jeremy. He was more than a friend to me, he was a dear brother." Mary's voice trailed as Patience's sobs began anew.

The door blew open as hurricane-strength

wind and summer rain swept in with Lizzie Fanning's arrival, nearly lifting one of her own hat creations from her silvery curls. Mary's older sister and Patience's business partner, Lizzie looked in control as she slid the burgundy wool from her head, gave it a good shake, and settled it on a hat stand. "Mary told me on her way over here. I'm so sorry." She enveloped her friend in a hug, her own tears trickling from violet eyes. She looked up at Mary. "I came immediately after I got my loaves out of the oven. Zeke is on his way to your house."

Patience did not try to hide her pain as tears escaped in rivulets down her cheeks. She'd never told them in so many words of her love for Jeremy, but the two sisters had pulled her into their family long ago, and matters of the heart were understood rather than spoken.

Her sobs subsided into soft hiccups, and she drew in a breath. "What now?" was all she could whisper.

Mary reached out to smooth Patience's locks. "Barnabas said he would talk to Reverend Youngs about a service for Jeremy. We should have a dinner." She looked at her sister.

Lizzie nodded. "He shall not be forgotten."

Patience shook her head. "We don't know that he's dead, though. Why would he not listen to me when I begged him to stop sailing? To stay here? Why could he not see that this would happen?"

"He was doing what he loved." Mary didn't look Patience in the eye as she uttered the sentence.

"You don't believe your own words. Why do people always say such things? It does not help. I just want him back. Happy or not, I want him here."

Mary blinked. "I know, I know. We all loved him. But I know for you 'tis especially difficult. He loved you. I know he did." She pulled a fresh handkerchief from her apron pocket and mopped Patience's cheeks.

"I treasured the time we spent together. But it wasn't enough, was it? Why could he not love me enough to stay by my side and be my husband?" She took the embroidered cloth from Mary and delicately blew her nose, then turned to Lizzie. "I cannot work with you today. I'm sorry. I should like to spend the day by myself." She looked from one to the other. "I love you both dearly, but I need time alone."

Lizzie wrapped her arms around Patience's shoulders. "Of course. But allow us to bring you a crock of soup or some tea

10

and biscuits. You must eat." She turned to Mary. "Could you help her upstairs?"

"Of course. Come, Patience." Mary led her to the staircase. "Let me build you a small fire while you change into a robe. It shall bring some comfort to the room."

Mary padded down the stairs. She sniffed. A savory scent filled the house. "That smells good. Patience is sleeping now. I should go home to see how Barney is faring. He and Jeremy were so close — I fear he is taking this very hard. Will you be all right?"

Lizzie stirred the simmering soup, then tasted the broth. "I have enough work here to keep me busy while she rests. I need to take stock of my supplies. When Heather Flower came last, she brought two large bags of beads." She nodded toward the shelves Ben had built for her.

Mary stood on tiptoe and peered into one of the bags. "Beautiful. She is amazing, and she's never forgotten to come back and visit." Heather Flower was the daughter of the Montaukett sachem — a princess to the English — and had almost married Mary's son Ben. In a strange turn of events, she instead married a Dutch lieutenant from New Amsterdam. But she remained loyal to her English friends, too, and Dirk had kept his promise to bring her back often.

Mary took her cape from the peg and slipped into it. "Very well, then. I'm off. Thank you for staying with Patience."

"She will be all right. There's much to keep me busy in the hat shop. Tell Barnabas I am so sorry."

"I shall." She opened the door to the wind whipping outside and hurried down the lane, pulling her hood close against the slanted rain. She paused at the parsonage and cemetery on the left and thought once more of poor Jeremy before she crossed over to her home.

In the foyer, she brushed the raindrops from her cape and hung it near the hearth. It was still early and the house quiet. Barney would be in the back kitchen, having his devotions and stirring up the fire — perhaps putting the first loaves in the oven.

She mounted the stairs and stood quietly as she watched her daughters. Hannah, her firstborn daughter and quite the little mother, brushed and braided Mercy's hair. At four years old, Mercy was the youngest of their nine children and loved the attention her siblings bestowed. Mary smiled as Sarah, eleven, smoothed and aired out the bedclothes, while young Mary — her namesake — helped Abbey's daughter, Misha, change the wash water in the basins.

Abbey was like a daughter to Mary. The eldest child of Winnie, a Corchaug woman, and Mary's dear friend, she'd come to live with the Hortons when she was fourteen. She helped Mary in birthing and raising her children, and learned to read and write and bake in an English kitchen.

Mary came down the stairs and moved toward the back of the large house. The lively voices of her sons carried down the hall from the kitchen. It was amazing to her that her youngest boys, Caleb, Joshua, and Jonathan, were grown men. Well, Jonathan was almost a man. At sixteen he was also the tallest of the Horton men, save Jeremy. Her brow wrinkled at the reminder that her brother-in-law was gone.

As she drew close, she heard Barney telling them the tale of Mary and Jeremy working together to bring his blue slate over from England with the epitaph he'd written engraved on the slab. They'd heard the story hundreds of times, had they not? Yet each time they thrilled at the tale, and today the story was particularly poignant.

Mary entered the kitchen and slid in next to Barney at the table. She squeezed his hand. "I'm thinking we need to get a stone for Jeremy. It won't be a blue slate, but do you think we could get a piece of marble? Something nice so he shall not be forgotten?"

"Aye. I don't know if we can come by marble easily. We might be able to find a nice slab of granite. The reverend is preparing a sermon in his memory, and if we had a church dinner between services, then we could set the stone in the cemetery and have a prayer service afterward."

Caleb stood up and fetched a platter of ginger cakes, offering his mother one before setting them on the old oak table. "Are you sure Uncle Jeremy died? Is it not strange to have a funeral for someone when you don't know where they are?"

Tears sprang to Mary's eyes. "Patience said the same thing."

"He died a watery death, I fear. The service will be for your uncle, but even more for those he left behind. We who loved him." Barnabas ran his fingers through his thick, white hair. He was every bit as dashing as he'd been the day Mary had met him at the Webbs' store so many years ago in Mowsley, England.

Jeremy was nine years younger than Barnabas. The image of her brother-in-law leading her around his ship the day they left England played in her mind. He'd been so

young and exuberant and full of life. The
last time she'd seen him, he hadn't changed
a whit. Not a gray hair on his head, his
tanned skin emphasizing the green of his
eyes, the burnished gold of his hair, the
scent of the sea that clung to his clothes.
"He was too young to die." She set the
uneaten ginger cake on the table and tipped
her face into Barney's shoulder.

"I know, my sweet. But God knows the
plans He has for each of us." His eyelids
sagged, and he leaned his forehead against
hers. "Jeremy included. We must put our
faith in that knowledge. Would you like to
accompany me out to see John Corey? He
might have a suitable stone. He came back
from Gloucester last year with several."

She pulled back. "Yes, if we take the
wagon and Stargazer."

"Of course." He gave a nod to Joshua,
who promptly departed to the barn.

Half an hour later, Mary watched Joshua
lead Stargazer around to the front of the
house with the wagon. She wanted the best
for Jeremy. He'd done so much for her and
Barney.

Lizzie busied herself with work in the
kitchen and the hat shop, only stopping
when Barnabas and Mary brought their

girls over, along with two barrels of dried apples from the orchard. The harvest the year before had been a bumper crop, and Lizzie loved that she could still make apple butter and pies throughout the summer, especially on a stormy day such as this.

Barnabas rolled in the last barrel and heaved it upright. "The wind out there is fierce. We might be in for a real storm, a hurricane." His shoulders drooped. "How is Patience?"

"She has not stirred, poor dear. I think the news has drained her."

" 'Tis good she sleeps. She needs to build strength to get through the coming days."

After Barnabas and Mary left in search of a stone for Jeremy, Lizzie set the older girls to simmer the dried apple slices in cider while she and Abbey let little Mercy help them mix flour and lard for pippin tarts.

Patience woke but remained in her chamber, refusing the trays of tea and soup Lizzie brought to her.

As the tarts baked, the rest of the apples went into the large copper pot over the fire, and Abbey helped the girls take turns stirring them with cinnamon, nutmeg, and cloves using a large wooden paddle. The apples simmered down to a dark golden sauce. The storm blew outside, and the sweet smell of fall scented the house. The girls worked together to ladle the thick apple butter into crocks, and when they were done, Abbey and Hannah scrubbed the kitchen.

The stairs creaked as Lizzie climbed up to Patience's room once again, a tray arranged with sage tea and warm pippin tarts in her hands. "Here now, Patience. This should be just what you need."

Patience looked up, her blue eyes puffy but dry. "You may leave it, Lizzie. Thank you."

"I'll set it here." She carefully lowered the tray onto the table before she sat on the edge of the feather bed. "Would you feel better if you came down to the kitchen? Mary's girls are here."

Her voice faltered with regret. "No, I shall stay here. Tell them Auntie Patience is not feeling well."

Lizzie pressed her arms around Patience in a gentle hug, then rose. She looked back at her friend as she quietly closed the door.

Darkness came early due to the storm, and Lizzie lit candles in the kitchen below. The wind abated, but a gentle patter of rain on the shingled roof added coziness to the house while the girls waited for Mary and Barnabas to return with the wagon.

For the tenth time that day, Lizzie wandered into the hat shop and fussed with her displays, turning a hat on a stand one way and then moving it back to its original spot. She checked her inventory for the third time. Nothing had changed. She picked up one of the bags of beads Heather Flower had brought her and several of the glass vials Jeremy kept her and Doctor Smith supplied with and took them to the kitchen. "We can sort these beads, if you girls don't mind."

They chattered as they admired the different shapes and colors, and Hannah told the younger girls what she remembered of Heather Flower and Dirk's wedding. Lizzie's curls bounced as she shook her head. What turns life could take.

"Uncle Jeremy was here when they got married," she heard Hannah say. "He officiated because he was a ship captain."

Lizzie smiled. "Yes, he was. And such a good man."

They heard the clop of Stargazer's hoofs, and Lizzie went to open the door for Mary and Barnabas. They came in shaking the wetness from their cloaks and went to warm themselves in the kitchen.

Lizzie loaded several baskets with tarts and crocks of apple butter. "I'll bring more

18

to you on the morrow, Mary, but these you can put in the bakeshop first thing in the morning."

"Oh my, they look delicious!" She gazed around the table at her daughters. "You have all been busy today."

Their faces lit up as Mary and Lizzie gushed over the girls' abilities in the kitchen. But it caused Lizzie to recall Mary's youthful attempts at the womanly arts of hearth and home. Lizzie had been patient as she attempted to teach her, but it was Barnabas who truly brought out the domestic side of Mary. Memories of growing up in Mowsley rushed in. What a shock it had been to learn that Jeremy planned a voyage to the New World and intended to take Mary and Barnabas with him.

Lizzie turned to her nieces. "Get your cloaks, girls, and help us carry these out to the wagon."

Mary helped Mercy lift her hood over her hair. "We found a beautiful stone for Jeremy. Mr. Corey says he can carve a proper epitaph on it. Barney is going to write it." Her eyes became moist as she spoke, and she leaned into her husband's arms. "We'll wait for the service for Jeremy until the headstone is ready."

"Yes, of course," Barnabas murmured.

As he opened the door, Patience came down the staircase and paused just before the landing. "Mary? I thought I heard you."

Mary rushed to her. "I didn't want to disturb you. Are you all right?"

Patience's straight blond hair hung loose about her shoulders, and she pulled it around to the side, twisting it like rope. "Yes. I think. Did I hear you say you bought a stone for Jeremy?"

"Yes, dear. Reverend Youngs will say a sermon for him on Sunday, and then we'll gather in the cemetery in a few weeks when the stone is ready and have a small remembrance service."

Lizzie could sense the tension, like the prickle on one's skin just before a lightning strike.

"How can you do that? You don't know he's dead!" The words pounced from Patience, and everyone stood silent, mouths agape.

Mary bit her lip, and Barnabas stepped up to wrap his arm about her shoulder. "Patience, we all grieve. Prithee, do not make this more difficult. We must bring some closure to Jeremy's life. We owe him that, do we not?"

She lowered herself to a stairstep and buried her face in her robe. Lizzie rushed to join Mary and the two pulled Patience into their arms.

"Oh, dearest. We all feel the same way you do. Truly we do." Mary looked at her sister. "Right, Lizzie?" She pressed her cheek to Patience's. "But the water has given up nothing but a bit of wreckage and some of the bodies. Most of the crew is simply swallowed by the sea, and we must face that with courage."

Barnabas gathered the girls by the door, picking up Mercy as she began to whimper.

Lizzie drew Patience closer. "I shall take her back to her room, Mary. You go with Barnabas and the girls. I'll stay here tonight and come to you on the morrow. Patience needs time. Let me take care of her."

Mary's eyes glistened as she left them and followed her family out the door.

Lizzie put her arm around Patience in a gentle hug and led her up the stairs. She tucked her friend under a thick quilt. The room was already dark, with not a candle lit. Lizzie sank into a chair near the bed, and in a moment she drifted into fitful dreams.

Patience lay awake, fingering the edge of her quilt. Her eyes were wide, as if they were propped open by her lashes, stiff with dried tears. Sleep would not come. Nor did she want it to. She needed to think of a way to find Jeremy. He couldn't be dead. She would know it if he were. And even if she could not be certain, she would not give up on him. No, never. She could not.

# 2

*One month earlier*
*Atlantic Ocean, off the coast of Barbados*

A swell of warm water washed over Captain Jeremy Horton's body, and he clawed at *The Swallow*'s hatch door with bloody fingers as he fought to cling to his makeshift raft. The saltwater stung his eyes and swirled in his mouth. He choked as he gasped for air and spat out the brine.

He laid his cheek against the rough wet wood, the thought of sleep both blissful and terrifying. He struggled to keep his eyes open, fixing them on the chunks of decking and broken mast that bobbed in the choppy sea. Sails that once billowed in the wind now floundered in the water. He searched amongst them for his crew. He lost track of how many times he shouted at a form as it drifted close, only to discover it was yet another piece of splintered deck or an empty cask.

How long he'd been in the water he did not know. Still, he forced himself to seek signs of life, to count the lap of the incessant waves, to scan the skies for birds, clouds, or stars — any form of concentration to keep him from drifting into a sleep from which he'd never awaken.

Hours spent calculating how far he might be from Barbados proved futile, as he came to a different conclusion with each attempt. His mind formed thoughts in slow motion, and he gave himself permission to remain in each moment rather than plan the next one.

Night fell, and he lay on his back and grasped a handle on the hatch with one hand. Fatigue clawed at his eyes. He promised himself he'd close them for ten minutes. And he would count the minutes out. He woke with a start as a sudden downpour jolted him from sleep. Did he ever say five? His hand was loose from its grip, and his legs were in the water. There was one horrifying bump on the back of his thigh, and then another. He turned himself in the water and scratched at the hatch with his fingers, splinters digging in deep as he clawed to pull himself high on the wood.

A shark was circling. He felt a bump once more. He tried to make himself small on the square door, difficult for a man of his height. He would not sleep this night, nor even close his eyes. Still, as the rain came to an abrupt end — much as it had begun — he prayed thanksgiving.

He began to count the bumps on the bottom of his make-shift raft. When they finally ceased, he counted the stars in the sky. When the sun came up and there were no more stars, he imagined there were clouds and rain, and he counted the drops that fell until he began to try to catch them on his tongue. His tongue felt like a dry rag.

The torrid heat from the summer sun parched his throat and cracked his lips. His chuckle at the absurdity of thirst amidst all of the water sounded hysterical even to his own ears. The puddle of rainwater he'd sopped into his felt hat during the deluge last night became diluted with saltwater with each wave that crashed over him, and he prayed for more rain. The bright blue sky held no promise.

His stomach twisted with hunger, and he tried to remember what he had eaten last. But all he could remember was Mary's feasts. He tried to remember every supper she had ever cooked for him. And as the sun began to go down at the end of another day floating in the middle of nowhere, he began to panic. Would anyone find him? With each day, nay each hour, that passed, he came that much closer to dying. And it couldn't be from thirst. No, not in all this water. He wanted to laugh, but then he knew he'd already made all the jokes he could think of about this situation. And so he prayed. He prayed God would give him the means to survive against all of the odds.

Instead of counting the stars that night, he looked to them for navigation. He named every star he saw, and some he made up. When the sun rose again, he didn't move. His strength seemed sapped from him, and any effort to move a leg or arm was just too much and beyond his comprehension.

He let his head fall back to the hatch and listened for the slap of the water. *One. Two. Three. Must count. Four. Five . . . I should sit up. The water . . . six. Seven. Eight . . . need to breathe.*

He rolled over with ease and gulped air. Strong hands and deep voices jostled him from a state of confusion, and he fought his way to murky consciousness. He was on a ship. He'd been saved from certain death. *Thank you, Lord.*

"He's alive." A voice echoed like thunder on an empty oak cask.

"I am, sir." Did he say that? Or mayhap

he thought it. Try though he might, he could not open his eyes, but he wanted his rescuers to know that indeed, he lived.

He succumbed to sleep, and when he next woke, a smallish man dressed in a plain linen shirt and breeches sat beside him with a bowl of pale broth that bordered on swill. "Drink it fast, mate, and ye won't notice th' taste." He shrugged as he said it and added, "I wish it were a slab of mutton or beef, but 'tis what we got."

Jeremy pushed up on his elbow but teetered to and fro. Was it him or the ship that swayed? His mouth opened to speak, but his throat burned with the attempt, and his tongue felt glued to the roof of his mouth. He swung his legs over the side of the cot and anchored his bare feet on the floor.

"I fear ye are not ready to get up. Just sit there." The man pushed the bowl into his hands. "This will give ye strength."

He took the broth and dipped a spoon into the thin liquid. He gave thanks and took a big gulp. Despite an impulse to spit it out, a surge of renewed energy surprised him, and he ladled another spoonful into his mouth. He swallowed quickly. They served better slop in jail. He studied the little man. "What's your name?"

"Samuel."

"Thank you, Samuel." He pushed from the cot, only to find his legs would not cooperate.

Samuel grinned and stood up to leave. "Not now. Rest a while. I'll have more for ye later."

Oh, wonderful. A stale biscuit would be better. "Yes, thank you." He croaked the words and received an odd look from the sailor before he scurried out. Perfect. The turnkey couldn't understand him even when he got the words out.

He scanned the small cabin and figured he was in Second Officer's quarters. He finished the broth and ran his hands, raw and burnt from exposure, through his hair, which was stiff with salt, then rested them on his knees. He stared at the floor and contemplated standing. Most likely the captain would seek him out to interview him and would expect to find him here. And most likely his legs would not work for him, so he lowered his head back to the cot to wait. His body shivered, and his head throbbed. Sleep claimed him anyway.

He woke to three faces peering at him through the early-morning gloom, all with worry lines creasing their foreheads and pursed lips.

"He's awake again. His fever's broke." It was the short man from the night before — Samuel. Missing half his teeth.

The one nearest his head straightened to his full height. He was over six feet tall and wore a British officer's uniform, his hat neatly tucked beneath his arm. "You are a lucky man, indeed." He rubbed the length of his long nose, his voice terse. "Less of one would not have survived. If I'd been a betting man, I would have bet against it."

Jeremy struggled to sit up, but his head swirled and the little man pushed him back to the cot. Still, he struggled to answer. "I don't believe in luck, Captain, but God has spared me another day, for which I am grateful."

A smile cracked the corners of the captain's lips. "Ah, you are English, eh? Well, sir, you are aboard HMS *Providence,* and I am Captain Stone. It is my duty to inquire of you who you are and what your business was before you landed in the pond." His brown eyes bore into Jeremy.

"Providence I do believe in, sir." He tried to chuckle, but it worked its way into a coughing fit.

The third man present stepped forward and studied him as his cough subsided. "There's much fluid in the lungs after swallowing the seawater, and the lungs are inflamed. I shall be watching for pneumonia," he said to no one in particular.

Jeremy raised an eyebrow. "And you are the ship's doctor, I gather?"

"Aye, that I be. And 'tis by God's grace indeed that you are alive. You were in the sea a long time. You are not out of danger yet."

The captain scooted a chair closer and sat down. "You know who we are. Now, sir, your name?"

"I am Captain Jeremy Horton, my ship is *The Swallow.* Or was, I should say. It wrecked off the coast of Barbados." He spoke with as much pride as he could muster. "I was on a sugar run to Barbados, loaded with pelts and lumber. My crew was lost. I stayed with the ship whilst they took to the shallops. I never thought I'd be the one saved. Violent waves smashed the boats against each other, and I clung to the mast as my ship listed and broke apart. The mast did me no good once I was in the brine, but a piece of the hatch floated by, and I lunged for it. I don't know how long I drifted. Days. Were you sent from Barbados on a rescue mission for *The Swallow,* Captain Stone?"

"Nay. We are now out of St. Lucia. *The Providence* is a frigate, a gunner ship with thirty guns. Indian Warner has claimed the island for England, and we sailed into St. Lucia with three hundred men aboard for defense against France. We are now bound for Boston."

"Who is Indian Warner, pray tell?"

"He's the son of Sir Thomas Warner, the former governor of St. Christopher Island. His mother was a Carib, but he grew up in his father's household with an English stepmother. After his father died, he went to live with his mother, but he always remained loyal to the English."

Jeremy considered all the events Captain Stone described, but his own predicament demanded answers. "Never a dull moment on a gunner, eh? You will be stopping at New Haven on the way? Or mayhap Winter Harbor?"

"We sail straight to Boston Harbor. You will be confined to this cabin for the duration. You have no papers. There is no method to confirm if you are who you say you are." He pressed his fingers together into a tent and leaned forward.

"Aye. I have nothing." What a state to be in. Did the captain suspect him to be a pirate? Surely if this ship had just left St. Lucia he would have learned of *The Swallow*'s disaster.

"You are not a well man, in any case. Doctor Clarke will attend you, and it shall be at his discretion as to what you may eat and what exercise you may have. Feel free to voice any concerns or complaints directly to me."

The captain stood, the meeting concluded. Jeremy longed to stand and shake his hand, to reassure this man he was everything he claimed to be, but his body clearly protested at even the thought. His strength had drained into that interminable ocean, and it wasn't returning in a day.

Boston. He loved it, but he needed to get to Southold.

# 3

*July 17, 1664*
*Southold*

Patience stood at her looking glass and pinched her cheeks. Her porcelain skin looked a ghastly white. It didn't bother her, but everyone else would notice. She didn't want the comments or the pity. Pink sprang to her face, and she bit her lips to give them color, as well. Cold compresses subdued the puffiness around her eyes somewhat, but she shook her head at her overall appearance. She'd have to keep her chin up. The service this morning would be difficult, and she wanted her friends to think she was in control, though she didn't trust herself enough for that to be true.

As she smoothed her long hair into a knot at the base of her neck, someone knocked at the door below. She glanced at her burgundy brocade. Everyone would wear black today, in their mourning clothes for

Jeremy. But she would wear color and pray for his return.

She raised her skirt and hurried down the stairs. "Patience?" someone called as she lifted the latch and pulled the door open.

"Mary!"

Mary stepped in and grasped her hands as she pressed her cheek to Patience's. "I thought I'd come and walk with you to church. I know this is hard for you, and I didn't want you to come alone."

Patience blinked back a tear and hugged her friend. "Thank you. I'm truly all right, though. But I do cherish your company." She grabbed her hat, a blue wool with a burgundy sash Lizzie had made for her. She set it firmly on her head and tied the ribbon beneath her chin.

"My, that looks so pretty on you. Not that your eyes need be any bluer, but it does make them pop."

"I need that today, I suppose. I could barely open my eyes this morning." Really. If she wanted Mary to think she was fine, why provide her with details that would say otherwise?

Mary studied her. "Oh, Patience. Could you not sleep? Of course you couldn't. Prithee, come stay with us after church tonight. Do not come home to this big empty house."

"I couldn't stay, you know that. I have the little girls coming for Dame School in the morning. I need to ready their lessons before they arrive." Her shoulders sagged as she retrieved her Bible from the table near the door, and her chin dipped. Though Dame School had its breaks, it differed from the boy's school that quit for the summer so the lads could help their fathers in the fields during growing season. The littlest girls continued through, and it helped their busy mothers to have them occupied in such a manner.

"We'll just get Little Mary and Mercy ready for school early, and we'll all walk over with you. And goodness, if you need to take a break, Patience, we shall understand."

They walked down Town Street arm in arm. A warm breeze caused the leaves to dance in the branches of the oaks that lined the street. Fall was not far off, and still Jeremy was not with her. Never would be, if what everyone said was true.

The church bell began to ring, and Mary's arm tightened. In the service this morning, Reverend Youngs would give a sermon dedicated to Jeremy's passing. According to the town officials and her dearest friends, and even Jeremy's family, he was dead. How could they give up so easily? Why were they not praying for his safe return? She could not believe this. She could not. The rain began to fall in a sideways pelt as they rushed into the sanctuary.

She took her seat in the women's pew several rows behind the Horton box, and Mary scooted in next to her. Mary often sat with someone who needed a little extra comfort or cheer, and Patience was thankful for her nearness. Lizzie and Zeke sat two rows ahead, with Benjamin Horton and his wife, Anna, in front of them.

The congregation rose as Reverend Youngs walked to the front, and Patience picked up her psalm book. Voices blended together, but she could not sing. Instead, she bowed her head in prayer and asked God to bring Jeremy home. Safe to her.

As the service progressed, she listened to the reverend and his stories of the honorable life Jeremy had led. Sniffles and the swish of handkerchiefs blotting tears swept through the worship hall, combined with smiles and nods as his life's story was remembered. His strength and courage were legendary, and his love of family and dedication to serve friend and foe alike were Horton traits he did not regard lightly. In the early days in Mowsley, growing up, she'd admired Barnabas for those very qualities. When he'd wed Mary, her infatuation with him almost broke her tender young heart. And she'd promised herself she'd never marry unless she found someone just like Barnabas.

It didn't take her long to know his brother Jeremy was the one. But Jeremy was in love with the sea, and it would have been easier to compete with another woman than with the wild and unpredictable ocean.

Mary nudged her, and she realized everyone was standing again, this time for the closing hymn. It was too cold and rainy for a dinner on the church grounds, but Mary insisted that she come across the road to her house. She'd cooked the day before and there was plenty.

Patience filed out with the rest of the parishioners and numbly shook Reverend Youngs's hand. He was grieving for Jeremy, too, of course — but he needed to be the one to hold them all together. "Thank you for the sermon, Reverend. I — I can't tell you how unhappy I am, though, to be talking about him in the past tense."

"My child" — he'd been calling her that since they'd first come to the island — "I know how distressed you are. I do believe when we have the memorial service and lay the stone, you'll have some closure. My purpose today was simply to celebrate his life, which ended too soon for those he leaves behind."

Her head spun and her knees almost buckled, but she caught herself.

"Are you all right, my dear?" His words were kind, but it took her a moment to focus on his face. Concerned eyes waited for her.

She raised her chin. "Yes, I'm quite all right, Reverend. I think I just need a bite to eat, and at Mary's house that is easy to accomplish, is it not?" She attempted a smile.

He patted her shoulder as he turned to the family behind her.

Lizzie waited for her outside. "Mary and the girls went on to the house to set the table. Are you doing all right, Patience?"

Her chin edged a little higher. "Everyone is asking that, Lizzie."

"We are worried about you."

"Because I refuse to give up on Jeremy? 'Tis my decision to make, yes?"

"Of course. Forgive me, we are all upset by this, but we must come to terms with it anyway."

They walked in silence the rest of the way, their skirts rustled as they tiptoed through the mud. Thankfully, the rain had stopped.

"Lizzie, I'm all right. I shall come to terms with it, I shall. But not today, I suppose."

Lizzie nodded and pushed Mary's door open. "Hellooo." They were greeted by the smell of bacon and cinnamon, and both smiled.

Mercy ran from the parlor and grabbed Patience's skirts. Patience picked her up and cooed, "Oh, come here, sweet thing. You are too big to carry, but let me hold you for a moment." She gave the little girl with auburn curls and big hazel eyes a hug. "Who do you look like?"

"Mama!" Mercy giggled and batted her thick eyelashes.

Patience rolled her eyes upward. "And who does Jonathan look like?"

She squealed, "Mama!" More giggles.

"And who does Joshua look like?"

Mercy was beside herself. She could barely squeak out, "Papa!"

Lizzie shook Mercy's little foot and looked at the girl with scolding eyes. "All right, enough. We shan't go through that whole routine. Not while your mother needs help in the kitchen, Miss Mercy."

Mercy's answer was more giggles. Patience set her down, and the three made their way to the large kitchen in the back. The release of laughter calmed her nerves. She might be

39

able to make it through the day, after all. Lizzie always had some concoction to cure ills, but for Patience, Mary's children always had a therapeutic effect on her.

Mary stirred a pot on the fire. "Barney and Jon went out to fetch some more wood. We just need to get everything on the tables." The long, worn oak table they'd hauled over from England, and the shorter one Barnabas had made for Mary as both their family and bakeshop grew. They always seemed to have room for company.

A warm ham and chunks of cheese and bread were already on the longest table, and to that Mary added a big crock of beans that had simmered all night with thick slabs of bacon. After Barnabas and Jon came in and stacked their logs by the fireplace, they all joined hands around the tables. Barnabas led them in thanksgiving, and they settled while he read from Scripture. He dished up a plate of food for Mary, who sat at the opposite end from him, next to Mercy. He heaped each plate and passed it on until everyone had one.

Patience sat next to Mercy, with nine-year-old Mary on the other side, Lizzie across from her. Jonathan sat on Lizzie's left, with Caleb and Abigail Hallock on her right, and then Joshua. Caleb was courting

Abigail, and she spent much time with the Hortons. She gave a sympathetic smile to Patience, and Patience tried to return it. Did Abigail know how lucky she was to marry into this family?

The younger Hortons ate quietly, while the women exchanged pleasantries. Patience picked at her food, moving it from one side of the plate to the other, listening to their chatter. The conversation turned to Jeremy, which of course it would, but wasn't the talk futile?

When they began to discuss the ceremony with the gravestone, she shifted in her chair. "Barnabas, have you discussed with Reverend Youngs or your lawyer, Mr. Wells, the notion of putting out a search for Jeremy and his crew?"

Forks and spoons paused in midair as everyone — save Mercy, who quietly snuck bits of ham to Muffkin, the cat — turned to Barnabas.

He cleared his throat and looked at Patience. "I know how deeply you grieve, my dear. I do, as well. But where would we even begin to look? Nathaniel said they sent some of the Caribs out in their canoes. There were just small chunks of wood where the ship must have been. It's sunk. There are no survivors, Patience. None."

His eyes were moist as he searched her face.

Mary patted her mouth with her linen napkin as her own tears welled. "He would have been the last to try to leave that ship." She pressed the napkin to her eyes to stop the flow.

Patience looked at Lizzie, and the alarm in her violet eyes told her she knew what she was thinking. She pressed on anyway. "Were there not ships in Barbados that could have been sent out? English ships?"

Barnabas shook his head. "I'm told there were, actually. There were warships in the area that delivered troops to St. Lucia. But we would know if they'd found any survivors."

Patience scooped Mercy up suddenly, and surprise registered in the little girl's eyes as Patience moved to the end of the bench and stood up. She kissed Mercy's little cheek and set her back at her place. "Sorry, little poppet." She looked up at Mary and then shifted her gaze to Barnabas. "Pray pardon me, but I fear I need to be alone."

Barnabas leapt to his feet, and he and Mary both were at her side in less than a moment. "I am so sorry. We are all trying to work our way through this. But I cannot give you hope where there is none. You must know that."

Mary hugged her. "Oh, sweet Patience. We want him back too. If there were a ship that would take us to find him, I'd be right with you going on board."

Patience's eyes flew wide. "But does not God give us hope? Are there not seafaring men who would search for him?" She turned to Barnabas before the tears burst forth, and he took her in his arms.

"I know how you loved him. And he told me you hated the sea, hated him leaving and risking his life. But he did. And it took him. And now we must learn how to carry on and depend on God to do it. God *is* our hope, Patience. That is true. Would you like Lizzie to walk you home? Would you be more comfortable there?"

Her eyes had puffed again, of that she was certain, and her throat ached. "I'd rather walk by myself, if you don't mind. I must skip services this afternoon. I shall be all right, truly. I just need to be alone. Give my apologies to Reverend Youngs, please."

She slipped out the door, and they let her go. Thank goodness. She loved them all to death, and they were well-meaning, but they did not understand what she needed. And she didn't expect them to. She needed Jeremy.

# 4

Jeremy stood on deck, his hands wrapped tightly around the glossy wooden rail. The dark blue water was frosted with glimmering whitecaps, and a salty breeze pricked at his face. A thin, gray line of land lay on the horizon, and he studied it without aid of a spyglass. He didn't need one. He'd sailed into Boston Harbor many a time and could probably do it with his eyes closed.

How he'd longed to jump ship as they'd sailed past Long Island. Not even a shallop had gone ashore. The captain did not give a fig about sending word to any authority about his rescue. Or was it capture? Hard to tell from the confinement he'd spent most of his days enduring. He'd been told it was to afford his recovery, but he suspected there was more to the story. And after days of gruel and hard biscuits, he was ready to be on his way.

Now he could not wait to disembark and make arrangements to travel to Southold. He paced as he formulated a plan.

Captain Stone appeared at his side. "Good morrow, Captain Horton. I pray the exercise on the deck is beneficial?"

"Yes, I believe so, Captain. When do you expect us to be ashore?"

"I'll send a party ashore immediately. You will, of course, be detained until the governor has relayed his wishes regarding your interrogation."

"Does *aghast* mean anything to you, sir? For that is what I'm feeling at this moment. How can you even presume that I would permit you to detain me once we are ashore? You've taken precautions whilst we are at sea, and though it has pained me to endure it, I would do no less if it were you on my ship. But I have no business in Boston without my ship, and I will make haste to be on my way as soon as possible."

"Soon is not possible, I'm afraid. It is not I who detains you, Captain Horton, but the governor himself. Governor Bellingham shall be here posthaste to discuss your predicament. Governor Winthrop of Connecticut shall accompany him. Good day, sir."

Captain Stone withdrew, and Jeremy watched as he strode to the stern and disappeared into the great cabin. He leaned back onto the rail and strummed his fingers on the wood he'd polished just a few hours earlier. He wouldn't go against the orders of the captain, but he didn't have to like it either. He proceeded to his own cabin — not much more than a cell — and sat on the bunk to await his summons to speak to the governors. John Winthrop the Younger was an acquaintance, and that was in his favor. All would be well.

He closed his eyes and pictured Patience. Her long blond hair pulled up, and sparkly blue eyes that danced whenever she saw him walk into the shop. She was the picture of elegance, save for a few wisps of hair that were forever escaping. And she was not averse to pushing up her sleeves and doing the work a husband would do, if she had one. When he was in Southold, he made sure her woodpile was split and stacked, her home in good repair, and her crops planted or harvested — depending on the season. He was in Southold but once a year, sometimes twice. Why had he thought what he did for her amounted to much?

He heard a commotion on the deck, and he sprang to his feet and dug his fingers through his hair. One tap on the door and Captain Stone came in.

"Captain Horton, may I present Governor Bellingham and Governor Winthrop?"

"He's lost a few pounds, but I'd know this man anywhere, Stone." Winthrop stuck out his hand. "Horton, so good to see you alive."

Jeremy clapped his back. "Governor, I am particularly glad to be alive. And thankful you are here to vouch for me and straighten out this mess."

Governor Winthrop turned to Governor Bellingham. "The Hortons and I go way back. This is Barnabas's brother."

The Massachusetts governor studied Jeremy for a moment. "Pray, forgive us. You've given us a start, I'm afraid. And the good Captain Stone has followed the Crown's protocol, as he should. Please be our guest for supper. You as well, Stone." He furrowed his brow. "Join us at five o'clock on Wednesday."

Jeremy started. "Wednesday? I should think it would be today, sir."

Governor Bellingham shook his head. "That gives me sufficient time to make arrangements for your travel. I expect you shall want to leave for London as soon as possible?"

"Long Island, actually. I was expected

there weeks ago, and I gather the news of my death has traveled there, has it not?"

"No doubt, no doubt. I believe we received the news from Nathaniel Sylvester, and he, of course, would have informed your brother. I sent him a note of condolence myself, and I expect he's read it by now. It was a terrible tragedy for the crew and their families." Winthrop frowned, but then his eyes brightened. "I'm thankful you survived. I would like a full report, of course, at supper. It shall be written up and sent on to the Crown."

"Most certainly."

As soon as Captain Stone left with the governor, Samuel brought him a clean linen shirt and a pair of dark blue breeches. He pulled the clothes on. A sash held the shirt in, and he looked much like a pirate. "All I need is a handkerchief around my head and the captain's gleaming sword."

A grin split Samuel's face. "I can get ye the kerchief, but the sword never leaves the cap'n's side."

"No doubt." He grunted a chuckle. "I know you hear much, and most likely speak little, eh?"

"Might be."

He measured his words. "But I know you have thoughts. What do you think about what's going on here? What's the truth behind why I've been kept little more than a prisoner?"

Samuel's grin slid from his face. "Why do ye think they'd tell me?"

He knew something. Jeremy could see it by the sideways look, and his eyes had narrowed to slits. "They haven't shared the information with you, Samuel, but you've heard them talk. They treat you like you don't understand, but I know different. That makes it all right for you to tell me, does it not?" Lord forgive him, but he needed to know what was going on here before he dined with the governor.

"This ship will be readied in Boston for an attack on New Amsterdam. They feared if ye were given full use of the ship and dined as a guest ye'd find out."

"England is attacking New Amsterdam?"

"Aye. But no one kin know." The man's eyebrows drew together until they were one thick line. Jeremy figured poor Samuel regretted his words at once.

"I cannot promise you I won't share what I know, but I can promise you that I shall never divulge where the information came from. You have my word."

If Samuel understood, it wasn't evident, and he scampered from the cabin, knocking over a chair in his haste. He didn't look back.

Jeremy looked down. He couldn't return to Southold dressed like this. Yet he had no coin, nothing to barter for a good suit of clothes. He did have news, however. Very important news. But could he reveal to Captain Stone and the governors that he knew their plans?

# 5

Patience rose early to work on the lesson plans for her young ladies. She'd slept poorly since the news of Jeremy, and last night had been no exception. She splashed cold water on her face and slipped into a linen chemise. She pulled her petticoat over her head, allowing the folds to drift down around her legs. Her gray skirt followed, with the panels open in front, and she finished her outfit with a matching bodice, pulling the laces tight at her waist. Her classroom was downstairs, off of the work-room for Lizzie's Hat Shop, and she took the steps quickly.

Her girls would make lace-edged handker-chiefs this morning, and she laid a linen square at each place along the wooden table. Little hands needed large needles and thick thread, and she looked through her supply for the right size.

She set out the samplers her class had begun and smiled at their beginner's stitches. She never tired of teaching her classes each year. She sighed. Today was bittersweet. Today she would write a note to her students' parents, explaining she would take a temporary absence. She disliked doing so. She hadn't missed a day of Dame School since her first class. But her mind would not stop thinking of Jeremy and where he might be and how he might need help. And Mary had said if she needed time, they would understand.

After the lessons were ready, she climbed the stairs to her room and laid out a woven valise. Many of her belongings she treasured because they were her mother's, but the bag recalled the most precious memories. She remembered Mother packing the valise before they left Mowsley, and she could so clearly see her mother clinging to it as they struggled to get ashore the day the shallop brought them to Long Island.

She layered an extra chemise, a garden frock, a brush, and a looking glass into the bottom of the valise. She picked up the set of ivory combs Jeremy had given her and brought them to her lips. She gently put them in the bag, folded the top, and buckled the latch. Oh, her heart ached. She prayed God would ease her pain, and then she prayed He would ease Jeremy's, too.

She stood with her eyes closed, the bag clutched in her hands, until a small voice broke the silence.

"Auntie Patience?"

She looked down at her white knuckles as she released the valise and dropped it gently onto the bed. "Why, Mercy, I didn't hear you come up the stairs. Is everyone here?"

Mercy grabbed her hand and pulled. "Yes, everyone except Julia. Mama says Julia is sick today."

"Oh, sweet one, you will miss her, won't you?" The two girls were the same age to the month, and they were inseparable.

"Like you miss Uncle Jeremy?"

She squeezed her eyes shut against the pain. She could not explain, so she simply said, "Yes. Let's go down now. I have a lovely morning planned. You may take Julia's supplies with you, and when she is better, you may help her make her own handkerchief."

"We're making our own handkerchiefs? That will be fun!" Mercy skipped ahead down the stairs. "Mama, we're making our own handkerchiefs!"

Mary smiled as Patience entered the

room. "I see you're feeling better this morning. And I love what the girls will be making. Is Lizzie helping?"

"No, she's got some hat orders to finish up, so she'll be here, but not with us. I shall be busy, and that is good. I'm grateful for the time I spend with my girls."

"I brought you some ginger cakes. And here's some fresh bread for the girls and a crock of my strawberry jelly for your class once they've put their work away. Sarah will come to walk them home."

"Very good, Mary. Thank you for these." She watched as Mary left and then put the gifts of food in the kitchen. Back in her classroom, she sat in between Misha and a squirmy Mercy. Misha was finished with school, but she liked to help with the little ones.

"I thought we'd begin this morning practicing stitches on our samplers. Once your fingers are warmed up, we can begin edging our handkerchiefs with lace. Who remembers which letter comes next after *L*?"

Mary's daughter and namesake smiled shyly. "*M* is for Mary."

Patience clapped her hands. "That is right!"

When the girls had one row of lace around their linen squares, Patience led them through practicing the days of the week and the months. "Thirty days hath September, April, June, and November. How many days do the other months have?"

Young Mary jumped to her feet and danced a circle. "Thirty-one!"

"You are so right. Just like your mother, you are. So good with numbers. And February, does it have thirty or thirty-one?"

"Twenty-nine!" they called out in unison.

"You are most correct for this year, my ladies. Who knows why it was twenty-nine this year?"

Everyone was silent. Misha finally spoke up. "May I answer that, Miss Terry?"

"Why, of course, Misha. Tell these young ladies why we had twenty-nine days in February instead of twenty-eight."

Misha recited a perfect discourse about how the calendar year must be able to catch up with the solar year.

Patience smiled her approval. "Thank you. Now let us practice writing our numbers."

Misha stood to gather hornbooks for the girls to write on. The students bent to their task. They strove for perfection in shaping their numbers, and most had them in order.

When they were done, Patience beamed even as sadness gripped her. How could she look so happy when her heart ached and her stomach twisted like a wrung-out dish rag? She sighed. She looked at the precious faces of her young girls. Only selfishness would allow her to burden them with her sorrow. No, for these sweet girls, she would give them a smile. Give them hope.

She smoothed her skirt as she rose to her feet. "You have all done well today. Follow me to the kitchen." As they ate their bread and jelly, chatting with one another about their needle-work, Patience sat at the end of the table, dipped her quill into the inkpot, and poised it over small sheets of parchment.

Dearest Parents,

I regret that I shall not be able to perform my duties as your daughter's teacher for an indeterminate amount of time. Please know that I enjoy teaching your dear child, and I long to return to that endeavor as soon as possible.

I have sent with them today the sampler and handkerchief they have worked so hard on. They should continue to practice their stitches at home whilst I am away.

I remain your faithful servant,
Miss Patience Terry

She dipped her pen again for a postscript.

P.S. I do apologize for the inconvenience of my actions. I pray your forgiveness.

She folded the pages and dripped puddles of red wax on the seam. Each circle she pressed gently with her stamp, sealing the letters. The parents could read her note at home. She had no desire to discuss the content with anyone. Writing it was difficult enough.

The chatter of her young students drew her attention, and she watched as Mercy used her pudgy finger to get the last drop of jelly from the crock and then put her finger in her mouth. "Manners, Miss Mercy. Sit up now and wipe your fingers on your napkin, please." She could not help smiling. How she would miss her darling girls.

Her class this year was smaller than the year before, but she liked that. Mercy was younger than the girls she usually instructed, but she was bright and already knew her alphabet. And she tried so very hard. Toward the end of the year, she taught her students to read, and it made her sad to think she might not be able to give Mercy her first glimpse of reading. But she would not be able to devote herself to teaching anyone until she knew where Jeremy was.

Patience wrapped each girl's hornbook, sampler, and handkerchief with a single row of lace in a piece of linen and tied them with a length of pink ribbon. Under the ribbon, she tucked the letter she'd written, with instructions for the girls to give the packets to their mothers. Sarah arrived to gather her sisters for the walk home, and Patience gave each of them a warm hug and waited until they were halfway down her flagstone path before she let the tears well.

She swiveled from the door, sank onto a chair, and sobbed into her apron. Long moments passed before she drew in a determined breath. She would not waste time on crying. She must be single-minded in her purpose and rely on God to see her through. Relying on her own strength would get her nowhere. She dried her eyes. There. Enough was enough. She sank to her knees on the wooden floor and prayed. "Dear Lord, give me strength and a clear understanding of what I must do to bring Jeremy home."

A gusty wind hit the roof, and she heard a shingle rattle. Jeremy considered it his job to repair such a thing. He'd always been her helper, now she must be his.

She picked up her skirts and flew up the

58

stairs. Grabbing the bag, she scarce gave a look around her room before she bounded back down. To the sack of ginger cakes she added a bit of cheese and bread and folded the top over with a gentle twist.

She banked the fire, scooped water from the pot, and ladled it over the ash. She draped her red cloak over her arm. Thankful Lizzie was late today, she hurried out the door without even a backward glance, straight for the south harbor, where the founders and their families had first waded ashore. Thank goodness there was a dock for the ships now.

She stood, her face tilted up, and gazed at the tall ship, sails yet hoisted, sides creaking with each lap of water on the wood. She'd overheard at church services that *The Rosemary* would leave port for Barbados. It was the merchant vessel Nathaniel arrived on, and her hope was to gain passage. Now she stood, the cool salt breeze rustling her skirts, and stared at the tall hull with a sick feeling in the pit of her stomach.

What a far-fetched plan it was to disregard her fear of sailing. Her heart ached, and she could not do it. She clutched the valise to her chest as tears flooded her eyes, coursing down her cheeks. She wanted to find Jeremy. Oh, why could she not just walk up that plank and beg they take her with them? She'd earned a meager salary from her Dame School, but she'd always been thrifty and had saved what some would call a pittance. Surely it was enough to purchase passage on *The Rosemary.* She would give it all to find Jeremy. But not on a ship. Not on the ocean.

# 6

Jeremy pushed up from his chair as muster was called to join all hands on deck. With everyone accounted for, Captain Stone invited Jeremy to walk with him. As they strolled along the upper deck, Jeremy said, "I'm hoping the good governor will see his way to offer me a hot bath. And mayhap accept a bill of credit toward a proper coat, breeches, and boots."

Captain Stone studied his garb. "Aye. You look like a crewman on a pirate ship. Is that all Samuel could find for you?"

"Apparently." He tightened the sash. He could not wait until supper with Governor Winthrop and Governor Bellingham. He'd give his report and be gone as soon as he'd bathed and donned a proper set of clothes.

"I'll leave you to your report then, Captain Horton. We shall go ashore at half past four.

61

Our supper is at five o'clock." He turned on his heel and left Jeremy to return to his cabin.

Jeremy took one last look over the rail and fought down a great urge to make his departure right then. Back in his cabin, he sat at the small writing desk. Paper, a billowy pen, and ink sat ready for his report. Samuel must have returned while he'd been out.

He sat and wrote with a flourish everything he could remember, from the first gust of the storm to the moment he awoke in the bunk on board Captain Stone's ship. He shook his head as he recalled each detail. Why was he not dead like the rest of his crew? Mayhap it was because he'd stayed with his ship until the end. So appalling, really. He would have given his life for his crew. He'd clung to the hatch and searched for them to no avail. Everyone perished, but he prayed that was wrong. He begged God to tell him why he'd made it when the others had not. He might not ever know. Only God knew when his days on earth were to be done. And it hadn't been the day he'd landed in the ocean on a piece of wood. He'd prayed then that if he ever made it home, he'd do whatever the Lord called him to do. He bent his head to the paper once more and finished the account.

He sat back while the ink dried. His arms folded behind his head, he let his thoughts drift to Southold, to Patience. She must be upset, but she always knew he'd never settle down, did she not? She'd cry, certes, then she would busy herself like she always did. She loved the children she taught. But what would she do when he returned? She would want to hit him, most likely. But she was too much of a lady, thankfully.

He drifted to sleep and dreamt of Patience until the door swung open with a thud. Samuel stood there, the corners of his mouth turned down, his hands twitching at his sides. "You're expected on the deck now. Cap'n Stone waits for ye."

"Of course." He stood and rolled his parchment into a scroll. "Lead the way." His long stride caught up with Samuel's newfound swagger. "And Samuel, by the way, you needn't worry. Your job here is secure. They won't find you out on my account."

Samuel's nervous laugh was like a twig scratching a window.

"Truly. I won't be telling." No, in fact he'd rather them not know that he knew.

Captain Stone looked resplendent in his red dress coat embellished with his sash and medals. His sword gleamed at his side. Jeremy fell in next to him, and the two walked down the plank like old friends. He couldn't help but notice his legs were weaker than he'd realized. He'd been through an ordeal, but surely the lack of exercise and the meager food he'd been given did nothing to restore his vigor. At least he'd been given a hearty supper last night — so that Captain Stone couldn't be accused of starving him, most likely.

He needn't have worried about his clothes, bills of credit, or whatnot, for Governor Bellingham's man led him immediately to a bath and handed him towels and a new suit of clothes.

He folded the borrowed clothes into a pile and lowered himself into the hot water. His head rested on the back rim of the tub, and he inhaled the steam. A deep sigh escaped as every muscle in his body relaxed. He allowed himself a good soak until the warmth of the water dissipated and then, with brisk strokes of a towel, he dried and dressed. The day was warm, but he finished with the coat left on a peg for him. It fit snugly and was of dark blue cloth with shiny brass buttons and gold epaulets. It would do, he guessed, though he looked like he'd just been commissioned a captain in the Navy.

He entered the parlor, and Captain Stone and both governors stood. "Hear, hear. From pirate to gentleman." Governor Winthrop beamed.

Jeremy's eyebrows rose with his chortle. "I think 'thank you' is the appropriate response." He tugged at the hem of the coat. "A bit dashing, wouldn't you say?"

"Yes, yes — I do say." Captain Stone nodded, and the governors moved to the chairs grouped by the window. They sat to discuss Jeremy's return to Long Island.

Jeremy would be provided with a horse and a scout to accompany him. The man would return with Jeremy's mount. A bell was rung, and the conversation moved into a long, narrow dining room, furnished with a gleaming mahogany table and sideboard. They were served a supper of pheasant and root vegetables roasted in a marmalade sauce.

Governor Winthrop stabbed a slice of meat, and with his fork in midair, he pointed to Captain Stone. "I want you to tell Captain Horton the plans for *The Providence* after you leave Boston."

Captain Stone's brows knit together. "Why would the captain of a merchant ship need to know such high-level information?" He met the governor's glare. "I mean, if I may ask, sir? We've gone to great lengths, have we not, to guard our intentions?"

"Oh, Captain Stone, you do not understand who you fished out of the sea." He grinned at Jeremy with a nod. "You know he is a Horton. He's the brother of Barnabas Horton — the magistrate from the east end of Long Island, and we need their militia. We'll be sending their troops in by land as you come in by sea." He chuckled as if it pleased him to have to explain.

Jeremy's eyes shifted between the two. "The Southold Militia? You'll be sending out the troops?"

The governor turned his fork toward Captain Stone. "Yes, to support *The Providence*. Tell him, Stone."

"We are but one of four gunners sailing into Long Island Sound to take New Amsterdam."

"You don't say. It's about time. We've put up with them long enough." He stabbed a bite of pheasant and chewed the morsel with gusto.

Captain Stone put down his eating utensils. "It is of utmost importance that this information is not leaked to the Dutch or those who would inform them."

"Why certainly, Captain. And I think you shall find those on the east end most eager to give you their full support."

The governor grunted his approval. "Aye, they've champed at the bit ever since the Dutch captured Johnny Youngs."

Captain Stone tilted his head and cocked an eyebrow.

Jeremy jumped in. "Our reverend's son. He was always getting himself in a sorry plight. He rescued himself, you might say. It is quite a story — I shall tell you it one day."

Stone grinned. "In a pickle he was, eh? Why does it seem the son of a preacher is always the troublemaker?"

A smile played across Jeremy's lips as he remembered growing up with Johnny. He shook his head. "But he is a willow among the grass now. You know the Bible verse? Isaiah 44:4?"

Both men nodded. Governor Winthrop added, "John's son is that."

Governor Bellingham swallowed and cleared his throat. "Brief him, Stone."

Captain Stone pushed his plate away. A servant stepped forward to clear the table, and as the plan to take New Amsterdam unfolded, a dessert of baked apples encased in a sweet crust was served.

"Three ships are in position now to enter the Long Island sound," Captain Stone said. "We sail on the morrow to join them in for maneuvers in the east sound to finalize plans to force a surrender. Word is that it will be an easy takeover. The people are weary of Stuyvesant, and they want peace — and under English rule, if that is what is needed. There's not much more to know."

Governor Winthrop turned to Jeremy. "I want you to be my point man in Southold. You shall train with their militia for a month. I want you to lead them into western Long Island. Do not be quick to shoot. Be there in an advisory capacity, but mostly to guide them into an easy transition after the takeover."

The last thing Jeremy wanted to do when he returned to Southold was to leave again. How many times had he said good-bye to Patience as she pleaded with him to stay? But surely she would understand it was at the governor's request. And surely she would give thanks that he would go by land, with the horse troop. "But why me? I haven't even trained with the Southold Militia."

Governor Winthrop began to answer, but Bellingham waved him silent. "Your good friend here has convinced me you're our man. Johnny and Benjamin are hotheads who have wanted to run the Dutch out of

New Amsterdam for years. We need you to keep a clamp on them. Keep them from taking things into their own hands and forcing a fight. We believe we can do this without a drop of blood. We need the horse troop, but we don't trust its officers. Simple as that."

Jeremy considered the argument. It was true that Johnny might go too far, and he could lead Benjamin astray. He had seen it before. Mayhap this was what God had saved him for. "It would be an honor, sir, to serve you and the Crown." He turned to Captain Stone. "You have my full support for the attack, and my prayers for a bloodless takeover."

Governor Bellingham stood. "Very well. *The Providence* sails at dawn, and I will dispatch you with a scout as soon as word arrives that she's underway."

Governor Winthrop stood, as well. "Give my regards to Barnabas when you see him."

"Aye. I shall do just that."

It was a long, sleepless night. Jeremy could sleep like a duck on water in a cabin bunk, cramped though it was. But a soft, feather-stuffed mattress made him toss about like a bass in a fishnet. Though he and the governor's scout left at a gallop, the ride would take days, and the fast pace would not be suitable for the long haul. He was glad to be on their way, and it was Patience who occupied his thoughts, not Stuyvesant or the Dutch people, as he and the scout rode toward New London and the ferry.

His mount was a tall mare with a sleek brown coat. Her stride was even and comfortable, and she tossed her head from time to time with a snort that said she'd go faster if he'd give the signal. He gave her no slack of rein, though, and settled back for the ride. A summer rain began to lightly pelt them, and he released the cocked brim of his hat and pulled it down.

A vision of Patience came to him. She faced away from him, blond tresses coming loose from their combs, as they were wont to do. He wanted to reach out and gently touch her to ease her grief. For she grieved, he was certain. The last time he'd left, she'd told him how upset she was, her clear blue eyes pools of tears. She'd confessed her love and told him only God knew how long they might have together. She'd confessed her love, and he had betrayed it by leaving anyway. She wanted him to stay, and now she thought him dead. Was her grief racked with pain or anger?

Or did she feel anything at all? What happens to a love lost? Once it is mourned, does it wither and die, blown away by the wind as if it were dust? Did she still love him, or had he lost her the moment he'd chosen to walk out the door? What would happen when he walked back in? He knew her well. She would fly into his arms and want his promises. He would kiss her tender red lips and tell her he would stay. After the siege on New Amsterdam, he would stay.

That night he and the scout rolled out their bedrolls under a stand of oak. The branches wove a thick ceiling of leaves above their heads, and Jeremy scooted to the bottom of the roll and closed his eyes to the damp black of night.

The next morning Jeremy fried some ham over a smoldering fire and they broke their fast with the crispy meat and a handful of dried currants. Cleanup consisted of wiping his small iron pan out with a couple of pieces of bread. He munched the greasy chunks as he kicked dirt over the fire and wrapped the pan in his bedroll all in one smooth motion. With a foot in the stirrup, he swung up in the saddle and studied the trail in front of him while he waited for his scout to mount.

The forest moved with wildlife, and he thought he'd enjoy the ride if he had more time to hunt, or even just to sit still and listen. But with thoughts of Patience grieving in Southold, there was not a moment to spare. They'd be at the ferry tonight and across the sound before the following afternoon.

With no idea when the ferry might run, they urged their horses on to make the landing by nightfall. As the sound came into view below, Jeremy scanned the horizon. In the warm glow of the setting sun, he saw the outline of the large, flat barge making its way toward the Connecticut shore. The ferry was large, but still it was tossed about in the water like a cork. He couldn't help but remember his first time coming to Long Island with *The Swallow.* Reverend Youngs and Barnabas had called this sound the North Sea, but seagoing captains had come to call it Devil's Belt. He'd taken the long route around the east tip of the north fork and sailed into the safe harbor of Peconic Bay.

Still, this would be the shortest way to Southold. They camped that night near the ferry landing, ready to leave at first light. Tonight there were stars overhead, and he studied them with a captain's eye. Sirius was the brightest star in the sky. How many times had he navigated across the ocean under Sirius's guiding light? He closed his eyes as he began to drift into sleep. The star became Patience's porcelain face, surrounded by her halo of yellow hair. He would see her on the morrow.

# 7

*July 24, 1664*
*Southold*

Patience sat opposite the two sisters in her parlor, the same room that served as the display room of Lizzie's Hat Shop. They were both dressed in black — Lizzie in a shiny black taffeta and Mary in a more subdued black linen, though it had cream lace at the wrist and neck.

Patience had chosen a purple gown, edged in white lace. "I am not going to the cemetery. That is much like saying he's dead. Why should I be there if I do not believe it?"

Lizzie buried her face in her hands and tossed her silvery curls as she shook her head. "No, Patience. 'Tis not that you must agree. But you need to come out of respect, don't you think?"

Mary nodded. "Besides, sweet one, we cannot trust you by yourself anymore. We are worried. What would we have done if you'd gotten on that ship? We could not have come after you."

"I should not have wanted you to!" Her face warmed as she said the words. She hated taking such a tone with her friends.

Mary rubbed her forehead and twisted back the stray lock she found there. "We love you too much to leave you, Patience, so we are taking you with us. I think your dress looks lovely, and it shall make your statement well enough. But you need to be there, and we shall carry you there if we must. Won't we, Lizzie?"

Lizzie stood. "Yes, we shall. Now come."

Mary rose, and the two took Patience's arms and helped her rise. "Oh, thank goodness, Patience. Come now, I shall pick out one of Lizzie's hats for you."

She let them fuss over her. The idea of her colorful dress making a statement appealed to her, and she smoothed her skirt while Lizzie tied the sash under her chin and Mary tucked errant wisps of hair beneath the hat. They walked to the church through a dreary shower and joined the small crowd in the cemetery. A spot near the stone had been saved for the three ladies, and her friends stood close while the drape over the stone was removed.

75

Her throat tightened, and her nails dug into the skin of her palms as she listened to Reverend Youngs laud Jeremy's life. Quiet tears gathered on her lashes, and she let them fall. After the eulogy, Barnabas's deep baritone led them in singing the Twenty-third Psalm, but when they sang the words "still waters," she could not continue. The waters would never be still for her. Had she not prayed all those years for Jeremy to be safe? She'd never liked the sea, but now she would never trust it again.

A short song service in the sanctuary followed the stone laying, and as she settled in the family pew at the front with Lizzie and Mary, images of all the times Jeremy had arrived into Southold tumbled through her mind. She pictured him the first time she'd seen him after they'd arrived in Southold. She'd been helping Winnie and Mary pick dried corn off the cobs. They sat on the ground outside their huts, looking up as he approached, his trunks in tow. Always bringing his trunks filled with gifts from England or France or the Caribbean. Always with a big grin on his tan face and the sun gleaming on his dark blond hair. Her heart beat now like it had then — fast, with a skip every so often.

He would not be walking up the path

anymore, and the only thing she had left of him was the cold stone in the cemetery. It was a beautiful, large, polished stone the color of the sea in a storm, wide at the base and sloping up to a point like a graceful sail — so befitting of a sea captain.

The congregation rose to sing the final psalm, but she remained seated, her shoulders drawn forward, her hands clasped in prayer. She allowed herself sobs, so drowned out were they by the notes of the hymn, and she imagined her tears were many enough to course their way to Jeremy and wash over him like the salty waves of the sea.

He rode down Main Street, his horse winded and lame. His clothes were soaked and clinging, his hair wet and matted under the hat he'd been given. He dismounted and instructed the scout to lead the horses directly to the livery, where he'd find a hot meal and a room at the boardinghouse to the rear.

Jeremy walked toward Lizzie's Hat Shop and Patience. Pure, sweet Patience. Surely she lived up to her name. How many times had she waited for him? Waited for him to stay. Waited for him to take her hand in marriage. He prayed she still wanted to hear those vows.

77

As he neared the church tower, he heard the music. Almost keeping time with the rain, it sounded like a dirge. Still, the light that poured out from the windows was warm, and he stepped to the ledge to peer in. A sea of black stood with their psalm books in hand, but a splash of light purple huddled in their midst. It was Patience.

He darted for the door and swung it open. No one turned, but rather all of the heads bowed as Reverend Youngs began a prayer. For him, for his soul, may it rest in peace. His feet did not move, as if fastened to the floor with glue. He was attending his own funeral, and for a moment he had to ask himself if he'd drowned when *The Swallow* sank, and only dreamt his rescue. His eyes riveted to Patience's trembling back. Moisture pricked his eyes. He stepped toward her, brushing past the people who stood between him and the woman he loved.

Everyone turned to stare at him, except Patience. She remained folded in a tearful prayer, oblivious to what people around her were saying. "Is it him?" "Can it be?" "Thank You, Lord!"

He touched her shoulder, but still she cried into her handkerchief. He lifted her arm until she rose to her feet, and then he pulled her close in an embrace. She sobbed on his shoulder, and he was certain she did not know it was he who held her.

"Patience. I am so sorry. I am here, do not weep."

Her head bobbed as she took a breath and looked up. Her big blue eyes widened with wonder, her mouth formed an *O,* and he could not tell if she believed it was truly him. But her words were a balm to his soul. "Jeremy! I knew in my heart if you were dead I would know it. I could just not believe it." Her arms encircled his waist, and she clung to him as if he'd leave if she didn't.

Suddenly the congregation was rejoicing, with claps on his back and hallelujahs. Barnabas and Reverend Youngs rushed to his side, and Mary and Lizzie hugged both him and Patience. When the fervor of the welcome settled into an earnest clamor, the reverend directed everyone to join him in concluding the service with thanksgiving.

Barnabas joined the reverend at the pulpit. "We were to meet at my house after services for a mug of warm cider, and I want you to know that you are all still invited. Most of all, you, Jeremy."

They walked across the road and up the flagstone path to the Horton house. It was not unusual for the house to be filled with townspeople on occasion, and tonight it seemed the entire town was here. There was always room. Barnabas insisted Jeremy sit at the head of the table in Barnabas's chair. Mary guided Patience to a seat next to him. She smiled, but there was a quiver to her lips, and her eyes remained riveted on his, as if she thought he might disappear. Indeed, seeing his funeral had the same effect on him — he wondered if at any moment he might be drawn up to Heaven after this last glimpse of earth.

Mary had prepared his favorite meal — roast turkey with mashed pumpkin, and he realized to be there to share it with them was nothing short of a miracle. After having second helpings, and everyone's attention, he stood to speak.

"Thank you all for this warm welcome on my return. I cannot begin to explain to you how much it means to witness your love and concern. At some point, I desire to tell you what happened the day the storm sank *The Swallow,* but for tonight I have other news that I must share with only a few." He turned to Barnabas. "May we withdraw to the parlor? Reverend Youngs? Zeke? Benjamin? Could you come with us?"

The men rose quickly to their feet and followed Jeremy and Barnabas out of the kitchen. "By the by, where is Johnny?" Jeremy asked.

Reverend Youngs cleared his throat. "I have a new granddaughter, Jeremy. Johnny is at home with his wife and their new baby, Martha."

Jeremy extended his hand to the reverend. "Congratulations. Johnny must be ecstatic."

"Yes, but he shall be sorry to find he missed your homecoming."

Barnabas chuckled. "It was a homecoming of a different sort, was it not?"

They all chortled as they settled in the parlor. The rain had cooled the days sufficiently to enjoy the fireplace, and Barnabas poked the logs to revive them before he turned to his brother. "Now, pray tell, what's on your mind for the chosen few?"

"I shall get right to the point because I fear we are deprived of time. The ship that picked me up was a British gunner. Captain Stone was in command, bound for Boston. I was treated much like a prisoner on his ship, which at this point is neither here nor there. We met with Governor Winthrop, who was most relieved to see that I lived and gave me a hearty welcome. He informed me of a plan from the Crown to invade New Amsterdam. Captain Stone was there to receive orders to join three other gunner ships already poised for attack. It seems the good governor of New Amsterdam will not surrender, though we have heard the people do not support him."

Barnabas stood and began to pace, a spot in the oak floorboard creaking each time he passed over it. "So one more ship will make the difference? Or are they to fire when Stone arrives?"

"Their intention is to take Amsterdam as peacefully as possible, but they will not withhold fire if provoked. What concerns us more, however, is that Governor Winthrop is sending in the Southold Militia as supporting ground troops." He turned to Reverend Youngs. "Is Johnny prepared to lead the troop?"

"They meet every week and train. Even with little Martha, he hasn't missed a week."

The fire snapped, and a shower of sparks landed on Jeremy's boot. He kicked the embers back toward the hearth. "I'll stop by his house after I walk Patience home. We need to gather the troop on the morrow and begin training in earnest."

Benjamin stood next to his father. "Count me in, Uncle Jeremy. But it's hard to take all of this in. You here, alive, but the troop will be leaving immediately to attack New Amsterdam? There was a time when we'd all jump at the chance. But in the past few years, we've learned to live with them. Dirk Van Buren, for one. He did more to achieve peace in these parts than anything Parliament has ever done."

Reverend Youngs rose. "He and Heather Flower. What's to become of them if there's a war?" He looked at Jeremy.

"Part of the troop's mission, as I see it, is to facilitate the safety of those not opposed to the takeover. Dirk and Heather Flower should return to Southold until New Amsterdam is secure. Do you agree, Benjamin?" He was curious about his nephew's opinion since he'd been engaged to Heather Flower at one time.

"Dirk might not agree to that — who knows? He might even want to stay and fight with us. But I can't speak for him, and he needs to be informed. We should make that our priority as we ride in."

Barnabas spoke up. "I agree. Captain Stone and his warship will be taking care of themselves. We need to take care of our own."

Jeremy stood now. "Then it's decided — the horse troop will meet tomorrow and we'll begin training. We ride out in one month. Now, I have a lady who is most likely suffering shock at the sight of me, and

I must take her home. From there, I will meet with Johnny and discuss our plans." He bowed and went to seek Patience.

He leaned in the doorway leading to the kitchen and grinned. The ladies still sat where they were when the men left, ginger cake crumbs on the table in front of them.

Mary leapt to her feet. "Jeremy, would you like a ginger cake?" Her ever-changing hazel eyes twinkled green.

"I could not leave without one." He put his hand out toward Patience. "But make it two. Patience, may I escort you home?"

She looked as white as the lace on her sleeve, but her cheeks colored as she rose. She swept a tendril from her face and tucked it behind her comb. "Yes, please. I would like that very much." She smiled at Mary and Lizzie with a look of apology.

Mary popped several of the crisp cakes into a bag. "No need to feel badly, Patience. You have no idea how happy we are to see you on the arm of Jeremy. 'Tis where you belong." She looked up to her brother-in-law, and her eyebrows shot up. "You have no idea. She almost went off on a ship to look for you. We were beside ourselves with what to do with her."

"I was right, though, Mary, was I not? Here he is, alive and well. Jeremy, I was so afraid you were hurt and could not help yourself."

He held his arm out, and she laced it with hers. They started for the door. "I have much to tell you, Patience. You are not far from the truth." They looked back at Mary and Lizzie and smiled their goodbyes. Then they stepped onto the road. The rain had stopped, and through the dripping trees, sunlight dappled their walk.

Patience hugged his arm. "Tomorrow you must come and tell me everything. And promise me, Jeremy, you won't be leaving me again. We've been blessed with another chance together. I cannot believe how we've been blessed." Her eyes danced with merriment as she gazed up at him.

"Patience, there's so much to tell you. But it shall have to wait."

"Wait? Why would we do that?"

He guided her around a puddle in the road. "I'm here on a mission. The Crown is ready to seize New Amsterdam, and I am to lead Johnny Youngs and his militia into Flushing and beyond to aid the warships that wait in the sound." He could not look at her face while he delivered this news.

She stopped and took his arm with both hands. "No. I cannot believe this. Why would we attack New Amsterdam now? And don't you see the danger of just riding in there when chaos shall be breaking loose? Don't you see? You cannot mean that you shall go."

He looked up as the rain began again. Black thunderclouds mounted high in the sky to the west. "I have to do this, Patience. It is not something I would have chosen for myself. But I have to go. I'll be back. I promise you."

Tears pelted her cheeks faster than the raindrops. "You cannot promise that. You don't know! I can't bear to lose you, Jeremy, not again."

"You won't. I won't let anything happen to me. Now, let me take you to your house." He put a finger under her chin. "And be thankful I did not drown." He studied the blueness of her eyes. "You have the most beautiful eyes, Patience. Do you know I think of them whenever we are apart?" He lowered his lips to hers and kissed her both hello and goodbye. Why was it always like that? He pulled her close and breathed in her fragrance. He loved the scent of honeysuckle and starch that lingered in her hair, in her clothes. "We have a month together. And I promise — it won't be this way forever." But he did not know how to change it. And it frightened him to think he might never know.

# 8

*August 27, 1664*

Saturdays were wash days for Patience, and she stood above the tub, the sleeves of her garden frock pushed up to her elbows. Washing clothes and her linens was her therapy, and today proved no different. With each shove of the garment into suds, she thought of Jeremy leaving again with no thought to how she felt. She brushed at a blueberry stain on the sudsy apron, then dipped it again into the soapy water. He could go then, she would not try to stop him.

He'd promised to come by to say goodbye before the militia rode out, but she almost wished he would not. How much simpler to not see him at all. And she might say something she did not want to say. Perchance he needed to hear it, though.

Sweat dribbled down her cheek, and she swiped at it with her sleeve. She held the cloth up to the light, and it was spotless. Each piece wrung tight, she bundled the twisted laundry and gathered it up, pushing the kitchen door with her hip.

Outside, the sun warmed her back. She shook out a jumper and draped it carefully over a rosebush. She pricked her finger, and as she drew it back to inspect the pinpoint of blood, the familiar suntanned hand of Jeremy closed over hers and brought it to his lips.

"You should be more careful when you hang your wash. Or choose a different bush."

"Are you speaking of my laundry or my heart?" She felt a warmth wash over her cheeks and could not suppress a giggle. She gathered her wits and added, "Do not come here just to say farewell, Captain."

He stepped closer and brought her into his arms. "I must leave, but I could not go without seeing you once more. Wait for me, Patience, and I will return to life here in Southold."

"Southold and me? Will we marry?"

"Yes, I want that very much, my love. Please say you will wait for me."

He kissed her, and her heart took flight like a flock of swallows. The church bell rang, and she squeezed his hands. Each clang beckoned the troops to gather. She wanted with every fiber to hold on to him, but he would go. This time she could let him, with his promise to marry her when he returned. "Yes, Jeremy. Oh yes, I shall wait for you."

"It is said we shall capture the city quickly. I pray that is true and I shall return soon."

She took a deep breath and stepped back. "Then go with my love and hurry back to me." Tears gathered, and she blinked to keep them from falling. She watched him walk away. Her heart throbbed as she returned to her pile of wet clothes. She'd keep busy. Tomorrow would be Sunday, and she would be surrounded by her friends. Many of them would have husbands, brothers, or sons who were in the militia, and they would have one another to hold in prayer. Poor Mary Youngs had just given birth to baby Martha, and Jeremy had said Johnny would be going, too. Guilt nipped at her like a hungry puppy, and she scolded herself for being selfish. There were women here who endured far more than she.

The island would be better off under English control, and she knew people like Dirk and Heather Flower would welcome the change. There were many others who would welcome it, too, and be there to support the horse troop when they arrived.

She smoothed the last gown over a bay-berry bush and dried her hands on her apron. When she went back inside, she found Lizzie at work in the hat shop, busy stitching a brim to the crown of a straw hat. She sat down opposite her, picked up a pink ribbon, and began twisting and turning until a rose emerged. She'd become quite good at making fabric flowers for Lizzie's creations.

"Mary was worried about you, Patience, but I see you have taken the news well that Jeremy shall ride with the horse troop. Quite a shock, was it not, to have him come home? And another to find he would leave us again so quickly."

She laid the rose in a box and picked up some soft yellow netting. She folded the fabric into daisy petals. "I was almost overcome with grief, but then I remembered all of the women here who will have their men gone, and my own sorrow seemed self-indulgent. We'll all be together tomorrow at church, and I imagine Mary's group on Wednesday shall be overflowing. We'll make it through somehow, won't we, Lizzie? And as Jeremy said, God willing, the men shall return soon."

Lizzie paused with her needle halfway

through the seam. "Yes, we shall. You have a good perspective, my dear, and I wonder if you have told me everything." Her violet eyes sparkled.

Patience's pursed lips slowly spread into a grin. "I should wait and tell you and Mary together." She enjoyed Lizzie's look for but a moment and then added, "But I won't. Lizzie, Jeremy said we would be married when he returns." Her grin blossomed into an even fuller smile, her joy lit like a sparkler.

Lizzie leapt to her feet, the hat and needle falling to the table. She rushed around and grabbed Patience in a hug. "Why, that is wonderful! How could you sit there chatting with me and not tell me first off?"

"It — it feels so very much like a dream. So unreal. It's very strange to even say the words." She shook her head. "Now, we must not waste a minute in going to Mary and sharing my news with her, too. She shall be upset with me if we don't. I'll go change my gown." She rushed to the stairs, hair tumbling down her back. She pulled the comb from her hair and gathered the loose tresses in one fluid motion, without missing a step. Never had she felt so sure on her feet.

She skipped back down the stairs, tying the pink ribbon lace on her bodice. She checked her hair once more in the looking glass, then turned to Lizzie. "I think I am ready."

Lizzie's laugh sounded like a chime tinkling in the wind. "I see. I am so glad to have my old friend back. Mary and I did not know what to do with you." The two went out the door arm in arm.

They chattered all the way to the Horton house, pausing to sniff the cinnamon that wafted from the kitchen as they approached. Mary opened the door before they knocked. "I heard you halfway down the lane." She smiled and gave each woman a kiss on the cheek as they entered. "Patience, are you all right? I'm sure it's shaken you as much as it did us to have Jeremy come back, and then off he went."

Patience took Mary's hands and squeezed them. "Yes, a shock, but I'm getting used to it."

"You are?"

"To be sure, only a bit. Mary, I have something to tell you."

Her friends exchanged a look. Mary started to say something, then looked at Patience. "Yes? I see Lizzie knows, so please — tell me now."

"Jeremy. He asked me to marry him."

Mary's eyes twinkled, and she squeezed

Patience's hands in return as she danced in a bobbing fashion. "He did? He did? I knew he would. How did he ask you? Tell me every word. Oh, your mother would be so happy."

Patience laughed through tears. "Truth be known, I think I brought up marriage. But in the end, it does not matter, does it? He was thinking it, if not saying it."

"You are right. And now we must pray without ceasing that the men return safe. Come, follow me to the kitchen. I've baked some new bread, almost like cake. You must taste it and tell me what you think."

Lizzie and Patience settled around the oak table with mugs of lemon thyme tea and Mary's sweet bread swirled with cinnamon. They could hear the Horton girls out the back window, chasing each other. Mary looked out and waved to Misha and Sarah, who watched the little ones. Satisfied all was well, she sat next to Patience, her eyes brimming with excitement. "So we have a wedding to plan."

For the first time since she'd told Lizzie, Patience's exuberance diminished. "I want Jeremy to be here. I want him to know all of our plans, to help me every step of the way."

Lizzie looked at Mary. "Oh." She turned

to Patience. "Is there a particular reason you feel this way?"

She nodded. "We are both older, and neither of us have our parents anymore. I just think I do not want to act like a silly young bride all in a swoon over marrying her shining knight." She took a sip of tea and let the warm liquid soothe her senses. "I've lived on my own a long time, made my own decisions. It's my wish that Jeremy will respect that and always take my desires into consideration in all of our decisions. I want to do the same for him, beginning with the wedding plans. But 'tis more than that. I need him home from this battle before I can believe our marriage really will happen."

Both sisters grabbed her hands and held tightly. Lizzie spoke up first. "It will, Patience, truly. Jeremy shall be all right. He knows how to take care of himself. We should have believed you when we thought he'd drowned. We all need to have faith."

"That's right, dear. We need to have faith like you showed to us when *The Swallow* sank."

Patience nodded. "The faith of a mustard seed. That's what it is. You both make me so grateful for friends like you. Mary, you know you will have a full house come Wednesday. Every woman in the town shows up when the men are gone."

"I know, but 'tis a good thing. I remember all those years it was you and Lizzie and Winnie. I wanted to give assistance to ladies who found it difficult to cope — we were all in this wild, raw land together. But mostly it was the four of us. I suppose we did not cope as well as the other ladies."

Lizzie shook her head. "No, I think they enjoyed gossip more than something constructive. They can meet over a fence for that."

Patience nodded. "We all like a little of that from time to time, but we've been able to solve some real problems here in your home, Mary. I'll be forever grateful for that."

"I think that is why God put us here. And we've been blessed by friends like you. And now a wedding. You may not be a swooning bride, but the wedding shall be beautiful, Patience. Shall it not, Lizzie?"

"Oh, it shall. I can see the celebration now. All of the others we have planned were but practice for this one. It shall be magnificent."

"Pinch me, for this seems unreal." She wanted to believe her marriage would happen. It didn't have to be the most beautiful wedding the good people of Southold had ever beheld. She just wanted Jeremy. To be his wife. Forever and ever.

# 9

*August 27, 1664*

Jeremy went directly to the front of the church, joining Barnabas and Reverend Youngs at the pulpit. Benjamin sat at the clerk's table, and Joshua Horton, now a lieutenant in the militia, arrived with Captain Johnny Youngs. They sat with Benjamin and waited for the rest of the troop to fill the pews.

At length, the sanctuary was filled, and the reverend cleared his throat before calling the room to order. "Gentlemen, we are sent today on a mission of extraordinary importance in the history of Long Island. Captain Horton has been dispatched by Governor Winthrop to facilitate the Southold Militia in an attack against New Amsterdam. Our ground forces are to support the British naval ships that are gathering in the sound as we speak."

A murmur rippled through the troop, but

they settled to listen as Jeremy unrolled a large map of the island and laid out the course of action.

When all questions were thoroughly answered, Johnny stood to close the meeting. "We've all known our militia could be called up at a moment's notice and we can be proud to say we are ready. You all have one hour to say your goodbyes to your families, and then you are to report to the livery. We'll mount and ride out at that time. If that is understood, you are dismissed."

Everyone began to mill about, keeping their comments low under their breath. As they dispersed to their homes, Jeremy started for Patience's house. She would roll her eyes, he was certain, and tell him he'd said goodbye already and once was enough. But he'd not expected another chance.

He stepped out of the church, musket in hand, into the sunlight. There she stood, with a blush to her cheeks and her eyes riveted to the ground. Could it be she was shy to seek him out? "Patience, I was just coming to look for you. We have an hour before I must meet the troop at the livery."

Her dark lashes fluttered as she looked everywhere except at him. "I have something for you. 'Tis not much, but a remembrance of me." She held out a lock of her blond hair, tied with a curled pink ribbon. Her wide eyes darted to his as he took the gift.

A pang jabbed at his heart, and his throat constricted as he began to speak. "I . . . I will hold this close to my heart and treasure it always. I wish I had something to give you, but all I have is my word that I will return."

She pressed her fingers to his lips. "Hush. Do not even think that is not enough. That is what I cling to — the hope you shall return to me safely. 'Tis all I need."

"Would you walk with me along the village green to the livery?"

"I should be delighted, Captain Horton."

She slipped her arm in his, and they walked in silence, with no sense of urgency. By the time they arrived at the livery, horses had been saddled and fit with the required supplies. The men were gathering, muskets at the ready and bedrolls wrapped around provisions of biscuits and dried venison.

Lizzie, Mary, and Barnabas were there to say goodbye to Benjamin, Joshua, and Caleb. Jonathan made it clear that he was old enough to go fight at sixteen, but Mary insisted — and Barnabas agreed — that their youngest boy would remain home. It was only right that a family should not be in jeopardy of losing all their sons to battle.

Jonathan could train with the reserve troop but would not be sent to the battlefield.

Mary's hazel eyes danced as she took Jeremy's arm. He didn't have to guess that she'd been told of his proposal.

"You must return at your first opportunity. Don't be the hero, just come home. I hear there's a wedding taking place when you get back, and you mustn't keep us waiting."

"You've found me out. Of course I will be returning posthaste, but not without all of our troops. You must take good care of her. For me. Will you?"

"I have all of these years, and I'm not about to stop." She looked at Patience, who remained quiet at his side. "We look out for each other, do we not?"

"We do. Always." Patience's blue eyes brimmed with tears. "Look at me. I wasn't going to cry today." She pulled a handkerchief from her pocket.

Jeremy touched her chin and drew it up. "Save your tears for ones of joy when the men come home." He bent to kiss her lips. "Until I return, my love." He bowed to Mary and Lizzie and shook Barnabas's hand before the man pulled him into a Horton bear hug and clapped him hard on the back.

Amidst tears and handkerchiefs, Jeremy

101

gave the final salute as Johnny and his men filed down the road behind him. The ride was rough to Wading Creek, and the troop made camp quickly to relax under the stars before heading to Flushing and the start of battle. In his bedroll, Jeremy pulled the ringlet of blond hair from his chest pocket and tucked it between the pages of his Bible. He went to sleep dreaming of a girl — a woman — whose yellow hair smelled of honeysuckle and crisp starch.

The ride into Flushing was fast, and they delivered the news quickly. Governor Stuyvesant must surrender to the British forces or face a bloody battle. Those who chose to support the takeover would be allowed to sign a petition and remain in their homes. Those who did not must face consequences if war broke out.

As Johnny and Benjamin delivered the message, Jeremy sought out Dirk Van Buren and his wife, Heather Flower. Dirk had left his post as a Dutch lieutenant when he and Heather Flower married. Over the years, he'd become sympathetic to the English and involved with the people of Southold. Jeremy considered him one of his closest friends.

He rode to the Van Buren farm on the

outskirts of Flushing. The house itself was set back from the public road and had a long, private lane. Heather Flower opened the door before he could dismount from his tall gelding, and he grinned at her deerskin tunic, bedecked with beads and feathers. She had not forgotten who she was or the ways of her people, even as she adopted her husband's way of life. The stark elegance of their home, immaculate and beautiful in its simplicity, was much admired by her Dutch neighbors he'd heard tell.

"Heather Flower, so good to see you." He took her shaking hands and pressed his lips to them in greeting.

"*Aqui,* friend. Is it truly you? We were told you were dead and with our Father in the heavens. I fear I see the ghost of you."

A fluffy gray wolf-dog with inquisitive blue eyes stood close to her, and Jeremy knelt and stretched his fingers in greeting. The pup sniffed, then nuzzled his hand, and Jeremy grinned up at Heather Flower. "Aye, it is me. But I was the only one to survive the wreck of *The Swallow.* My crew, all was lost."

"I am so sorry, Jeremy. Dirk is too, but he will be so thankful to see you live." She tugged at his arm to bring him inside and led him to a walnut table, decorated with a small square of delicate embroidery and a tall vase filled with sunflowers in the center. "I must give you some tea while we wait for Dirk. He returns every day at this time for dinner. I've made a rabbit stew, and you must eat with us."

He watched her dip water from the large pot at the back of the fireplace into two mugs. She had not aged in the least, her glossy black hair in a braid down her back, her lips in a pout even while her tall figure was confident and elegant. She picked clumps of bright green sage from a little bowl sitting on the window sash and dunked them in. With silver shears, she shaved chunks from a sugarloaf and stirred them into the steaming tea. She took the lid off the Dutch oven and stirred the stew before she brought the cups to the table.

He stood as she took a chair opposite him, and then they sat together, chatting about Southold and Montauk and the life she'd left behind when she married Dirk. In a funny twist in the path of life, Jeremy had wed them, and he'd been honored to do it. She was the female sachem of the Montauks now, but in name only. Her parents were dead, and her brother, too. The numbers of her tribe had dwindled from illness, and only a few remained on the tip of the south fork of the island.

"My friend, I want to hear about the shipwreck. I want to hear how you live."

Jeremy grinned. "It's a long story, and I think it should wait for Dirk." No sooner had he said that than the door swung open and Dirk stood, his mouth agape, his boots glued to the floor.

"Hallo! How is this? Jeremy — we thought you dead. It is you in the flesh, *ja*?"

Jeremy jumped from his chair and closed the distance to the door in four long strides. "Of course — Dirk, how are you, my friend?" He clapped him on the back, and the two embraced in a bear hug. The only kind of hug the Horton clan knew.

"I have never been better since I married Heather Flower and left the cavalry. I enjoy scouting much more as a civilian." He patted his wife's hand and sniffed the air. "Hmm, rabbit, and it smells wonderful." He looked at Jeremy. "Heather Flower has made you agree to dinner, *ja*?"

"Oh yes, of course. I've much to tell you, but I am famished. If it's ready, I would be the first to say 'let's eat.' "

Heather Flower put chunks of stew meat in a bowl and set it on the floor for Mosh, her wolf-dog. She ladled the rest, swimming in gravy with turnips and onions, into bowls, and Dirk helped her set them on the table. She passed a basket of *poffertjes* to Jeremy, and after the meal they ate *koekjes.*

"These are just like Mary's ginger cakes." He crunched a couple more, one after the other.

Dirk chuckled. "You don't like those, do you?"

Heather Flower refilled the plate and set it in front of Jeremy. "These cookies have the same spices as Mary's. My neighbor gave me the recipe."

Dirk helped himself to another, then leaned forward. "But I know you did not come for our good company. I do hear rumors of British ships lurking about. Does this have anything to do with your disappearance?"

"No. I was on a trade run. One of the worst storms I've ever faced moved in, with no hope of outrunning it. *The Swallow* sank, and I was the only one to survive. My crew, God rest their souls — gone." He covered his eyes as he shook his head. A long moment passed before he could continue. "I was rescued by a British warship, *The Providence.* They kept me confined. She was bound for Boston, and once we were in port, Governor Winthrop vouched for me. The secrecy aboard ship made sense when the governor briefed me about a planned attack on New Amsterdam. Four ships, including *The Providence,* are sailing into the harbor now. The militia from Southold is here, in Flushing, to give support for the attack. It is well known to the English, as well as Governor Stuyvesant, that many in Flushing would not support a battle. They don't want to fight. Simple as that."

"So you were rescued and then put into service without your ship."

"Aye. I'm sick about the ship. But I have no time to lament, which is a good thing. Barnabas and Mary desire you to take Heather Flower to Southold until the fighting is over." He looked at Heather Flower. "It won't be safe here. Most likely it will only be a matter of weeks. Mayhap days, and then you can return."

She stood and moved closer to Dirk. "I will do as you wish, my husband." She looked at Jeremy with fire in her black-opal eyes. "But *my* wish is to stay by his side."

Jeremy ran his hand through his hair and nodded at Dirk. "Barn was thinking you would be a good choice to train the reserve militia in Southold. He said Mary would love to have you stay with them, but Patience tells me she would like to have you stay with her. She always feels that big house her father built is too big for her."

"I don't know. My loyalty is not with the Dutch anymore. You know that. But I rather thought I'd fight with the horse troop when the time came. Sending me to watch over the left-behind militia seems like a retirement or quarantine. I want to be in the tussle."

Heather Flower stiffened and raised her chin. "My husband, if Barnabas requires you in Southold, I would like us to go there. He has always been very kind to us, and to return his favor would be my greatest desire." She exchanged a look with Jeremy, and though her eyes still held the fire, he could see the pleading in them, too. She did not want her husband to fight. She'd lost one husband to a violent death years ago. Jeremy understood she could not lose another. He studied Dirk, willing him to acknowledge her fears.

"I understand. We will go to Southold." Dirk kissed her hand and leaned across the table toward Jeremy, creases deepening around his eyes. "You should apprise me, and I you, before we leave."

Heather Flower pulled away. "I will be gathering what we will need to take with us. We will take the cart, yes, Dirk?"

"*Ja*. We won't need much. But we'll take

the cart and a team of two horses."

"I will take my shells to make beads. It will be a time of working with Patience and Lizzie. It would be good to spend time with them and help with the hats."

Jeremy spoke up. "The ladies will welcome that." He watched as Heather Flower disappeared behind a bearskin curtain, Mosh close to her heels. "She is rather brave, is she not?"

"She is. She's been through too much not to be. I fear she would have perished had she not been so resolute and courageous. I admire her because of those qualities. The day I found her abandoned in the forest, I knew she was a woman I could love. But she is sachem of her tribe, what little of it is left, and I must protect her for her people."

"She has led with elegance and grace, and that says much about her. We want her out of the line of fire if we attack New Amsterdam. And I know she won't go out to Southold without you. Thank you for agreeing to go. I know it is a hard decision for you — one you're not completely happy with. But the right one."

Dirk rubbed the stubble on his jaw. "It isn't difficult when it comes to Heather Flower. I will do what's right for her. Now, tell me what the plans are for this attack. I want to know what I'm training the relief troop for."

Jeremy pulled the plate of koekjes closer and broke one in half, popping a piece in his mouth. "I will tell you the details, which of course must be kept to ourselves. It is believed that there won't be a fight, though."

"There have been rumors of war around here, of course, and I can tell you Governor Stuyvesant has declared he will fight until the end if it breaks out."

"Do you think his military is prepared to do that?"

"I am not on the front line for information anymore, but personally, no, I don't believe they are. Too many are disenchanted with him and his notions. He has built a strong trade with the natives to the north, but he has pitted tribe against tribe in his effort to turn them against the English. I could not be married to Heather Flower and still support his policies. That is why I left the army."

Heather Flower entered the room, and both men stood. She smiled. "When do we leave?"

Dirk looked to Jeremy, who raised one brow. "I think you should leave even tonight. Tomorrow the ships will show their force, but you know how it is. One cannon pops off early, and that is all it takes. War breaks out."

"*Ja,* I agree." He turned to Heather Flower. "We will leave tonight."

Jeremy hauled trunks as quickly as Heather Flower could fill them. He rolled casks to the cart filled with food that would perish if left behind. Dirk gathered his ledgers and secured the livestock. Mosh, of course, would come with them, but Dirk made a quick visit to their nearest neighbor and arranged care for the livestock. Dirk's buckskin, Miss Button, stood hitched to the cart.

The three bid one another a hasty good-bye, and Jeremy watched until the cart rounded a corner, with Mosh hanging his head over the back rail, and then they were out of view. He pulled his hat down on his brow and mounted Ink, the solid-black horse that Barnabas had lent him. Ink was the first descendent of Starnight — a Great Black owned by Mary's father — born without a star or blaze. He was of sturdy stock and had a comfortable gait.

He urged Ink up the long lane and onto the well-traveled highway toward New Amsterdam. He'd camp out on the outskirts of the city, and before first light, he'd be down at the harbor to view the situation firsthand before gathering his troops. The horse troop, reinforced with Dutch soldiers from Flushing — who long favored British rule — would be at the ready.

# 10

*September 1, 1664*
*Southold*

Shadows crept across the room as the sun lowered in the sky, and Patience's fingers shook as she struck the flint to light a tallow candle on the hearth.

Lizzie hovered close to her as Mary brought the family Bible to a chair in front of the window. Mary thumbed the worn pages. "I'll read some Scripture while we wait for Barney and Zeke."

Patience burnt her thumb, and as she fanned her hand, she leaned over Mary's shoulder. "Something to calm our nerves. I can't bear to wait for Barnabas and Zeke. What takes them so long?" She straightened to look out the window into the growing darkness.

Lizzie paced. "Do you think the war has begun? How shall we know?"

Mary peered above the top of the page

she'd turned to. "They will send someone. A runner, perhaps. Barney will know we are worried." She pulled the Bible close to her nose and squinted at the verse. " 'He maketh wars to cease unto the ends of the world, he breaketh the bow, and cutteth the spear, and burneth the chariots with fire.' "

The corners of Patience's mouth turned upward. " 'Be still and know I am God.' That's the next verse. Psalm 46, verses 9 and 10." She took a deep breath. "Quite right. We should remember that."

But still she jumped when the door swung open and Barnabas and Zeke came in.

Mary jumped, too. "Barney, is there word? Do we know what is happening?"

"Dirk and Heather Flower have returned with some news. They will stay here during the attack on New Amsterdam. Dirk is assigned to train the reserve troop." He looked at Patience. "They wanted me to inquire of you if they may be your guests."

"Certainly. I shan't allow them to stay anywhere else. Where are they now?"

His mossy green eyes crinkled as he smiled. "They are at the church, still briefing Reverend Youngs. They are tired, so I imagine they won't be much longer. It is good to have them back."

"I wish they would stay." Lizzie pulled on

Zeke's arm. "Did they say if the war has begun?"

He nodded. "They left in the night. Jeremy told them that on the next morn he would be down at the harbor, with the ground troop ready. They believe the attack has begun by now."

Barnabas took Mary in his arms as he addressed the ladies. "Pray there is no bloodshed, nor life lost. The last few years have been quiet ones on the island, and I believe the Dutch would just as soon live side by side with us in peace. But it has been the intent of the Crown to claim New Amsterdam from the time we settled the east end of Long Island. And the time has come."

"And Jeremy? He put himself in the thick of it by going down to the harbor in New Amsterdam?" Patience's voice trembled as she spoke, and she put a hand to her lips.

Mary pulled back and looked into her husband's eyes. "I cannot bear this, Barney. He just came back to us."

"Jeremy knows how to manage in danger. He's proved that over and over."

Zeke chuckled. "He's got the cat's nine lives."

Lizzie's gray curls bounced as she shook her head at him. "You know that is not true. 'Tis God who has spared him, and only

God knows when He will call him home."

"Reverend Youngs will have a dedicated service on the morrow for prayers for our troops and the war." Barnabas let go of Mary and stepped toward Patience. "We all will be praying for Jeremy. With Thomas and my parents gone, he's all I have."

His words pierced her heart like tiny arrows. "I know — we all grieved so very much when we thought him dead. It was too much for me, I fear. I cannot take much more, but I know this must be so very hard for you. I do not mean to sound as if I'm the only one who matters. I only want him back home with us. By my side."

"He shall be, Patience." Lizzie took her arm. "Now come. Let's go to your house and ready a room for Heather Flower and Dirk. We have much to keep us busy as we wait, do we not?"

Patience took Mary and Barnabas in her arms as one and kissed each of their cheeks. "Please do bring me any word, good or bad. I shall worry constantly."

Barnabas nodded. "I — or Zeke — will bring you whatever snippets of news we receive. Beyond what Heather Flower and Dirk will be able to share with you, I don't believe we'll get much information until the fighting is over."

"Thank you." Her eyes misted as she and Lizzie walked up the lane. The pretty house in front of them, a tall two-story with a center chimney, stood out from the other homes. The neat flagstone walk was lined with colorful flowers. Built by her father and Barnabas when they first arrived on Long Island, the home was a place she loved sharing with her friends. But she longed to share it with Jeremy. They'd lived for years with the Dutch on the west end without major problems. Oh, why did the King decide to attack now? Why now?

"It will be over before we know it, Patience." Lizzie's chin tilted up as she looked at the house. "We'll have the wedding, and you will have Jeremy here with you, by your side, as you said."

"You've read my mind."

" 'Tis not hard to do. I shall make you some tea, and then we must fluff the mattress and set out a pitcher of fresh water and some towels. Can you think of anything else they shall need?"

"Some candles and something to light them with. I would bring in another chair, but perhaps I should wait and see how many trunks they've brought. Oh, a rug for Mosh. He will surely sleep in the room with them." They hurried inside as her list grew, eager to have everything ready before the guests arrived.

An hour later, with the room prepared, they greeted Heather Flower and Dirk. Patience was beside herself with questions. "When did you last see Jeremy? What was he doing? Where was he when you left?"

Dirk smiled. "Why don't we sit for a while, and we will tell you everything we know. It won't take long, and then we should all get some sleep. It will be a full day tomorrow."

"Yes, shall we go sit outside? It will be cool there." She took Heather Flower's arm as they wandered along the path to her English garden. The prickly-headed purple echinacea were still in bloom, and the sweet-scented butterfly bush with its arms loaded with lilac-like flowers formed an arch over their heads. Two oak benches, flanked by blue aster and spotted bee balm, faced each other at the end of the path, and the four sat down to talk.

Heather Flower pulled her thick, dark braid forward over her shoulder to cool her neck. "Where is Zeke?"

"He's still with Barnabas. There is so much happening so quickly, they must have a lot to discuss. I wanted to walk Patience home and see you." Lizzie leaned forward to pat her hand.

Patience watched a tiny hummingbird hover before flitting after a smaller one that threatened its territory. It swooped after the little one, chasing it away, then returned to the top of a small willow to keep guard over the flowers. Apparently he would rather starve than share the nectar.

She turned to Dirk. "Why can we not keep everything simple? Why do our men have to go off to war? Jeremy just returned to us. To me. Why can't the English and the Dutch just live side by side?" Her eyes grew round as she spoke.

He straightened on the bench before he answered. "The fact is, many — if not all — of the people living under Dutch control dislike Stuyvesant and his policies. They welcome change. They will not support a war."

Lizzie's brows shot up above her wide violet eyes. "Do you mean to say they will not fight for the Dutch? That the English will take over without a struggle?"

"*Ja.* I have no doubt that the English ships will not retreat. But I do not think Stuyvesant will find too many to risk their lives for him."

"Does that mean that Jeremy and the rest of the horse troop are risking their lives by putting themselves in the midst of it all? Wouldn't their presence be taken as aggressive?" Patience fingered the handkerchief tucked into her sleeve. "I mean, isn't that why you've brought Heather Flower to Southold? 'Tis too dangerous for her to remain in Flushing?"

"I don't believe they are terribly at risk, Patience. But yes, Heather Flower is principal sachem for her people. We must do everything possible to secure her safety. In the event there is gunfire or bloodshed, she needed to be far from that."

Heather Flower took her friend's hand. "And Jeremy requested Dirk keep the reserve troop at the ready."

Patience squeezed her hand as she stood. "That is not at all the encouragement you mean it to be. But come, let me show you your room. I know you are tired, and Lizzie, you must get home. Zeke shall wonder whatever happened to you." She led the way into the house as dusk settled over the yard and fireflies flew before them, lighting their path. Would that God would light Jeremy's path back to her the same way. With little fireflies of light. *Please, Lord.*

# 11

*September 10, 1664*
*New Amsterdam*

Jeremy rode out first, before the rest of the troop. Two days earlier, the Dutch governor Peter Stuyvesant had surrendered to the British. Jeremy stopped Ink near a pond for a deep drink of water. He removed his water pouch from the saddle and took a swig of water. Warm water was better than pond water, to be sure. He splashed some at the sweat on his temples and ran a hand through his hair, curly from the damp. Sweat and water trickled into his eyes, and he pinched the bridge of his nose as he blinked to see clearly again.

A runner had been sent out, so he could ride directly to Patience. He'd done his duty, now he only wanted to hold her in his arms. It was time to put her first in his life, was it not?

He camped for the night at Wading Creek,

and the next morning, he rode hard, pushing Ink as fast as he dared. He rode past the Corchaug Fort in a blur and continued on at a gallop until he reached Southold's town green. He pulled in the reins and walked his horse down the lane to Patience's home — and her arms.

In the early evening light, she looked pretty in her yellow garden frock. She wore a white linen apron and pulled weeds from her rosebushes with a vengeance. If she heard him coming, she didn't give a clue. He eased himself from the saddle and came up behind to touch her shoulder. She turned, her eyes a question, and tears sprang into their blueness as she cried out. "Jeremy! How could this be? You were needed in the war." She looked him up and down, as if expecting an injured arm or leg. "Are you all right?"

His joy at seeing her spilled into his eyes, and his grin could not be contained. "Yes, yes I am. The war is over, Patience. In fact — there was no war. The people would not have it. Governor Stuyvesant locked himself in his office and did not want to come out until they agreed to fight. But they would not and forced him out to raise the white flag. The Dutch surrendered without one shot from the English cannons. We have claimed New Amsterdam for the Crown."

She fell against him. "Thank goodness you're home." She pulled back and looked into his eyes. "Does Barnabas know? Reverend Youngs? Where are Johnny and Benjamin?"

A chuckle escaped as he drew her back to him and held her close. A blond wisp of her hair brushed his cheek. "A runner is bringing the official news. I may be ahead of him, but no matter — they will know soon enough. I did not want to tarry in coming to you. Johnny and Benjamin are still with the horse troop. They will remain there during the transition."

"Do you feel they are safe?"

"I would not have left if I thought not. The English have long had support from those who lived under the unstable rule of Stuyvesant. It is said he will retire to his estate and not cause one whit of a problem. No, they remain more to facilitate the change than to defend the takeover."

They walked hand in hand along the path to the garden. Her laughter pleased him as they watched a small fluff of a rabbit nibble on a grass blade. He'd like to hear the music of her giggle every morning and every night. "Patience, we've known each other for a long time, but in many ways we are just beginning together." He rolled his eyes at how inane his own words sounded and tugged her arm so that she sat with him on the bench. "I mean, thank you for waiting for me. In some ways, I've been such a fool. I could have lost you to a number of men that mayhap deserved you more."

He expected a light laugh again, but she turned to him instead and studied his face. After a long pause, she began to answer him, but then stopped, as if deep in thought.

He lifted her chin with his finger. "You haven't changed your mind, have you?"

"No, of course not. I was just thinking, I've never met a man who measures up to you. Oh, Barnabas — but he's never counted. But I would have waited forever, I think, sadly. Don't you know that?" A smile flit across her lips and disappeared quickly. "Don't you?"

"When you tell me like that, I do. I love you. I always have." She laid her lovely head on his shoulder, and he bent to kiss her. "We have a lot to get ready for. Lizzie and Mary will be thrilled to know they have a wedding to plan."

"Oh, I imagine. And Heather Flower."

"Where are she and Dirk? They are staying with you?"

"They are. They went over to Mary's. But

I'm the wedding planner. I shall be making all of the decisions, and they will delight in helping me, to be sure. But what of you, Jeremy? What are your plans here in Southold — besides marrying me?"

"What? You shall not provide for both of us?" He chuckled. "I rather thought I'd be a kept man."

She teased right back. "I rather think you should tire of that quickly."

"I haven't had much of a chance to think this through, but you know I had much to say about how *The Swallow* was built. I'm thinking I might be a shipwright and build or repair ships. What do you think of that?"

Her blue eyes flew open wide, and dimples emerged in her cheeks. "Why, that is a wonderful idea. Ships have been the love of your life, have they not?" Her grin took on an impish delight. "I'm not afraid to share you."

"You could say they were my first love, but *you* shall be my last."

She leaned into his embrace. "Tell me more — would you be building at Hallock's Landing?"

"Possibly. But I'm more inclined to inquire at Winter Harbor. I've docked there from time to time, and I think the fellows there might be open to another shipwright.

125

I don't know — we shall see."

"It seems the big ships prefer it over Hallock's."

"The fact is, Hallock's is almost too well-protected. And the water in the bay is deeper on Winter's end. I've had a few conversations with the master shipwright in the past, and he says he's close to handing over the sail iron, so to speak." He watched her as she studied an ant that ran one way and then another as if it were lost. "What say you?"

She looked up, a blush flooding her cheeks. "Why, I think it is a grand idea. Winter Harbor is not far from here. Handing over the sail iron is much like handing over the kitchen tongs." Her eyes misted.

"What's wrong? You are crying."

She dabbed at her eyes with the corner of her apron. "I'm not weeping. It's just, it's just . . ."

"Go on. What is it?"

"It made me remember we have no parents between the two of us. They're all gone. No one to hand me the tongs when we marry. Perhaps that is not so important anymore."

"That is not true. Certes. It's important." Mary would present her with the tongs, he would see to that.

"My mother and father would have been delighted that you have proposed. They would have welcomed you to the family. Oh, Jeremy, we shall be so happy!"

"That we shall. Now, first things first. I should look into employment at Winter Harbor. Once that's settled, we need to decide where we will live."

"Where we will live? I thought you would move in here, with me, after the wedding."

He smiled at her. "I did not want to assume, but I had hoped you might make that offer. The other option would be to ask Benjamin to build a house for us. Thomas Mapes is surveying some land out toward Thomas Benedict Creek and some near where Johnny Youngs lives. There's a hill above the port. It would be perfect for our house."

Her eyes flew open. "What about Dame School?"

"You could use this property for your school and Lizzie's Hat Shop, just as you do now. We have time to think on these things." So many decisions. Very well then. They would take their time. There was no hurry. He was here now, and they had the rest of their lives to think things through. They could take each day as it came. "There's no hurry to decide. With your school and the wedding plans, you have much to keep you busy."

Patience looked over her rosebushes and settled on the pink cabbage roses nodding their heads in the light breeze. Jeremy had brought the plant over from France, just for her. She snipped several blooms and took them in to arrange in a vase. Barnabas had come in search of Jeremy the moment he heard the news of his return, and the two had left for a meeting with Reverend Youngs.

She looked about her kitchen. She loved this house. But perhaps building their own house was the proper way to begin her life with Jeremy. She wasn't certain she would continue her school for little girls — as much as she loved them. No, it might be time to expand the hat shop. Lizzie had indicated for a while now that she could easily do that, if she had the space.

And if Heather Flower and Dirk remained in Southold, their friend could have her own workroom and become a full partner with Lizzie. Would Dirk want to return to Flushing? Most likely. But perhaps the hat shop would entice them to stay.

Her mind swirled with the turn of events. Not only were her prayers being answered, but the prayers of the entire village of

Southold. And Jeremy seemed to be taking everything in stride, as if he had prayed for this, too. But he hadn't, she was sure of it. But at least he had accepted it with enthusiasm. She would be open to change too — wasn't that love? For with love came sacrifice. That much she knew.

# 12

*September 14, 1664*
*Southold*

If Patience hoped to remain in control of the wedding plans, those thoughts were quickly revised by Mary, Lizzie, and Heather Flower. After a morning relishing the memory of Heather Flower's wedding, the ladies dove into preparations for Patience's as they stitched pretty lace onto linen napkins.

They all agreed her dress should be of the finest ivory brocade and pure pink silk. French lace and gossamer ribbons would drape her like icing on a cake. Lizzie would place an order from Boston on the morrow. If *The Margaret* was still in port and headed for Boston, perhaps they could send their list with the captain.

Nothing was decided about her stick-straight hair, though it was much discussed. Heather Flower's was straight, too, and had

130

looked gorgeous on her wedding day with the curls ironed into it and flowers woven through. Perhaps she would request the same treatment.

Mary looked over her list. "You do think the wedding will take place before winter, do you not, Patience?"

"That is the thing. Perhaps not. Jeremy is going to Winter Harbor to seek employment as a shipwright."

Lizzie nodded her approval. "That would be perfect for him."

"Yes. It seems he has talked, some time ago, with the master shipwright. It may be time for him to retire, and he thinks Jeremy would be a good replacement. At least he did back when they first talked."

"Well, he shall want to get that settled first, I am certain. As I said, we shall be ready, no matter what. I'm just thinking a wedding in warm weather is so much nicer. Not that a wedding at Christmastide would not be beautiful."

"I hope we do not wait that long. But we do want Benjamin and Johnny back before we wed. And Joseph to come home with Jane and the children."

Mary sat next to Patience. "The event of the year, my dear. We shall have as much fun as you."

The kitchen door opened, and Barnabas entered, followed by Jeremy and Dirk. "Heigh-ho! I hope we do not intrude?"

Barnabas most often commanded the attention of the ladies, but today all eyes were on Jeremy. Mary was the first to speak. "Of course not. In fact, you have arrived just in time. We have many questions for you."

Jeremy grinned at Patience. "Mayhap we have arrived at the wrong time." The men chuckled.

Mary nudged Patience. "Go ahead, dear. You first."

Now everyone watched Patience. Her cheeks burned. "We are wondering if you might, when you are over in Winter Harbor, find out if *The Margaret* is still in port?"

Jeremy's eyes met Barnabas's before he answered. "Patience, I must delay going to Winter Harbor."

"But why? What about your plans?" Patience's throat ached once more as she waited for his answer.

Barnabas cleared his throat and ran a hand through his thick, white hair. "The truth is, Patience" — he nodded to her and then the room — "ladies, Jeremy is needed here at the moment. We've just had a meeting with Reverend Youngs, and although the initial word is the takeover of New Amsterdam was peaceful, we've been instructed to prepare the reserve troop for backup in the event things turn ugly. It has almost gone too smoothly to not be prepared for an ambush of some sort."

Jeremy smoothed the hair on the back of his neck. "I am going to be working with Dirk in training the horse troop that remains here. We must be ready for an attack from the Dutch along the sound. We have no idea how long this will take, but we must be prepared for anything. I'm afraid I will need to delay my plans to go to Winter Harbor."

The sadness in his eyes did not escape her, but her own sadness clawed at her throat, and her heart ached. Why did this seem like one more delay in their happiness?

Mary was quick to fill the silence. "Why, in a way that is good news. Why don't we proceed quickly with the wedding? By the time everything is resolved politically, you could be settled."

Jeremy's brows rose, and Patience noted the tender smile he gave his sister-in-law. They'd always been close, even throughout the difficult early years of Mary's marriage to Barnabas. He was about to say something neither she nor Mary would care to hear. She could see it coming.

"Mary, we cannot proceed just yet. It's

my duty to Southold and the Crown to defend and protect it. Surely we cannot celebrate in the midst of this turmoil, no matter how safe we have always deemed it to be here."

Barnabas held up his hand. "The facts are, it's more than supporting the takeover. We on the east end are wide open for an Indian attack from the Narragansett whilst our attention is on the west end." He looked at Heather Flower. "We can't risk it happening again."

Lizzie put a hand on Heather Flower's shoulder. "At least we could prepare for the wedding so when the time comes, we are ready."

Patience looked from Mary to Heather Flower and then to Lizzie. They appeared stricken. Well, she was a little stricken herself. "I think we need to support the military rather than plan a wedding, Lizzie. There is much we can do to provide meals and clothing for the soldiers. And you should prepare some of your concoctions in the event sickness or injuries overcome our troops."

Jeremy came quickly to her and pulled her to her feet and into his arms. "Thank you, my love, for making all this easier. Just as soon as this matter is put to rest, I will go

134

to Winter Harbor." He pulled her close and lowered his lips to hers.

She caught her breath, and his kiss sent tremors down her spine. For a moment, she desired to remain in his arms, but just as quickly she remembered her friends who sat agape. "Oh!" She smoothed a wisp of hair from her cheek. "Well, now. Before we are accused of impropriety, I think I should remind everyone we are pledged to each other." The delighted faces staring back were both amusing and disconcerting to her, and her cheeks grew warm. "I think 'tis time I went home and began to make a list of what I can contribute to the cause."

"I will escort you, of course." Jeremy offered his arm.

"Thank you, but there's no need. My goodness, it is just down the lane. I need a little time to myself. Surely you understand." She smiled, but she feared her eyes gave away the sadness that engulfed her.

Lizzie stood. "I shall go with you."

"No, Lizzie. Truly, I want to be alone." She slipped out the front door. The clouds that had been gathering throughout the day opened, and she walked through the rain without so much as a glance to the sky. Even a rumble of thunder did not faze her, so alone she was in her thoughts.

The insistent cadence of the rain on her shingled roof caused her to look down at her soaked clothes, and she climbed the stairs to change into a dry gown. How could he insist on waiting? Had she not waited for him a lifetime already? Would there always be a reason they could not marry?

# 13

*September 15, 1664*

Jeremy started immediately to organize the ragtag troop left behind when the cream of the village rode out to Flushing. It was now on his and Dirk's shoulders to train them into a militia Southold could be proud of.

He picked through the assorted muskets and ammunition while Dirk put the small band of men through physical training at a good pace. He looked out the window of the meetinghouse and watched as the troop tossed weighted balls back and forth. They might make something out of these men yet.

A messenger brought word that Joshua Hobart would be arriving the following day for a short visit. Jeremy did not know him well, but he knew of his interest in Long Island and particularly Southold. He was the son of Peter Hobart, the venerable minister of the church in Hingham, Massachusetts. Joshua was a minister himself, most recently in Barbados, where Jeremy had met him. His wife had died there some years before, and he was looking to relocate his ministry.

Mayhap it would be on Long Island. Joshua liked the isolation they seemed to enjoy here. He shared his father's inclination to have a more inclusive church, and that was easier here than up in Massachusetts, to be sure. And Southold had become more tolerant over the years. Nathaniel and Grissell Sylvester were a good example. Everyone knew they were sympathetic to the Quakers, but still they were welcome to worship in Southold. Tolerance was not about suspending their own beliefs but knowing how to love those who did not share those beliefs.

But the somewhat cloistered existence had been shattered when their King decided to invade New Amsterdam and left the island vulnerable to a counterattack. Would Joshua feel the same when he visited and found the troops training and an attack on their end of the island imminent?

Jeremy folded the message and stuffed it in his pocket. He was certain Ester had an empty room at the boardinghouse. It was not good timing for a visit, but he could take it in stride. God might have a purpose and a plan in all of this.

He returned to cleaning the guns, a chore familiar to him since he'd been a youngster on his father's estate in Mowsley. He and his brothers grew up with guns, and his father taught them to not only respect them, but to keep them in good working order, as well. He rather enjoyed the process.

Barnabas appeared as Jeremy polished the last musket with strong, gliding strokes. "What say you we go down to the meeting-house. Reverend Youngs came by and requested that we join him and bring Dirk with us."

"By all means. I just finished up in here, and if the shouts of elation I heard a few minutes before you came are any indication, I believe Dirk to be finished with the troop. He put them through their paces today."

"Very good. Let's find Dirk and walk on over."

They went outside and did not look long for Dirk, as he was on his way to find Jeremy.

"How goes it?" Barnabas clapped his shoulder.

"It's only day one, so we should not expect a lot. But young Jacob showed much promise. As for the rest of the lot, they have a long way to go." He looked at Barnabas. "I will tell you, though — our Jonathan is the best of the lot. He'll make a fine soldier. He'd go in a heartbeat if you would let him."

"His mother will not allow it, and I have to agree with her. Four sons on the battlefield are enough. Even if it is a non-battle."

The three strode toward the meetinghouse. A drizzle kept the lane muddy and a gray cast on the day. Jeremy cocked his head toward Barnabas. "Do you know what John wants to talk to us about?"

"Nay, not really. But methinks it will be about the military situation and the implications for Southold."

The rest of the walk was in silence, save for their boots trudging through puddles. What more could they do but pray and prepare the troop? If there was something else, Jeremy wanted to know.

John Youngs stood in the doorway as they approached. "Good to see you. Come right in." They filed in and sat around the clerk's desk. "I called you here because I've received some news from New Haven."

"Oh?" Barnabas leaned forward, and Jeremy glanced between the two.

"Yes. It seems as New Amsterdam is assimilated into an English colony, King Charles intends the whole of Long Island to fall under the jurisdiction of New Amsterdam. We shall lose our place with New Haven."

Barnabas scraped the chair against the wood floor as he stood, his hand raking through his hair while he paced. "Then we shall object. That is not right. We haven't a vote? We haven't a say? Well, that is not acceptable."

"Now, settle down, Barnabas. This is more rumor at this point than fact."

Jeremy rubbed his chin. "What are the implications if this happens? Why is this not better than having the Dutch in control of the west end and Southold having to answer to New Haven?"

Dirk leaned forward. "The Dutch left Southold alone. And New Haven does the same. They have ignored us almost from the start, for which we have been thankful."

"Southold, and every village on the east end, will be under the scrutiny of the Crown. That is not what we desire." Barnabas sat back down.

"And I repeat, it hasn't happened yet."

"Very well, but we will fight it. I will go home and write a letter to New Haven at once. Dirk, you should write one, as well. From the Dutch point of view." Barnabas looked at Jeremy. "And you should, too. Use your influence with Governor Winthrop. Write him a letter. We have to do all in our power to put such notions to an end."

Jeremy nodded. "That I can do. But that reminds me. I had a message from Joshua Hobart. He will be here two days hence for a visit. I know this is not the ideal time, but I would like to suggest that we have a dinner in his honor. I would be volunteering you and Mary for that, Barnabas, but I think it is advantageous — especially in light of your news, Reverend Youngs. His father is quite good friends with Governor Winthrop, as well."

"Of course. Mary and I would be honored. We cannot let it interrupt the training, but certainly we can have a small feast and make sure he sees things our way. What is his business, though, if I might ask?"

Jeremy arched an eyebrow. "Well, I am not sure. I think he's on a mission to find a place where they need a minister. That won't be Southold, now, will it, Reverend?" He grinned.

"Not for a while yet, anyway. I intend to serve this congregation until the good Lord calls me home. As long as the people are willing to have me."

Barnabas stood again. "Hear, hear. Of course we will have you. If this Reverend

Hobart desires to preach on Long Island, he shall have to inquire over at Easthampton. Thank you, John, for keeping us informed. Now, we have letters to write, meals to prepare." He chortled and clapped Dirk and the reverend on their backs. Jeremy fell in with him as they crossed the road to the Horton house.

"This Hobart chap is a scholar, you know. I think you will like him. Graduated Harvard."

"If he can help us retain our allegiance to New Haven, I will like him very much."

They circled around to the back entrance into the kitchen. Mary looked up from the pot she stirred as they entered. "Why, hello. You are just in time for a little stew, Jeremy. I know I need not ask if you are hungry." She smiled at both men.

"It smells good, and you know I would never turn down one of your meals, Mary."

Barnabas draped his arm across her shoulders and pulled her near. "Two days hence, we shall have company for dinner, and he is someone who could prove to be important to the people of Southold. If I offer my services, will you prepare the meal? Reverend Youngs and his wife will be coming, as well as Dirk and Heather Flower. And of course, Jeremy and Patience."

Her face brightened. "That would be lovely. Shall we have a ham? Or perhaps I should roast a joint of beef? And we shall have pheasant."

Jeremy chuckled. "It will all be good no matter what you prepare."

"We will be in my study. We've a couple of letters to write. Call us when the stew is ready."

"Letters? What letters? You cannot be so mysterious with me and get away with it."

"You may read them when we are done, my sweet sister-in-law. But it is better for us to write them first, then discuss them with you over dinner."

Barnabas led the way down the hall. "To be sure."

Mary called after them, "When I send you back to rewrite them, you shall wish you had talked first." Her giggle followed them into the study.

Barnabas sat at his desk. "She may be right, you know."

"Aye, I am sure she is. We must not let her know it, though." He looked around the room, so well appointed, and knew her hand was in it. Many of the pieces in the room she'd asked him to bring on his voyages from England and France. He ran his hand over the soft, worn leather of the chair he'd brought from Italy for Barnabas's birthday, at Mary's request.

Barnabas proffered the chair with a wave of his hand. "Sit. You write a letter first to Governor Winthrop. We must make it clear to him we desire to remain under New Haven in all government matters."

Jeremy removed the cap from the ink bottle and dipped the quill in, stirring with the tip. "We need to state that this is just to inform him of our intentions, not that we anticipate a change. He disclosed the plan of attack to me in order to have the backing of our ground troop, but he did not come forth with the consequences of what he intended."

"He might not have known himself. We have all wanted the Dutch rule defeated, but to what end?" Barnabas walked over to the window and watched the orange and yellow oak leaves shiver in the breeze, droplets of water from the recent rain shedding from their surface. He clasped his hands behind his back. "State our concerns from a positive standpoint. That we rejoice in New Amsterdam for the Crown, but we expect little change on the north and south forks of Long Island."

Jeremy bent over his paper and let the words flow. He dotted an *i* and a period before he signed with a flourish: *Your humble servant, Captain Jeremy Horton.* "There. I think Mary shall be proud."

Barnabas looked over his shoulder and scrutinized the letter. "Very good."

Jeremy stood and swept his arm toward the seat. "It is all yours." He watched his brother pick up the quill and dash off two letters in succession. One to the New Haven authorities and one to the King himself.

"Well done." He clapped Barnabas on the back, and they trotted down the hall, letters in hand, to find Mary. She was in the kitchen, ladling chunks of venison into bowls. She dipped the spoon back in the pot for extra gravy and bite-sized pieces of carrots and potatoes. Mercy sat at her place at the table, and Hannah, Sarah, and Mary brought bread, cheese, and crocks of butter to the table.

Mary smiled at the men. "Barney, you may call Jonathan for supper. He is in the stable."

He set the letters on the sideboard and motioned Jeremy to sit. "I'll fetch him."

Jeremy helped Mary place the steaming bowls of stew around the table before he took his seat.

When everyone had gathered for the meal, they joined hands and Barnabas led them in prayer. He thanked the Lord for the good harvest that year, the food prepared, and the hands that cooked it.

Jeremy listened as his brother asked for guidance in the coming days, for wisdom to meet the challenges before them. For change was here, and some was needed and welcomed, but not without difficulty laced with emotion. He added his hearty "Amen" to the prayer. "Someone once told me we must accept the things that cannot be changed but strive to change what we must. It seems that is where we are with this. As I see it, we have only one choice."

Barnabas paused as he brought a spoonful of stew to his mouth. "We wrote our letters, Mary, and when we've finished eating, we'd like you to read them."

"I should like that." She smiled at her husband, then Jeremy. "I'm beyond curious."

Jonathan sat ramrod straight like his father and uncle. He set his spoon down. "Father, are your letters concerning our fight in New Amsterdam?"

"Not so much the fight, son, but the aftermath. It is important that Southold has a say in how the government is restructured, for it will be, without a doubt. We must not lose our voice."

Mary stirred Mercy's stew and blew on the steam before she gave the spoon to her little girl.

"There you are, my poppet. It's not too hot." She turned to Jeremy. "Patience and I shall be so happy when everything has settled and you may turn your thoughts to her and the wedding."

A pang of guilt played with his heart. He knew Patience waited on him to finish his business and get on with their life. But had they both not waited for each other a long while? Would a few more weeks matter? Not really, not with so much at stake for Southold and their future.

After eating, the children set about their chores. Jonathan went out to bring in wood for the fireplace, and even Mercy helped her sisters clean the table and put away the dishes. Mary cut fat slices of apple pie for everyone and took bites of her piece while she pored over the letters.

"You men are very bold, are you not? But I like it. You must show these to Reverend Youngs and send them off at once." She glanced at them over her spectacles.

"When did you start reading with spectacles, Mary?"

"Oh, I've had them for years now. You just have not been around to see. I started using them after Mercy was born. Everything started falling apart then, I fear."

Jeremy stood and kissed her cheek and turned to bid good night to the children and Barnabas. "Well, I shall be much closer now. Keeping an eye on all of you." The children shrieked their delight and ran to hug his legs as he inched toward the door.

He turned to take in the warmth of the fire, the aroma that lingered from the fine meal, the children gathered 'round. He'd waited too long to have such a family with Patience. But he could be thankful for what they would share. And a passel of nieces and nephews would be among those things.

# 14

*September 16, 1664*

A cool, wet wind lifted her hair and skirts as Patience walked the path to Mary's orchard. It was the most established grove in Southold, with trees brought over years ago from her papa's orchard, and Mary took joy in it. She shared their bounty with all in the village.

Patience breathed in the damp air, happy for the change in season. The apple harvest was already in progress, but today she'd promised to help Mary and the children tidy the groves. After they removed the bad apples, the boys could come through quickly, filling baskets with the good ones. School would begin again soon, and she'd spend her days planning and teaching — and dreaming of her wedding.

Mary helped Sarah out of a tree, small withered and wormy apples on the ground beneath. Patience waved and called, "Good morrow — I remember when Caleb and Joshua used to do this chore. Where is Jonathan? Does he not help?"

Mary pushed at her sleeves. "He is off with Barney out in the woods by the sound. They took Thomas Mapes out with them to do a little surveying. Someday Barney might build another house out there."

"Oh! I did not know he had intentions of that sort. Is this new?"

"It is, in a way. But I think he's thought of doing this ever since John Budd left for Rye and gave Ben and Anna the house he built here. Barney would never leave Southold, but he rather likes the idea of leaving the old house to the next generation. Sooner rather than later."

"But what of the bakery?"

"Why, it could stay right here, I would think." Mercy ran by chasing Muffkin, and Mary raised her voice. "Now, don't chase that mouser — he's much too old for that."

They both watched as Mercy fell in a heap on the ground, tearful at the reprimand but rolling over with giggles as Muffkin came to investigate her condition and planted licks on her cheeks.

Patience turned back to Mary. "I have not seen Jeremy for a few days now. I know he has much to occupy his time, though."

"He had a meeting with Reverend Youngs and Barney yesterday. Did Dirk tell you about it? He was there."

"Oh yes, he did. 'Tis troublesome about New Amsterdam. At first it seemed wonderful news. But truly it is so much more complicated." How could they begin thinking of their life together when the recent events consumed the thoughts of the entire village? Her sigh gave her thoughts away. "Governor Winthrop told Jeremy that King Charles gave New Amsterdam to his brother months ago, even before he sent the warships. 'Tis why everyone worries that Southold will fall under the Duke of York's realm rather than New Haven."

"Is that possible? I don't know. But life goes on, Patience, and soon Jeremy will come to you. In fact, he brought us news yesterday that Reverend Hobart's son, Joshua, is coming to Southold on the morrow. Barney asked me to prepare a meal for him, and I told Jeremy to invite you. I'm certain he will be stopping by today to ask you. Heather Flower and Dirk are invited too, of course."

"Really? That is delightful! How can I help you?"

"Just come. Perhaps cut some flowers from your garden. You have the prettiest in all of Southold."

Patience looked at the sky, the clouds scuttling across like little ships. "I shall do that, if a storm doesn't come through during the night and the petals all blow away." Jeremy could be at her house right this instant, and here she was chatting away with Mary. She surveyed the orchard. "It looks rather fine here. Do you still need my help?"

Mary's giggle eased her guilt over abandoning her. "The children love this chore, and they were up before first light in anticipation. I appreciate that you offered, but truly I understand your need to go home and tend to your own chores. Even if that includes worrying over Jeremy." Her hazel eyes shone green as she spoke.

Patience grabbed her friend's shoulders and kissed her cheek. "Thank you. You know how dear you are to me."

"Yes, yes, I know. Now go. Do not tarry — Jeremy could be at your door as we speak."

Patience's feet flew beneath her as she hurried to the road. Behind her she heard Mary call, "I did not say run — you shall fall" right before she started to tumble.

Strong arms caught her, and she looked up into Jeremy's gorgeous green eyes. "I . . . I . . ."

"Are you all right? Did you twist your ankle?"

He held her close, and all of the doubts aggrieving her mind released like fuzz from a dandelion blowing in the wind. "I'm fine. Mary said you might be coming to see me, and I thought I should be at home."

"I did go to your house, and Heather Flower said I'd find you at Mary's. Would you like to go back to her house, or shall I walk you home?"

She peered back toward the orchard and could see Mary had already turned back to the children. No doubt she'd seen Jeremy save her from her graceless fall and hoped they would spend some time together at last. "I rather think I'd like you to walk me home."

He opened the gate to her backyard, and they followed the path to the garden. They'd just settled on a bench when Mosh entered and curled himself at her feet. She bent and ran her fingers through his thick gray fur, and he thanked her by nuzzling her knee with a damp nose.

"Oh, Mosh." She lowered her face into his furry neck and pulled him partway to her lap. "I see why Heather Flower loves you so." She looked up at Jeremy. "She shan't be far behind him."

154

"Then I must tell you quickly."

She held her breath.

"Joshua Hobart, a minister I met in Barbados, is coming to Southold tomorrow."

Her breath gave way to a laugh, and Mosh wiggled as if the laugh were for him. "I know. Mary told me. And we are to have dinner with him at the Hortons'."

"Yes, and did she also tell you that there are likely to be changes in the way we are governed because of the changes in New Amsterdam?" His earnest eyes searched hers.

"No, Dirk told me that last night. I've caught up on all of the news, Jeremy. Why did you wait so long to come to see me?" She watched him as he studied a rose bloom. One drop of moisture still clung to the whorl of petals.

"I imagine because I thought the news would be upsetting to you. Not only must we prepare to defend Southold, but we must find a way to restructure that is acceptable to both our people and the Crown. It is very complicated, and I know that you long for everything to be resolved so that we may turn our thoughts to our wedding."

She stretched her finger to the flower and brushed the droplet away. "I may long for peace and security for Southold, but prithee, why must we wait for it all to be resolved? Why must we?" She could not look in his eyes as she asked the question. The fear that she would see his answer, stark and unadorned, kept her from it. Surely he would soften it with gentle words.

"Patience, my love —"

"Mosh! There you are." Heather Flower came around the bend in the path. "Oh, I am so sorry. I didn't know you were here, Jeremy. I'm sorry if I am intruding."

Jeremy stood. "Of course not. Please sit down with us." He swept out his arm to the other bench.

Was he relieved that Heather Flower had kept him from saying what he must? Her friend took the seat offered by Jeremy, and Mosh moved immediately to her side.

Jeremy lowered himself next to Patience. She shook her head. "I know what you intended to say, but I can assure you I understand. You needn't explain, but you must know I shall be waiting for you. I always have." She looked into Heather Flower's dark eyes. " 'Tis all right. You have not interrupted. In truth, you came at just the right time."

"You are angry with me, Patience." Jeremy picked up her hand and kissed it. "I'm so sorry. I should have come sooner."

Heather Flower rose. "Do not be afraid to talk to each other about matters of the heart as long as you use loving words meant to heal and not destroy. Neither angry words nor silence are good ways to communicate. Come, Mosh. These two must talk." Her lips gave way to a small, pouty smile as she turned to follow the path back to the house.

Patience looked up at Jeremy. "Of course, she is right. I should have let you finish. I'm not angry, I'm just a little sad, I suppose."

He pulled her into an embrace. "Yes, you are, and that is all right. I am, too. It won't be like this forever, Patience. Give me some time, and we'll be wed. Just let me finish up my duties to Southold, and then I shall turn my attention to finding work."

She tilted her head back, her lips near his. "I shall do that. I shall let you finish what you need to do. Just hurry, please." She felt his breath on her cheek, then his lips on hers. She clung to his kiss, making him be the one to end it — hoping he never would.

He rested his chin on the top of her head. "I will hurry, my love, with every breath."

# 15

*September 17, 1664*

Patience hummed as she snipped late blossoms from her garden and piled them on the linen cloth. Frost would soon wreak its havoc on them. She would bring an armload of flowers to put in the many vases Mary kept about the house. The bouquets would be colorful, filled with roses and chrysanthemums, asters and anemones. And she plucked sprigs of mint to scent the rooms.

Heather Flower and Dirk had walked over earlier to help Mary with her roasts. When Jeremy came, she was ready to go. The day was bright, with a crisp blue sky, trees dressed in vivid color, and the smell of wood smoke in the air. He carried the flowers, and she clung to his hand. She wore a favorite dress, simple with small blue flowers woven into the linen. Her hair was twisted and pulled up in the back, and she wore a white cap with the ties loose and flying in the fall breeze.

Mary and the savory scent of roasted meat greeted them at the door. She brought them into the parlor, where Barnabas sat with their guest. Both men stood for introductions. The young Reverend Hobart bowed deeply over Patience's outstretched hand, and for a moment she was unsure what to say or do next. But the tall reverend with warm brown eyes and wavy nut-brown hair filled the silence by telling her how pleased he was to meet her and could he just say he'd never seen such pretty dimples.

A warmth blossomed on her cheeks, and she turned from both Reverend Hobart and Jeremy to hide her response.

Reverend Youngs arrived with his wife, Joan. Lizzie and Zeke came a bit later.

The young Horton girls had taken their supper early and now remained upstairs with Abbey and Misha. It made for lively, uninterrupted conversation at the table, and Patience enjoyed sitting back as she listened to the men discuss the latest news from New Amsterdam. Everyone was grateful there had been no bloodshed, but they all, Joshua Hobart included, feared what would become of the east end.

Presently, after Mary pressed him to take

second helpings of everything, including the sweet potatoes she'd laced with cinnamon and molasses, Joshua shared his plan to travel to Easthampton and visit with Thomas James, the minister there. "As you know, I am intent on finding a ministry here on Long Island. But after hearing about the recent events, I'm thinking that they affect the south fork as much as the north fork. Mayhap some of you should accompany me on my trip tomorrow."

Barnabas rubbed his chin and looked from John Youngs to Joshua. "Who else will you be meeting with?"

"Charles Barnes, the schoolmaster."

Barnabas chortled. "Charles and I go way back. John, Dirk — what say you? Jeremy?"

"All of us on the east end need to stay united. We should go." Reverend Youngs turned to Jeremy. "And we should take Nathaniel Sylvester with us."

"I quite agree. Dirk, how do you feel? You have a unique position here, being Dutch but fighting with the English."

"We should go and talk. Governor Stuyvesant often said the south fork is like a different country. We need unity from them, not contention."

Barnabas nodded. "Then it is set, we shall go with you. And by way of Shelter Island."

"I have some berries and cream if anyone would care for some before we leave the table." Mary stood halfway up. "Barney? Reverend Hobart?"

Joshua waved a hand. "Oh no, thank you. What a fine meal, though."

Barnabas scooted his chair back. "Gentlemen, shall we remove to the porch to finish the conversation?"

"Splendid idea." Reverend Youngs stood.

Jeremy was the last to file out and gave Patience a kiss on the cheek as he left. She turned to help Mary and the other ladies clear the table and wash the dishes. Heather Flower had been quiet during the meal, and she moved next to her as she wiped a wet rag over the table. "Has it been a long time since you were in Montauk?" Patience asked.

"*Nuk*. Yes, it has. I was just thinking I would like to go with Dirk and the other men. To see Grissell and my people."

Lizzie ran a dry cloth behind Patience's wet one. "You should tell them you want to go."

Joan nodded. "They will let you. But you need to tell them that's what you want to do."

Patience's brow wrinkled as she turned to Heather Flower. "You must tell them. They cannot say no. Those are your people."

The ladies finished up in the kitchen and took bowls of berries and cream outside. They wandered around the yard, eating their berries and examining plants. Mary led the way to the stable, where Stargazer's newest foal stood on wobbly legs next to his mother, Moonbeam.

"We haven't named him yet. We are out of 'star' names." Mary giggled. "If you have any ideas, please tell me."

Patience ran her hand down the foal's face. "Look, he has three white blazes all the way down. Like falling stars."

"Call him Starry Night, Mary."

Patience patted his nose. "Very good, Lizzie. Yes, Starry Night suits him."

"That is his name, then. Papa would have liked that, Lizzie."

Mary's eyes were misty as she spoke, and Patience hurried to hug her. "Shall we go tell the men our plans for Heather Flower?"

"Let's." Mary led the way to the porch. "Barney, Heather Flower would like to go with you tomorrow. It shall be her chance to see Montauk and her people again."

"You do know that many have left, do you not, Heather Flower?" Barnabas cast an uneasy glance at Dirk.

Dirk answered for her. "We are in constant

contact with the people of Montauk. We send runners back and forth from Flushing, and we know there are few left. So many have died from disease, and others have left because they fear they will be stricken, too, or to find new hunting grounds far from the English fences. But you find the same true with the people of Corchaug, *ja*?"

Jeremy spoke up. "True. In fact, Benjamin talks of moving his house out toward the old Corchaug fort. It's deserted, and there's much good land out there. I thought of building out that way, too, but if I work at Winter Harbor, methinks it would be better to live close."

Heather Flower stood tall, her black-opal eyes serious. "My people who remain need to see me. I must give them hope. But even more, I must remember and give honor to the elders who have gone before me."

Reverend Hobart spoke up at once. "Yes, come with us. Perhaps your husband would escort you to Montauk after our meetings?" He looked toward Dirk.

Dirk stood and put his arm around his wife. "Of course, and thank you. I agree completely with Heather Flower. She needs to visit Montauk."

Jeremy stood and took Patience's hand. "The evening is still young, and the weather is chilly but clear. May I take you for a stroll on the green? Or to the beach?"

"I would love that." She took his arm after they said their goodbyes, and they walked toward the beach where Patience had first come ashore many years ago. A place they now called Hallock's Landing.

The sun was low, sending light across the water's surface. Jeremy wrapped his arms about her to keep her warm as they gazed at the rippled gold. She rested her head against his shoulder. She could stay here just this way, forever. "Jeremy, tonight is lovely."

"It is. I'm glad we have a moment to ourselves."

"What do you think you shall find out tomorrow? Do you think the people of Easthampton agree that it is not in their best interest to be so closely ruled by the Crown?"

"They do not like to be in much agreement with us on anything, but I cannot imagine they would disagree on this."

She shivered, and he rubbed her arms. "You shall return tomorrow night?"

"Most likely two days hence. That depends on the discussions. I don't believe they need to be long and drawn out. But we will take it as it comes. I should walk you home."

They walked arm in arm. Patience sighed. "Reverend Hobart is very nice, do you not agree?"

His pace slowed. "Well, yes, I do. I noticed he was quite taken with you."

"I think he was being polite. Truly, it was generous of him to agree to take Heather Flower on the journey over to the south fork."

Jeremy shook his head. "I'm not sure I'd say it was generous. He couldn't really say no, could he?"

They came up to her door, and Patience turned to look up into his face. He looked so serious, and she could not suppress a small giggle. "I suppose not. But you do agree he's a very honorable man, don't you?"

He pulled her close and lifted her chin toward his lips. "Yes, I would say that, if I must. But you find me to be an honorable man, too — don't you?"

"Yes, Jeremy. But if you don't kiss me now, I shall freeze to death."

His kiss was long and warm, and she did not want it to end. When he drew his lips away, she clung to him for a moment. She did not want him to leave tomorrow. But if this was the last time she would say goodbye, if he would come back and marry her, she could let him go.

# 16

September 18, 1664

Jeremy arrived at Patience's house at dawn. A light frost on the flagstone made it slippery beneath his boots. He warmed his hands inside by the fire while he waited for Dirk and Heather Flower.

Patience paced about, poking at the fire and straightening the crocks on the table, but finally paused a moment. "Would you like something warm to drink? Or a bite to eat?"

"Nay, I ate. Ester had set out some bread and cheese for me on the table. It was enough. Come, let me hold you or you will wear out the floorboards."

She fell into his arms, and he brushed back the hair that fell into her face. "That's better now. I shall not be gone long, you know."

She looked up to him. "I know."

Dirk and Heather Flower entered the

kitchen, with Mosh at their heels. Patience gave them each a bundle of cold meat and berries. "I know you said you would not eat this morning, but take this with you to eat when you are hungry."

"Thank you. We will." Heather Flower bent to her dog and showered him with hugs. "Be good for Patience. We will be right back." She rose, and Patience gave her a hug.

"Don't worry about Mosh. I'm falling in love with him, and he seems happy with me. We'll be fine together. Won't we, Mosh?" She took a sliver of turkey from the table and dropped it as he lunged, nabbing it midair. He sat and looked at her with adoration. "See?"

Jeremy chuckled. "Well, of course. You know the way to a man's heart. Feed him."

"If that is the case, Jeremy Horton, I shall make you sit down right now whilst I feed you a meal fit to break any king's fast."

"Then we would be keeping the good reverends and Barn waiting."

"And that would never do." Dirk helped Heather Flower with her cloak. "But I'm glad to know Mosh is in good hands."

Jeremy took one last look at Patience as they went out the door, and she blew a kiss to him. The three trudged through the cold to the meetinghouse, and Jeremy scanned the sky. It looked like they would have precipitation, but mayhap it was not quite cold enough to snow.

Inside, Reverend Youngs and Reverend Hobart discussed the plan with Barnabas. As magistrate of Southold, Barnabas would lead the small delegation. They would take the ferry to Shelter Island and visit with the Sylvesters. Hopefully, Nathaniel would make the trip over to the south fork with them.

They mounted the horses, Jeremy on Ink and Heather Flower sitting in front of Dirk on Miss Button, and rode for the ferry. It would be noon by the time they got to Grissell and Nathaniel's home. Jeremy had not visited there before, but he'd heard Benjamin and Heather Flower talk of the beautiful estate they lived on. Mayhap he'd pick up some ideas for his and Patience's new home.

The ferry ride was cold but quick. Jeremy watched as Heather Flower ran up the slope to the large house perched on the rise and a young woman ran down to meet her, arms open wide. They met and spun each other around. Four young children, the eldest a girl about ten years old, waited at the top for their mother, who slowly walked back up with Heather Flower in tow.

He glanced around at the massive hedges and tulip trees that gave the grounds a fortress-like appearance. The house itself was two stories and built much like a castle. Barn had seen the place before, but Dirk and the reverends stood in awe with him. "I suppose this is how one may live when he has an island to himself," Jeremy said.

He walked up to the house with the reverends behind him. Most of this visit would be Heather Flower and Grissell catching up on lost time, he could tell. But it would give them a chance to convince Nathaniel to come with them. If he were here. They didn't even know that yet.

When the men reached the terrace, Grissell greeted each of them and told Reverend Hobart that she had heard not only of his father, but him too. She brought them into the massive house and went to find Nathaniel. Before they returned, a housemaid brought a tray of cider and savory meat tarts.

Reverend Youngs gazed out the window, taking in the view. "As strategic as this island is, we need to be certain Nathaniel agrees on resistance to jurisdiction under New Amsterdam."

Barnabas shook his head. "I don't think

we'll have a problem there. Nathaniel will have a sympathetic ear towards us. And if he doesn't, his wife will. Trust me." Barnabas and Jeremy exchanged a nod.

Heather Flower turned as Nathaniel and Grissell entered, and all eyes followed. Jeremy remembered them from Dirk and Heather Flower's wedding. They were a striking couple, difficult to forget. He strode quickly to them and extended his hand to Nathaniel and bowed to Grissell. "So good to see you again."

"Yes, quite a surprise — I'm shocked, really — but pleasantly. It was terrible news about *The Swallow.* Terrible. My condolences on your crew."

Jeremy closed his eyes briefly and nodded. "Thank you. That means much to me."

Nathaniel turned to Reverend Youngs. "Reverend, so good to see you." They shook hands. "And Heather Flower, we are delighted to have you here as our guest again. Grissell tells me it is only for the day? Surely you must all stay the night, at the least. Please, everyone sit."

Reverend Youngs spoke up as he took a chair. "We are on our way to meetings in Easthampton, and we wanted an opportunity to discuss recent events that affect us all out on the east end."

"You mean the overthrow of the Dutch in New Amsterdam?"

"Precisely." Jeremy leaned forward in his chair and tapped his fingers on his knee. "And are you aware the colonies in the east end may be removed from New Haven's jurisdiction and fall under New Amsterdam's?"

Nathaniel leaned forward, as well. "I've heard nothing about those plans. Is this what the meetings in Easthampton are all about, then?"

Reverend Hobart cleared his throat. "Presently I am of Barbados, but I'm visiting Long Island as I seek a place in need of a minister. When I heard about the current situation, I invited Reverend Youngs and these gentlemen to accompany me to the south fork. There's much at stake, and it seems prudent to take this up with the good gentlemen of Easthampton."

"We thought you may want to come with us." Jeremy stood and went to the window. "These affairs have importance for you, as well." He looked back at Nathaniel for his reaction.

Nathaniel looked at Grissell, then studied his guests as if to decipher their hearts and minds. "Yes, I shall go with you." He stood and leaned into a brief bow. "You will excuse me while I put together a few things? And darling, I will plan on returning on the morrow once our business is concluded." He kissed his wife's hand, and the men rose as he left the room.

Grissell crossed the room to sit by Heather Flower. "You look so well and happy. I am so glad you've come for a visit, no matter how brief. But you must come back and stay with me."

"*Nuk,* my friend. I will. For now, I need to return to Montauk. It has been too long for my people, too." She pulled a beautiful length of wampum from her belt. "This I made for them. It tells the story of Heather Flower and her warrior, Keme. It is a way to have my story handed down through the generations and to say *ooneewey* — thank you — to my people."

"I understand how important that is to you." She turned to the rest of her guests. "Our friendship goes back to the time when Nathaniel and I first came here and Heather Flower was the first friend I made."

Barnabas smiled at Heather Flower before he turned back to Grissell. "Her aunt Winnie was Mary's first new friend on Long Island. Heather Flower represents her people well and is a friend to all. I'm told that the Dutch people of the west end share those sentiments."

Heather Flower's lashes covered her dark eyes, and a pink tinge spread across her coppery cheeks. "You say too much, my friend. I love the people of Long Island. I consider all to be my people."

Reverend Hobart stood. "You are a legend, Heather Flower. Many people in these parts say they have heard of my father, Peter Hobart. But I can say that I have heard of you, and you are loved and revered even by those who don't know you."

She rose at once. "Thank you, Reverend. Thank you for your words of kindness."

Nathaniel reappeared, and everyone said goodbye to Grissell. She and Heather Flower walked arm in arm as the men rode ahead toward the ferry on the south side that would take them to Easthampton. At the shore, the two women clung to each other.

"I shall miss you, Heather Flower!"

"I miss you too. I will come back. We will have a long visit before I return to our home in Flushing." She stepped onto the ferry with Dirk at her side.

When the ferry arrived at the other shore, Jeremy watched as Heather Flower took in the beach she had left so long ago. He knew the story the wampum told. It was tragic, and Benjamin and Dirk — though it was Dirk who won her hand — were both blessings to her at that time.

Dirk helped her up on Miss Button before he climbed up himself. When the entire party had mounted, Jeremy swung onto Ink and fell in beside Barnabas. They would dine with Thomas James and stay the night as his guests, but any meeting to be put on the schedule would be discussed at breakfast. Jeremy prayed the decisions would be quick in coming and that he could get back to the life that awaited him in Southold. From the moment he'd been tossed into the ocean, he'd felt as if his life had come to a standstill. He was ready to begin living it again.

## 17

*September 19, 1664*
*Easthampton, Long Island*

Jeremy woke early and came down from his room to the parlor. Reverend James and Mr. Barnes, the schoolmaster, rose to greet him and offered him a chair by the fire. "I trust you slept well," said the reverend.

"Good morrow, gentlemen. Yes, indeed, very well."

"Mr. Barnes and I were just discussing the meeting you so desire."

"Yes?"

Mr. Barnes lowered himself into a chair. His ruddy face was moist, and he took a handkerchief from his coat and wiped his brow, then his upper lip. "It seems it is very short notice and —"

"It is, but of great import. The Court of the Three Men has the authority to call a meeting within a half hour. I hardly see the difficulty in that, given the gravity of the situation." Jeremy adjusted his collar while he awaited their answer. He glanced toward the door. He needed a little support here. Where was everyone?

"The fact is, we haven't been under the jurisdiction of New Haven for years. Oh, they keep posturing like we are, but we don't pay taxes — never have. They try to tell us to answer to the magistrates of Southold — to Barnabas, mind you — and we've never done that either. And there is not a freeman here who worries New Amsterdam shall be any different. Let them lay claim on us, but we do not send anyone to assembly in New Haven, and we will not send anyone to New Amsterdam."

Reverend James took his seat, and Jeremy followed in taking the chair they'd offered him. Mr. Barnes shifted in his and brought his hand to his temple. He looked ill. Or did he object to what Reverend James had said? Jeremy looked back at the reverend. "Do you mean to —"

Everyone turned as Heather Flower and Dirk came down the staircase and made their entrance. The men stood.

"Good morning." Heather Flower, dressed in deerskin adorned with jingle shells and eagle feathers, bowed slightly to the group. A long wampum belt made of deep purple and creamy white shell beads crossed her dress. The belt was the one she'd made to tell the story of her life. Her bearing was regal as she walked to Reverend James. "Thank you for keeping us for the night, but I feel I need to continue to Montauk and my people. My husband will take me there today."

"Ah, we shall regret that you must take your leave, but most certainly do not without sharing a meal with us." He nodded to a room with a long table already laden with several meat and egg dishes.

"*Nuk,* yes. We will break our fast with you." She fell in beside Dirk and followed Reverend James as he led the way with Mr. Barnes.

Jeremy paused at the door to the dining room and waited as Barnabas joined the group. They allowed Nathaniel Sylvester, Reverend Youngs, and Reverend Hobart to file in. He watched as Reverend James sat at the head of the table and Barnabas sat at the far end. Heather Flower took a seat next to Mr. Barnes, and Dirk sat opposite her. He couldn't help but notice the beet-red face of Barnes as he took his own seat. Beads of sweat dotted Barnes's forehead. Was he uncomfortable with the north fork delegation being here, or was there something else wrong with him?

Conversation was light as they ate, which suited Jeremy, and he supposed Barnes, as well. It gave them both a moment to plan their strategy. He found it surprising, in a way, that Dirk was willing to leave before the talks. But mayhap as a Dutchman he'd rather not engage in the conversations. He could add an interesting slant, however.

Heather Flower put her hand on Mr. Barnes's arm and leaned toward him. "Are you all right? You are not eating."

"Fine, fine." He poked at a mound of eggs, and as he lifted a spoonful to his mouth, it clattered to the floor.

She leaned over and scooped up the mess as the maid hurried to help her.

Jeremy stood. "Do you need to lie down? You don't look well."

Mr. Barnes tossed his head. "Nay. I am fine. If everyone is finished, we should remove ourselves to the parlor, where we can bid Mr. Van Buren and his lovely wife goodbye." He stood and walked out.

Jeremy looked to the reverend, his brows raised.

"As he said." Reverend James stood and walked out, and Youngs and Hobart followed with Barnabas.

After the farewells, Jeremy headed outside

with Dirk and Heather Flower. He placed a hand on the bridle as Dirk swung up into the saddle, then bent to help Heather Flower. "I guess I thought you'd stay for the meeting. How long will you be?"

Dirk shook his head. "I don't know. A fortnight, perhaps." He looked at Heather Flower, who nodded her head. Her dark eyes were serious, but a small, pouty smile played on her lips. She looked forward to this visit.

"Sounds right." Jeremy grinned at Heather Flower. "Your people will be glad to see you."

"*Nuk.* And I will be glad to be there."

He watched the sooty-black tail of Miss Button swish with each stride as they disappeared around the bend before he walked back to the house. As he entered, he heard a commotion in the parlor and quickened his pace.

Mr. Barnes was on the floor, and all three reverends kneeled over him. Reverend Hobart unfastened his collar, and Barnabas worked at removing his boots.

"What happened?" Jeremy rushed to their side.

"He just keeled over. He's burning up — has a fever." Reverend Youngs looked up. "Can you see if there's a doctor nearby?"

He started for the door, but Reverend James called to him. "We haven't a doctor. We shall have to do our best here. Let's get him to bed."

The men gathered around him and carried him up the stairs.

Nathaniel went to haul in some fresh water. The good reverends tended to Mr. Barnes while Jeremy paced, arms folded. They all had a bit of doctoring experience, as the reverends frequently tended the dying, and Jeremy, as a ship's captain, was often the only one available to treat an ailment. He knew in his gut Mr. Barnes was a very ill man. He'd thought him lethargic the night before, but then everyone had been tired, had they not?

After making the poor man as comfortable as possible, Reverend Hobart determined it best for the north fork party to return home, for which Jeremy and Barnabas were grateful. The likelihood of something good coming from their meeting seemed rather bleak regardless. They made haste on the return home, stopping overnight at Shelter Island. Grissell asked about Heather Flower, and Jeremy assured her that Heather Flower would be stopping by in a couple of weeks.

As they led their horses onto the ferry, his

thoughts turned to Patience and home. The ship had always been his home. That Southold was now home was a new thought. One that he prayed he could get used to.

Patience awoke with a shiver and welcomed Mosh up to the bed. His fur was warm, and she hugged him close. The men would return today if the talks had been successful and not unnecessarily long. And Jeremy would be home.

She swung out of bed and pulled on her robe. She laughed as Mosh tried to race her down the stairs. "Are you hungry, boy? Or are you just cold like me? Shall we poke at the fire and start it up? Yes, we shall." She ruffled the fur between his ears with her fingers.

She took the iron poker and urged the embers to life. A bucket of fresh water stood by the fireplace, and she heaved it up and poured it into the large pot. After she gave Mosh some leftover venison from supper the night before, she pulled her robe about her and went to the window that overlooked her backyard.

Her hand went to her cheek as she gazed at the beauty of the trees. She loved fall, for just when the flowers lost their radiance, the elms and oaks blazed in glorious golden yellows and fiery reds and oranges. She held her breath in awe until she sighed and turned to Mosh. "Do you want to go out, pup?" She followed him out so she could inhale the fresh air and give thanks for the day. When she could take the chill no longer, she went inside to dress.

It was a day filled with chores, but she was thankful for them, for they filled the moments until Jeremy would return. As she soaked a ham in water, she chopped squash and onions. She hummed as she worked and let her thoughts drift to her wedding dress. She and Jeremy could begin plans in earnest. She'd not let him put it off. On the morrow, after they talked, she would sit down with Mary and Lizzie.

She heard a horse out front and rushed to the door. She swung it open before Jeremy could knock and threw herself into his arms. He swung her around, and the joy of his arms around her made happy tears escape from her clenched eyes. Mosh was barking circles around them, and they both laughed as Jeremy set her down.

"Hey, boy, are you glad to see him, too?" Mosh licked her hand as she reached to pet him. She looked at Jeremy, and he bent to pat him on the head. "See, he's glad to see you, too."

Jeremy led her into the kitchen. "It smells good in here."

"I'm not sure why. I think you are just saying that because you must be hungry. I'm only getting tomorrow's dinner started. Mary invited us for a supper at her house. We didn't know exactly when you would be back, but she thought Barnabas would want to have you and Reverend Youngs over tonight to discuss the meeting. Oh, and Reverend Hobart, too." She saw his frown and looked away.

"Very well. Barn didn't mention having us come over tonight, but then nothing went as we'd hoped. There's not anything to discuss, except that Mr. Barnes became ill. There's not much point in going back. They aren't interested in what we have to say."

"How interesting. Well, at least Heather Flower and Dirk have made their journey to Montauk. Do you know when they shall return?"

"Within a fortnight."

"Mosh stays busy all day following me around, but in the evening, after we've had a bit of supper, I can tell he misses Heather Flower. He shall be happy to have her back. Me, too."

She sent Jeremy to her cellar for a crock of cream to take to Mary's while she checked the water level over the ham. She hoisted the pail and added water until there was a full three inches covering the meat.

"You should have waited and let me do that." He set the crock down and took the empty pail from her, returning it to the corner beside the hearth.

"I'm so used to doing things myself, and if you are here long enough, you shall discover there is plenty to do without following me around and helping me with my chores."

He chuckled as he went to retrieve her cloak from a peg next to the door. "While that may be true, I would say enjoy it whilst you can." His green eyes twinkled as he helped her with her wrap.

She tied a bonnet under her chin and flashed her own smile back at him. "I shan't argue with that."

They left her cottage hand in hand, forgetting the crock on the table as Mosh dashed out ahead of them.

As they walked along the village green, Patience noticed Joshua Hobart coming out of the meetinghouse. He didn't notice them, but Jeremy obviously spotted him, for he swept her into his arms and drew her near for a kiss. Men. They would never admit to insecurity, but was this not just that? But he held her with such tenderness and his lips were so gentle on hers that her objections fell away and she returned his kiss like they were the only two people on the island. At last she pulled back and could feel the flush that crept across her cheeks. "Oh my. I shan't argue with that either."

Her heart pattered the rest of the way to the Hortons' front door. She had prayed so much for this, and now it was coming true. Soon she would be Jeremy's wife, and how thankful she was she'd waited for God's timing and not hers.

# 18

*September 21, 1664*
*Southold*

On Wednesday, the ladies gathered at Mary Horton's house for their weekly prayer and sewing meeting. But today was not just any Wednesday meeting. Today they planned to work on Patience's wedding dress. Heather Flower could sew on the beads when she returned, but the ladies had plenty to do until then.

Mary's daughters joined Anna, their sister-in-law, each Wednesday at her house to give their mother time with her friends. Anna enjoyed having them, and they found it quite a treat to be her guests.

The night before, Barney had told Mary that Dirk intended to return to Flushing when he got back. He said Jeremy planned to go with him, at least for a time. Patience expressed her dismay, but Mary said they should go ahead with the gown. And perhaps that was for the best. If her dress was ready when he returned, he might like the idea of a wedding before he left again for Winter Harbor. After all, they had work to do, and Jeremy would cooperate if she had anything to do with it.

Mary glanced out the window. The day was cold, with heavy, dark clouds low in the sky. She stacked fresh logs over orange-hot embers. Blue-tipped flames sprang up and licked at the new wood with a crackle. The ladies scooted their chairs closer to the heat. Lizzie and Abbey cut cream brocade and pink French silk with silver scissors while Mary and Patience heated irons in the fire to smooth each cut section of the dress.

At last they were ready to hold the pieces up to Patience before they began stitching. She stood with her arms out to her sides. "It feels like it could snow out, does it not?"

Mary smiled. "I think so. Winter is early this year, but 'tis my favorite season."

Lizzie's eyes flew open. "Why, it is not, Mary. You like to be out with the flowers and sunshine. Spring is your favorite."

Patience watched the two sisters, a grin playing on her lips. "And cannot Mary have more than one favorite season?"

"Why, I think that is it. I have more than one favorite. Spring has so many choices, so many new and delightful things that one could do. But winter comes and there is really only one good choice."

"What is that?" Abbey leaned forward, eager to know.

"To keep warm near a good fire. Preferably with a good book and a cup of peppermint tea. Or perhaps with friends like you."

"Very good, but my favorite is fall, and I'm sad to see it turn so soon." Patience flapped her arms. "But you need to finish pinning. I can't stand here like this forever."

Lizzie giggled. "So sorry. Here, let's take it in a little here at the waist, just a snip. You can breathe, Patience, it is allowed. And Abbey, check the length on the sleeve."

When it was all pinned, Patience twirled about. "Do you think Jeremy will love this?"

"Oh yes, he will. But I think he will love any gown that has you in it." Mary smiled with satisfaction.

"I cannot stand him being gone, you know. I think that when he first came back to Southold, the notion that he would be here from now on settled in on me. And yet all he does is go away."

Mary shook her head. "It is just the way Jeremy is, I'm afraid. Always finding something he must do. Always leaving. 'Tis his duty calling, he thinks. Always his duty. I should think you would be used to that by now."

She stood still while her friends carefully took the pins out. "That's just it. I thought after all these years he'd finally come home to stay."

They all took their seats and began to stitch the pieces together. Mary stabbed her needle into the silk and pulled the thread through. "He has, Patience, truly. But it is a big adjustment for him, I think, and you need to give him a little time."

Patience put her work in her lap and bit her lower lip. After a moment, she looked up with tears in her eyes. "I guess I just have to wonder — when will I be his priority? Why doesn't he feel a sense of duty toward me?" She wiped at a tear. "There are times when I think he does, like when he first comes home after a long absence and he is very attentive to me. But then there is always something that calls him away, and I'm left with this feeling he will never truly put me first."

Lizzie frowned. "You should pray."

"Oh, I do. And I know that he should put God first. And he does. But I think God left room in there for a wife, before all those other duties."

Lizzie smoothed her piece before continuing her stitches. "Quite true. But Jeremy is an honorable man, and some of what troubles you so much is exactly why you love him in the first place. Mary is right. He's settling down, but 'tis a big adjustment for him. Give him time. Have patience."

They erupted in giggles over her pun. "I think that is what my mother hoped for when she gave me that name, but I do recall trying hers many a time growing up."

Mary shook her head as she tsked. "Not just hers." They sat giggling again, sewing needles hovering in midair.

They sewed the rest of the afternoon, eventually setting their work aside for refreshments. Then Mary bid her friends goodbye and turned to revive the fire in the hearth. She'd meant what she'd said about winter. She loved friends and good books around the fire. But she was thankful, too, for her husband. Had she not prayed that Patience would find that kind of love, too? And Jeremy needed Patience just as much as she needed him. Perhaps he needed to be told.

She threw on a cloak and marched out to the barn. The men were bent over Stargazer's hoof, and Barney looked up as she approached. His mouth opened but then relaxed into a grin when she walked straight up to Jeremy.

"Can we take a walk in the orchard?" She didn't wait for an answer but heard Barney tell him to go as she left the barn. Barney and Jonathan could handle Stargazer.

She waited under the spread of the huge corner apple tree. As he joined her, she took a deep breath and looked up into his face. "I remember you telling me long ago Barney loved me, he just didn't know how to show me. Now it seems you are right there where he was all those years ago. Jeremy, you cannot keep Patience waiting. You make her feel like she is not important to you. We've always been able to talk. I love you like a brother, and I want you to be happy. Prithee, tell me what is wrong. Why do you run from marriage? Because that is what you do."

His face was pure panic. She'd not meant to cause him pain. But he needed a jolt.

"I don't know, Mary. If you want to talk about long ago, I can do that. When Barn lost Ann, I saw how fragile life is. And he couldn't stop loving her, but he married you, and that seemed so unfair to you. I saw Barn with his pain, and you with your pain, and I couldn't do anything about it. I just decided life was so much easier at sea. I didn't feel pain, and I didn't inflict pain. It became a way of life for me, even after I fell in love with Patience. She knew I would come back, but she always knew I'd be leaving, too." He shrugged his shoulders. "Does any of this make sense?"

"Life is fragile, and none of us have a promise that we won't lose someone we love very much. But to not let love into your life out of fear does not make any sense. Most of us would not accomplish anything in our life if we let fear guide us. That's where we depend on God."

"It seems when my ship wrecked and tossed me into the ocean, God was telling me He had more in store for me than sailing the high seas, does it not?"

Mary softened her gaze. "I think He spared your life for a purpose."

"I've given it much thought and I've promised God to go where He leads. I do need to ride out to Flushing with Dirk when he returns. You must understand that there are responsibilities that come with living here." His green eyes pleaded with her.

She let out a deep sigh. "That is just one of the things that makes Patience feel unimportant. You'd best be ready to marry her when you get back. Promise me?"

He chuckled and took her arm as they

walked back to the barn. "You can tell Patience that I will be a lucky man when she is mine to have and to hold."

## 19

*October 2, 1664*
Patience was wandering the aisles at the mercantile, looking at supplies for Dame School, when Jeremy rushed in, alarm in his eyes, his mouth rigid. She nearly dropped a bottle of ink. "What? What is it?"

"Dirk and Heather Flower just arrived from Montauk. It's Heather Flower. She's ill. Let me take you home. Dirk is already putting her in bed."

She put the ink back, and they rushed to her house. Dirk was upstairs, and he called to them when they came through the door. Jeremy took the steps two at a time, and she hurried up after him, clutching her skirts.

She was saddened by what she saw. Heather Flower lay on the bed in her soft deerskin dress. Her glossy black hair spread out on the pillow like a dark cloud. Her eyes were closed, her breathing labored. Her creamy copper skin had taken an ashen hue and was moist with sweat. Mosh lay beside her on the bed, his chin draped over her arm, lids half closed over his blue eyes.

Patience grabbed Dirk's arm. "What happened?"

"She was fine when we first arrived at Montauk. She was with her people, and she was celebrating with them. They had a pow-wow and feasts. She presented them with her wampum belt. But she began to feel very tired. She just wanted to sleep. We'd been there about twelve days and planned to stay a day or two longer. But I could see she needed to get back here and see the doctor."

Patience turned to Jeremy. "Does Doctor Smith know? Is he coming?"

"Yes, he should be here soon." Jeremy rubbed his arm across his forehead. "I'm going to get some cold water from the well."

"Very good — I'll get some cloths. I can bathe her with the cold water and get her into some bedclothes while we wait for the doctor."

Dirk shook his head. "I think she has smallpox. When we came through Shelter Island, Nathaniel told me Mr. Barnes is very sick with the pox. Heather Flower must have caught it from him. We were there the morning he fell sick."

Jeremy shook his head in disbelief. "No. I hope not."

"I've had the smallpox — back when my family was in Boston, before we came down to Long Island. I can take care of her. But Dirk, you may already be infected." Worry etched its way across Patience's brow.

"I don't care. *Ja,* I might be sick, but even if I'm not, I wouldn't leave her side."

She turned to Jeremy. "Have you ever had the pox, Jeremy?"

"Yes, and so have Barn and Benjamin. Joseph, too. We all got sick the year Ann died."

Dirk looked up. "Barnabas's first wife?"

"Yes. I think even Mary had the pox that year — so many in Mowsley did — but I'm not sure about Lizzie. And that's the thing to remember, Dirk. People do survive this." Jeremy headed for the stairs. "I'll get the water."

Heather Flower moaned, Dirk sat on her bedside, and Patience ran to get the cloths. After Jeremy returned with the cold water, he took Dirk down to the kitchen to find something to eat.

Patience pushed Mosh out the door and made him follow them. "You need something to eat, too, boy. Then you can come back. She will be here waiting for you. Go now."

She closed the door and began to gently pull the dress off Heather Flower's limp body. She bathed her with the cold water, dipping the cloth back into the pail with each stroke. When she finished, she pulled the fresh bedclothes on and pulled back the covers of the bed. She remembered Doctor Smith's advice for fever and decided not to tuck her in, but left the quilt at her side.

She sat down next to her on the bed and leaned over to wring out another cloth for her forehead. She heard the doctor on the steps with Jeremy and Dirk and stood as they entered. "I am so glad to see you. She's very sick. She's not stirred at all while I gave her a cold bath. But I don't see any blisters on her, so how could this be smallpox? I remember the blisters."

Doctor Smith shook his head. "We won't know right away." He looked at Dirk. "When did her fever start?"

Dirk looked so weary, but he roused himself to look at the doctor. "Just today. Before today, she was all right. Well, not completely. She was tired. But she sat next to a man a couple of weeks ago who came down with the pox. He was sick the day we saw him." His voice trailed.

"Then we need to watch her closely for the next few days. If she has the pox, she'll start breaking out with red spots. They won't be blisters at first. But we won't know for sure until we see the spots."

Mosh came to her bed, but this time he jumped up on the end and settled at her feet. He rested his muzzle on his paws.

As the doctor bent over Heather Flower, Patience picked up the deerskin dress and brushed the dust from it before she folded it and put it in the trunk at the foot of her bed. To keep busy was best, but she was running out of things to do.

Jeremy offered his hand, and she stepped over to him and into his arms. He led her out of the bedroom and held her on the landing. "Russell is the best physician in all of New England. If anyone can save her, it is he."

"I pray so. But I was thinking while we waited for him how the native people here seem to react to illness in a much more severe way than we do. Look at Winnie and Winheytem. Gone before we knew it. I hope Heather Flower is stronger than they were."

"You need something to eat. Let's go downstairs, and I will set out some cheese and bread. That's what Dirk and I had. You need something, too."

She looked down at her yellow linen dress, now dotted with water spots. "I'm not hungry. I think I shall just wait here until the doctor is finished. Perhaps you should go and tell Barnabas and Mary. She will want to come."

He pressed her close to him, and she closed her eyes against his chest. His strength buoyed her, and as he left for his brother's house, she took a deep breath. As she waited for Doctor Smith to come out, she prayed for strength for Heather Flower. And she prayed for her own strength, no matter what came her way.

When she felt she could not pray any longer, nor wait any longer, the door finally opened. Doctor Smith smiled at her. "She's awake now and would like to see you. Dirk told me you've had smallpox, as have most of the Hortons, so I will not restrict you from visiting and caring for her. Dirk will need a lot of help and support. He could be ill and we just don't know it yet. I can't convince him to stay away."

"I know. I pray he won't get sick. But I fear that's all we can do."

"Very well, but if you can convince him to sit downstairs and allow you to give her direct care, then that would be best. But I'm leaving it up to him."

She watched him go downstairs, then went into the bedroom to see her friend. "I'm so glad to see you awake. Let me get you another bolster so you may sit up, and can I bring you a cup of water?"

Heather Flower gave her a weak smile and stretched out her arms. "Sit, my friend. Sit beside me for a moment."

She sat down and held Heather Flower's hands. "You must get well. And you must tell Dirk to go downstairs so that he stays well for you." She smiled up at Dirk.

He didn't say a word. Just sat in his chair, pulled as close as he could get it.

"My husband, this does us no good. Not you and not me. Go, like Patience says. Sit downstairs. I am feeling better already. Take care of yourself. For me, like she says." She nodded toward Patience.

He stood. "I cannot argue with the both of you, and I'm encouraged to see you so much yourself this evening. I'll be downstairs." He looked at Patience. "Call me if she needs anything at all."

"I will, Dirk. And you can bring her a cup of water before you get settled. We shall let you do that."

His eyes lit with pleasure, and he bowed and went to get the drink.

Patience found an extra bolster and propped it behind Heather Flower's back. She settled in the chair Dirk had vacated.

After he delivered the cup of water, along with a full pitcher, Heather Flower took a long drink, then set the cup down on the little table beside the bed.

Patience settled back, and without too much prompting, her friend told her all about the visit to Montauk. Of the little children running circles around her, of the old ladies smiling broadly and wanting her to wear one of her silk dresses. They were disappointed when she told them she'd brought only her deerskin tunic. But they were pleased when she explained how much her native dress meant to her. The men enjoyed Dirk's company, and they all celebrated her return.

It was a solemn occasion when she presented the wampum belt to the medicine man. But when she began to feel tired and the dread of illness gnawed at her, she found she did not want to seek help from the medicine man. She wanted to keep her fears from her people. And so she asked Dirk to take her back to Southold. To her friends.

"I am so glad you came back. You might have died there, but here we have Doctor Smith, and he is wonderful. You already look better."

There was a tap on the door, and before Patience could respond, Mary peeked in.

"May I come in?"

"Yes." They answered as one, and Mary smiled as she entered.

"You are looking so much better than I expected, and I think it must be an answer to prayer." She patted Heather Flower's knee as she sat on the end of the bed by Mosh. He looked up, and she scratched his ear. "Not you, dear Mosh." He put his head back down, this time on Heather Flower's feet.

"We were just talking about her trip to Montauk and how glad we are she's back here in Southold."

Mary nodded. "We are. We shall take good care of you, Heather Flower."

Heather Flower gazed at the window for a moment, then turned her eyes to her friends. "I was able to visit with Keme's mother. It meant much to see my warrior husband's mother again. We talked much of his memory. I watched his younger brother, who is such a good son, like Keme was."

Mary leaned toward her and let her hand rest on Heather Flower's. "I'm sure it was good for her to see you. Did you give her the wampum belt?"

"No. It is with the medicine man. He will tell the stories and keep the history alive. It is his duty."

"You will too, Heather Flower. You must get well first, though. Patience and I will go make some broth for you. You rest, dear." Mary stood up and handed Patience the cloth from Heather Flower's forehead before testing her temperature with her fingers.

Patience dipped the cloth back into the water and wrung it out. She patted it across Heather Flower's brow. "I shall bring fresh water, too. You rest now."

Before they left, Mary turned to their friend. "Lizzie wants so much to come see you, but she cannot. She's never had the pox, and the doctor has sequestered your house from anyone who has not had the disease. 'Tis the only way to protect Southold from an epidemic. She's at my house in tears, poor thing."

Heather Flower's black eyes grew wide. "She must stay well, she must stay away."

"She will. I just wanted you to know she wants to be here too. She is very sad to know you are so sick. But she will be cheered when I tell her how much better you are tonight." Mary smiled, and Patience followed her down the stairs.

"I have a joint of beef in the cellar, Mary. Let's have Dirk bring it up and get us fresh water. I shall boil it and make a quick broth."

They looked in on Dirk and found him asleep in a chair in the parlor. He looked so haggard and worn out.

Mary touched Patience's arm and held a finger to her lips. "Let's go to the cellar ourselves and let him sleep. We can manage." Her voice was a whisper, and the two tiptoed out to the cellar door, without their cloaks. They reached the cold room and shivered.

"What were we thinking?" Patience picked up a cloth-wrapped package. "This is the beef." She handed it to Mary. "I shall get the water." Mary followed her to the well, and Patience hauled up a bucket filled with icy water. They lugged their burden to the warmth of the kitchen and set about making a simple broth.

"Lizzie sent some yarrow with me and said to be sure to make her a tea with this, for the fever." Mary put the sprigs of the dried herb in a mug and ladled boiling water over it to steep.

Mosh wandered in, and Patience bent down. "You poor thing. You didn't want to leave her either, did you? But you must need to go outside." She took him to the back door. " 'Tis cold out. You shan't want to stay out long, Mosh."

When they had a rich broth, Mary ladled it into a large slipware bowl, and Patience put a bone aside to cool for Mosh. He hadn't stayed out long and had hurried back to his mistress.

They assembled a tray, and Mary carried it while Patience lugged the pail of cold water. Heather Flower was sound asleep, Mosh already at her side.

They looked at each other as they set everything down. "Do we wake her, Mary? Or let her sleep? Doctor Smith said to watch out for the deep sleep."

"We should wake her and have her take some broth and tea." Mary shook Heather Flower's shoulder gently. "Wake up, sweet thing."

Heather Flower didn't stir, and for a moment Patience sucked in her breath in fear that she was gone. But then her lashes fluttered, and Patience let out a sigh. "You are awake."

Their friend looked from one to the other. "Did I close my eyes? It seems you just walked out the door."

Mary brought the broth to her and sat on the bed. She dipped the spoon and offered her a small sip. Heather Flower smiled. "Mmm. That is good." But she could not eat much and only took two sips of the tea that Patience brought to her.

Heather Flower settled back on her pillow. "Dirk. Is he in the house still, or did the doctor make him leave?"

Patience adjusted the pillow for her. "He's still here, Heather Flower. He won't leave, and because he might already have the disease, Doctor Smith felt it best he stay here, though not in the same room as you. He's asleep downstairs."

"I miss him."

Mary set down the bowl. "I know he is missing you." Her hazel eyes held a teary blue tint as she looked at Patience. "I'm going to get a chair from your room so we don't have to use her bed to sit." Patience saw her face crumble as she swept out of the room. Mary needed a cry out of Heather Flower's sight.

Patience kept her back to Heather Flower as she willed herself to contain her own tears. "We won't leave you, Heather Flower, and we shall keep Dirk informed of your progress. Now, let's work on getting you well. Would you take another sip of tea for me?"

She nodded, and Patience held the cup for her.

The three settled in for the evening,

reminiscing and dozing off and on. By midnight, they slept soundly, only waking at daybreak. When Patience opened her eyes, she could see Heather Flower was staring at the window, and she said a prayer of thanksgiving that her friend was all right for another day. She prayed that today would bring more healing and strength.

She moved her stiff legs and arms, and Heather Flower turned to her, her usual fiery eyes were dull. "You poor things, sitting all night as you sleep. You should have gone to your beds."

Mary sat up straight, rubbing her arms. "We wanted to be near in case you needed something."

"We won't leave you until you are able to be up. How do you feel?" Patience stood up and took the dried-out cloth from Heather Flower's forehead. She noticed the flat, red splotches right away and turned to Mary.

Mary jumped up. "Heather Flower, you are beginning to break out in a rash."

Patience moistened the cloth and gently stroked her friend's face and arms with it. "You feel very hot too. Doctor Smith said the red spots will blister after a day or two. That shall be the worst part of it, and you must take broth and tea to get you through this. I hope you will try. You have Dirk and

Lizzie waiting for you." She smiled and hoped her words encouraged her.

"I will, my friend. I do not give up."

Her courage and dignity even when faced with this horrific disease did not surprise Patience. This was a woman who faced all trials in that manner. She was indeed royalty — not only among her people but to everyone who was graced by her presence.

## 20

*October 6, 1664*

The ladies spent the next few days in Heather Flower's room, chatting, praying, and singing hymns. Patience took turns with Mary, preparing broth, tea, and compresses for Heather Flower. When downstairs, they comforted Dirk.

Barnabas and Jeremy made visits to Heather Flower's bedside and spent time with Dirk to pray for her recovery. Doctor Smith came daily and told Patience that Dirk was definitely worn out, but he didn't appear to be ill. At his orders, Reverend Youngs and Reverend Hobart stayed away but held regular prayer sessions for Heather Flower at the meetinghouse.

Patience learned from Barnabas that Lizzie was beside herself. Never had she felt so useless. She couldn't work at the hat shop, but he said that was not what troubled her. She wanted to be there, helping her friend. And so she busied herself with supplying dried herbs and elixirs to Patience and Mary to administer to Heather Flower. In Mary's absence, she took care of the girls, with the help of Anna and Abbey, and cooked meals for them and the boys.

When the red splotches turned to pus-filled blisters, Heather Flower took a bad turn and lapsed into a coma. Her fever raged. Prayer groups met every hour at the meetinghouse, and Barnabas and Jeremy stayed by Dirk's side.

Patience directed Dirk to keep her supplied with the ice-cold well water, and she and Mary worked diligently to bring the fever down, but it would not abate.

She took Mary beyond the bedroom door and spoke in a low whisper. "Mary, I think it is time to let her people know how ill she is. And I think it is time to send word to Joseph and Jane. I don't think we should wait any longer."

Mary put her hands on Patience's arms and held tight as her eyes pooled. "I don't want to lose her."

Patience couldn't hold back her tears either, and they collapsed in each other's arms and cried. "I don't want to lose her either, Mary, but I'm afraid to wait to get everyone home. What about Benjamin and

Johnny? Dirk and Jeremy were going to ride out and help them finish whatever it is that they are doing. Dirk can't leave. I don't want Jeremy to either."

Mary patted Patience's shoulder. "Dirk won't, but I believe Jeremy will go. I think he and Barnabas have been discussing that. He probably should go, Patience, and I'm the last one who would say that. But he can get word from there to Jay, and he can ride back with Ben and Johnny. I don't think we should say anything to Dirk yet."

Mary left to talk to Barnabas and Jeremy. Patience entered the bedroom again and sent Mosh down to stay with Dirk while she sat to wash pus that oozed from the lesions on her friend's body. She tried to spoon elixir-infused tea into Heather Flower's mouth, but it trickled to the pillow, and her efforts were for naught.

She took her friend's hand and leaned forward until her forehead rested on top and said prayers for her as her tears fell. A rattle from Heather Flower's throat brought Patience upright again, and she took her face in her hands. "Don't leave us" was all she could whisper. "Please don't leave us."

She ran to the staircase landing. "Dirk! Come quickly!" She dashed back to Heather Flower's side. Dirk was right behind her.

He took Heather Flower in his arms. "No! No! You can't!" He held her close and wept.

Heather Flower stirred and opened her eyes. They were dark but luminous, and Patience wondered if it was the light of Heaven she saw in her friend's eyes.

"My husband. I love you." Those were her last words.

Dirk drew her to him and buried his face in her hair, sobs wracking his shoulders.

Patience left him to private moments as her own sadness gripped her heart. She crept down the stairs to Mosh. He was hovering in a corner, as if he knew his beloved mistress was gone. Patience sank to the floor and hugged him, rocking back and forth, shedding her own tears.

She knew Heather Flower was in Heaven this day, and the angels rejoiced. She knew she joined her aunt Winnie, and that should be a comfort. The loss of her own parents had taught her that God could heal the hurt. But for now, she only wanted to cry and mourn her dear friend — her sister, as they'd declared so long ago with Mary. Founding sisters of Southold.

Patience was unhappy Jeremy left for New Amsterdam, but she understood his obligation to bring the horse troop home, and he was charged with notifying Joseph, Benjamin, and Johnny of Heather Flower's death, as well.

The funeral was delayed until friends and family could gather, and now the long procession of mourners wound from the meetinghouse, out past the village green, to the hill above the Corchaug village. It overlooked the bend in the river where Heather Flower loved to sit.

On their shoulders, six young braves carried a litter that bore her body. Keme's brother was one of them, and his mother walked directly behind with Patience, Mary, Abbey, and Lizzie. Mosh remained close to Patience's side.

Jeremy walked with Barnabas, Joseph, and Benjamin, followed by the younger Horton boys. Patience watched him and was glad he was home again. This time for good. He'd gotten back the night before, and they'd not had a chance to talk yet. But she knew he was as devastated as she over their friend's death, and it would take a while for the pain to ease and life to return to normal.

She looked beyond him to the form of Heather Flower, who lay on the bier with hands folded. She was as beautiful in death as she was alive. Mary and Patience had first bathed her in rosewater and then dressed her in her softest deerskin, bejeweled by Heather Flower herself with rich purple beads, peacock and eagle quills, and red ink swirls.

They braided her hair, entwined with silk ribbons, and draped it over her shoulder. Her eyes were closed, but they would never forget the fire and beauty that were so unique to those dark opals. Her lips were frozen in a small pout, and Patience smiled through tears at the thought that, though she'd gone on to grander things, she most likely would have stayed a bit longer if given the chance.

Lizzie nestled two vials of beads — one deep purple, the other creamy white — into Heather Flower's arms, and Mary added a bayberry candle. In the tradition of her people, the braves lowered her into the waiting grave in a sitting position, facing the east, for her final repose. As Keme's mother placed wampum, a treasured blanket, and a tomahawk in her lap, Patience whispered, "God knows best for us, sweet sister. Go in peace."

Reverend Youngs and Reverend Hobart each said a prayer as her grave was covered with earth, and afterward Barnabas gave a eulogy. Patience noticed that Dirk was silent throughout, his hat clutched in his hands, a void in his eyes she was certain came straight from his heart. Heather Flower's burial blended all of the cultures that came together on this island — she had been a friend and leader to so many, and was loved by all.

The men accompanied Dirk to Winnie's old hut, while Patience, Mary, Abbey, and Lizzie went with the native women to the little clearing by the river. Their grief gave way to wails and chants. Only after the last tear did they manage smiles and talk of the legendary life that was Heather Flower's.

When they left the riverbank, they walked to the longhouse. The birch-bark structure was caving in, but Patience and Mary managed to clean off space to put out the food baskets and cold meats while Lizzie went to Winnie's hut to call the men for supper.

Patience brushed away the fallen leaves and pieces of roof that had collapsed over the years. Her eyes stung, and she wiped them as tears gathered afresh. So many of her memories here at the fort were sad ones. But she would cling to the good memories. She bent down and wrapped her arms around Mosh. She would not forget.

# 21

*October 11, 1664*

Jeremy rode up the lane to the big yellow house at the end of the green. It looked hauntingly empty now. Dirk left immediately after the funeral for Flushing, and he left a heartsick Mosh behind. The dog cowered in the room where Heather Flower had died, though Patience urged him to come out. Dirk most likely would never come back. He'd told Jeremy that Southold would forever hold sad memories for him.

He turned Ink toward the boardinghouse on the opposite corner. He would get a bath and then go gather Patience. Barnabas had relayed an invitation from Mary to come for supper. No doubt Patience knew about it already. He loved the closeness of family and community here, something his years on the ship never afforded. Unless he counted a couple of the youngsters who sailed with him and called him Papa.

He entered his small room, much like the master cabin on *The Swallow,* except that it had a tub in the middle of the floor. A caldron of hot water sat over the fire, which burned low in the corner hearth. He dipped a bucket in the water and began to transfer it to the bath. Soon he was sitting in the steamy tub, planning the new house with a room just for this purpose.

He almost went to sleep in the water but caught himself and climbed out to dry and dress. He pulled on his breeches and boots, then a white linen shirt, and headed out the door to Patience's house.

She was not at all ready. She sat in a heap on her kitchen floor, Mosh happily trotting this way and that over her. Her laughter cascaded over his gleeful woofs, and Jeremy had to pause at the door and enjoy the moment before interrupting. When she noticed him, she shyly held up a bone she'd hidden beneath her to explain what was going on.

"No explanation needed, my love. Except did you not know we are expected somewhere for supper?" A grin wreathed his face.

"Oh! I did forget, and Mary told me. Just one moment." She tossed the bone to Jeremy. "Here, play fetch in the yard with Mosh and I shall be right out."

He led the dog out with the bone, then

218

threw it with all his might. It went sailing into Ester Bayley's yard and smacked the side of her house, but that didn't deter Mosh and he retrieved it in a flash. "Good boy," he said as he eyed the windows of the boardinghouse. His transgression was, thankfully, unnoticed.

Patience danced out the door. "You look terribly guilty about something, but I shan't ask. I'm too eager to go to Mary's. We have a surprise to show you." She called for Mosh to follow, and they set out for the Hortons'.

"Very well. I'm looking forward to the evening, too. It is time the town relaxes and celebrates, don't you think? We've had our share of sadness and trouble."

They walked down the lane, arm in arm. Jeremy patted her hand. "Did I ever tell you about the time I was sailing for England and wound up on the coast of France?"

Patience glanced at him, her blue eyes wide. "No, you haven't. What happened?"

"There was a terrible storm, and it threw me off course, and I found myself in French waters. A French warship detained me and searched *The Swallow*. They released me, of course. It was all a misunderstanding."

"Why, the ocean is not a safe place at all. Weather, pirates, warships. So very harsh.

I'm so thankful you are here in Southold, Jeremy."

He chuckled as they walked up the flagstone path.

Barnabas came to greet them when they arrived, and Mary joined them in the parlor. Patience immediately took her aside to whisper in her ear.

Barnabas chortled. "They have plans for you, I can tell."

"Patience says they have a surprise." Jeremy watched the two ladies.

"We do have a surprise for you, Jeremy, and we shall go get it." Mary led Patience out of the room.

The two brothers did not wait long. With Mary humming a tune — not her forte — Patience entered in a gorgeous pink-and-cream gown. Jeremy stared at her, his mouth open but wordless.

"Do you like it?" Patience twirled for him.

He rose from his chair and took her hands. "Do I like it? Patience, you look like an angel. How is it that I am so blessed?"

Mary ran her fingers over the lace of the sleeve. "Lizzie stayed up a whole night just so it would be done when you got back from New Amsterdam."

Barnabas stood, too. "You are beautiful, and what a beautiful gown."

Tears popped up on her lashes, and she blinked. "Thank you, both. 'Tis the thought of a wedding that makes me seem beautiful. I am so happy."

Mary tsked. "Nay, you are always beautiful. And you never change. How do you do that? Still the same blue-eyed beauty that turns all the men's heads. Jeremy, you had better wed her soon, before someone else does." She winked at Patience.

Barnabas said, "Well, you know, as magistrate I could perform the ceremony now. She is in her dress, Jeremy. What say you?"

His surprise was drowned out by the ladies' laughter. "Oh no you don't, Barney." Mary gasped between laughs. "Patience will have her day as the bride — the whole day, with all the festivities and guests. She has waited too long to let you get away with that."

Patience joined in. "Yes, I will have my little ladies-in-waiting and be queen for the day. I've already promised your daughters."

Jeremy put his arm around her. "Rightly so. I want it to be perfect for you. Once I return from Winter Harbor and I begin work on our house, you may begin with your plans."

Mary looked from Patience to Jeremy. "But we have made the plans. Why wait until after all of that?"

Jeremy watched Patience's face go from light to cloudy. "That is only to say I would like to have a place for us when we wed. A place of our own. But, my love, if you and Mary want to plan, do that with my full approval. Our wedding day will come quickly, and we will share a beautiful life together."

Her smile sent him reeling again, and he could not imagine being without her. "On the morrow, I go to Winter Harbor. Once it is settled that I will be the next master shipwright, I will bring you out to see where we will begin to build our new home."

She threw her arms around him, and he held her close. He forgot his brother and Mary and saw only his bride. Soon they would be married. And from that day forward, his duty would be to her, and he would love her forever.

# 22

---

*October 15, 1664*

Patience stood at her trunk and took her gowns out one by one. She spread them on her bed and picked the green linen dress. With the dress held up in front of her, she spread the skirt with her free hand. She looked back over the other dresses. This one would do. She liked the conservative cut of the collar, and it was one of her more comfortable frocks. She slipped it on over her chemise and pulled at the laces.

Mosh sat watching her, his head cocked and his tail thumping on the floorboards, for he knew a walk was in the making. "Yes, dear boy. We shall go for a walk. I've a list of items I need from the mercantile for my class. The girls start school again in a few days. You shall love playing with them, Mosh, and they shall love playing with you."

She skipped down the stairs with Mosh almost on top of her. She set out her breakfast and gave Mosh his morning bowl of meat chunks — rabbit this morning, leftover from her rabbit stew. She ate some porridge and grabbed her list as they set out for the shop.

After searching the shelves, she finally collected everything and piled her supplies on the counter in front of the proprietor.

"Did you find everything, Miss Terry?"

"Oh yes, I believe I found everything and more, Mr. Danbye."

"It is hard to believe that harvest is over and school is beginning. Another year. Where do they go?"

"I don't know, Mr. Danbye. They do seem to go quickly." Right now it could not go too quickly. The urge to tell him of the wedding was strong, but she bit her bottom lip and signed the account for her purchases. "Thank you, Mr. Danbye."

"Have a good day, Miss Terry."

She bolted from the store and ran straight into Reverend Joshua Hobart. He caught her from falling, but Mosh jumped between them and her bag went flying. Quills and parchment flew everywhere. "Oh my, Reverend. Forgive my clumsiness. Mosh, behave."

"It is my apology, dear Miss Terry. I fear I was in a rush to enter the shop and did not see you coming out. Let me retrieve your purchases." He gathered the quills, and she held the bag as he placed them inside. He gave Mosh a pat. "Did you tell me you are the schoolmistress for the young girls?"

"Yes, I have the Dame School here."

"Why, you are too young to be occupied with that, are you not?" He bent to gather the parchment papers that threatened to blow away.

"Why, no. I love the girls."

He straightened. "May I carry your package for you?"

"Thank you so much, you are very kind. But no, I am not far from here." The wind whipped at her cap and skirt. "But thank you again. Good day, Reverend."

He bowed. "Good day, Miss Terry."

She hurried home, Mosh at her heels. She had not heard that Reverend Hobart had returned to Southold. Why would he have come back? They had no need of another minister. He knew Jeremy, but as far as she could tell, he had only acquaintances here, no actual friends. But she could be mistaken. She would ask Jeremy when he returned from Winter Harbor.

She entered through the kitchen, but heard Lizzie in the hat shop talking to someone. She put her bag on the table and went to see who was there. Lizzie was bent over the drill table, working on the wampum beads. "Hello, Patience — I was just showing Misha how the drill works for the beads. She tells me she would love to work here, helping me with the orders, making beads."

"Wonderful." She turned to Misha. "I'm so glad you'll be here. We've been somewhat out of sorts, and with Dame School starting back up and the wedding to plan, Lizzie and I didn't know what we might do."

Misha's smile reminded her of Winnie. "I'm glad you need me. Mary's girls are growing up, and I need something to do. It is such an honor to work with Heather Flower's beads."

They spent the day together, laughing and recalling the early days of the hat shop. Benjamin had built the counters and shelves. Heather Flower was the one who'd said the shop must be named for Lizzie, and Benjamin had made a sign, Lizzie's Hat Shop.

The quills and paper sat on the table where she'd left them. She would have tomorrow to set up her classroom — today it was more important to spend time with friends who were really more family than anything else.

Mosh was curled by the fire, occasionally sighing in his sleep. Lizzie told Misha the story of how Mary and Barnabas met.

"That reminds me, Lizzie. I ran into Reverend Hobart today."

"Really? What is he doing in Southold again?"

"I don't know — I did not ask. I did think it odd, too, though."

Misha put down the drill. "He is hoping to find a church in need of a minister on Long Island. He likes Southold very much."

"Well, he need not tarry here. We have a minister, and we love him. He will be with us a long, long time." Lizzie shook her head and set her curls bouncing.

Patience tucked a stray lock behind her ear. "He is a very nice man, and his father is quite famous in Boston. I hope he finds a church close by. It would be good to have him near, don't you think, Lizzie?"

"Perhaps. I don't know. Yes, as long as he knows Southold is not up for the taking." She giggled at herself. "And Jeremy, what do you think of his looking for work at Winter Harbor? Why not at Hallock's Landing?"

"He's a bit out of sorts without his ship, I think. And if he is to be a shipwright, then Winter Harbor is the right place to work. I wish it were a little closer, but 'tis not so far that I cannot come here to work. I won't give up Dame School. At least not at first."

"And what of this house? Why does Jeremy not move in here?"

"He would like one of our own. I think that 'tis rather nice. I'm thinking, Lizzie, you can have the whole of the downstairs. Expand your hat shop. Your business has flourished. Even the ladies of Easthampton come here for your hats."

"Lovely idea. But what of Dame School? You said you would keep on with that."

"I shall, but upstairs. The upper rooms will be for the school. And I can still bring the young ladies down for their lessons with you."

"Excellent!"

Lizzie was pleased with her plans, and she sighed. The light was getting short as the sun lowered, and supper had bubbled in the pot long enough. "Shall we go to the kitchen for a bite to eat?" Patience raised her brows as she looked from one friend to the other.

Misha's eyes lit up. "Yes, I'm starved."

They left the shop and Mosh followed, not to be left out when food might be involved. Patience cut thick slices of bread and tossed the crustiest parts to him while Lizzie ladled the pottage. They sat at the table bathed in a golden haze, and Misha lit a beeswax candle before they joined hands in prayer.

They ate their simple meal, chatting about the plans for the hat shop. Patience patted her mouth with a napkin as she turned to Lizzie. "Are you glad you did not give up in the beginning?"

"Oh yes. It was hard at first, was it not? Grissell kept me in business, if I remember correctly. And Mary and Mrs. Wells. But it took a bit of time for our little town to catch up with my big ideas."

Patience leaned back in her chair. "You succeeded because you persevered. And I believe that is what sets the people of New England apart from the homeland."

Misha rested her spoon on the side of her bowl. "How is that?"

Lizzie set down her spoon, too. "Those of us who came did not see an ocean that could not be crossed. We saw an ocean that challenged us to cross it with the promise that we would become who we were meant to be should we make it to the other side. And Patience, 'tis true for you, as well. You have never given up waiting for Jeremy."

"But there were times when I wanted to. And that is the difference between the matters of the mind and matters of the heart. I love him. I couldn't simply decide to give up on him." Her eyes stung, but she smiled bravely.

Jeremy reined in Ink and studied the bay below. The deep water at Winter Harbor lent well to the whaling activities that predominated the port. Merchant ships arrived regularly from France, Italy, and England, and once their cargo was dispensed, the wares bound for the Caribbean were brought aboard and the ship readied to sail again.

The surrounding land, rich and productive, was owned by Captain Johnny Youngs. Jeremy hoped to purchase a lot on top of the hill that overlooked green marshland. When his future was secured, he'd bring Patience out to look at both the hill property and the lots Mapes had mapped out by Thomas Benedict Creek. They would choose the lot together and begin their plans for building. He'd ridden out to both locations, and they each had excellent appeal.

He continued his ride to the dock. Captain Dunning's years of sailing had ended when he lost a leg, but his love of ships led him to a livelihood in shipbuilding. Jeremy hoped to follow in his path. He'd been involved with every aspect of *The Swallow* when she was built, but that had been years ago. Still, he'd maintained her, and his confidence in his ability to learn the trade buoyed his determination.

Captain Dunning labored over a curved length of oak but looked up as Jeremy approached. A wide grin spread across his face as he recognized his old friend. "Why, Captain Jeremy Horton. So good to see ye." He straightened and held out his hand.

Jeremy shook it as he clapped him on the back. "So good to see you, Harry. You look as busy as ever."

"Aye, but never too busy to swap stories. And as I recall, ye are a champion of sea stories, eh, Jeremy?"

He chuckled his approval. "True, true. What is that you work on?"

"It's part of the keel I'm repairing for that whaling ship over yonder." He nodded across the bay at the big whaler up on dry dock.

Jeremy studied the dock and spotted a weathered trunk perched at the end. "What say you we go sit a spell and catch up on each other?" He nodded toward the chest.

" 'Tis what the trunk sits there for. The stories it could tell." He winked, and Jeremy followed him out.

After they settled on the trunk, Jeremy leaned forward, his elbows on his knees. A fresh sea breeze ruffled his hair, and he ran a hand through it. "I guess you know I'm here to inquire about working here at the dock. I'd like to be a shipwright, like you. With you." He cocked his head to watch the man's reaction.

"Ah, I've been expecting ye. You might say I've been praying for ye to come." He had round red cheeks that nearly closed his bright blue eyes when he smiled. His gray hair had specks of the black it used to be, and grew long into his thick beard. He appeared strong despite a wooden leg — and far from ready to give up his love of ships.

"It's been a few years, but as I recall, we talked of a day when you might need someone to learn the trade, to keep the yard going when you're ready to quit. But it looks to me like the day has not arrived." He turned his shirt collar up around his neck as he listened to the icy water gently lap at the dock. As he waited for his friend's reply, he spotted the fin of a coastal dolphin, rare for this time of year. White triangles of light glinted from the surface as the sun played with the ripples in the bay. He could like it here very much.

"Don't be quick to your conclusions, old friend. I have pains that don't go away come nightfall, and I eye this chest every day and think of sitting on it without a care. The day is not far off." He shook his head.

"I could begin on the morrow — that is, if you agree."

The old sea captain's eyes watered. "That is what I prayed to hear. I can give ye a bunk, and Mrs. Sweeney cooks fish like ye've never tasted."

Jeremy stood, his hand outstretched. "Deal, if I may buy you a plate of that fish now. I believe I smelled it before I ever entered town."

Harry stood and shook his hand. "Ye won't regret your decision. And I won't either."

They trudged to Mrs. Sweeney's House of Fish, where many of the harbor's workers already sat out in front on rocks or any other surface they could find, their laps filled with greasy fish wrapped in parchment. It would be different for Patience, living here, but they would be together. He would build her a fine house and a cart she could use to go into Southold. She could teach and visit with Lizzie and Mary each day and come home to his arms each night.

They found an empty table inside and sat down. Mrs. Sweeney cleared away the litter as she offered her fish of the day. When the steaming platter arrived, Jeremy let his cool as they discussed the details of his apprenticeship. It would be accelerated, to be sure, and in the end, the dry dock could be his.

He tore a chunk from the tender fillet and savored it while Harry talked of what he would do with his free time. "Your timing is good, lad. I've inherited me a bit of money. I'm going to build a ship. A ship with three square masts." He winked at Jeremy.

He put his fork down. "That's an ambitious plan, Harry. I haven't forgotten how you helped me when *The Swallow* had a hole in the keel large enough to put her down forever. There was no one who could fix her. But you believed you could, and you put your heart and soul into it. She had many a seaworthy year after that. I told you then if there was ever anything I could do for you, I would in a heartbeat. And I meant it."

"It is ambitious. It is my last hurrah."

"Last hurrah? No, don't think that, Harry. If that is what you truly want to do, think of it as a stepping stone to an easy life, sitting on the trunk and eating Mrs. Sweeney's fish. I will help you do it."

Harry sat there with tears twinkling like diamonds in his eyes. "Bless you. I was praying you would say that. When I heard you didn't drown, I prayed for this."

"I need to find some land to build a house for Patience, so we can get married. But I want to work with you. We'll build your ship, Harry."

"Ah, welcome aboard."

Jeremy shook the captain's hand, the firm grip of the old man impressive. "I will return to Southold to settle with Mrs. Bayley and pack my belongings." He hadn't much, since everything went down with his ship. He'd be leaving Patience's arms once again, but this time to move forward to the day when he would hold her forever.

## 23

*November 4, 1664*
*Southold*

With the harvest complete and plans for a community day of thanks in the making, Patience spent the last day before Dame School commenced after the fall break working at the bake shop with Mary, Lizzie, and Abbey. Misha and Mary's eldest daughters watched Mary and Mercy upstairs, having pretend school in preparation for classes on the morrow.

The women baked four different breads. Patience made the thirded bread — a third wheat, a third rye, and a third corn. It was easy and quick to put together. Lizzie made her wheat bread fancy with chopped onions and garlic added to the dough before she twisted it like a rope. Abbey flattened her dough out and sprinkled it with cinnamon and brown sugar before she rolled it up. All of the loaves would sit overnight, and Mary and Barnabas would begin a day of baking on the morrow.

Lizzie chopped more onion. "Perhaps you and Jeremy should wed on the thanksgiving day."

"How could I be a queen for a day if I must serve food and be thankful?"

Mary looked sharply at her. "Patience! Of course you want to be thankful. And we would not make you serve, we would serve you."

Patience laughed. "I only jest. But truly I think Jeremy will say that it's too soon. I'm anxious to hear what transpired at Winter Harbor. He says once his job is decided, he will bring me out to look at some lots we could build on."

"That seems so far away." Abbey punched down her dough.

"Well, I shall not be able to walk over like I do now, but we'll have a cart, and I'll come every day for Dame School. And whilst I'm in town, I can stop by for a bit of mint tea."

Mary wiped her hands on her apron. "Of course, dear. Jeremy shall make sure you both visit often. He promised me."

"Your dress is ready, we've planned the meal. There won't be flowers, but we'll have lots of greenery and red berries for Christmastide, if you wait that long." Lizzie got a piece of paper and a quill. "I should start writing these things down."

"I do think it will be close to Christmas when we marry."

Mary's eyes lit up. "I love a Christmas wedding. So pretty. But you don't want to wait until after Christmas, because then it is just cold and bleak. Not a good start to a marriage."

The ladies all looked at Patience, and she returned their stares. "I shall be certain to tell Jeremy that." She tried to remain serious, but she knew her eyes were dancing with glee. She loved a good reason to tell Jeremy why they should not postpone any further.

Lizzie was the first to respond. "Well, I, for one, would like to make it known that in your beautiful pink wedding gown, you shall not look the least cold or bleak. Your very presence will warm the hearts of your subjects, Queen Patience."

"Oh, Lizzie, that was so very sweet of you." Mary's smile was as wide as Patience's eyes.

"That it was, Lizzie. Thank you."

Lizzie looked up from the list she scribbled. "So, 'tis decided? Tree boughs and red berries? Bayberry candles? What else shall we need?"

Patience shook her head. "I think we should wait on Jeremy. He shall have news. And hopefully then we may plan."

Mary thanked the ladies for their help. Patience walked to her house but turned on the flagstone to watch the sun sinking beneath pink-tinted clouds. She opened her door, but instead of going inside, she let Mosh out and the two made their way back to the garden, where she could sit and watch the sunset.

She pet Mosh behind his ears, thankful Dirk had left the wolf-dog in her care. She felt close to Heather Flower in a way she never would without Mosh. He laid his head in her lap. "Where do you think Jeremy is, my pup?" He looked up with sad eyes, and she laughed. "Oh, it is all right. You don't have to tell me. He shall be here soon, I'm sure."

She remembered her bag of dough and hurried into the house. She slipped it into a pan and set it by the hearth to rise during the night. She leaned against her table, and the same sense of waiting for Jeremy engulfed her as it had for years. She'd thought he'd be back by now.

She moved into the classroom and went over for the seventh time the supplies, the arrangement of chairs, and the schedule

239

she'd carefully written out. It had not changed for years, but still she felt better with a fresh document detailing each day of the week.

She sat down in her chair at the head of the class. Mosh settled at her feet, but only for a moment. His bark was friendly, and she suspected it was Jeremy at the door before she ever opened it. She threw herself into his arms. "I'm so glad to see you!"

He rocked her back and forth before he kissed her. "I am so glad to see you, my love. I have good news."

"Come to the parlor and tell me all." She pulled on his arm, and they sat close on her velvet pumpkin-colored couch.

"I have an apprenticeship with Master Shipwright Harry Dunning. I begin on the morrow, he is so eager to have me. The harbor is beautiful and the village charming. I think you will like it there, Patience."

"How wonderful. And when shall you bring me to look at the lots?" Her thoughts were spinning. "At the end of the week, after Dame School?"

He chuckled. "Yes, yes. That would be best. I will have a week done with Harry, and your classes will be off to a good start. We'll celebrate with a ride out to Winter Harbor. Now I should go and gather my clothes. I'll let Mrs. Bayley know she may rent my room. And then I'll be gone for the week."

"You're staying in Winter Harbor?"

He pulled her near. "Harry has a bunk for me. We'll be working long hours. But this is not goodbye. This is just the next step toward our marriage."

"That is so very good. I've waited so long for this, Jeremy. Please kiss me one last time so that I might dream of it through the week." She tilted her chin up toward him, and their eyes met. His were so deep a green. How many times had she looked into those earnest eyes when he told her goodbye and she did not know if she would see him again? It always brought tears. But this time she could drown in those eyes and still smile. For this was not goodbye. This was only until they met again. In a week. His lips caressed hers with a tenderness that spoke to her heart. He was happy, too.

Cold morning light poured into the window, and Patience sat up with a start. She threw her quilt aside and pulled on her robe. "Mosh, why did you not wake me? The girls will be here before we know it." He looked at her with questions in his eyes. "Oh, 'tis all right. Let's go down and have a bit to eat, and then I'll get dressed. Lizzie shall be here soon, too. I could not sleep last night, so much I thought of Jeremy and our life together. I wish this week were over."

She hurried down the stairs and checked the shop first to see if Lizzie was there. She was not. The kitchen was cold, and she shoved a split log into the embers and poked until she had a flame. Mosh gulped down the meat and bread crusts she tossed to him, and she had a bit of cheese and bread before she let him out and ran back up the stairs to dress. She must remember to put a fire under the oven and bake the dough she'd brought home from Mary's house. The girls would enjoy it after a morning of lessons.

She picked a dark maroon gown and threw it over her head and pulled the skirts down over her petticoat. She brushed her hair and twisted it into a knot, held with her ivory combs. After pinching her cheeks for a little color, she took a breath and went down the steps.

Lizzie was just coming in with stacks of felt and ribbon that had arrived from Boston on the last ship. "Good morrow to you," she called.

"I woke up late, and it seems I have been scampering like a mouse ever since." Patience heaved a sigh.

Lizzie peeked in the classroom. "Well, you made good time by the looks of things."

"I've been ready for days, actually."

"And Jeremy, what do you hear from him?" She took off her cloak and hung it on a peg near the door. She tossed her head to shake out her curls.

"He was here last night but left again almost immediately for Winter Harbor. He has the job. He begins today. It all is happening so quickly."

"Well, *at last* is all I can say." She smiled at Patience. "And I am very happy for you."

"He gave up his room at the boarding-house, and this Saturday he will come and take me out to look at building lots." She wanted to pinch herself, it all seemed like such a dream. "I'm not dreaming, am I, Lizzie?"

They both laughed. "No, you are not. But I fear you might walk through today as if you are in one. How will you concentrate with the girls? Do you want me to take them for a sewing lesson?"

"No, no. That is later in the week. We shall be fine. I think." She could feel her face warm with a blush.

"Well, I am here if you need help. And nothing I have to do today is more important than you are to me." The crinkles around her violet eyes deepened as she smiled.

Patience wrapped her arms about her friend. "Thank you. You mean much to me, too, Lizzie. Oh, I'd better start the oven fire. I want to bake the bread I brought home."

Young girls' voices sounded on the walk. Lizzie put out a hand. "I shall tend to the bread. Go meet your students."

She opened the door to Mercy, Little Mary, and four more girls from the village, all in pretty dresses freshly ironed for their first day of school. Their faces had a well-scrubbed glow, and their eagerness was palpable. Mosh followed them in with the same enthusiasm, his tail all a-wag.

"Good morrow, my ladies." Patience waited for their response. With none coming, she gave a prompt. "Each morning, when you come to school, I shall say, 'Good morrow' and you shall say, 'Good morrow, Miss Terry.' And you shall curtsey — just a small curtsey, for you are small girls. Do you see? Like this." And she grasped her skirt and tucked one foot behind the other before she dipped. "Can you do that?"

The girls did almost perfect curtsies. "Oh, you've been practicing at home, I can tell. Very good! Now remember, you shall do that each morning. Now follow me to our classroom, and I shall show you your writing instruments, and we shall talk about the rules for our class."

Little Mary stopped before going through the classroom door. "Miss Terry, may Mosh come to our class, too?"

Mosh wagged his tail at the sound of his name but waited for a summons.

"Well, yes, I do think we should have Mosh with us, as long as he does not make a nuisance of himself. Right, Mosh? You promise to behave yourself, don't you?" He leapt to his feet and followed the girls. "I suppose that was a yes."

Watching Mosh watch the girls gave Patience an idea for an art project. She took out large sheets of Lizzie's parchment and sketching pencils and sat the girls down. She told them to sketch the wolf-dog. When Mosh moved, the girls would cry out "stay" and tell Miss Terry their picture was ruined. But she showed them how to put the dog in their picture into movement, and soon they delighted every time Mosh so much as scratched. And if he sat too still, Mercy would get out of her seat and run to move his foot. She squealed with delight when he jumped up and ran after her.

The week flew by, and Patience was grateful she had her girls and the classes to help her get through it. They were smart girls, and already they were farther into their lessons than she had planned. By the time they finished with Dame School, the girls would be proficient at reading their Bibles and reading and writing recipes. Lizzie helped by bringing them into her sewing room to work on samplers and, weather permitting, they went outside to learn about the forest animals and plants. Mosh seemed to think he was an expert in that field of study.

Patience climbed into her bed on the last night of the school week exhausted but happy. On the morrow, she would see Jeremy, and they would ride out to Winter Harbor. She would get her first glimpse of her new life, and that would be enough to get her through the ensuing weeks. She closed her eyes and said her prayers, then snuggled into the covers. But it wasn't long before her eyes popped open and she lay there remembering Jeremy's last kiss.

## 24

*November 12, 1664*
*Winter Harbor, Long Island*

Jeremy hitched the wagon to Ink. "Let's go, boy. I know you'd rather not haul the cart, but Patience will be with us on our return." And Mosh, too. The woman and dog had become inseparable. He prompted his horse into a trot and enjoyed the scenery, if not the chill of the air.

He came into Southold and drove straight to Patience's house. He tied Ink to the gate out front and walked briskly to the door. A knock brought no answer. He thought it odd he did not hear Mosh. He waited a moment and knocked again. He opened the door a crack. "Hello?" There was no answer, but he could see her reticule on the table.

On a hunch, he walked around to the back and was greeted first by Mosh. "Why, hello there, boy. Where is she?" As he asked the question, he spotted Joshua Hobart on the adjacent road, stopped at the fence, in conversation with Patience. Both turned as he called and strode across the corner of her property to reach them.

"I was worried for a minute there, but I see you are in excellent company. Good morrow, Reverend." He stuck out his hand, and the two men shook before he draped his arm around Patience.

"Jeremy! We were just talking about you. I was telling Reverend Hobart about the lots we shall look at by Winter Harbor."

"Yes, there are a couple of choice locations I'd like to show her today. Have you been out that way, Reverend?"

"Please, call me Joshua. No, I have not. It sounds like it would be worth a trip. Certainly, once you've settled I should be pleased to come to call."

"Yes, indeed. Well, my love, are you ready to go?"

She shivered. "Yes, but I think I need to bring a quilt for the ride. Reverend Hobart, it was very good to see you again." She turned to Jeremy. "The reverend had some good news. He has located a church over near Flushing that is looking for a minister, and they are interested in having him come preach."

"Wonderful news, Joshua."

"Why, thank you. Good day to you now, and enjoy your ride."

"Thank you." They walked back to the house, and Jeremy waited while Patience fetched a quilt and her reticule.

Mosh jumped in the cart before he was even invited, and Jeremy helped Patience up to her seat. He climbed up beside her. "I was surprised to see the reverend still in these parts. For some reason I thought he was just traveling through while he looks for a parish."

"He was. But I think he rather favors the north fork. But he's not been able to find a church in need of him."

"Well, any church would be blessed to have him, of course."

"Reverend Youngs is fond of him. Who knows, mayhap someday he will want to retire and Reverend Hobart shall take his place."

The oak and chestnut trees that lined the road, long since bare, looked like tall, dark sentinels with arms outstretched as Jeremy steered the wagon through the winter gloom.

Patience shivered under her quilt. "I almost wish it would snow than look so gloomy."

Jeremy looked at the leaden skies. "You

may get your wish before our journey is over. Pray we do not get stuck."

"Except that tomorrow we have designated as the day of thanksgiving, and we need to be back. You are staying for the dinner tomorrow, yes?"

"I should tell Harry if that is what I plan. To tell you the truth, I think he and I both forgot. Mayhap he would like to come back with us and stay for the dinner, as well."

She leaned against his shoulder. "That would be very nice. Do you like this Harry?"

"Well, I do. I think he might seem a little rough around the edges to you. But under all his gruff, he's a good man. He is excited to help me with a start in shipbuilding. And it seems I can help him, too. I'm certain he could do this himself, but he seems to think he needs me."

"Then I know I will like him too."

The road led them closer to the water, and the terrain changed quickly to sand and beach grass. The oak and chestnut trees were replaced with gray birch and bayberry.

Jeremy looked down at Patience and kissed the top of her head. "I thought I could show you the dock and we could have dinner with Harry at Mrs. Sweeney's. Then we will ride out to the hill first and look at the spot I've fallen in love with. You can see the bay from one side and the marsh from the other. After that we can go to the river, and I will show you the lots Thomas Mapes laid out."

"And then come back to the village to get Harry?"

"Yes, I suppose we would have to, unless he tells us no."

The large dockyard appeared as they rounded a bend, and he stretched his arm and pointed out the boat shop where he worked with Harry. "There, that's him, sitting over on the trunk."

"He looks cold and a little lonely."

Jeremy shook his head. "I don't believe he ever gets cold. In the morning when I get out of my bunk I'm freezing — he's already been up an hour and no fire. It's like he thrives on the cold." He reined in Ink. "Whoa, boy."

He helped her off the cart, and Mosh followed as they made their way out onto the pier. Harry leapt from the trunk, excited to see Jeremy again and make Patience's acquaintance. Perhaps he *had* been a little lonely.

They dined on fish at Mrs. Sweeney's, and Harry and Patience could not stop talking. They took to each other in the way two people who know loss do. When she invited

Harry to the thanksgiving dinner, he accepted without hesitation, and Jeremy promised him they would circle around to get him before heading back to Southold. Hopefully, Mrs. Bayley still would have a room or two.

On the ride to the top of the hill, Jeremy noticed Patience's pale-knuckle grip on the side board. But after they climbed down off the cart and gazed down at the still-green marsh, her expression softened. She ran to the other side, Mosh at her heels. "Oh, Jeremy — look, the bay. There's Mrs. Sweeney's. And the dock. I think I could watch you work from here." She smiled up at him, her blond hair escaping the comb's hold.

He spread her quilt among maidenhair ferns and bearberry bushes with reddish-purple leaves studded with red berries. With Mosh between them, they sat for as long as they could in the cold, and he knew they both dreamed of their life together on this hill.

He brought her to him and kissed her lips firmly before pulling back and looking deep into her blue eyes, bright with cold. "Are you ready to go and see the next lot?"

"Oh yes, but I don't know how it could be lovelier."

He stood and held out his hands to pull her to her feet. "Well, let's go look. You will have to tell me."

They climbed back into the cart after Mosh, and Jeremy eased it down the hill. It was a short ride to Thomas Benedict Creek. The river ran slowly here, and he led her by the hand to the shore. He pointed down at the river's edge. "That's where we would build a house, and up behind it I'd build an icehouse. This river will freeze come January and February, and I should be able to cut blocks of ice from it and store them in the icehouse." He pointed in another direction. "And over there would be your kitchen garden."

She stood close to him as he pointed out these things, and he had to remind himself about all he wanted to tell her. Otherwise he would just have to kiss her again.

Mosh took off through cordgrass and sedge after a rabbit, but it proved quicker than he. They turned back to the river and he grabbed her hand. "We are a little like the river, you know."

Patience looked up. "How is that?"

"Well, it runs slow and steady, but it gets there. Look at us — we've been slow and steady, and we are going to get there."

Her laughter tinkled on the cold air. "I'm

not so certain about steady, but I shall give you slow." She stood on her tiptoes and kissed his cheek.

"Patience, this is difficult for me to say, but I want you to know I truly want to spend the rest of my life with you. I know sometimes it doesn't seem like it. It occurs to me that I never properly asked you to marry me." He lowered himself to one knee while holding her hand with both of his. "Patience, will you?"

She laughed. "Will I what? You must say it if you are going all the way down on one knee."

"You are going to make me, aren't you?" He took a breath. "Very well, Patience Terry, will you marry me?"

Her voice was but a whisper when she said, "Yes, yes!"

Her crystal-blue eyes twinkled as he stood to kiss her. It was warm and wonderful, and he knew he'd done the right thing. He let his lips linger on hers, and he could feel the tremble in her fingers as they caressed his neck. As she pulled back, a slow smile spread across her face.

He grabbed her hand and whistled for Mosh. The ride back to Winter Harbor was quiet, and Jeremy wondered if Patience thought the same thoughts as he. It might take some time to plan the wedding and get settled out here, but they would do it and be happy. It hadn't seemed like much of a blessing when he'd been thrown into the sea, but now he could count it as one, for it had brought him back to Patience.

Harry was waiting for them when they got back to the dock, and soon they were all on their way to Southold. Jeremy enjoyed listening to the captain chatter with Patience and learned a few things about the old man, as well. He'd had a family once — a wife and four loving children — back when he lived in Massachusetts. But they'd been killed in the Indian wars while he was out to sea. He could still remember the day he returned, only to find the village gone. He went back to sea and vowed never to return. And he hadn't. When he lost his leg, he'd come to Long Island and never looked back.

Patience turned to him. "I'd forgotten the terrible creaking of the ships."

"The creaking?"

"Yes. 'Tis the awful sound of wet wood against wet wood. When you are on a ship, the sound is constant."

Jeremy looked at Harry, one eyebrow cocked. "I suppose when one spends as much time on the sea as we two, one does not notice so much."

When they arrived in Southold, it was late, but Mrs. Bayley gave him and the captain a room. After making sure that Harry was settled, Jeremy walked Patience and Mosh home. He stood at her door and took her in his arms. "I enjoyed spending the day with you. I can't remember when we last did something like that."

"I'm not sure we ever have." Patience's eyes were soft, and a small smile played on her lips.

"Well, we'd best start planning days like this. Tomorrow, for one. I'm looking forward to the dinner after church."

"I am too, but I'm not feeling very ready. It shall be an early morning for me." She looked down at Mosh. "And I am depending on you to get me up."

He rested his chin on the top of her head. "We shall take these next days a day at a time. Tomorrow, Harry and I will go back to the harbor after dinner. Next Saturday, I imagine he and I will work straight through. It might be that way for a few weeks. Can you manage that?" He drew back and looked at her. Her eyes were a blue mist.

"I'd rather have you here, I know that. But if that is what you must do, I shall spend my Saturdays as I always have, doing my wash and preparing the next week's lessons. But I shall be dreaming of you and this day while I'm working."

"Thank you. You've made it easier for me to do what I need to do." He gave her a warm kiss in farewell. "Now go, warm yourself by the fire and then get some sleep."

"Good night, Jeremy. I'll see you tomorrow."

He watched her slip inside with Mosh. As he walked back across the road to Mrs. Bayley's, he prayed the next few weeks would go quickly. Then he and Patience could begin building their home and their life together. He wanted this, did he not? There was a time he would have said no, but at this moment it never seemed so right. It was, wasn't it?

## 25

*November 13, 1664*
*Southold*

Patience's Sunday morning walk was brisk as she hurried in the crisp cold to church. She pulled her red cloak tighter around her. There was no way to carry everything for the large dinner planned between services in the hall. It was an abundant harvest this year, and following the tradition of many of the colonies, today would be a special day of thanksgiving. Perhaps she could persuade Jeremy to come back with her immediately after the morning service and help her tote the delicacies she'd prepared for the feast.

She rushed through the door just as the second bell rang. There was a buzz in the vestibule as families moved to take their seats. She saw that the Hortons had gathered in their pew box, but she didn't see Jeremy. When they were married, she would sit with him in the Horton row, but for now she took her seat with the other single women.

As she waited for the service to begin, she glanced across the aisle. Reverend Joshua Hobart sat in the single men's pew. His warm brown eyes met hers, and he smiled and nodded. She returned his smile, but with downcast eyes, and a warmth crept up her neck. Where was Jeremy? She strained to look at the back of the room. He should be here with Harry.

Reverend Youngs stepped up to the pulpit, and the congregation rose to sing Psalm 95, her favorite. "Let us come before His face with praise: let us sing loud unto Him with Psalms."

After prayers of praise and thanksgiving, they all settled back into their pews. She loved this particular service, but without Jeremy present, she found it hard to concentrate. She sensed her eyes wandering and constantly snapped them back to the front. Once she glanced sideways at Reverend Hobart. Why had she been heedless of the fact that he was a very eligible widower?

At last the long service ended, and she turned to file out with the congregation. The ladies began to gather to set up the dinner almost at once. She inched her way toward the door so she could go retrieve her contributions to the meal. Joshua Hobart fell in step beside her.

"Wonderful service, do you not think?" he asked.

"Why, yes, I do. I love this time of year."

He stopped and nodded toward the ladies across the hall. "Are you staying for the dinner?"

Her eyes darted about the room once more, searching for Jeremy. She wanted his help. Where could he be? "Well, yes, I am, but I'm afraid I must hurry home and fetch the food I've prepared." How she wished she'd brought at least some of it with her so she could manage the rest on this trip alone.

"May I be of assistance?" His brown eyes had flecks of gold that gave her a feeling of warmth and sincerity whenever he addressed her.

"I would like that. I'd hoped to find Jeremy, but I haven't seen him this morning. Have you?" He helped her with her cloak, and they walked together down the lane.

"No, I have not. But then, I'm not at Mrs. Bayley's anymore. I've been staying with Reverend Youngs."

They entered her kitchen, and Mosh wagged his way to her. "Mosh, I shall give you something to eat, but you must stay. Be a good boy." She tossed some meat into a bowl and set it down for him. He devoured it before she and the reverend had their arms loaded with her dishes. "No, no more. I shall be back, you silly dog."

She led the way out and stopped to shut the door before Mosh could run out. She set her armload down on the rocker and pulled the door shut.

Joshua stepped close. "Would it be forward of me to ask if you and Jeremy are courting? At times I think I know the answer, but . . ."

Her mouth gaped, and she hesitated to pick up her dishes. "Oh no, it's not." She giggled as she scooped everything up and started down the lane. "I think Jeremy struggles with that question, too. I would say yes, he is courting me . . . when I can find him." She flashed a smile as Joshua matched her long strides. She thought to add "we are engaged," but before she did he pushed the door to the meetinghouse open with his shoulder, and as they tumbled through, Jeremy ran straight into them.

"Patience, I've been looking for you." Jeremy held his arms out and took her bundles.

"We went to get these for the dinner." She searched behind him. "Where is Harry?

Where have you been?"

He glanced at the reverend. "Good day, Joshua. I was with Harry at the boarding-house. He took ill last night. I had to find Doctor Smith this morning."

Her horror overcame her annoyance. "Oh no. Is he all right?"

"Yes, he will be. He is still in bed, but Russell thinks he ate something tainted."

Joshua shook his head. "Well, that can make one deathly ill. Thank goodness he shall get well."

They carried the goods over to a table already laden with platters and dishes of food, most of it fresh from the harvest. Mary and Barnabas had their own table laid out with breads and sweets of all kinds. The Corchaug people had been invited to join in the feast, and many had come and provided roast venison, pheasant, and turkey.

Reverend Youngs offered a blessing for the food and a prayer of thanksgiving not only for the harvest, but the safe return of the horse troop. The people of Southold made their way around the tables with bowls and plates to fill before finding a place to sit, eat, and visit.

Patience and Jeremy sat with the Horton clan, celebrating Benjamin, Caleb, and Joshua's homecoming. Patience couldn't help but notice Johnny Youngs and Joshua Hobart sharing in their own celebration with Reverend Youngs and his wife, Joan. The two pretty Youngs girls, Rachel and Mary, sat with them. Of course. Rachel would be the perfect match for the eligible Reverend Hobart.

Doctor Smith arrived at the dinner in time to get a plate of food and deliver an update on Harry. He would be able to travel in the morning, provided he didn't relapse. Patience scolded herself for not welcoming that news. She'd have liked to have Jeremy stay a little longer, but in the end it was good for him to get back to work so they could keep moving forward on their plans.

As she left after the evening service, she stared at the door where the banns would be posted. How she longed to see them hang there for all the world to see they were to marry.

Jeremy knocked on Patience's door and heard the woof of Mosh. The wolf-dog knew who was on the other side, that was obvious, and he chuckled at the mock ferociousness. He listened as Patience arrived at the door and shushed the dog before opening it.

"Hello, pretty lady. I'm here to see if you

have any of those mashed yams left? The ones with the maple syrup?"

Her laughter was good to hear, and she pulled him inside and led him to a chair in the kitchen. "Where is Harry?"

"You care more about him than me, but I can tell you he is up and preparing for the ride back. He is not hungry, though, and tells me he might not eat again, so sick he was."

She put a bowl of yams on the table and handed him a spoon. "I'm sorry he got so sick, but 'tis good he's recovered so quickly. I shan't worry about him, but I do like that man."

"And he likes you. He gives his regards and looks forward to the next time you are out in Winter Harbor." He dug into the yams. "Mmm. So good."

She tapped her fingers on the wood table. "Well, it seems to me I shall have to find my own way out there, so intent you are to bury yourself in work."

"Do you remember the year that Harry helped me rebuild *The Swallow*? The year the storm about destroyed the harbor? He gave up everything he was working on to help me. Everything. I want to help him build his ship, Patience. Like he helped me. And in the end, he is truly helping me once more. Because without *The Swallow,* I am lost. And yes, I have the means to buy a new ship, but that would not be fair to you. And I will never be content to be a man of leisure. Nor will I ever be a farmer like most of the Hortons. Harry is giving me the chance to do something with my life that I love. And in the end, it is all for us, because it keeps me home, close to you." He smiled at her, and she graced him with her own grin, her blue eyes sparkling.

"Wow. I did wonder why you were so determined to get right to work." She stood. "I want that for you, and Harry, too. And I want you here, safe and on dry land." She wiped her hands on her apron. "I'm going to wrap up some food for you."

He put out a hand. "No, that's too much trouble."

"No, it's not, and I have so much from the dinner yesterday. Besides, you cannot eat Mrs. Sweeney's fish day in and day out."

"True, though her fish is very good."

He watched her as she pulled venison and turkey from her larder and wrapped big chunks in sackcloth. She did the same with the rest of the yams and several meat pies.

He perused the kitchen while she finished wrapping. There were open shelves at one end, filled with crocks and wooden bowls.

Along the bottom shelf she kept black iron pots, some with legs and lids for cooking directly in the fire. A beeswax candle sat on the table, unlit, next to a stack of sieves. On the opposite wall, shelves held stacks of baskets with a number of different uses. "Did you make the baskets, Patience?"

She looked up at the wall. "Oh, some of them. Winnie made quite a few of those, and Mary. Often we would get together and make baskets." Her voice held a wistful lilt. "I guess I have enough now to last a lifetime. And I'm glad — I like knowing that something I'm using had a history, and someday I'll pass it on to someone close to me and it will continue on."

"I'm going to like being married to you, Miss Patience Terry. I like your kitchen, I like watching you flutter around it, and I like how your connection to the past gives you a hope for the future."

"Why, Captain Horton, I believe I'm going to like being married to you. And I shall like fluttering around you in my kitchen. You are the one who gives hope to my future. It has always been you."

He stood and kissed her, and when he left her standing at the door, he was thankful she had waited for him. Thankful she looked to him for hope. Mayhap the years apart

266

made their moments now all the richer. For did not even the stars need some darkness to shine?

## 26

*November 14, 1664*
*Winter Harbor*

It was a snowy day as Jeremy and Harry started working on the plans for the largest vessel Harry had ever built. Most of his money had been made building small coastal schooners, but with his inheritance he planned what he called his "masterpiece."

"If ye learn on this one, ye can build anything," Harry told him as they gathered their tools and sorted the lumber.

Jeremy watched as Harry pinned a half model of the three-masted rig. When the design was perfected, he removed the pins, and after careful measurements, he drew the full-sized hull on the floor.

After a dinner of cold turkey and yams, they started on the keel. Jeremy listened while Harry talked nonstop of how the keel was the backbone and the strength of the ship. These things Jeremy knew, but he listened anyway, and when the old shipwright began to speak of scarfing and bolting, he paid attention, for his memory was dim on some points.

The days turned into weeks, and Christmastide approached, evident by the green boughs Mrs. Sweeney draped from every ledge and the scent of her bayberry candles. No doubt Mary and Barn would be baking, and Patience decorating. But Harry had asked him to stay on through the season, and he had said yes. As a sea captain, he was used to being absent at Christmas, but more than that, he wanted to work on every aspect of this ship.

The two worked on the ribs of the ship, and there was an art to choosing correctly shaped timbers, straight and curved, and then refining them with an adze.

After a long day's work, he and Harry would sit on the trunk, telling endless sea stories until they froze. Mrs. Sweeney saved a place for them by the fire, and they ended each evening with fried fish and more stories.

When Jeremy climbed into his small bunk in the corner of the lofting building at night, he often wrote a message to Patience and sent it in the morning by way of a messenger. Mostly they were notes to tell her he thought of her each day, and sometimes to apologize for his absence. Occasionally he described the work they were doing or a funny thing that Harry had said that day.

On the rare day when Harry quit early, Jeremy would ride Ink to the top of the hill and plot out the grounds for their new estate. He had not purchased it yet, and in fact he and Patience might decide the river lots were more to their liking. But he took satisfaction in the ride and the view.

Finally, he and Harry hoisted the frame and began to lay the deck beams, and soon they were planking and caulking. He tapped oakum into seams with a mallet and did not hear Patience as she walked up behind him. He turned at her voice. She wore a deep green velvet gown, with layers of lace at the sleeves and neckline.

He threw the mallet aside and stepped toward her. "You look like a Christmas present all wrapped up in finery." His arms embraced her and he pulled her close.

"I thought if I were to ever see you again I would have to come to find you." Her voice had a tremble to it that almost broke his heart.

"Hey, now. Do not weep." He turned her to face the big skeleton of the ship. "What do you think? Are you amazed at what we have done here?" He tried to keep pride from his voice, but it was difficult.

"She is beautiful." She walked around to the other side. "Where's Harry?"

"He went to get food from Mrs. Sweeney. We didn't want to both quit working, so he was going to bring me something back. But now that you are here, methinks we should walk over and eat with him."

"Jeremy, you should know that working on the Sabbath is not right." She shook her head.

"Well, I must confess that, as a sea captain, I've worked more Sabbaths than I have not. And Harry is committed to finishing his ship." He leaned toward her. "Are you hungry?"

"Yes. But mostly I want to see you, so if you want to keep working, I shall just find a box to sit on and stare."

Her grin teased, and he offered her his arm. "There will be ample time for you to stare at me while I work. Let's get something to eat, and I wonder if you've given thought to your ride home in the dark?" There were no rooms to rent in this harbor town.

"I have. Reverend Hobart drove me out after church services."

He cocked his head toward her. "Joshua?"

She smiled and patted his arm before they stepped into Mrs. Sweeney's. "He wanted to bring Rachel Youngs out and invited me to come with them. I'm a chaperone of sorts for them."

He hoped the relief that coursed through his body was not apparent to her. "Ah, very well. I'm glad you don't need me to escort you home, although, by all means, I would like to. But Harry is depending on me to keep him on schedule."

Harry sat by the fire inside the fish house, and Jeremy took Patience's elbow and guided her toward him. "Where are Joshua and Rachel?"

"They took the cart up to the top of the hill."

He and Patience pulled out chairs next to Harry, and she bent to kiss the old captain's cheek as she took her seat. "How are you, Harry? The ship looks beautiful."

Harry beamed. " 'Tis because of Jeremy's expert help. He tells me he is apprenticing, but his skill gives him away."

Patience put her hand over Jeremy's. "While he's slow in matters of the heart, I am not surprised that anything that has to do with the sea he's quick to learn."

Jeremy feigned hurt but couldn't keep the chortle out of his voice. "I suppose I'm forgiven? In matters of the heart, I mean?"

"There is nothing to forgive. Except the two of you completely forgot this is Christmas." She turned. "Does she have a name, Harry? Your ship?"

"Didn't Jeremy tell you? She's to be *The Annabelle.*"

She caught her breath. "That's a beautiful name. Does it have a meaning?" She looked from Harry to Jeremy.

"Aye, it does. It means 'God has favored me,' and He has." Harry's blue eyes were soft.

Mrs. Sweeney put down bowls of fish stew and plates of meat pie. "They might have forgotten, but I have not. There will be plum pudding on the house tonight." She winked at Patience.

Jeremy grinned. "Thank you." Following the splendid meal and a tip left for Mrs. Sweeney, the trio walked back to the dry dock, and Patience did as she'd promised and found a box to perch on.

He caulked and smoothed and worked on the ship like she was his own. He glanced from time to time at Patience, expecting to find her asleep sitting up, but each time he peeked at her, she watched him attentively and even had questions now and then.

As the sun settled behind clouds in its

273

descent, Joshua and Rachel came to find Patience. They spent some time admiring Jeremy and Harry's craft and then climbed into the wagon for the ride home.

Jeremy watched until the cart rounded the bend, and for a moment he wished he were with them. But he turned his attention to the work before him and soon was lost in pounding oakum and sealing with tar. Choosing to do one's duty was not without its downfalls, but hadn't he promised God after the shipwreck that he would follow wherever He led?

Patience sighed when Revered Hobart brought the horse and cart to a stop outside of the livery. She was glad she'd spent Christmas with Jeremy rather than at Mary's once again, wondering what he might be doing.

After Joshua tended to the horses, he offered her and Rachel each an arm and walked Rachel home first. Since he was staying with the Youngs, Patience assured him she could walk the rest of the way home alone, but he insisted she be accompanied. At her door, he bowed. "Thank you for the use of your cart and the opportunity to bring Rachel out to see Winter Harbor. She tells me that she's been wanting to see that area, as her brother has owned property there for quite some time."

"I should thank you for taking me with you — I wanted to see Jeremy very badly, and this was quite possibly the only way to do it." She smiled, and he took her hand. She fretted he might kiss it, but a friendly pat was all she received. "Goodbye, Joshua."

"Good night." And he was gone.

Mosh was beside himself with wiggles. "I am so sorry I didn't take you. Next time, all right?" She brought him to the kitchen to give him his Christmas dinner and pulled a big bone she'd been saving out of the larder for his special treat.

She went to the parlor and put a split log on top of the embers. She curled into a chair and watched the flames leap to life. Mosh padded out with his bone and settled for a good chew on the rug in front of the hearth. Contentment wrapped her like a thick shawl, and she went over each minute she'd spent with Jeremy today. It was the right thing to do, to go and visit him. He seemed happy she had.

On the morrow, she would go visit with Mary. Her friend had been disappointed when she'd told her she'd not be coming today for the festivities. But Mary wanted her and Jeremy together as much as Patience wanted it, so she'd understood. Under one condition. That Patience would come over and tell her every last thing that happened. And that she would do.

## 27

*December 26, 1664*
*Southold*

Patience sat with Mary, Lizzie, Abbey, and Anna and watched the younger Horton children exchange gifts. Muffkin played with the ribbons while Mosh watched from beside the hearth. It was the second day of Christmas, and the children exchanged either small handmade gifts or a kindness of some sort. Misha had helped the children make the presents, and they surprised Patience with one, as well.

Mercy put the small package on her lap. "For me? Why, thank you."

"Be careful." Mercy's eyes danced.

Mosh looked up from his post as if he expected one too. Patience pulled the ribbon and pushed back the cloth that wrapped it. Inside was a tiny pot with a little unidentifiable sprout.

She held it up. "I love it. I shall water it

and tend it. And what shall it be?" She looked from one sister to the next.

Sarah smiled. "It is a little apple tree from Mama's orchard. She said it came over from Mowsley."

Patience's eyes grew wide and misty. "I know that tree. Thank you. I cannot tell you how much this means to me. Are you girls anxious for school to be back in session?" The classes would resume in a few days.

Little Mary giggled. "May we say no?"

"Oh, of course not! But I love my little tree. Thank you, girls."

Mary spoke up. " 'Tis for you to plant in Winter Harbor. Not before. When you and Jeremy are married, you shall plant your little apple tree."

"Oh, I shall. And I shall love it and care for it." She took her apron and dabbed her eyes.

With all of the presents opened, the children gathered their treasures and scrambled upstairs, leaving the ladies to converse.

Lizzie put her fists on her hips and raised her brows over her pretty violet eyes. "Now, we've some important things to discuss."

Patience knew what was coming.

Mary's grin grew wide. "Yes, we need to know if Jeremy has set a date for your wedding. When shall the banns be posted? Has he started building your house? And if he has, why hasn't he asked Ben to help him?"

"Oh, so many questions. Let me see now, where do I begin?"

Abbey sat next to her and pressed her arm. "You should start with the first one. Do you have a wedding date?"

Her shoulders sagged. "No, not really."

Lizzie tossed her curls. "And he was working on Christmas?"

"What should we do with our Jeremy?" Mary stood and paced. "I have counseled him and pushed him to take care of this very important step, but I must admit I truly am at a loss as to what to do."

Patience shook her head, and straight blond tendrils fell against her temples. "Do nothing. There is no amount of coaxing for this man. And I don't want to push him into anything. Truly."

They all looked at her with the same puzzled expressions, and she knew it was not the answer they longed for. But it was all she had to give them. And thankfully Barnabas, Zeke, and Benjamin walked in — Caleb, Joshua, and Jonathan behind them — and all eyes turned to the men.

Barnabas's face was lit with expectation. "I have your surprise, Mary. It is in the barn." He gave her little presents on each

279

day of Christmas, but he usually saved the biggest gift for Twelfth Night. "Come, children. You must see this too."

Mary rushed to him. "In the barn? Oh my. This is exciting." Her eyes shimmered like emeralds.

Patience smiled as the girls jumped from the floor. Mercy grabbed her father's legs. "In the barn, Papa? Is it a horse?"

"No, no. We don't need another horse." Starry Night was just the latest of several to descend from the Langtons' Great Blacks. "But I will tell you it involves Stargazer, and methinks everyone should dress warmly. Get your capes and muffs. Mary, you and the ladies might want to gather blankets to bring."

Patience went with Mary to the rooms upstairs in search of wraps and blankets. "What do you think he has planned?"

"I cannot imagine. But I know he and Benjamin have been up to something. We shall need warm coats for the barn, certes, but I am a bit perplexed about blankets."

They took several from a trunk and joined everyone in the kitchen. Benjamin and his brothers were already gone, and Barnabas stood by the door. He pulled it open. "Mary, ladies, girls —" he bowed — "this way please."

They stepped outside, and Patience blinked at the thick blanket of snow glittering in the bright winter sunlight. A path had been dug to the door of the barn, and she followed Mary until she stopped at the door with a gasp.

Patience peered over her shoulder. There stood Stargazer, bedecked in a harness trimmed with bells that jingled with each move of his head. At the end of the yoke sat a shiny red sled, long, with rails along the sides. The runners gleamed.

Tears ran down Mary's cheeks. "Barney, how did you do this? Those bells — they are beautiful. Where did you get them?" She threw her arms around him, her eyes not leaving her gift.

"Benjamin and the boys helped me. He made the sled, and Caleb and Joshua painted it. Jonathan worked hard to polish it. Jeremy brought me the bells last year, on his last trip to England, and I took the harness down to the cobbler and had him stitch them on."

Mary and Lizzie stepped over to Stargazer and touched the bells, setting them to tinkling.

Patience followed them and ran her hand over a rail. "How many may ride in the sled, Barnabas?"

"I should think I could take five or six of you at a time. Mary, let's start with you — and Patience, Lizzie, Abbey, and Anna. Hannah, you come too. We'll go out Horton Lane and look at the building site out by the sound. Then I'll come back for Misha and the little girls. Jonathan and Joshua can come with us on that run. What say you?"

Sarah spoke up. "I'm not a little girl, Papa."

He chuckled. "Of course not, my sweetling. But Misha needs help with the little ones."

Sarah looked at Patience, and they exchanged a smile. Patience often told her she was growing up, even though Sarah complained that no one noticed.

"Very well, it's arranged," Barnabas said. "When I get back from the second run, Benjamin, you may take Caleb and Zeke out for a ride."

Patience stepped back from the sled as Benjamin led Stargazer outside. Jeremy would have loved to be a part of this. He'd missed getting to see Mary's face when she saw the horse bells. He'd missed so much over the years, and now he was so close but still missing family times, happy times. It made today bittersweet, and she'd promised herself she would not allow those kinds of thoughts anymore.

She put her chin up and took Mary's arm as they walked to the sled. "All the way out to the other side, is that what Barnabas said?"

Mary patted her hand. "Yes, we shall go see where he is clearing for a new house."

Barnabas opened the side of the sled, and the six ladies climbed in and huddled close. They spread the blankets over their knees and looked out in anticipation. They all fell backward when Stargazer stepped out with a quick step, and they giggled hard as they struggled to right themselves.

The horse kept a good pace as they jingled their way through the woods. With snowy boughs shaking wet droplets as they passed underneath, they pulled their hoods over their heads, and a fresh round of giggles rippled the crisp, quiet air. Patience saw Barnabas turn with a grin to see Mary's face. He most likely enjoyed this more than any of them.

Barnabas's early years with Mary had not been easy. He'd grieved so for his first wife. And though he'd tried to be kind to Mary, sometimes it had seemed he did not know how. Or perhaps he just could not see through his pain. But he was a sweet, honorable man, and he'd come to love Mary in a powerful way. And with that same stalwart devotion, he'd loved and served his church and his township.

Jeremy was so much like him, and that was why she loved him. Oh, how she wished he were with them today. She leaned close to the rail and watched the blur of shrubs and trees whip by. She pulled back after only a moment and smiled at Mary. She would not let sad thoughts ruin this day, this ride, this time with her dear friends.

They spent an hour at the clearing and stood in awe of the beach at the bottom of the cliff. Across the water they could see a strip of land Barnabas said was Connecticut. Mary told her that when they first came to Southold, Barnabas had brought the boys out here, and the three had hiked down to the shell-strewn shore.

When they could not take the cold any longer, they bundled into the sled again, and Barnabas guided Stargazer back along the narrow road. Mary chattered about a warm kitchen filled with Christmas breads and hot tea. Misha surprised them all by having just that waiting for them when they returned. And Patience promised her they would do the same for when Misha and the girls got back. She settled with her warm mug at the table and stared out the window as Benjamin, Zeke, and Caleb waved to Barnabas as he left on his next tour. Only Jeremy was missing.

## 28

*January 8, 1665*
*Winter Harbor*

Jeremy stood back and admired their crafts-manship. They'd worked hard and steady, but still they were not even close to finished with the ship. Harry knew Jeremy would be going over to Southold on the morrow. It was Plow Monday and the beginning of the farming season. They wouldn't actually plow — too much snow on the ground for that — but they would get all of the imple-ments in order — cleaning, repairing, and oiling — so when the snow disappeared even for a day, they would be ready.

No doubt he'd been missed, even scolded in absentia, during the Christmas celebra-tions. But he and Harry had accomplished much in that time, and he did not regret seeing through the smelly job of caulking.

That night he looked at his clothes, stinky and in a heap. Living in a hole did not afford him opportunity to keep things neat and orderly like he preferred. He wished anew that Patience were here to tend to laundry and meals. But he imagined she thought he'd come home each day smelling of saltwater and fresh wood, not tar and greasy fish.

He picked up his clothes and took them to the water's edge. He swished the breeches and shirts in the icy water, then took them close to the fire to dry overnight. He'd smell like smoke, he guessed, and that would be an improvement. Mrs. Sweeney had said she could take in his laundry, but Harry had warned him he might not ever see it again.

He was up before dawn and pulled on a broadcloth coat and neck cloth over his stiff but clean clothes. He walked with Harry to Mrs. Sweeney's, and she cooked them thick slices of bacon and served it with crusty bread and chunks of cheese.

After the meal Harry shook his hand and then he swung up on Ink. The ride was not long, and soon he was trotting down the town green, with Patience's house standing out at the end. With each step closer, he realized how much he'd missed holding Patience in his arms. He'd thought they ached from all his labor, but now he knew they ached for her.

He jumped from the saddle, and before he could reach the door, it flew open and she was in his arms. Mosh ran circles as Jeremy hugged her and twirled her about before setting her back on her feet. He held her back to look at her. "I have missed you, Patience."

"I am so glad to hear that, for I have missed you, too. And I didn't expect you home so soon. Are you finished? Is the ship complete?" Her blue eyes searched his.

"Nay. We have a long way to go, my love. But it is Plow Monday today, and I know Barnabas would appreciate me helping." She shivered, and he added, "Should we not go in by the fire?"

"Yes, come in. But Jeremy, you would have been appreciated here during the Christmas holiday, too." She held his hand as she led him to the hearth. Mosh darted in front of them and lay by the fire.

He sat in the chair opposite her and stretched his foot to rub Mosh's side. "We had begun caulking, and once you start that, you cannot take a break. But we've finished, and I have a day or two before I must be back to start planking."

" 'Tis my first day of classes after the holiday. It shall be hard to concentrate, knowing you are at the Hortons'." She looked at him from beneath her lashes.

"Mayhap you should bring the girls there."

"And teach them what? This is what a plow is?" She wiggled her eyebrows.

He chuckled. "Well, no. The bakery. Teach them about the bakery and show them all of Mary's tools."

It was her turn to laugh. "Half of my girls were born in that house."

Their eyes met, and time paused until they broke into uproarious laughter and stood to embrace again.

Patience was the first to speak between her giggles. " 'Tis so wonderful to have you here."

"Walk with me, Patience."

She took her red cloak from the peg while he banked the fire. Mosh wagged his tail. "Yes, you may come, boy." He dashed ahead of them.

Jeremy held out his arm, and as they walked, he wondered if he should even return to the harbor and shipbuilding. Mayhap he should stay right here, with Patience on his arm and Barnabas and Mary down the lane. "Ask Mary if you may learn cheese-making in her kitchen. Mary makes the best cheese. She can demonstrate to both you and the girls."

They passed the meetinghouse and crossed the road. "Nay. Lizzie is dyeing wool and felt today, and I promised the girls we could watch."

He paused for a moment at the front door before knocking. "Very well. I will miss you, then, and you must promise me to come dine at Mrs. Bayley's with me."

"And you don't think Mary will insist you stay to eat?" She rolled her pretty blue eyes.

"I will tell her we have previous plans, and we do." He pounded on the door, and it was but a moment before Barnabas opened it wide.

"Heigh-ho. I wondered when we would see you again. Good of you to come on Plow Monday."

"Have I ever missed one?"

Barnabas clapped him on the back. "I cannot think of a time you've been here for even one." He winked at Patience. "Come in. This is a surprise. Mercy and Little Mary are getting ready to come to class. Follow me to the back kitchen."

The bakery was warm, and the scent of spices and yeast permeated the air. Mary was elbow-deep in bread dough, punching and turning it. She looked up with a smile. "Oh, good morrow. I would hug you both, but then you'd be covered with flour."

Jeremy opened his arms. "I can think of worse things." He brushed his coat after they embraced. "I've been trying to convince Patience to stay here today and hold her Dame School in your kitchen."

Patience held up a hand. "Of course I've told him no. I'm taking your girls with me, right back to school. Lizzie will be showing them how to make dyes today. We'll be dyeing wool and felt."

"Oh, they shall like that very much."

"They can each bring a sample home."

Jeremy eyed the fresh-baked ginger cakes on the shelf.

"Go on, have one." Mary pointed at them. "And Patience — put some in a bag for the girls."

Jeremy picked up a cloth bag and layered several crisp cakes in it, then popped one in his mouth.

"Thank you. The girls always like it when we have your baked goods, Mary."

Mercy and Little Mary ran into the kitchen, followed by Sarah and Hannah. Barnabas handed them each a piece of cheese and placed a platter filled with slices of bread, spread thick with butter, on the table. He took his Bible off the sideboard, and the girls sat still as he found a verse.

Jeremy glanced down the hall. "Where are

the boys?"

Barnabas looked up. "We had our devotions earlier. They are already out at the barn. We find it easier to have the boys eat first. So much commotion in the bakery every morning, it just works better."

They all fell quiet as Barnabas leafed through the pages of the Bible. "Listen to 2 Timothy, chapter 1, verse 7: 'For God hath not given to us the spirit of fear, but of power, and of love, and of a sound mind.' Now, bow your heads as I bless our food."

Jeremy took Patience's hand and bowed his head. He often forgot how a family should be, living so many years with a crew of men. Prayer and blessings had always been important on the ship, but it was the sense of belonging to other people, rather than just being responsible for them, that touched him on this morning.

The girls ate their bread and asked if they might bring the cheese with them to school. Soon Patience was out the door with them in tow.

Jeremy followed Barnabas through the snow to the barn.

"How is the shipbuilding coming?"

"Slow, it seems to me, but Harry thinks it's coming along nicely." Jeremy shook his head. "I'm thinking we have months to go on it."

"Mary tells me that Patience would like to have the wedding soon."

They stepped inside the barn. "I don't see how we can get married before I finish this ship. And I rather thought she was in agreement." He looked at his brother in the dim barn light. "Do you think it is more Mary than Patience who wants it?"

"I would not be the one to question either of the ladies." They both laughed. "You will just have to take it for what it is worth. I will tell you, Caleb and Hallock's daughter, Abigail, plan to marry at the end of the year. In that regard, I'm certain Mary is thinking sooner is better for you and Patience."

"I wondered if they might. He has been smitten with her for a long time."

The Horton boys had spread out the shovels and rakes and hoes. Barnabas studied them and nodded his approval. "We'll begin with the small implements and work our way up." He turned to Jeremy. "And I think you can apply the same principle to your present situation. Begin with the small decisions — those can be dealt with quickly and be put aside, removing the clutter. Then you may turn to the large issue with no distraction."

Jeremy ran his fingers through his hair. "Barn, you are getting wise in your old age."

Barnabas chortled. "No, I think you are just noticing. But seriously, do you intend to marry Patience or not? Because it is beginning to seem like you have excuses and the women are champing at the bit."

"Don't beat about the bush, Barn." He chuckled, but how could he tell his brother that it was Barnabas's own marriage, early on, that had changed Jeremy's view on marriage and commitment? "I mean, I want to marry her, and then I have to wonder if I'm making a mistake. Or is she, for that matter? How do two people know that they've each found the one person they are meant to be with forever?" He shook his head. "I'm almost there, and then I feel myself hold back. It's like an instinctive move I can't stop."

Barnabas stared at him for a moment. "That's a sorry excuse. After all the years Patience has waited for you, and you've been coming here and telling her you love her, now you are having doubts? I would say pray about it, brother. Because to me it looks like God booted you out of *The Swallow* so you would get on with your life. It might be time to figure that out."

"Point taken. One of the things I told

myself when I was fished out of the sea was that I'd be open to what God had saved me to do. Mayhap I've taken Patience for granted."

Barnabas clapped him on the back and turned to his sons. "Your uncle and I will build a fire to forge the blades. You boys begin checking them, but look at the handles first. Make sure they are not coming apart. If they are, they need to be repaired before we fix the blades."

They worked the rest of the afternoon, right through to the heavy plows and wagons, and it wasn't until they finished checking the last wheel and bolt that Barnabas took Jeremy to see the sled.

"Patience told me about this. She said you gave everyone a ride out Horton Lane to the sound."

"Aye, I did. Mary loved it. But you haven't seen the best part."

"What's that?"

"Remember the horse bells you brought back for me? I had them stitched to the harness. Look here." The bells clattered as he pulled the harness from a wooden box. "We won't be running into anyone in this sled. They hear us coming from miles away."

Jeremy held the harness and gave it a shake. "Excellent. You amaze me, brother.

You give me much to live up to."

"How is that? You brought the bells back for me."

"It is the spirit in which you give, Barn. The joy you have in making someone happy."

"You have heard it said, have you not, that the gift is in the giving? Well, it is true."

The boys wiped the last of the crusty mud from the plow's moldboard, and they all dipped their hands in a barrel and splashed their faces with a shock of cold water. Jeremy handed each a ragged cloth to rub away the grime, and they stomped through the snow for supper.

"It smells very good, Mary, but I've promised Patience I would take her over to Mrs. Bayley's."

Mary's eyes flew wide. "The boarding-house? I've not known you to pass on one of my meals, no matter how simple it is. No, bring her here. Go fetch her now."

Jeremy shook his head. "It's been too long since I've seen her, and we must sit and talk." He put his arm around Mary. "Surely you understand."

Later he sat across from Patience, chewing dry slabs of venison. "I'll not tell you how good Mary's kitchen smelled tonight."

She laughed, and he watched as her eyes

smiled along with her lovely mouth. "Mary's kitchen always smells lovely. I wanted your company tonight more than a good meal."

She was beautiful. And kind. He set his fork down, stretched his hand across the table, and wrapped his strong fingers around hers. "I was hoping you might feel that way." They sat that way a long while, taking each other in, ignoring the cold food on their plates.

She squeezed. "I hate that you are away in Winter Harbor, but thankful 'tis close enough we can find a moment here and there to feel your touch on my hand."

"It will be several more months, I fear, before Harry's ship is complete. He is thrilled to have me working with him, and I believe that is because he knows he could not do it by himself. I think he knows it is his last ship."

Droplets of tears collected in her eyes like the snow crystals gathered in the spent rose blooms. "Then I am glad you are doing this for him."

They walked to her porch. Jeremy put his hand on her arm. "Will you sit with me a while? It's cold, but you look so pretty in the moonlight."

Her eyes shone like stars in the cold moonlight and as she took a seat on the steps she pulled her cloak tight around her.

He sat beside her, an arm about her shoulders. "Did I ever tell you about the time I was sailing with my uncle when I was about fifteen, and we sailed from London up to Southwold?"

A smile flickered on her lips. "Well, I remember something about it. But tell me again. I can't remember how the story ends."

He chuckled and told her sea stories until they were half frozen.

He kissed her warm and long on the lips before he crossed the road back to Mrs. Bayley's. The memory of that kiss would be what kept him to task through the coming weeks. He must finish the boat so they could marry.

## 29

*May 10, 1665*
*Southold*

Four months passed by, and for Patience the change of season magnified the passage of time and her longing for Jeremy. Her little students and her friends kept her busy, but her life truly seemed on hold until the ship was ready to sail.

She stood with Mary while Barnabas led Stargazer around from the barn. The snow had melted long ago, and the sled remained behind, but the horse jingled with each step, his harness full of bells.

Abbey and Misha were there, and Lizzie and Zeke joined them. The men helped the ladies into the back of the wagon and then climbed up to the board in front. Benjamin and Anna would bring their own wagon, and Benjamin's brothers and sisters would ride with them.

It was the middle of the work week, and it

was springtime, with all that entailed, but they'd made this journey to Fort Corchaug every year on this date since Winnie had died. Several of the townspeople made the same journey, including the Youngses, and it was a daylong celebration of Winnie's life.

Over the years, it had grown into a celebration of her people, so keenly were they aware of their dwindling numbers. Patience gazed at Abbey and Misha as the wagon bumped over the road filled with puddles from spring rains. She thought of the sad loss of Winnie and Heather Flower. Fever and pox were killing the native people faster than any wars with the Narragansett.

They rode past the meadow and into the forest, fragrant with beach plum blossoms. Tall tulip trees danced in the wind, adorned with white flowers and flanked by white oak and tall chestnut trees. Mosh happily sat in the wagon with his head over the rail, mouth open and tongue out, flying in the breeze.

As they entered the old wooden gate of the fort, now hanging open wide, Patience's heart was heavy. She breathed deeply and said a prayer for the native people. Barnabas's strong arms lifted her down, and then he turned to help Mary. They took Abbey and Misha's hands, and together they walked toward the longhouse. It had a covered area like a large porch that in years past had served as a place for the women to boil maple syrup or make shell beads. Old buckets lay abandoned, and the ground was littered with broken oyster shells. Large chunks of the roof lay on the ground, and she thought back to the last time she was here, at Heather Flower's funeral.

Patience put her hand to her throat. It ached with grief for the people who had been here before. She missed Winnie and Heather Flower so. She struggled as she tried to talk to Abbey and Misha. "I just want you to know how sorry I feel to see your people go. I know the Hortons and the Youngses and all of the families who were here to found Southold must feel as I do. But it seems there is no going back, and we can only move forward. And it makes me wonder why, in order to achieve something great, good things die. We try to do the right thing. But we are far from perfect. We make mistakes, and I fear this was one of them. May God forgive us."

Abbey and Misha took Patience and Mary in their arms, and soon Lizzie and Anna came to join the weeping women. They walked down the path to the river, wailing and mourning their loss.

Patience settled on a stone ledge overlooking the river, with Mosh at her side. She spread her skirt over her knees and hugged them close to her body. A log, half submerged, bobbed with the river flow. Abbey pointed upward, and all eyes traveled to a majestic bald eagle sitting high on a nest as wide as Patience was tall.

Mary spoke in a soft voice. "Winnie used to tell us that the same eagles came back here year after year. Do you think he is the same one? Where is his mate?"

Abbey nodded. "It might be. He probably has eggs in that nest. His mate would not be far. They are sacred birds to my people."

"They are beautiful." Patience's voice was low like Mary's, in awe of the bird.

Lizzie, Mary, and Patience told stories to Abbey and Misha about Winnie and Heather Flower. They talked about the early years when they learned so much about survival from Winnie and the tragedy of Heather Flower's wedding to Keme and then the craziness before she married Dirk. Anna said the most amazing thing to her was God's timing. It was so hard at the time to know why things happened as they did, but God had a plan for each of them.

Jeremy had officiated Heather Flower and Dirk's wedding. It was the only thought of Jeremy that Patience allowed herself as they sat there. He'd come for two brief visits since Plow Day, and it almost hurt worse to see him for what seemed like moments than to have him gone. He worked hard in Winter Harbor so that they soon could be together forever. She clung to that and loved him all the more for it. But it didn't make the separation any easier.

As the sunny day turned to dusk, they listened to the crickets compete with the incessant call of the whippoorwill. They could see wood smoke rise in a curl above the tree line, and the aroma of meat roasting reminded them of their growing hunger.

Patience came up the path lighthearted and glad she had this connection to these wonderful people. Mosh mirrored her mood and trotted beside her. Mary and Lizzie returned her smile as they entered the hut that had once belonged to Winnie. The few families who remained at the fort had brought together the bounty of their hunt and the dried corn and apples from their larder to provide a feast for their guests.

The spring evening was cool, and they sat near the fire, listening to the Corchaug people share their own memories. Mercy, Little Mary, Sarah, and even Hannah leaned into the arms of Mary, Lizzie, Abbey, and Patience. As the evening grew late and

Mercy fell asleep, they said their goodbyes and climbed into the wagon. Mosh curled at Patience's feet. She could hear Barnabas singing in his beautiful baritone, but she couldn't make out the words. She leaned her head back and saw the stars ablaze and looked over at Mary.

Mary smiled. "Yes, I'm searching the heavens for a new star. Heather Flower looks down on us, I just know, with Winnie, and they're smiling."

Lizzie laughed. "Or tsking us."

Patience grinned and settled back. She was happy this night. True, she'd be happier when Jeremy was with her. But that time would come. She just prayed it would be soon.

She slept soundly, hugging Mosh close, and when morning light broke through her window, she threw back her quilt and ran to the window. She pushed open the casement and breathed in the brisk, cool air. "I love a new day, Mosh. God gives us a fresh start every day we wake."

She settled in a soft chair and read her Bible and said her morning prayers. She ran down the stairs to let Mosh run in her garden, her robe pulled close about her as she watched him romp through rambling honeysuckle and roses and drifts of foxglove and lavender. She needed to spend a day in her English garden, nipping spent buds and pulling weeds.

But her little girls were coming for their last day of class. They followed almost the same schedule as the boys' school most weeks, but during planting season, they returned to classes while the boys helped their fathers in the fields. Today she planned a special day for her girls.

She wandered back to the kitchen and scooted a chair over to her shelves. From the top shelf, she took six of her mother's blue-and-white Delft cups and plates and brought them down to the table. She took six of her finest white napkins from her linen trunk. Her students were invited to bring their very favorite poppet and wear their church dresses.

She went back up the stairs to change into her own gown, a pretty yellow floral with much lace about the neck. She let her hair down and brushed through it twenty times and then twisted it back into place and secured it with her ivory combs. She finished her ritual with a quick pinch on her cheeks and pressed her lips together to bring out their color.

She floated down the stairs and went to

check on her wolf-dog. He chased a rabbit under the fence as she stepped out. "Mosh! You leave him alone." He trotted to her and followed behind as she plucked some pretty coneflowers and daisies to make a bouquet for the table.

As she entered the back door, she heard the girls arriving at the front. She'd invited Lizzie, Abbey, and Misha to the party. Mary and Anna would be working in the bakery. Mosh ran ahead to greet them, and she listened to their happy chatter as she dipped the vase in the bucket for water and added the flowers. She set them on the table and admired them for a moment. Flowers reminded her of pretty weddings, but she still had no idea when hers would be. Perhaps she should make a trip to Winter Harbor on the morrow. She had not been there since Christmas Day. It would be nice to see how the ship looked.

She set out scones and crocks of butter as the girls made their way into the kitchen. "Oh my. Look at you young ladies."

The little girls curtsied. "Good morrow, Miss Terry." Their faces were scrubbed, and their dolls had been cleaned and pressed, too — she could tell.

"Good morrow to you," she answered and swept into a deep curtsey.

She sent each of her students to the shelf for jam and honey while she set a bowl of berries on the table. She had made lemonade like Mary taught her and had hot sage tea she hoped they would at least try if she added enough milk.

When the three girls were seated around the table, each with their doll next to them, Patience instructed them before they ate that they must make introductions, and after the introductions they must wait for the blessing.

Mercy was the youngest, but she always was ready to talk. "I am Mercy, and this is my poppet, Marcy." She dissolved into giggles when she said the doll's name.

Abbey and Patience hid a laugh while Misha oohed over the doll. "Is her name part Mercy, part Mary?"

Little Mary spoke right up. "Yes, she thinks it's funny, but I think it's a pretty name."

"Why, I do, too." Patience had Mary and Lilly, the last of the three, recite their introductions, and then they folded their hands to pray. The little girls looked so much like angels, and she would miss them over their short break.

After their refreshments, they went to the garden to play games. Their poppets were propped up on the bench to watch, and Patience and Abbey sat with them as Misha helped the girls line up. Falling Bridge was their favorite game, and they played it over and over again, chasing one another with Mosh right in the middle of the fun.

They played hoops until everyone was sufficiently worn out, and then Patience presented each girl with their certificate for a year complete. She'd started the year with six girls, which dwindled to three, but it was not unusual to lose half. Often, as young as they were, a mother would need her daughter at home to help with some of the chores. It made her sad because it seemed a waste of a precious mind, but she understood how difficult it was in this land to raise a family.

She sent her charges home and looked about her house. Lizzie had gone home for the rest of the day, and it was empty and lonely. It occurred to her that Jeremy and Harry needed something to eat besides fried fish. She would make them some meat pies and go to the bakery to buy some nice loaves of bread and cakes to take to them.

She would do her shopping first. Perhaps stop by the mercantile and pick out some nice currants to put in her pies and then go on to Mary's. Cooking could wait until tonight. She took off her apron and ran her

308

hand over her hair. It seemed to be in place. "Come, Mosh. You may go with me." He wagged half of his body with his tail and followed her out.

She bustled about the shop, scooped some currants into a bag, and stopped to admire the beeswax candles. No doubt Mary had made those. She stepped to the counter behind the gentleman Mr. Danbye was assisting. He turned slightly, and she exclaimed, "Reverend Hobart, why, what a surprise."

"Indeed, and a pleasant one. You were going to call me Joshua, remember?"

Her neck was warm, and she put a hand up to her collar. "Yes, Joshua. Good morrow to you." She turned toward the shopkeeper. "And you, Mr. Danbye."

Mr. Danbye nodded his greeting. "Miss Terry."

"I am so surprised to see you back in Southold, Reverend."

"Reverend Youngs was good enough to invite me back to speak this Sunday in church. Will you be attending, Patience?"

"Yes, definitely yes."

"Very good." Joshua took his bag from the shopkeeper. "Good day, Patience."

"Good day, Joshua. I shall see you Sunday."

He nodded and stepped out.

She stepped up to Mr. Danbye with her purchase and rolled her eyes at her own feeling of ill ease. She did not know whence it came from, but by the time she got to Mary's, she breathed a sigh of relief.

Mosh settled on a rug in the parlor, and Muffkin plopped next to him. Mary led her back to the kitchen. "You are going to Winter Harbor?"

"Yes, and I cannot wait. 'Tis been too long since I saw Jeremy, and even longer since I've seen that ship they are building. And I enjoy Harry so much."

"Wonderful." Mary's eyes lit up. "You must take some of the best bread — I put some onion and cheese in this one — they shall love it, and take some ginger cakes, too. And he especially likes these apple tarts, so let me put some in with the cakes."

They flitted around the kitchen with cloth sacks, filling them with the baked goods. "You know, Jeremy loves the clotted cream," Mary said. "Let me put some in a crock for you."

"Mmm. I love it, too." Patience dipped her finger in it for a taste as Mary skimmed it from a large earthenware pan.

"This has sat for two nights now. It should be very good." Mary handed her a loaf of sugar and the sugar shears. "Here, shave some of this over the top. Make sure he stirs it."

"I shall want to make this for him often, I think. How do you make it?"

"Oh, 'tis easy. Let me write it for you."

While Patience topped the cream with sugar, Mary took her quill and a piece of paper and sat at the table.

### Mary's Clotted Cream

Set two gallons of the first milk of the day over a hot fire. When it boils, pour in a quart of sweet cream. Take it off the fire and pour through a fine sieve into a large crock or earthenware pan. Let it stand in a warm place for two days and two nights without stirring. Take it off with a skimmer and strew with sugar before serving.

"Thank you, Mary. I shall put this in my recipe book." She folded the paper and tucked it inside one of the sacks. "Now, I should be off to bake the meat pies. I bought some currants to put in them. I'll be baking all night, no doubt. Did I tell you I spoke with Reverend Hobart at Mr. Danbye's?"

"Nay. He's back in the village?"

"Yes. He shall be giving the sermon this Sunday. I think he rather has a sweet spot for Rachel Youngs." She smiled and looked at Mary sideways. "Don't you think?"

Mary shook her head. "While that would be a good match by any standards, and Rachel is very charming, I hear the reverend thinks of her more as a friend — and a child, at that. At least it does not seem he will be courting her."

"Oh." She turned from Mary so that her friend would not see her raised brows. "Well, then, with that, I shall be gone." They kissed cheeks, and Patience hurried out the kitchen door.

She walked home at a brisk pace with her packages. There was much to do, and she would like a good night's sleep for her short journey on the morrow. She tended the fire first and built one beneath her oven with the fattest logs. It would need to be hot. Thank goodness the spring nights were still cool.

The meat larder was a little bare, but she found some good pieces of elk to chop for her pies. As she trimmed the pieces, she tossed scraps to Mosh, who sat at the ready to catch anything thrown or dropped.

She boiled the meat and minced it before stirring in suet, chopped apples, and currants. She added cider and then sprinkled in cinnamon, nutmeg, and mace. She set the mixture aside to make her pastry. Mary had taught her a simple crust, but still she pulled out her book to consult the recipe. She wanted these pies to be perfect.

### Pastry for Pie

To a quarter peck of flour, rub in half a pound of butter, a little salt, and make it into a light paste with enough cold water to make it just stiff enough to work up. Then roll out flat. Stick a few more pieces of butter on top. Strew some flour and roll up. Roll it out flat again. Do this about twelve times, until you have rolled in about half a pound of butter.

She followed the directions and had enough for two pies. Satisfied with her results, she filled her finished pastries with the meat mixture. The oven was hot with white ash, and she slid the pies onto its floor. While they baked, she took a bottle of rosewater and beat a few spoonfuls into an egg. Halfway through the baking, she'd open the oven door and brush the crusts with the mixture. Mary had taught her the method, and she loved the golden color it produced.

She cleaned her kitchen as the pies baked and thought about what she might wear for her visit. She decided on a very simple blue linen gown with narrow bands of lace trim. She'd wear her favorite Lizzie hat — a straw one with blue ribbons. The horse she would use belonged to the horse troop, but with the worry of an attack somewhat alleviated, they could loan a horse and wagon for the day.

At last she could smell the pies, and Mosh followed her to check them. She brushed her rosewater mixture over them and then busied herself in the kitchen while they finished baking. When they were done and out of the oven, she cooled them on a ledge high enough that Mosh could not reach them, if he were so inclined during the night.

With candle in hand, she climbed the stairs so exhausted she wanted to close her eyes before she made it to the top. She removed her apron and slipped from her dress, crawling with gratitude into her bed. Her prayers were brief, so tired she was, and she drifted to sleep still thanking the Lord for the day to come.

# 30

*May 12, 1665*
*Winter Harbor*

Jeremy and Harry sat on the trunk and wiped sweat from their brow. If Harry were a rich shipbuilder, he'd have hired spar makers. His inheritance money would go only so far, though, and as it was, he'd spared no expense on materials, but it was Jeremy who'd crafted the foremast, mainmast, and mizzen, and a bowsprit from the straight white pine shipped from Boston. They'd installed them today, and Harry was thrilled with the result.

"I could hire a joiner to do the finish work, but that would take our profits. What do ye think of building the deck houses? And the galley?"

"Truly, I'm not a carpenter," Jeremy said.

"Pshaw. Look at those masts. Finer work I haven't seen done." Harry struggled to turn and look back at the planked ship in dry dock. Undaunted, he continued. "We need hatches and of course the master cabin." He finally looked at Jeremy, his blue eyes bright above his ruddy cheeks.

"You do not see this is quite possibly beyond my scope of ability? What say you I ask Benjamin to lend us a hand?"

"It will take him the summer." Harry stared out at the water.

"That is my calculation, as well. But without him we'll be lucky to finish at all." What would Patience think about all of this? He studied the sun, low on the horizon. "I'm thinking Patience should have arrived by now, Harry. She sent a message and gave me the impression she'd be here early."

"Why, I think she should have. 'Tis about time for us to be finding some supper at Mrs. Sweeney's."

"Methinks you should go ahead. I'm going to mount up and go take a look." He didn't wait for Harry to get up. He clapped his shoulder and trotted to the livery to fetch Ink.

He urged his horse to a gallop down the main road on the way to Southold. The oaks and chestnuts, now in full leaf, were but a blur. He rounded a curve in the road, and his surefooted steed almost stumbled over the cart. Patience sat in a heap on the ground beside it, reins still in her hand. The bay she had borrowed from the livery stood quietly. She looked up at Jeremy with swollen eyes, a patchy red complexion, and tearstained cheeks.

Mosh sprang from her lap, but when Patience did not stand, Jeremy threw himself from Ink and ran to her. "What has happened?"

"I — I broke my ankle, I am sure. We hit a rock, and I fell from the wagon. I think the wheel is broken, too. I was so frightened that it would get dark and no one would come."

"I could not let it get dark, knowing that you should be on your way." He bent to her ankle and ran his hand over the tender swelling. He pressed and moved her foot up and down. "I don't think it is broken. I think you have only sprained it, but I know it hurts." He strained to look over his shoulder at the wagon. "I see. I think we need to leave the cart and take the horse with us. I'll put you on his back and lead him with Ink."

"Oh no, we cannot, Jeremy."

He pushed himself to a standing position. "Why not?"

"I have so much to bring with me. I have bread and jams and clotted cream. And two meat pies. All for you and Harry." Her eyes were watering again.

"That sounds wonderful, but it will have to wait. The important thing is to get you off this foot and get it wrapped. You might have to see Doctor Smith yet." He reached down to wipe her tears with his finger. "There, let me unhitch the horse, and I'll get you out of here. Does he have a name?"

"Yes, Chester."

"Oh ho." He patted the horse's nose. "Well, Chester, you've behaved remarkably well." He released the cart and turned to gather Patience. He put his arms around and beneath her and swooped her atop Chester.

She winced and groaned.

"Do you hurt anywhere else? Is it just your ankle?"

"Prithee, I'm all right. 'Tis just my ankle."

She looked so pathetic he forced himself to reevaluate the situation. He removed one of the side boards and lashed it to the harness. After securing her bundles onto the board, he stepped back. That would work. He looked up at Patience.

She gave him a small smile. "Thank you. This means much to me. I stayed up so late last night to bring you these gifts I fear I am exhausted now. How shall I ever get home?"

He swung up into his saddle. "Don't think about that yet. We are not far at all from Winter Harbor. Mrs. Sweeney will have to agree to let you stay the night. I'll fix the wagon in the morning and escort you home. I think the doc will still need to look at you."

They rode into Winter Harbor, Jeremy holding a lead tied to the harness and Mosh trailing the whole contraption. Mrs. Sweeney jumped into action when she saw Patience's condition. She wrapped a poultice tight around her ankle and soon had her propped up on her own bed. When Patience queried where Mrs. Sweeney would sleep, she hushed her and said not to worry.

Jeremy saw her arrange a pallet in the parlor before he and Harry left for their own bunks. "Thank you for taking care of her, Mrs. Sweeney."

"Oh, 'tis nothing" was her reply, but he knew she would not do that for just anyone.

The next day, Jeremy carried Patience from Mrs. Sweeney's to the dock and set her on Harry's trunk. He swept his arm toward the ship. "She is almost finished. Do you like her?"

Her eyes grew big, and she caught her breath. "She's beautiful, Jeremy. I cannot believe it."

"I don't want to leave you with the impression that she will be completed soon. Harry says it will take us most of the summer to do the final work. When I take you back to Southold today, I must visit Benjamin. I'm going to ask him for his help in building the cabins and galley."

"I think he will help you, yes?" There was a little-girl quality to her voice that made Jeremy want it to be so.

"Yes, if he has no other commitments."

Harry thanked her profusely for the meat pies, breads, and sweets, and Mrs. Sweeney came out for one last goodbye before they rode back to the wagon in much the same manner that they'd come. Determined to keep her off her ankle, Jeremy transferred her from Chester's back to the wagon seat after he'd made the repairs.

He handed her the reins. "I think you might have been going too fast. Take your time, let Chester take the lead." He looked down the road. "Actually, I'll take the lead, let Chester follow." She leaned toward him, and he put his hand behind her head and pulled her into a kiss. He grinned at her, then climbed onto Ink. "Let's go."

He took her straight to the doctor's house. Doctor Smith unwrapped her ankle and, after a brief examination, declared he'd not have done a thing differently. He rewrapped it and instructed her to stay off of it until she could step without pain.

As he helped her back into the wagon, Jeremy leaned close. "I didn't tell you that my years as a sea captain taught me many things. I was doctor, lawyer, and preacher to many a seagoing lad."

Next stop was the Hortons'. Jeremy did not wish to delay asking Benjamin to come work with him. Anna was with Mary in the bakery and told him he'd find Benjamin and Barnabas out in the lower cornfield.

He hesitated to leave. "Will you be all right, Patience?"

Mary's eyebrows shot up, and she put her hands on her hips. "And why would she not? We shall not let her even think of stepping on that foot." She turned to her friend. "I think a cup of lavender tea is what you need."

Jeremy backed away. "Very well, then, I'll go find Benjamin." Mosh followed him out.

He traipsed down through the orchard, the quickest way to the lower field. His brother and Benjamin were in the middle of the field, bent over the tender young stalks.

Puffy clouds sailed through a blue sky, and he was struck for a moment by the scene. "Heigh-ho there."

"Jeremy, what a pleasant surprise." Barnabas stepped over the rows to meet him. "What brings you out here?"

"I've come to talk to Benjamin." He watched as Benjamin caught up.

"Hello, Uncle. What can I do for you?"

Jeremy explained in detail what he needed done on the ship.

Benjamin's eyes traveled to his father. "What say you? I'd be here helping you if not in Winter Harbor. Can you spare me?"

Barnabas wiped a trickle of sweat from his cheek with his sleeve. "It would just mean I would use Jonathan more, and that's not a bad thing. He's ready to start doing a man's work. I've got Caleb and Joshua, too. You help your uncle." He looked at Jeremy. "You wouldn't ask if you didn't need him. And you won't find a better carpenter than Benjamin here."

"That I know. Thank you, Barn. And thank you, Benjamin. You tell me when you can start. We were ready for you yesterday." He clapped his nephew on the shoulder, then offered him his hand.

Benjamin cocked his head with a grin as he shook it. "I can tell Anna our plans tonight. And can you stay through tomorrow? That way we could finalize our plans after church."

Barnabas broke in. "And young Hobart will be delivering the sermon in the morning."

"Excellent. I will make sure Patience arrives at church safely, and after services we can go over the details."

"Is everything all right with Patience?" Barnabas frowned.

"She was thrown from the wagon, but she is all right. She sprained her ankle and will need some help for a while. Benjamin, perhaps Anna might do her the favor?"

"Good thought. I'll ask her when we talk tonight."

He left the two to figure out what to do with their corn and walked back to the house quite satisfied. He'd let Barn and Benjamin share the plans with their wives, and he'd take Patience and Mosh home.

"Did you talk to Benjamin?" Patience asked on their ride back to her house.

"Yes, and I thought he seemed eager. And Barn was fine with the plan, even though he could probably use his help in the field."

She settled her head on his shoulder. "That is wonderful. 'Tis a beautiful ship, Jeremy."

"And you are a wonderful, beautiful lady, Patience. Thank you for being so understanding in all of this. I know it hasn't been easy. But it won't go on forever."

# 31

Patience sat in the chair and directed Anna to the shelf with the butter crock. Anna had come last night to put her to bed and came again early to help her get dressed for church. Patience wore a gray dress with plain white linen cuffs and collar, to which she added a gray felt hat. It was one that Heather Flower had beaded, and she liked to wear it to church.

Jeremy arrived in time to sit down for a breakfast of eggs, and then he helped both ladies into the cart. It was a short ride down the lane, but this was the only way Patience could go. Oh, he'd suggested he could carry her, but she was quite sure he'd been teasing.

This was the first Sunday he insisted she sit in the Horton pew box, and it pleased her very much. Anna walked ahead to join

Benjamin, and Patience leaned on Jeremy as he escorted her to the front. That they had a guest to deliver the sermon this morning made it all the more compelling. She often found herself stiff sitting on the hard pews, struggling to pay attention. Often her feet felt cold even on warm May days. But today she was quite certain, despite her injury, that she'd be awake and attentive, so nervous she was to be in this pew.

Usually she could see most everyone, because the single ladies sat close to the back. As a hush fell over the congregation, she fought an urge to turn around and look. Instead she took a sideways peek at Jeremy, then darted a look to the right, where Anna sat. She welcomed it when Reverend Youngs stood to lead the first hymn.

Several hymns and prayers later, Reverend Joshua Hobart stood to deliver his sermon. Patience turned her face toward him, ready to listen to this man so many had been talking about. Certainly everyone in the room was interested in what the young Hobart had to say.

He put his open Bible on the tall table in front of him and stepped to the side. "This morning I will be talking to you about disappointment. How many of you have been hurt by the disappointments that follow each of us? We are plagued by 'if only' and 'I would have' instead of 'what does God have for me to do now?' Falling in the quagmire of 'should have' only leads to hurt and disappointment.

"And how much more hurtful is it when it is someone else pointing the finger? One of my favorite things I used to hear my father say — and actually he got it from another reverend, Mr. Cotton — 'Some men are all church and no Christ.' "

Patience looked at Jeremy. No one could ever say that about him or Barnabas. Truly, none of the Hortons. She settled back against the hard pew and said her own prayer. She thanked God for her friends, her community, and her church. They had all been through hardship, but they were blessed.

The morning wore on, and eventually they all filed out past both Reverend Youngs and Reverend Hobart, shaking hands. Jeremy congratulated Joshua while Patience leaned hard on his arm. "Excellent sermon, excellent."

"Thank you. And you shall join us for dinner on the ground? I hear the ladies have been working hard." Joshua looked at Patience with a question in his eyes.

"Oh, I am not ready for it, actually."

Jeremy spoke up. "She sprained her ankle on her way to Winter Harbor. Fell from the cart. She's supposed to stay off of it, but of course I could not persuade her to stay in this morning."

Alarm flashed in Reverend Hobart's eyes. "You fell? Were you alone?"

Her cheeks burned. "Yes, but I am all right, really. My ankle is feeling much better today."

"In the future, you must tell me when you desire to ride out to Winter Harbor. I shall be more than happy to accompany you." He patted her hand. "And do not even think of coming back to services this afternoon. By all means, stay at home — off that foot."

Jeremy put his arm around her. "I am taking her home now so that she may get settled. Anna Horton will be attending her." He steered her out the door and lifted her into the waiting cart. "And so that you know, with Benjamin working with me, he or I will always be available to escort you to Winter Harbor."

"I shall be taking you up on that offer, Captain Horton."

Anna stayed with her and Mosh that night, and the two giggled and gossiped most of the evening. They both thought Joshua Hobart would make the perfect husband for Rachel Youngs, and they could not understand why he did not see that.

Mary and Lizzie came in the morning to see how she was doing, which made the day even better than the previous one. Mary brought food, and Lizzie worked on some hat patterns. With her summer hats done and most of them sold, there would be a lull through the summer in the shop, which worked out well with all that needed to be done in the garden.

Patience sat with her wolf-dog, thinking if she did not get up and do something she might be bored to tears. Jeremy had returned immediately to Winter Harbor. Lizzie suggested she draw, in hopes it would distract her, and gathered paper and pen. She opened the door to the back garden. Patience could see but one wild iris in bloom and set about capturing it. "Do I start with the petals or the stem, Lizzie?"

"Why, I don't know. Do it how you want to." She fluttered her lashes.

"But you are the artist, are you not? Where would you start?" Patience was not letting her off easy.

Lizzie pulled a chair close and sat down. She looked out at the iris and took the quill. "What I would do is draw the bowl of the flower first — you know, the cup of it." She began to sketch. "Then I'd add the stem like this, and finally spend most of your time working on the petals." She gave the paper back to her. "Here, you finish."

She stared at the paper. Mary came out from the kitchen. "I've a stew cooking for you. It should last you a week." She wiped her hands on her apron and looked at the paper. "Very pretty, Patience."

"I think I shall go mad. I cannot sit around with this foot."

Lizzie and Mary looked at her. Lizzie spoke first. "Have you talked to Jeremy about having a fall wedding?"

" 'Tis not like I've had opportunity to sit down with him for such a discussion."

Mary tapped her index finger on her lip. "I don't think you should wait until fall, anyway. I think we need to go out to Winter Harbor and tell Jeremy that 'tis time to post the banns. He can work on that ship, but he can take a day to get married, too."

"I don't know." Patience closed her eyes. "He wants to build a house for us before we marry."

Lizzie waved her hands in the air. "Why? You have a house, and he can sleep in that bunk out at Harry's when he's working."

"He would say that's not a way to start a marriage. And while I agree with that, I

330

confess to you that I am so unhappy that he continually finds reasons to delay our plans."

Lizzie shook her head and sent the gray curls tumbling. "Well, he should not. If I didn't know better, I would fear he feigns affection. But he loves you, Patience. That I know."

"We must go to Winter Harbor. The three of us, and we shall take Anna. We shall visit and see his ship. And we shall tell him he must post the banns." Mary grabbed Patience's hand. "He cannot say no. My gracious, Patience, he wants to get married, too. Of course he will say yes."

Mosh looked up from his spot by the hearth. His eyes begged to go too. "Why, how can I say no to all of you? But what about my foot?"

Lizzie looked closely at it, pressing on her ankle with her fingers. "Well, you can sit in the wagon just as well as you can sit here. Only you won't be bored."

Mary chimed in. "And I shall ask Barney to make you a walking stick. He can do that tonight. That's it, then. We shall go on the morrow."

Patience winced. "Barnabas offered to make me a stick, but I said no. But would you be so kind as to bring some of your sweets? And a crock of the stew? Mrs. Sweeney is so very nice, and her fried fish is lovely, but . . ."

Mary's eyes opened wide in horror. "I would not think of going without taking food."

Lizzie shook her curls. "Those men need more than fried fish."

The next morning, Patience watched as Lizzie, Mary, Abbey, and Anna loaded the wagon with enough food to feed all the men who worked at the wharf. They'd petitioned Reverend Hobart to escort them to Winter Harbor and invited Rachel Youngs to come along. Both accepted with pleasure. Joshua lifted Patience up to the seat in front, and Lizzie climbed up beside her.

Rachel sat with Mary in the back, along with Abbey and Anna, who found spots amongst the food bundles. Patience turned to Joshua and kept her voice low. "I thought you would have Rachel sit next to you. You are sweet on her, are you not?"

He kept his eyes on the road in front of them, but she could see the corner of his mouth pull into a small grin. "She is very nice, Patience. And I know her father and you ladies would like to see a courtship, but the truth is, although I enjoy her company, my heart is called by another." He looked sideways, and his eyes were lit with delight.

Lizzie, on her other side, leaned in. "What did he say?"

Patience could feel the warmth of a blush across her cheeks and turned her own eyes to the road. "Oh!" was all she could say.

The ride was bumpy, and Patience clung to Lizzie's arm, but Reverend Hobart's expert guidance kept Chester on an even keel and the wagon upright. When they turned down toward the wharf, most of the dock workers stopped to stare. The reverend reined in the bay, and Patience saw Jeremy and Harry come out to see what had caused the commotion. Benjamin was not far behind.

Joshua Hobart jumped down and strode over. "Good morrow, gentlemen. I could tell you this was my idea, but you would know that is not true. When the ladies get a notion, it's impossible to dissuade them."

"I would be hard pressed to disagree with that." Jeremy stuck out his hand, and they shared a handshake. "Thank you for ensuring they traveled safely." He came up to Patience's side and lifted her off the seat. "What a surprise." He held out a hand for Lizzie. "I thought you would keep her off of her foot."

Patience leaned into his arm. "Lizzie

thought we should come out to see the ship."

"It seemed a good idea. And we brought food. Show him the food, Mary." Lizzie's violet eyes sparkled under her lashes.

Benjamin came over to help his mother from the cart and then assisted Anna and Rachel. Abbey had been the first one out. He leaned over the rail to look at the bundles. "Did you leave any food at home?" He chortled just like his father.

Patience noticed Harry hung back. " 'Tis so good to see you. You must come give me a hug, as my ankle still gives me pain."

He stepped up to greet her and bowed to each of the ladies.

Mary took his arm. "Harry, we've heard so much about the ship. You must show her to us. But first you must show me where your larder is. We've come to stock it."

His eyes lit up. "Come this way with me, and I'll show ye. We all like Mrs. Sweeney's, but we welcome a good home-cooked meal for a change, to be sure."

Benjamin helped the reverend carry the food, and Jeremy helped Patience over to the trunk. "It seems this is my chair when I visit." She looked out over the water, mirror still, and watched the seagulls swoop low over the surface. "But it is lovely."

"I'm afraid until that ankle heals it is the best I have. Or the box in the dry dock, if you'd like a better look."

She took his arm and pulled him down to sit next to her. "I'm afraid Lizzie and Mary have an ulterior motive to making this trip."

He smiled as he studied her face. "Other than seeing the ship and bringing us much-needed food?"

She nodded. "Mary and Lizzie wonder why we don't just get married now. And I wonder that, too. It doesn't mean you cannot finish the boat. You can still work with Harry."

"I see."

"And we feel 'tis time to post the banns."

"I see." He looked over his shoulder toward the ship. "And is that why the ladies are huddled over yonder, staring at us?"

She leaned a little so she could see past him. "I do believe so."

He ran his hand through his thick hair, and it glinted like burnished gold in the sun. She could not help but stare at his profile as he contemplated the request. He was so handsome when he was serious.

"I don't like the idea of us being so far apart, and I would like the distance even less if we were married. So I don't see how that helps." He gathered her hands in his. "I love you and want to marry you. Is that not enough for today? Can we not wait until Harry and I have the boat finished and I can build a home for us?"

She wanted to shout no, they had waited long enough. She held her tongue, and she did not even know why. "We've been together and yet apart for a long time, Jeremy. If I must, I shall wait for you. But I shan't like it."

He kissed her, and she heard the murmur of her friends, but she did not look at them. She should tell Jeremy how she really felt, and Lizzie and Mary were sure to point that out.

Jeremy pulled away and patted her hand. "Now, if we are going to all invade Mrs. Sweeney's, I think someone had better tell her. Shall I help you to the dining room?"

"Yes. I hope we aren't too many for her." She leaned on his arm as he helped her to the fish house, where they were greeted by the proprietor and cook herself.

"I've never known you to run out of fish, Mrs. Sweeney, but I have several friends here with us tonight."

Her grin spread wide. "Have them come in now, why don't ye? You'll get a table before the men clear the dock. Otherwise, you'll be sittin' outside."

He pulled a chair out for Patience and turned to find Benjamin and Anna already coming, with Harry, Joshua, and the ladies in tow.

Everyone raved about Mrs. Sweeney's fried fish, and Harry and Jeremy entertained the group with sea stories — some even Patience hadn't heard before. But she sat quietly, her thoughts on the conversation she and Jeremy had while sitting on the trunk.

When they left, Patience limped on Jeremy's arm and let Joshua and Benjamin walk ahead with her friends. Only Harry remained behind to walk with them. He spoke softly, his hat still in his hands. "Ye know, Jeremy, I dun't want the ship to stand in the way of you takin' Patience for yer bride. We could use a celebration here, and I have me reasons to see to it that ye get wed." He gave Jeremy a feisty look, and Patience didn't miss it.

She stopped so that they maintained some distance from everyone else. "What reasons, Harry?"

"Oh, me own."

Jeremy nodded. "Well, Harry, thank you, but I have some reasons that we need to wait."

"Aye, and I just want to be sure I'm not

one of 'em. Because I'll do whatever I can to see ye married." He winked at Patience.

She looked at Jeremy. "I've been thinking during dinner about what you said. It hurts me very much to tell you this, but I think we should not see each other anymore. Because what we are doing now is more painful than just putting this whole issue out of my mind. I think I need time to do just that."

His eyes snapped to hers, and his mouth opened, but no sound came out. He moved toward her, but she could see he hadn't a clue as to what to say.

"No, Jeremy. I need to go. Finish the boat with Harry. I shall not be asking you again about wedding plans. There shall be no wedding." She began to walk away, but the pain in her ankle reminded her she could not go without help. "Harry?"

His blue eyes had lost their sparkle, and that would have broken her heart if it wasn't already in pieces. "Harry, walk me to the wagon, please."

She didn't cry on the ride home, for she was beyond tears. Lizzie and Mary thankfully did not question her. And when Joshua carried her into her parlor and settled her on the pumpkin-colored sofa, he only wished her well and good night. But she felt his arms linger around her, and she knew he hoped that one day she might be ready to love again.

## 32

*May 16, 1665*
*Winter Harbor*

Jeremy watched the wagon pull away. His heart was a stone in his chest, and it was painful. He was right, wasn't he? It would not be a good way to start a marriage — living apart. But watching her ride away in that wagon with Joshua Hobart at the reins just made his stomach burn. Had Hobart finally won her over? Had she come here with the plan of breaking off their engagement?

He stared after them until the wagon disappeared and then turned to see Harry and Benjamin sitting on the trunk. He walked slowly out on the pier to join them. It was a warm evening, and the water gently lapped at the side of the planks. A silver slip of a moon had risen, and the thought of Patience and how much she'd love this evening occurred to him, and he hoped she was not enjoying it with Hobart.

Benjamin stood up when he reached the trunk.

"You don't have to get up."

"I think I'll go to bed, Uncle Jeremy. We've got a lot of work to do in the morning. Good night, Harry." He clapped Jeremy on the shoulder. "You all right?"

"Yes. Good night." He sat down next to Harry.

The two lingered there in silence for almost an hour. Finally, Harry spoke up. "I don't understand ye. I know ye love her. Ye won't find another lady like her." He turned to look at him. "Why don't ye marry her?"

"Harry, I want to. I do love her. Believe me, it's my intention. Over the years, I've always known that when I was ready to give up my ship, I would marry Patience. But now the time has come, only I didn't give up the ship — it gave up me. And what surprises me is, I'm torn. Not really torn, I know I want to marry her, but I fear something will happen and I will be hurt — or worse yet, she will be hurt."

Harry harrumphed. "Ye've already done that. She's hurt, if ye haven't noticed."

"I want to make everything ready for us. I'm not sure what's wrong with that. I'm training as a shipwright with you, and I thought that was a good thing. When we are done, you can retire and Winter Harbor will still have a shipbuilder. I'll build a home for Patience, and all will be good. Until then, I am going to have this fear in the pit of my stomach that I'm not doing this right and something's going to fall apart."

"Have ye told all this to her?"

He stuck his feet out in front of him, crossed at the ankles, and studied his boots. "Yes, I have. Mayhap not all of this. I did tell Mary that watching her and Barn in those early years really did make me stop and think about the risks."

"All of life has a risk, Jeremy. But God didn't give ye a love to see you run from it. And the risk of buildin' this ship is losing Patience. Dun't do it. Go to her. Tell her what yer afraid of, but tell her too that she means more to ye than anything else. Women need to hear that. Dun't lose her for a ship, my friend. And if 'tis in God's plan for ye to build the ship, ye'll find a way to have both."

"You always have given me good advice, Harry. I'll go see her." He leaned his head back and stared at the starry sky. "It might be too late, though."

Patience sat in a rocker on the front porch,

drawing paper on her lap, Mosh curled at her feet. She'd spent the morning trying to forget the night before in Winter Harbor, but to no avail, and finally she'd settled on sketching. She watched a butterfly with golden wings dotted with black wave its wings as if drying them as it rested on a blade of grass.

She poised her pen to begin drawing, but then she saw Joshua Hobart walk up the path from the road. A pang of sadness gripped her. Where normally she'd be glad to see the reverend, today he only reminded her that she and Jeremy had argued. And she'd broken off their engagement. She had been right to do that. Of course she'd been right.

"Good morrow, Patience. How is your ankle today?" He walked up onto the wide porch.

Mosh sat up, cocking his head, his blue eyes on Joshua.

"Much better. I was able to hobble out here completely on my own."

"I'm so glad. I was thinking the market is tomorrow on the green, and I was wondering if there was anything I could get for you. Or perhaps if your ankle is well tomorrow, you should like to accompany me?"

She looked up at him, the sun behind his

form. She shielded her eyes with her hand, as her bonnet was not doing much good in keeping the glare away. "I don't know. The market is always so nice, but my ankle might not be up to that. But thank you." She looked away, and he sat on the porch step.

"Is that better? So I'm not in the sun?"

She smiled. "Yes, much. But in truth, I've been in the sun long enough. I think 'tis time I go in." She gathered her drawing things.

He hopped up. "Let me help you." He offered her his arm as she stood.

She leaned on him, and he helped her inside. Mosh followed closely behind. Lizzie was at work in her hat shop, and she called out her hello. "I made some of that French lemonade, if you two would like some."

Patience looked up at him. "That does sound good, does it not?"

"Very good." He helped her to the kitchen. "See, it's still much easier to walk with a little help, isn't it?"

She looked into his warm brown eyes, and her breath caught as his arm came around her. He bent and kissed her lightly on her lips. Her arms embraced his neck, and it felt good to have him hold her. He put a finger under her chin and drew her mouth to his again. His second kiss was longer, more insistent, and for a moment she didn't want it to end. But she pulled away. "Joshua. I'm not ready for this. It would be wrong for me to let you think I want something more than your friendship right now."

Joshua didn't move. "I'm sorry. I'm not sure why I did that. Well, yes, I am — I've thought of kissing you since I first met you. But I had no intention of coming between you and Jeremy. And I certainly do not wish to rush you. Please forgive me." He reached out to smooth a stray wisp of her hair.

Her heart wrenched. "I'm sorry. I want to be your friend. I just don't trust myself right now to make any more decisions. I'm not even sure if the one I made last night was the right one."

She heard him begin to say something like "I understand" but something caught his attention beyond her, and she turned to look. She could see Jeremy through the window, walking up to her house. She wanted to faint. He would think the worst of Joshua — and he'd be close to right.

"Here, sit in the chair. No reason for you to hobble anymore. I'll let him in."

Mosh sat close and watched for Joshua's return.

She wondered if his going to the door was a worse idea. She listened to Jeremy's surprised "hello" and to Lizzie greeting him, too. She could hear the amusement in her friend's tone. No doubt she enjoyed seeing Jeremy and Joshua together under her roof.

Finally, both men came into the kitchen.

"Jeremy, we were about to have some of Lizzie's lemonade. Would you like some?" She nodded to the slipware jug on the counter. "I wasn't expecting to see you today."

He strode quickly to her cupboards, finding the mugs without effort. "I can see that. Lemonade for everyone?"

He was upset, she could see that. "Yes, Jeremy. And I know you are wondering why Joshua is here. I was out on the porch and he happened by, and I invited him in for a cool drink."

Jeremy poured two glasses and set one on the table for Patience and handed the other to Joshua. "You needn't explain."

Joshua waved the mug away. "No, thank you. I really must go." He nodded to Patience. "I'm glad to see you are better. If you decide you'd like to go to market on the morrow, have Lizzie get word to me."

"Thank you. I shall." She looked up at Jeremy as Joshua left. "Why are you here?"

"I'm asking myself the same question right now." His jaw clenched several times, and he rubbed his chin before he continued. "But I had a talk with Harry last night, and he got me to thinking I'd behaved rather like a fool. I have to say, I now feel even more foolish."

"Joshua is a friend, Jeremy. There's no reason to feel foolish on his account."

He rolled those green eyes of his and sat down opposite her at the table. Mosh finally left her side and sat next to Jeremy. He leaned down to pet the wolf-dog. "I came here to tell you something, and I've not gotten off to a very good start. Patience, I love you dearly. You mean more to me than sailing, than that ship, and than anything else on this earth. I want you to marry me, and if you insist it be tomorrow, I will do it."

She folded her hands as if in prayer and stared at him for a moment. "I'm stunned. You would do that for me?"

"Yes. It was all I could think about last night. I prayed and prayed. And now I'm here."

She'd promised herself she was done with him and the hurt he'd caused. But if he really meant he was putting her first from now on, she wanted that. She loved him so, and she wanted this to work. "You'd be willing to give up building the ship for me?" She saw pain in his eyes as he nodded. "I couldn't let you do that, because it seems I love you, too. Do you really think you and Harry could finish the ship by fall?"

"I do."

"Then build it. Help Harry. You know I will wait for you. I'm hopeless, am I not?" She smiled at him, and he smiled back.

He stood and pulled her to her feet. "You are not. Mayhap I am. Are you certain you want me to concentrate on the ship and we'll marry in the fall?"

"Yes, I'm certain." She nestled close to him and wrapped her arms around his waist, her cheek resting on his chest. "I shan't press you anymore. Do what you need to do with Harry and then let's have a wedding. Something tells me Harry will march you to the church himself by then."

He ran his fingers over the ivory combs in her hair and then the back of her neck, and she looked up as his lips found hers. She didn't want to tell him how horrid her night had been. And how she'd prayed and prayed. Here he was, and she was glad. They were meant to be, she was sure.

## 33

*August 29, 1665*
*Southold*

The summer wore on as slow as clouds on a windless day and had been one of the hottest Patience could remember. She donned a cream-colored linen — her lightest-weight garden frock — and her straw hat to venture into her flower garden in the early morning. She layered an apron over her dress and filled the pockets with her implements — a small spade and shovel — and went to attack the weeds with Mosh at her heels.

The shade of the white oaks and silver maples did not afford enough relief for the lobelia — its tall blue spikes had withered — nor the usually whimsical anemone with its puffy seed heads. Only the yellow horsemint and purple aster blooms seemed to survive the parched heat.

She lowered a bucket down the well, thankful she no longer hauled water from the stream, though her ankle was long since healed. She let Mosh drink from it before she carried it to her thirsty flowers. With the beds damp, she laid a worn-out quilt on the ground and kneeled to work the soil, pulling out weeds that did not protest. Even the most tenacious were weary from the heat.

Harry's ship was almost complete. Jeremy and Benjamin toiled long hours, and occasionally she went out to see their progress. But mostly they behaved as if it was a big secret. To be sure, they wanted to surprise her when it was done.

She stood and looked at the sundial. It was nine o'clock, and she hurried to brush the dirt from her hands, happy in the knowledge that the ship would soon be finished. The wedding had been planned and planned again, and if they had much more time she was quite certain they would find something to change. But the one constant that remained was her beautiful dress. She longed for the day she would wear it.

Inside, she changed her apron, and then she and Mosh left to help Mary and Lizzie with the baking. In the heat of summer, baking was done outdoors. Bread consumption did not go down during the summer. Indeed, the men and women worked hard in the fields, and bread was important to keep them nourished. Heavy, hot meals were avoided, and light, cool meals of fruits, vegetables, cheese, and bread were enjoyed. There might be a pottage simmering indoors, but the beehive oven kept the hottest heat outdoors.

Patience walked around to Mary's kitchen door and found Mary and Lizzie in the backyard, checking the ash in the beehive. "I see I am just in time."

Mary looked up. "It's not quite ready yet. I imagine the men will be coming up from the field soon for dinner, but I think we have time to sip some cool lemonade." She led the way into the kitchen. Lizzie helped her pour, and she added some fresh sprigs of mint to the cups.

"Where are Anna and Abbey? And the girls?" Patience peered down the hallway before she sat down.

"Oh, Anna wanted to get her house ready for when Benjamin comes home. Abbey took Sarah and Hannah to help her. Benjamin talks of moving the house out by the Corchaug fort, and she wants it ready for that."

Lizzie looked at Mary with a puzzled expression. "I thought Joseph and Jane will stay with them when they come home for the wedding."

Mary nodded. "They will. It will take some time to move the house. Benjamin won't start it until after Patience and Jeremy wed."

Patience sighed. "Oh good, then perhaps Benjamin shall urge Jeremy to get married soon." They laughed, and each took a sip of her lemonade. "And where are the little girls?"

Mary fanned her face with her hand. "Misha took them down to the water. 'Tis too hot for them."

"Have you been out to see the ship lately?" Lizzie wiggled her eyebrows.

"Yes, and he's beautiful. I mean she — ships are shes, correct?"

They all twittered. "You meant Jeremy is beautiful, of course, and he is," Mary said between giggles. "And most ships are shes, I think. And she is beautiful, too."

Patience felt a warmth wash over her cheeks.

The men began traipsing into the kitchen, and the women stood to give them a place at the old oak table. They'd washed in the barn, which Patience knew made Mary happy, and now they eagerly awaited some dinner.

"Heigh-ho." Barnabas kissed Mary on the

cheek and then took his seat. He nodded to Patience. "And why are your cheeks so red?"

Lizzie started the giggles again. "She is aflame with love."

Caleb, Joshua, and Jonathan all reddened at that and elbowed one another. Barnabas gave them a look and cleared his throat. "Very well, I suppose we shall all be glad when this wedding is over — most of all you, Patience, eh?"

She nodded. "And you should tell Jeremy that."

He chortled. "I shall. Now, let us say a blessing." They joined hands.

Patience and Lizzie helped Mary put cheese and loaves of bread on the table. They served baskets of blackberries and beach plums, and while the fruits were not as plump as previous years, they still were sweet and tasty. Platters of last year's pickled carrots and cucumbers completed the meal.

Mary put her hands on her hips. "There is a little pottage left from yesterday, if any of you want it."

Misha came in with Mercy and Little Mary. Sand-studded sweat trickled down their temples. Patience took a damp cloth and wiped their faces first, then their hands, and helped them to their seats.

"There's my girls," Barnabas said. "Methinks you are ready for a nap after dinner?"

They shook their heads no, but Misha smiled and nodded. "Up they go after something to eat."

The talk was lively, and most of it centered on the soaring heat and lack of rain. The damage to the crops could be considerable. Captain Johnny Youngs had trained the troop as a bucket brigade, and they delivered buckets of water to the fields as they stood ready for a fire that could destroy their homes and shops.

At length, Barnabas stood. "Well, men, as much as we'd like to stay here and visit with the ladies, it's time we get back to work." He kissed the top of Mary's head and led his sons out the door.

Mary jumped up. "If that oven was not ready before, it must be white-hot now."

Lizzie and Patience followed her out the door, and they all strained to look inside. The walls of the beehive were pure white.

Patience picked up the rake and started pulling what remained of the ash. "We should get those loaves in now. Good thing they weren't already baking — they'd be charcoal."

As the bread baked, they cleaned the kitchen, and with the table wiped down and

354

the bread cooling, they welcomed several of the ladies from town for a quilting circle. The quilt would be given to Patience as a gift, and each lady present signed her square. Most of the ladies could sign their names, even if they didn't know how to write, and Mary signed for the ones who could not.

Much discussion was made of whether Patience should sign her name "Patience Terry" or "Patience Horton." Patience was adamant. "I will be receiving the finished quilt as Patience Horton, so that is how I shall sign my name." Truly, she wanted to just sign it "Mrs. Horton" — so much she desired that name — but all of the other ladies were using their Christian name, so she bit her tongue and realized as she signed that it was still very satisfying.

After they had written their names, they settled back with their needles and thread and embroidered over the ink. Hers would be the center square, and this would be a quilt to cherish always. She could not help but look up from time to time and study each woman's face, so intent upon their work. Some of these ladies she saw only at church or occasionally in Lizzie's Hat Shop. But seeing them here today reminded her of something Mary liked to say. "Good friends are like the stars. Near or far, they twinkle for you."

They were still sewing when they heard the men come back in through the kitchen. Mary looked up as Barnabas entered the parlor. "Are you early or have we lost our sense of time?"

"Reverend Youngs came out with a message intended for Jeremy but which has import for us, as well." Lines etched his forehead, and his shoulders sagged as he rubbed his hands together.

Patience put her sewing in her lap.

"There's been a massive fire at the Horton estate at Mowsley." He dropped his arms to his sides. "We don't know how many died in the fire as of yet, but the word is that there has been great devastation."

Mary rushed to his side. "Barney, I am so sorry. Does Jeremy know yet?"

"Reverend Youngs is on his way to tell him."

Patience stood, her hands clasped but her fingers shaking. "Do you think Jeremy shall come back with Reverend Youngs?"

Barnabas shook his head. "That's hard to say. There's not much we can do from here, except to wait for further word, perhaps."

Mrs. Wells gathered her needlework. "I am so sorry, Barnabas. We should be leaving, to give you time to sort through this." She turned to Mary and Patience. "It was a lovely afternoon. I hope we do this again."

All of the ladies followed her out with their own apologies, except for Lizzie and Patience, who sat in the parlor with Barnabas and Mary.

Patience wanted to be helpful. "Shall I put something for supper on the table?"

"Nay, not for me." Barnabas looked at Mary and Lizzie. "Are you hungry?"

"I am not. Prithee, Patience, could you put out bowls of the pottage for Caleb and Joshua and Jonathan? The girls may have some bread and cheese. There is a ham in the larder. They could have some of that."

"I can do that." Patience went to the kitchen and tried to keep up banter with the children, but they fell quiet and watched her work with wide eyes. When they sat and ate, she kissed the girls and patted the boys. "Everything shall be all right. We are just a little disturbed by some news from England. But don't fear. Everything is fine here." She wandered out to the parlor, praying what she said was so.

# 34

*August 29, 1665*
*Winter Harbor*

The work on the ship had progressed to the point that Jeremy, Harry, and Benjamin could sleep onboard in dry dock. It was quite luxurious, with two large main cabins and a dining cabin, and they rather enjoyed it after sleeping for months in too-small bunks stuck in a hole in the wall. Benjamin and Jeremy planned to ask Lizzie to see to the draperies and bedcovers for the ship.

The three men — finished with their supper — were sitting in the dining cabin, discussing their plans for the morrow, when Reverend Youngs boarded the ship. Jeremy heard him first and went to investigate. "Reverend, what a pleasant surprise. Come in, please."

"I'm not sure how pleasant this will be, Jeremy. I'm afraid I have some disturbing news."

Benjamin leapt to his feet, and Harry wasn't far behind. Jeremy, who was pulling up a chair for the reverend, stopped, his eyes riveting to Reverend Youngs. "Is it Barnabas? Patience? Who is it?"

"It's not a person, Jeremy, it is the estate in Mowsley. Your estate."

"Pray pardon. What has happened?" He looked around at Harry and Benjamin. "Let's sit down."

"Your attorney sent me a letter. As you had instructed him, if an emergency arose, he wrote and asked me to notify Barnabas and then you. Assuming your brother and I knew your whereabouts, of course."

Jeremy nodded. "Yes. Go on."

"There was a devastating fire just outside of Mowsley that swept through and burned the entire estate. I'm sorry, but there have been several deaths, including your overseer, Elliot Gibson. Many more are homeless, and food and supplies have become scarce. The house and mill burned. All the surrounding buildings, the cottages of the workers, from the sound of it. Here." He pulled a letter out of his pocket. "This is the letter that explains all that is known right now."

Jeremy read the letter and then passed it to Benjamin. "My attorney requests that I return immediately. He says I am urgently needed." He sat forward, his hands clasped between his knees. He was sick at heart. "Harry, I trust we are sufficiently done for me to go posthaste?" When Harry nodded, he turned to his nephew. "And Benjamin, would you see to any of the accoutrements that Harry requires?"

"Certainly, Uncle Jeremy. This is horrible. Will Father go with you?"

"I don't know. He certainly may if he wishes, but he will not have to. To be sure, it would be better if he stayed to be strong for Patience. She will undoubtedly be upset by this news."

Reverend Youngs leaned forward. "I shared with Barnabas that the fire has destroyed the estate. I did not tell him of the request that you go back to Mowsley. I felt it better, especially in regard to Patience, that you personally give them that information."

"Thank you, Reverend. I should make haste to Southold. I don't want to keep Barn wondering, and I do not wish to withhold the request — as much as I'd like to."

Benjamin ran his hand through his blond hair. "Patience will not like this."

Jeremy stared at him for a moment. "I know. I have no idea how to tell her without upsetting her. I must go. People are suffering, and Elliot is gone. And it is not only my employees and their families affected. Mowsley depends so much on the mill. People are not only without work, they are without food."

Reverend Youngs put his hand on Jeremy's. "What about your attorney? Can he help?"

"I don't see how. He's in London. He can release funds on my behalf, but there's no one to receive them now — and no one to administer them."

Harry stood. "Go to Patience now. Don't ye worry about me. Or the ship. Benjamin and I will get her done."

Reverend Youngs stood, too. "Get Ink, and we'll ride back together. I suspect you'll find Patience with Mary and Barnabas."

Harry turned to Benjamin. "Ye go too, son. This is a tragedy for yer whole family. Go, and when ye're ready to come back, we'll finish my ship."

"Thank you, Harry. I think I should go. Anna will be upset, too."

They shook hands with Harry, and after the horses were saddled, the trio urged them into a gallop for Southold.

Reverend Youngs was right. Patience still sat with Mary and Lizzie in the parlor.

Mosh lay at their feet. Barnabas sat across from them, staring at the empty hearth. With the sweltering temperatures, they kept only the kitchen fire burning, and that was just low embers.

Jeremy was the first one to walk in, and Patience flew into his arms. He held her close and nestled his chin in her hair while he looked at Mary. He was helpless at the moment, and he knew his sister-in-law could tell.

The room had darkened, and Mary got up to light the candles on the table and the mantel.

Patience spoke first. "I'm so sorry, Jeremy. What an enormous loss."

He led her back to the chair she'd been sitting in. He pulled another one close to sit beside her and took her hand. "It is, Patience. And it is not just the loss of income."

"Oh, I know. There might be lives lost. It shall be good to receive a full report." She looked at Mary, shaking her head.

Jeremy turned to his brother. "Reverend Youngs did not give you all of the information in the letter, Barn."

Barnabas raised his brows. "He did not?"

"No, he gave you the account of what happened, but he did not tell you that my attorney has requested I return to Mowsley immediately."

Patience gasped, and Mosh jumped to his feet.

Jeremy squeezed her hand. "There is nothing I can do, and this was totally unforeseeable. I am so sorry, my love."

Lizzie and Mary began to cry, and tears began flooding Patience's cheeks, which reddened by the minute. "You cannot go," she said.

Her crystal-blue eyes searched his, and his heart tore. "I must. I see no other way."

She sobbed loudly now. "But they shall write to you again, and they will tell you everything. You can send letters of comfort to cheer them. You can send money to rebuild. Why would you go there?" Lizzie and Mary put their arms around her and peered at Jeremy with looks that asked the same question.

His throat was rough when he tried to answer, and it felt like he had a plum pit caught in it. He swallowed hard. "It will take a great deal of money to rebuild, and I can authorize my attorney to provide funds, but who would oversee the reconstruction? Elliot Gibson died. It's not the money. Many people are either dead or without their homes. Food is scarce — and medicine, too. I employed many faithful people who

363

worked hard to make the estate prosperous. I don't even know what I shall find once I get there. I have to go now."

Barnabas cradled his head in his hands and ran his fingers through his white hair. He looked up, his forehead creased with concern. "How long will you be gone? Shall I send Caleb or Joshua with you?"

"I cannot say when I'll return here. To restore the Horton estate could take years. Truly, until I get there, I don't know what the situation will be. If I need Caleb or Joshua, I will send for them. There's something I must share with you." He looked each of them in the eye, one at a time. "When I survived the wreck of *The Swallow,* I felt 'twas not fair to those who lost their lives that I lived. I asked God if He'd spared me for a reason. Somehow, that made it easier to bear — to think I'd lived for a noble cause. But I've not been able to see what it was God spared me for, though at first I believed it was to support the troop in New Amsterdam. But now I know. This terrible devastation is why I am still alive. Can you not see? This is what I'm meant to do, and truly there is no one else to do it."

Mary brushed back Patience's hair and turned her chin upward so she could look in her eyes. "May Lizzie and I take you home? I think we all need some sleep. Everything shall look better in the morning, or at least we'll be stronger with some sleep." She looked at Jeremy. "I understand what you are saying, but it doesn't make this any easier for any of us. I think we should walk her home, and you both can talk in the morning. Come, Mosh, you come, too."

He took Patience in his arms and kissed her wet eyes and then her lips. "Go get some rest. I will come to you in the morning." He watched the ladies leave with Mosh and then turned to Barnabas.

His brother sat with his head resting in his hand, and he looked sideways at Jeremy. "That was difficult."

"It all is, Barn. I don't know what else I can do, do you?"

"No. But you must ask her to go with you. She's loved you for a long time, Jeremy. You can't just leave her. Tell her to come with you. Marry her and take her with you."

Jeremy looked Barn in the eye. "I will do that. Thank you. Excellent. Why did I not say that to her? Of course." He walked over and clapped his brother on the back.

Barnabas stood. "Now, let's make a pallet for you, and you can sleep on our floor like you did in the early days."

"If that means getting up and breaking my fast in your kitchen, I am all for it."

Mary came home late, and he listened as she went up the stairs to the room she shared with Barn. How thankful he was that Mary and Lizzie had been with Patience tonight, but in the morning he'd go ask her to come with him. She would be so happy to know they could be together. He was, too. It was a blow to know he must go to Mowsley, and it gave him a lonely, empty feeling. But the moment Barn had said Patience should go with him, the pain had lifted.

Patience could not sleep during the night, and though the morning sun streamed through the windowpane, hot and insistent, still she did not rise. It hurt to open her eyes, so swollen and crusted with dried tears they were. Lizzie had wanted to stay with her, but she'd emphatically told her to go. Now she missed her.

Mosh came to lick her hand, and she pushed herself up to sit on the edge of the bed and hugged his neck. Jeremy had said he would come to talk with her today. And she knew already she would beg him once again to stay. But if he refused, she could bear no more.

She rose and went to her pitcher of water and poured it into the bowl. She washed and then slipped into a blue silk dress. She brushed her hair and twisted it into her combs. Whenever she looked at the combs he'd given her so long ago, she saw his handsome face.

Mosh followed her down the stairs, and she set some meat down for him, but her own stomach clenched, and the thought of eating was unappealing. She paced until he finished, and then the two went out to the thirsty garden. She went to the well, forgetting an apron to cover her pretty dress, and hauled up a bucket of water. After giving Mosh his drink, she lugged it over to her flowerbed. Some of the blooms perked up at the dousing, but most were too far spent.

She went back for another bucket, and as she drew it up, a strong arm reached in front of her and eased the load. She held her breath. Jeremy. She didn't move.

He set the bucket down. "Patience, I am so sorry. Come, let's sit on the bench and talk. No, we should go inside where it might be cooler." He led her by her hand, and she did not resist.

They sat in her parlor, and she wept when he began to speak. She shook her head and pleaded with her eyes for him to stop. It took a moment, but she worked to regain her composure and put her hand to her lips until they stopped trembling. After what seemed like forever, she told him what she had to say. "Please do not leave. Yesterday I gave you all of the reasons you should stay, except for one. I love you. Stay. Please, I beg of you."

He sat there looking at her, his mouth set as if he was going to say something but held it back. He looked at his hands clutched together in his lap. He extended his fingers out like a steeple. Finally he looked at her again. "I have to go, Patience."

"No! You don't have to."

He shook his head. "Hear me out. I have to go, but here it is. I want you to go with me. Come to Mowsley with me."

She sat like a stone statue. "I cannot."

"Yes, you can. We can be married before we go. Everything will be all right. We will be together. Is that not what you want?"

She looked out the window. Everything looked so ordinary. A blue sky, white clouds, tree limbs moving in a gentle breeze. How could he be suggesting something so absurd?

"I could never leave here, Jeremy. You must know that. How could you even suggest that?"

"Because of Mary and Lizzie? We could come back someday. If not to live, to visit. I would see to that."

" 'Tis not that, though it certainly is one of the things that pains me." Her tears began to flow again. "I cannot get on a ship. Never again. I can't." She threw herself into his arms, and he sat in the chair, his arms wrapped around her, rocking her.

"Ah, there now. Of course you can get on a ship, and I will be there, right by your side. Come with me."

She buried her face in his shoulder. "Jeremy, you said you loved me, and if you do, you shan't make me say no to you. You would stay, and we would be married. If you love me, stay."

He pushed her gently away and brought himself to his feet. "I will not stay, Patience. I want you to come with me, but if you won't, I still must go. There is no other way."

She stared at him with tears running down her cheeks, but no more sobs. She strode to the door and opened it wide. Mosh cowered by the hearth, unwilling to move. She reached up and pulled the combs from her hair. "Then go. But I must tell you, I shall put you from my mind from this day forward. I cannot continue on a path of ups and downs, hellos and goodbyes. One minute I think I shall have you for the rest of my life, the next you are gone for 'just one more time.' I cannot live this way, so I choose to live without you." She held out the combs. "Take these. I no longer can look at them."

He gazed at her, and something broke within her. But she could not do again what she'd always done before. She placed them in his hand and stood aside from the door. He left without a word.

# 35

*September 8, 1665*
*Southold*

The searing heat was relentless. Every family member worked to save the crops, and Patience appreciated the chance to work in the fields with Mary. She buried herself in the never-ending labor. Jeremy was the only Horton who was not out in the fields.

She overheard he was arranging passage and packing his few belongings for Mowsley. Barnabas said it was good Jeremy had always kept some of his money with the banker in Southold, because everything on *The Swallow* had been lost, and Mary answered that she was sure he'd have bought his brother's passage if need be.

Mr. Timms at the livery mentioned Jeremy had been going out to see Harry almost daily. But other than that, no one spoke to her of him. While happy would not be a word she would use to describe herself right now, she was glad they refrained from questioning her.

In the evenings, her muscles ached, she was bone-tired, and though it was hard to drift into sleep, when it came, she slept soundly. This evening she was particularly worn out, and Mary offered to walk home with her.

"Do I look tired, Mary?"

"You do. But there is something I must ask you, and I'd rather not ask you here."

The heat made her head ache, and she longed to be alone. She watched the sun slip low on the horizon. Dark treetops stood out against the orange glow. Soon the sun would dip low enough to ease the swelter of the day. "Of course, Mary. Walk with me."

They strolled in silence most of the way along the green to Patience's house. Mosh trotted behind them. Mary was the first to speak. "Jeremy shall leave tomorrow. He sails from Hallock's Landing."

Patience could not look at her. "I do not wish to hear of his going. Surely you understand."

They continued in silence, until they entered the parlor. As Mary sat in a chair, she laughed. "Do you remember how you were so infatuated with Barney when you were young, and I was so upset when we all came to Long Island because you flirted so with him?"

Patience's cheeks flamed. "I was horrible, Mary. How did you ever forgive me?"

"Ah, you were young, and in the end I could not blame you for loving my Barney. And we became dearest friends, did we not?"

"Truest of friends, Mary." Her eyes were stinging as she fought to keep her tears in check.

"Then you need to listen to me. Go with Jeremy. Reverend Youngs would marry you in the morning before you board the ship. On the morrow, put on your wedding dress and just go, Patience. We love you too much to ask you to stay on our account."

" 'Tis not that. I told Jeremy that is not what holds me back. I fear the ship. I quake at the thought of stepping onto one. I am a wreck even thinking of Jeremy getting back on a ship. I'd much rather he build them. If he loved me, he would stay here and do just that. He'd never step on another ship again."

Mary absently twisted a lock of hair that fell across her forehead. "He does love you, that I know. And I love both of you. This is not right to let this come between you."

Patience suddenly noticed how dark the room was, and she stood to light the candles on the hearth. "It is not right, but it is Jeremy who is wrong. He has put me through so much, for so long, and now he will leave me again."

Mary forced a small laugh, and Patience wondered if she was trying to make light of everything.

"I mean it. He is the one in the wrong. He is the one who could make everything right."

Mary shook her head. "No, prithee, I was only thinking. Have you ever noticed in life that men do what they want to do, and we women are the ones left with the difficult choices to make? And often 'tis not really even a choice."

"What are you saying?"

"Only that Jeremy has decided to go to Mowsley. And now you have a choice to make. Go with him or stay. If you love him, there really is no choice, is there? You must go."

Patience blew out the rush she'd used to light the candles and set it down. "Do you know what I truly feel right now? Would that he'd drowned when *The Swallow* sank and threw him into the ocean." Her throat ached, and the pain went straight to her heart.

Mary sprang from her chair. "No, Patience, you do not mean that. You cannot say that!"

"Why, yes I can, Mary. It would have been easier if he'd never come back." There, she'd said it. Because it was true. To have him back in her life had proved disastrous to her heart. So he could leave, but she never wanted to see him again. Or even speak of him.

"I can see I should go. But I hope tonight you think and pray about what you just said. There is still time to do the right thing." She bent to Mosh and petted his soft head, then turned for the door.

"Yes, there is, and Jeremy could say he will be here forever for me. Those are the only words I should like to hear him say. And since he has told me himself that he will not stay, I shall not spend another minute waiting to hear those words. Good night, Mary."

She could not bear Mary's sad hazel-blue eyes so she turned away as her dearest friend let herself out.

She curled up on the sofa, not caring to tread the stairs and climb into her bed. She covered her head with her arms and tried to hide the world away. Jeremy would leave tomorrow and be out of her life forever. Why was there a tiny piece of her heart that wished him to come to her and say he would stay? She wanted him gone. She wanted to get on with her life. She prayed her heart would heal around that tiny speck and seal it away.

It was a small gathering at the meetinghouse the next morning. Reverend Youngs held a special service to offer prayers for Jeremy and the people suffering in Mowsley because of the fire. No one wanted to see him leave, and his family and friends were somber. But everyone supported his decision to go. Everyone except Patience, and she was not there.

Benjamin and Anna gave him a blanket as a gift, and his nephew told him he would be back in Winter Harbor on the morrow to help old Harry finish the ship.

Mary's girls gave him small gifts of oranges and crystalized ginger. Lizzie and Mary gave him a hand-stitched leather jacket with fringe. He noticed they kept glancing at the door as if they expected Patience at any minute. She wouldn't come. He'd heard it in the trill of her voice when she'd told him to go.

Joshua Hobart was back in town and came to say farewell. Jeremy found it slightly odd that he'd returned at the precise time

Jeremy was leaving, but the man was cordial and genuine when he said his goodbyes. When he expressed his concern for Patience, Jeremy pretended not to hear and withdrew to the back of the room to tell Barnabas that it was time to board the ship. His trunk had been deposited by Benjamin and Caleb on the ship, and with so few things to carry, he insisted he preferred to walk down to the dock by himself.

He walked down the road to Hallock's Landing. *The Merrilee* was a three-masted schooner, much like Harry's. It docked in the same spot Barnabas and Mary had come to many years ago aboard the whaling ship that carried the thirteen original families. He'd been in and out of this port many times on *The Swallow.*

He had the same urge Mary and Lizzie had had in the meetinghouse to turn and look for Patience. How he'd wrestled with himself the whole of last night. Could he stay? No. How could he leave her? His steps were heavy as he trudged to the ship that would take him away from her forever. He must keep walking. Up the plank. He must do this.

He could offer his services to the shipmaster. He knew the myriad duties required to get the ship underway. But he was barely even aware when they hoisted the sails, and when the wind caught them, he was deaf to the flap of sailcloth. He stood affixed to the rail, and his eyes searched for a tall blond woman with sparkling blue eyes to come rushing to dockside. The fact that no one appeared could not keep him from looking again even as the ship sailed out of port and the shoreline faded. He grasped the rail until his knuckles turned white. It took all his strength to keep from jumping from the ship and swimming to shore.

He was still standing there when they headed for the high seas. His hat was tucked under his arm, and the wind ruffled his hair. The pain of knowing he'd never hold her again tore at his heart, but as much as he hurt, she hurt, too, and for that he was sorry. He thought of Reverend Hobart. He seemed to appear at all the right times, and he knew she could love again before the frost was on the roses if she would allow him into her life. Joshua would be a good man for her, certainly better for her than he'd ever been. It was a bitter elixir to swallow, but what could he expect?

His eyes stung as he picked up his bundle and went in search of his quarters. It would be a long voyage. When he settled in his cabin, he knelt at his bunk. He prayed that

Patience would find comfort; he prayed he would find strength and purpose in returning to Mowsley; and he prayed *The Merrilee* would have a safe and speedy voyage.

It was another sleepless night, but the morning broke clear, with a strong easterly wind. It seemed God was answering his prayer, and he was encouraged enough to seek out the captain of the ship and offer his assistance in whatever way was needed.

He found the captain at the master cabin, eating his breakfast. The captain's room was more than twice the size of his own on *The Swallow.* Captain Leonard Thornberger dined at a round mahogany table. He stood as Jeremy entered and waved an arm to the chair across from him. "Ah, Captain Horton. Join me." He sat back down. "Everyone was worried about you, but I thought you'd make a figure of yourself in due time. One has to eat, you know."

Jeremy extended his hand before he took the offered seat. "Please, Captain Thornberger, call me Jeremy."

"And call me Leo."

A cabin boy promptly placed a pewter plate filled with cold meats and pickled fruit before him. He dug in and enjoyed the unusual tang of flavors. "Leo, we have good wind, and the gulf tide is in our favor. What is your calculation for the journey? Four weeks? Six?"

"After we eat, I shall pull out the maps, and we can look at the charts again. The weather is good. I have high hopes we shall stay on course and make good time."

"Excellent."

"I'm curious, how does it feel to be aboard ship again after being thought drowned?"

"To be sure, I hadn't given it a thought. I suppose too much on my mind at the moment." He took a scone from a platter and broke it in half. He spread clotted cream on it and spooned strawberry jam on top. It dissolved in his mouth, but he barely noticed the taste. "So tell me, how did you come to be captain of your ship?"

Leo leaned forward. "No real story there. My father was a captain, and I followed in his wake, so to speak."

"And successfully, I see." He glanced around the well-appointed room. A massive bed and a chest with drawers took up the back of the room, and a desk sat to the left of the dining table. All were gleaming mahogany.

"And you, Jeremy? How did you find yourself the captain of a ship?"

Jeremy finished chewing. "Much like you,

except I rather careened into it instead of falling."

"Eh? How so?"

"It was my uncle who took me sailing as a lad, and I could never get the sea out of my head." He shifted in his chair. "Or my heart, as someone dear to me once told me."

Leo stood and brushed the crumbs from his breeches. "Ah, you've left a woman at home. Let's take a stroll to the stern." He led the way out, and they walked along the deck "Tell me about your lady."

It was not his intention to talk about Patience. "Suffice it to say, the lady in question is no longer mine. Nor will she ever be. It seems I determined that when I made the decision to return to Mowsley."

They stopped at the rail and watched the rhythm of the white-foamed caps peak with the current. Leo spoke first. "Ah, that is the way of it. I know it well. We are accused of being married to our ship, are we not?"

"I am afraid marriage is altogether out of the question for me. I go to Mowsley to see what waits for me there. God, it seems, has other plans for me." He fell silent for a moment, thankful Leo did not pursue the issue. "By the by, I want to offer my services to you. I know I have paid passage, but if you require anything of me, do say so."

"Thank you. We always do an inventory in hull once we are out to sea, and I may ask you to assist in that."

Jeremy nodded. "It would be my pleasure."

To keep occupied was his goal whilst on his way to Mowsley. He wandered back toward his cabin and paused again at the rail. He breathed the sea air in so deep his expanded lungs were ready to burst. It was his calling to go to the Horton estate in its time of need. It was a legacy passed down to him by his parents, and he could not ignore that. How he wished Patience understood that. There was a time when he'd thought, with Patience at his side and God at the helm, there would be nothing he could not do. Mayhap with God still at the helm, there was nothing he could not do — but he truly wished Patience was there to share it with him.

## 36

*September 21, 1665*

The apple harvest was in full swing, but the temperatures continued to scorch everything living. Patience noted the orchard grass crunched as they moved from tree to tree to pick the pippins, and tempers were as frazzled. Even Mosh seemed impatient.

She was huffy to her friends and blamed it on the excessive heat. Mary, as loving and sweet as always, acted like she'd forgotten their terse words before Jeremy had left. Mercifully, she did not bring him up.

After the last long, sweaty day of picking the apples, Barnabas suggested they pile in the wagon and ride to the beach. He asked Caleb to hitch up Stargazer, and Patience helped Mary pack a large hamper with cold meat pies and fresh-picked fruit for a supper on the beach. Mosh hopped up after everyone had climbed in.

Barnabas turned Stargazer toward the

sound side of the fork. Horton Lane ended at the cliff, but they'd found if they continued east of the property, there was a pretty beach that reminded the elders of the long-ago beaches of Southwold in England.

Benjamin was back in Winter Harbor, working with Harry to complete *The Annabelle*. Anna had busied herself with the apple harvest while he was absent and came with them to the beach. She took a blanket from the wagon, and Patience reached out to help her spread it. As they unfolded it, she saw it was a large, star-patterned quilt. What had become of the quilt the ladies had been stitching for her? Mayhap they were saving the squares with the names for another friendship quilt. All except for the square on which she'd written "Patience Horton." They'd most likely burned it.

She shook her head. Those thoughts were better chased far from her mind. How could she get on with her life if she constantly thought about Jeremy? Yet the fact that she was friends with so many members of his family made it difficult.

Once the quilt was spread and the hamper opened, the adults settled around, the children too interested in running near the waves to sit and eat. Anna began to talk of Benjamin's work on *The Annabelle*.

Mary put out a sack of ginger cakes. "Lizzie is busy making the bedcovers, drapes, and tapestries for Harry."

Patience tried to sound interested, and truly she was. "Oh really?"

"Yes, she is using a beautiful gold damask. The master cabin shall look so elegant."

Anna nodded. "Benjamin says it already does. Mahogany throughout. He's made the furniture and the bed is massive. It has four posts for curtains." Her pretty eyes grew wide as she spoke.

"We should all go out to see it." Mary uncovered the pies.

Patience watched her cut slices. "Should we not wait until 'tis done? It must be almost complete. It would be fun to see it with all of Lizzie's finery added."

Mary nodded. "Perhaps that is best. I shall ask her how close she is to finishing."

Barnabas took out his knife and sliced several pippins. They munched on the crisp fruit, and before they loaded the wagon back up, the ladies took off their slippers and ran down to the water's edge, skirts in their hands, laughing and dodging the waves. The children shrieked with glee at having the adults run and play, so infrequently did they see such behavior. Mosh was excited and confused at the same time.

He couldn't decide who to chase so he ran in circles.

Patience watched the others walk back to the wagon while she lingered and let the water lap at her toes. She drank in the fresh air. It smelled of salt and sand and Jeremy. She cried out and was thankful the noise of the waves drowned out the sound. She reached for a handful of seawater and splashed it on her face. No one would see the tears that cascaded down her cheeks.

Patience sat in the wagon with a wet Mosh in her arms, and as they turned away from the road that led to Winter Harbor, she strained to look over her shoulder, as if she could see the ship. Sometimes, if she let her thoughts get ahead of her, she imagined Jeremy still there, working on *The Annabelle.* It was like a slap in the face when she remembered he was gone.

The next morning, she woke up singular of mind. She needed to go see the ship. Granted, she'd been the one to suggest they wait. But perhaps she had just said that so she could go without company. "Come, Mosh. Let's get some water on the flowers, and then shall we go to the livery and go for a ride?" He followed her out, panting, and before she watered her plants, she set the bucket down and watched him lap half its contents.

Before they left, she went in to take off her apron and brush her hair. She twisted it back high on her head and pinned it in place. She set out with Mosh for the livery stable. A reluctant Mr. Timms harnessed Chester, and she watched as he led the horse out into the sunshine. Her dog jumped in the wagon without waiting to see if she followed.

She looked beyond the horse and saw Reverend Hobart. "Good morrow to you, Reverend," she said as he approached.

"Good morrow. And are you not supposed to address me as Joshua, Miss Terry?"

She did a small curtsey. "And you? Should you not call me Patience?"

He laughed easily. "Of course, Patience. If I'm not mistaken, you look to be ready for a ride."

She glanced at Mr. Timms and then back at Joshua. "I am." Alone, she hoped.

"Would you be riding out to Winter Harbor?"

"Yes. I thought I'd see how the shipbuilding is progressing." She turned to Mr. Timms. "Thank you so much. I shall return before dark." He nodded and went back into the livery.

Joshua's eyes became serious. "I should

go with you. We don't want any more injuries."

"I shall be fine. I really thought I'd just like to ride out by myself." She meant for her words to be kind.

He stepped closer. "I made a promise to Jeremy and myself that I would escort you when I could. I'm here now. Let me drive you."

Her heart was breaking, and she was certain her face gave it away. She barely got the words out. "I thought you promised *me,* and if that is the case, I release you from the promise."

He folded his arms. "You are in no condition to be going by yourself, Patience. I shall take you. And to be sure, I would like to see the ship, too." He picked her up and set her on the wagon's seat. He climbed up, took the reins, and clucked to Chester.

Patience did not say a word on the ride, and neither did Joshua. It was awkward, but she was thankful he did not press her to talk. She had no idea what she would say to Benjamin, but she longed to see Harry and see his ship. Mosh stuck his head over the backboard between their shoulders and panted the whole way.

Soon the dock was in view. Joshua guided Chester right up to the side of the dry dock.

Harry and Benjamin came out to see who'd arrived, then hurried to her side. Benjamin helped her down, and she turned to Harry for a big hug. It was awkward to have Joshua with her because Harry and Benjamin loved Jeremy, but she was glad for Joshua's company.

While Benjamin ignored Joshua to begin with, he rallied and gave the reverend a grand tour. The boat was beautiful, almost majestic, and Harry clearly was proud of *The Annabelle,* but Patience held back, not ready to see the ship that had so occupied Jeremy, and oddly Harry didn't insist she board. Instead, he asked her to come sit with him on the trunk and look at the water. Mosh lay at Patience's feet.

The water was a little rough in the breeze, but she found the waves relaxed her. "I like the ship very much, Harry. It surprised me how nice it is. Not that you couldn't make something so nice, but I remember how awful it was coming over in the hold of *The Swallow.*" The moment she mentioned Jeremy's ship she felt heat travel up her neck and blossom in her cheeks. "Not that he had a horrible ship."

Harry laughed so hard he held his sides. "I know what ye mean, child. No need to explain." He became serious. "Ye miss him, I see."

She tossed her head, and with a raised chin, she studied the water through half-closed eyes. "I don't think so. I do not give him much thought. I think that is how it should be from here on out." She could not look at Harry.

Harry didn't move a muscle except a slight twitch of his hands, which he had folded in his lap. "I don't pretend to know Jeremy as well as ye do. But I wager he is a lot like me. He does not deal well with matters of the heart."

Why did her women friends leave this subject alone, but the men seemed compelled to bring it up? She loved Harry dearly, but she did not want to talk about Jeremy. "May I say he does not and leave it at that?" She tried to smile, but it was a grimace.

"Aye, of course. I only wanted to tell ye: do not be too harsh on him. He is doing what he was meant to do. That's all." He faced her. "And I want ye to know, if I'd had me way, he'd a married ye ages ago. He was wrong on that one. Now, shall we all go over to Mrs. Sweeney's and have some fried fish?"

Relief washed over her like a wave on a

hot beach. Her eyes danced with her smile. "I would not come out here without partaking of her fish, Harry."

He clapped his hands at Mosh, who ran a large circle and barked enough to bring Benjamin and Joshua out. Harry called to them. "We are heading over to Mrs. Sweeney's. Are ye coming?"

The four gathered around a table, and though it was too hot for a fire, Mosh was polite enough to lie down by the cold hearth. They ate heartily of the crispy fish, and tonight Mrs. Sweeney served a fish stew, as well.

Talk was sparse, though Harry tried to begin several conversations. She was lost in thought about the times Jeremy had sat with them, and it was increasingly apparent to her that it had not been a good idea to come out for a visit. Too much Jeremy here.

At long last, Joshua said he should take her home, and she quite agreed.

"Harry, it was so very good to see you." She grabbed his hands, and he kissed her cheek. She stood on tiptoe to kiss Benjamin's cheek. "Anna shall be coming out for a visit with Mary when Lizzie brings the bedclothes and curtains. Pray understand if I decide to stay home."

Benjamin helped her take her seat in the

wagon. "Of course, Patience. I know this is hard for you, too."

Joshua took up the reins, and they were off.

"Why did he have to say 'too'? Of course 'tis hard on me. I am not the one who decided to leave."

Joshua nodded. "I don't think he meant it that way. Everyone is upset Jeremy had to leave. Most of all Jeremy, I suppose." There was silence, and they listened to Chester's *clop-clop* on the dirt road.

At long last she looked sideways at Joshua. "Are you siding with the men because you are one of them, or because you really believe I'm being unreasonable?"

His laugh was light. "I won't comment on that. But Patience, I wonder if you forgave him, perhaps you could move on?" His words carried a ring of hopefulness.

"I know we should forgive. And, truly, I believe I have. And I have moved on, Joshua. I have."

As they neared her house, Joshua said, "I should see you to your house and then return the cart for you." He slowed Chester and turned in the seat. "I'm not so convinced, Patience, that you are ready to move on, but I want you to know I've come to care deeply for you. If there comes a day that you might feel the same, know that I am here." He jumped down and held out his arms.

She thought for a moment about how easy it would be to let him be strong for her. To let him care. She put her arms out to his shoulders, and he lifted her to the ground. "You are right about one thing, Joshua," she said as she looked into his warm eyes. "I'm not ready to move on. And I should tell you, I might not ever be."

He slipped his arms around her and pulled her close. "You deserve more than Jeremy is willing to give you, you know that, don't you?"

Her heart was pattering double time, and she wondered if he could hear it. Why could she not just let go and accept his embrace? And then he kissed her. It was warm, and for a moment, she didn't think of Jeremy. And that was what she wanted, wasn't it? To not think of him anymore? But she pulled back. "I . . . I must go."

Mosh followed her into the house. She called a thank-you as Joshua drove away. Perhaps she did want to cling to the hurt, to live in the past. It was the last thing she wanted to admit, but mayhap that was where she was most comfortable.

## 37

*October 21, 1665*

With the crops in and a hint of winter in the air, Patience was glad to be in Mary's kitchen. Abbey and Lizzie were there, too. The room was warm and smelled of sweet spice and apples. Baking was once again in full swing leading up to a day of thanks for the harvest. All of the young Horton girls were with Misha at Anna's house, helping her get ready for the church supper. The pies coming out of the oven looked near perfect with their beautiful crimped edges and golden-brown crusts. Barnabas had baked bagfuls of crisp ginger cakes, and Patience had a large crock of beans loaded with onions and molasses baking at home.

Lizzie busied herself with making an encrusted roast of venison. She liked adding a French flair to their New England cooking. "Did I understand correctly that Joshua Hobart shall be preaching again?" She studied her pastry as she asked.

Patience waited for Mary to answer.

After a moment, Mary turned. She held a pie from the oven with two tea towels under it. "He is."

"It seems he's been doing that often. Is Reverend Youngs sick or anything? Tired of us?" She frowned.

After another long pause, Patience finally answered. "No, Lizzie. I think he knows that Joshua likes it here very much and enjoys giving him the chance to preach. Reverend Youngs is fine, but he won't be around forever. And Johnny isn't going to be taking over for him."

They laughed together over that thought.

"No, I would not think so." Mary put her hand to her cheek and shook her head.

Lizzie stepped back from her masterpiece. "Patience, is it true he comes to call on you?"

Both Mary and Abbey turned to look at her.

"No, he does not."

"Are you certain?" Lizzie persisted.

Patience wiped her hands on her apron. "It depends on what you mean by *calling*. If you mean he is courting me — and I do think 'tis what you are inferring — no. He has become a friend to me, in a time when

395

I need a friend like him."

Mary stood in front of her and took her hands. "We are your friends. What do you mean? You have friends."

"Oh yes, I do not mean you aren't. Don't be hurt." She leaned into Mary to hug her, then turned and gave Lizzie a hug, as well. "I love you both."

Lizzie put her hands on her hips. There were giggles in her violet eyes, however. "What do you mean, then, pray tell?"

"Oh, he has helped me with things — like when my cellar door went off its frame, he fixed it. He does things like that for me. Like . . . like Jeremy did when he was here." There, she'd said his name, and it did not even hurt. Much. "But if you are wondering if we have romantic feelings for each other, we do not. We are friends." Her eyes stung.

Mary shook her head. "Anna told me that Benjamin says that Joshua has a sweet spot for you."

Patience stared at the floor, afraid her eyes could give her away. "That might be true, but it does not mean we are more than friends."

"Well, perhaps that shall change for you. Because it would be lovely to see you happy again." Mary swept back a tendril of hair that fell across her forehead.

Lizzie nodded. "We both want you to be happy."

"I'm trying to be. I shan't be, though, if we talk of Jeremy. Or love."

Mary brightened. "Why not take our pies over to the meetinghouse? It shall be less to carry tomorrow."

Abbey took off her apron and used it to dust flour from the table. "Wait for me and I'll help you."

They pulled on cloaks, and each carried two pies. Mosh got up from his nap and followed them. It was cold and crisp outside, and they laughed at how this morning the warmth of the kitchen felt good and now, after a full day of working next to the oven, the chilly air was refreshing.

It took only a few minutes to leave their pies. Back out on the road, they said good night to one another and went their separate ways. Before Mary got far, she called back, "Look at that moon."

All four gazed at the big, white full moon.

" 'Tis beautiful, is it not?" Mary asked. "A sugar cake moon. That's what our mother used to call it, right, Lizzie?"

"Yes, she did."

They watched until they shivered from the cold, and then each hurried home.

Patience stopped and picked up a piece of

paper that lay tucked in the doorjamb. Mosh followed her in, and the sugary smell of beans greeted them. "It makes me hungry." She scratched his ears. "You, too? We must save the beans. Let's see what we have."

She set the note on the table and lit the candle. She pulled the beans from the oven and then put a plate of meat down for Mosh. She decided she wasn't really hungry herself. Most likely, she'd eaten too many apple slices intended for the pies. She sat down to read the note.

Dear Patience,
I stopped by to ask if you'd like to ride out to Winter Harbor on Monday. Harry says it has been some time since you came for a visit, and it would be my pleasure to take you. You can tell me in the morning after the service. I look forward to seeing you at the supper.

Your faithful friend,
Joshua Hobart

She held the note to her chest. She hadn't been out to see Harry since Lizzie and Mary had taken the curtains and bedclothes out. They'd told her it looked absolutely breathtaking. Benjamin was back home now, and

Anna was thrilled. Even Mary seemed happier with him back in Southold.

Mosh came over and laid his head on her lap. She scratched his furry ears. "What do you think, Mosh? Do you want to go see Harry?" He wagged his tail. "Ah yes, I should have known. Well, perhaps I do, too. I'm ready to see *The Annabelle*."

She carried the candle up the stairs, her dog right behind her. She slipped from her dress into a night shift and climbed under the covers. She tossed and turned, trying to keep her mind from Jeremy. She'd go with Joshua to see the ship. It would be good to see old Harry again. She knew he probably wondered why she did not come.

After Joshua's well-received sermon, Patience thanked him for it and told him, yes, she would be pleased if he'd take her out to see Harry.

He sat with her and the Hortons and Fannings during the church supper, and she let herself be amused by Lizzie and Mary's questions to him and their curiosity. It was either be amused or cry. Clearly they were going to get to the bottom of why Joshua was preaching so often and if it had any connection to Miss Patience Terry. When he mentioned he'd be taking her for a ride to

Winter Harbor, they looked rather pointedly at her.

"I want to see the ship and your beautiful bedclothes, Lizzie. Reverend Hobart is gracious enough to take me." She looked at Joshua. "Thank you for that."

"You are most welcome. Shall I pick you up early? Say nine o'clock?"

"That would be lovely. We can have dinner at Mrs. Sweeney's and still be home early."

Mary and Lizzie smiled sweetly at her, and she gave them a meaningful look in return. They apparently knew what she meant because they said nothing more.

After the last sermon of the day, she walked home to Mosh and went upstairs. Sleep would not come. She slid to her knees and turned toward her bed. Hands folded and eyes closed, she prayed. *Lord, please show me the way through this. Show me Thy path and give me the strength to follow. Amen.*

# 38

*October 23, 1665*

She heard Chester out front and called for Mosh. A moment later, Joshua knocked. She picked up her red cloak, grabbed a bag of leftover ginger cakes, and hurried to the door, opening it wide. Joshua took the bag with one hand and held up her wrap with the other. "Let me help you with that."

Chester pawed the ground, and Mosh ran over to sniff a greeting before leaping into the wagon. Soon they were on their way. Joshua was talkative, bantering about his sermon, his life on Barbados, and how he was hopeful of finding a church out near Flushing. Barbados had lost its appeal when his wife had died. "Not to change the subject, but Harry has missed you quite a bit."

She looked at him for a long moment. "I think he misses Jeremy, and when he sees me, he feels closer to him. And there's the folly."

Joshua cocked his head to the side while keeping his eyes on the road. "No. I do think he misses you. No need to bring Jeremy into it, unless of course you want to. But I hope you shall just enjoy the day and visit with Harry. And *The Annabelle.* You will not believe your eyes. She is magnificent."

"Truly?"

"Yes, truly. I won't tell you more, because I do not want to give it away." When she laughed, he looked at her and smiled. "I like it when you laugh."

She smiled back at him and then turned to watch the foliage fly by. She enjoyed his company, and he was a gentleman. He had a sweet spot for her, no doubt, but he did not impose it on her. Well, at least not anymore. He was a good friend, and she was thankful for him.

Harry was standing out in the road as they pulled up, as if he'd been waiting all morning. "Did you know we were coming, Harry?" she asked as he helped her down.

"Nay, I did not. I just heard the clatter and came to see what it was. I cannot tell ye how good it does my soul to see ye. Where have ye been?" Mosh jumped down

and wiggled up to him. "No, not ye. Her."
He patted the dog on the head and nodded
toward Patience.

She looked out at the dock, glistening
from the seamist. She breathed in the salt
air and could taste it on her lips. The sadness of her last visit was gone. "I've missed
you, Harry. But for a while, I couldn't come.
But I'm better now, and I'd like to see *The
Annabelle.* Lizzie and Mary have told me
much about her, and I had to see for myself."

"Bless ye. Let's go look."

They started toward the ship, and Patience
looked back over her shoulder to see that
Joshua hung back. "Are you coming with
us?"

"I think I will go keep Mrs. Sweeney
company." He turned with the dog on his
heels.

"Mosh is following you. He knows where
he can get food." She laughed as she
watched them go.

Harry was quiet. She followed him up the
plank as she eyed the gleaming sides. The
ship looked too pretty to put in the water.
"This is nice, Harry."

He nodded with a smile, watching her
intently. The sparkle in his eye gave him
away, and she knew he caught every shade

of her reaction. They walked along the main deck, past the forecastle, to the bow. She admired the linen cloth of the headsails tied to the bowsprit, ready to be raised. He led her around to view all three ramrod-straight masts. When they came to the mizzen mast on the aft side of the ship, they climbed down the steps to the galley below.

She gasped when she saw the ovens. There were two, side by side. Their walls and floors were made of brick, and each had a large copper caldron set into the top to boil fish and meat. He showed her the barrels that stored ship biscuits, fresh water, and salted pork and beef. There was a bunk in the back for the cook.

"Harry, this kitchen is grand. Fit for a queen." She smiled as she took in every detail.

"Aye, 'tis that. A queen of hearts, would ye not say?"

"Oh, I should say so." She followed him back up the steps as they climbed to the quarterdeck. The fresh scent of new wood tickled her nose with each step. "I've never had a love for ships, Harry, but this is one I could love." Jeremy's sweat was in this ship, but she was thankful Harry did not mention him.

He chuckled, his wooden leg pounding

the white oak floor as he trudged down the deck to the cabins. "I imagine ye would like to see what Mrs. Fanning sewed for me."

"Lizzie? Yes, very much."

He paused before an ornate wooden door, and his merry blue eyes danced above his round cheeks. "This is the master cabin." He pushed the door open.

She stepped in and ran to the middle of the room. Gold damask curtains hung from the window. Matching bolsters and bedcovers adorned the massive four-poster bed. "This is exquisite." She held her breath and twirled around, taking in the beautiful reddish-brown mahogany walls and the furniture Benjamin had crafted.

A sandglass and sundial were displayed on the desk. She ran her finger over the mirrored lid of the dial, and he removed it to show her the inside. "This one has a compass set inside."

"Beautiful, Harry. 'Tis true what Mary and Lizzie said. *The Annabelle* is magnificent."

"Ye haven't seen all of her."

"Do you mean the hold? I came across from England in a hold, and I shan't care if I ever see another." She peered into his face. She didn't want to hurt his feelings. "I mean, I could go see it if you'd like."

Harry's smile spread across his face. "Nay, I would not do that to ye. Come, follow me." He thumped his way out, and they crossed to a second cabin with a carved door. He threw the door open and stepped back for her to enter.

Her eyes flew wide, and she brought her hand to her mouth. "Oh! Look at this. Why, 'tis just like the other." She turned to him. "Why would you have two master cabins?"

He chuckled and tossed his head from side to side. "Ye never know when ye might need a second one. Come. Is it too cold for ye to sit with me a while on the old trunk?"

"If you'd like to, then no, 'tis not too cold." She followed him out and pulled her red cloak tight against the chill as they walked down off the ship. It was slippery on the dock, but they made it to the trunk and sat. She waited for Harry to speak.

"I had a dream when Jeremy and me were working on this ship. I never shared it with him."

She looked at him for a moment, puzzled. "You didn't? Why?"

"Oh, I hinted. But I knew he would tell me no." He stared out into the water reflecting the gray light of the sky. "I thought my sailing days were through when I lost my family, then my leg." She put her hand on his arm. "And I began having a notion Jeremy would sail in and talk of working with me someday. I began to dream of building this ship." He shook his head and paused.

"And look at that. You did it."

"Aye, we did it. But I wanted him to sail it for me, and I never told him that."

She blinked away the tears in her eyes. Slowly, his meaning became clear. "And he left before you could."

"Ah, well, aye, he did. And he needed to, mind ye. He was called to."

Her tears tumbled.

"But I put two cabins in — one for me. And I hoped he'd be my captain and he'd bring ye with him." His head bobbed, and she hoped he would not cry, too.

"Harry, Harry. Did he ever tell you he thought you could sail her? He told me."

"He did. We used to sit on this trunk, and he'd say, 'Harry, what are ye going to do when we're finished? Sail this boat, because ye could, ye know.' " He patted his wooden leg. "He didn't think this should stop me."

She blinked away her tears. "It shouldn't. You can do this, Harry. You can sail your ship."

He straightened and looked her in the eye. "Ye believe that?"

"Yes, I do." She reached over and hugged him. "What is more, I think you should. She's beautiful, and you should be the one to sail her."

"Well, I've got me a crew." He began to add something, but stopped. "Ye are hungry, are ye not? We should go get some of Mrs. Sweeney's fish before she sells out." He hesitated a moment. "But first I must tell ye I prayed ye'd come today. I need to ask ye something I couldn't ask Jeremy."

She froze.

"Sail with me to England." His eyes pleaded.

Tears threatened again. "I could not."

"Are ye not the one who just said, 'You can do this, Harry'? Then so can ye. Is it Jeremy? Because he loves ye. Go to him, Patience. He is yer North Star."

"Oh no. No, I cannot. You don't understand. 'Tis not only Jeremy. I fear being on the water so much. When I was a girl and we came across on *The Swallow* — it was horrible. But even then I did not understand the dangers. And over the years, so many people have lost their lives. I cannot bring myself to sail again." She was sobbing now, so sorry she was to say no to Harry. Why was Jeremy not here to say yes? "I'm sorry, Harry." She stood.

He rose and offered her his arm. She took it, and he patted her hand as they walked toward the smell of fish frying.

Joshua smiled as they approached the table. Mosh raised his head from his spot near the hearth, but only for a moment before he went back to sleep.

"Beautiful ship, isn't she?" Joshua said.

Patience sat next to him. "Oh yes."

He did not say a word about how long they'd been gone. Harry was quiet during their meal. Even Mrs. Sweeney seemed a bit serious. But her fish was superb.

After their meal, the trio took a long walk on the wharf with Mosh running ahead and then dashing back. They could see a storm coming in from the west, and Joshua said he should get her home before it hit. She hugged Harry goodbye. She hoped he would come to understand the things she'd told him out on the old trunk.

When they were on their way, Joshua glanced at her. "Did you have a good visit?"

She turned to look at him. "I did. Harry is a special man. I think you were right. He was happy to see me. I'm glad you took me — thank you."

He nodded. "You're welcome. I enjoyed the outing, too. Shall I take you to your house, or shall we drop off Chester at the livery and walk back?"

"Let's walk from the livery. I'd enjoy that."

They returned Chester and the wagon, and when they reached her house, Joshua offered to bring in some wood for the hearth, and they sat to watch the fire take hold.

He stood. "I should go now, Patience. Thank you for a wonderful day."

She followed him to the door. He took her hand in his and kissed it. She squeezed his hand before he released hers. "No, thank *you* for taking me to see Harry. I think you knew we both needed to see each other. That was very kind of you."

"It was my pleasure." He disappeared up the walk.

She went back to the fire and sat to think again about Harry. He had said something she longed to be true. Was Jeremy her North Star? She would never find out. Because she could never get on that ship.

# 39

*October 28, 1665*

In the early morning, Patience worked in the fields with Mary and Lizzie, bringing in the last of the pumpkins. She ran her sleeve over her damp brow and shared a few tears with her friends as Mary remembered the years Winnie and Heather Flower had worked alongside them. For the youngest Horton girls, running and merriment took precedence over picking pumpkins, and Mosh did his part by keeping up with the girls.

Excitement for Southold's Saturday market rustled through the townspeople like wind in the willows. It would open on the village green later that morning and was expected to be the largest one the town had ever had. But they'd not anticipated the scorching summer, and it was a scanty harvest. Still, there was much to do, with games and performances a part of the festivities. And the cooler weather was favorable for a celebration, so the festival continued as planned.

Barnabas and his sons were already down on the green with Zeke, Johnny Youngs, and Joshua Hobart, setting up tables for the ladies and special games for everybody, young and old.

Mary would bring her apple pies and Barnabas's ginger cakes. Lizzie would have a table for her hats. School had not resumed yet, but Patience had asked her young students if they would bring their samplers from last year and recite some of the rhymes they had learned. Mercy could not wait and sang every song they had learned last year at the top of her lungs in the pumpkin field.

Patience filled her apron with small pumpkins, and Mary and Lizzie each wrapped their arms around big fat ones. They trod over to the wagon with their loads. Patience wiped her forehead with her sleeve. "I cannot believe I have sweat on my brow. 'Tis like a little summer today."

Lizzie rearranged the pile of pumpkins, stacking the smaller ones on top. She brushed her curly tendrils from her eyes. "It shall be wonderful for the festival."

Mary shook her head. "I've heard it means a hard winter, though."

"If that means more sled riding, I look forward to it." Lizzie's laugh tinkled like a bell.

They walked back into the field to gather the next armload, Patience lagging behind. Mary turned and held out her hand. "Are you all right, Patience?"

"I am. A little tired, I suppose. I didn't sleep well last night." When did she sleep well? It seemed her nights were spent tossing and turning.

Lizzie turned to look at her. "Perhaps you should rest. If you are not sleeping well, you most likely have the malaise. When we go in for the festival, I shall stop by my house for a tonic."

"Oh, I shall be fine. I'm looking forward to the festival. It shall be great fun."

It took most of the morning to finish with the pumpkins. Caleb came out to drive the wagon to the market. Mary took her girls in to change their clothes. Patience reminded them to bring their samplers, and then she left with Lizzie to change their aprons at her house and fetch her hats.

By the time they made it to the village green, Caleb had pumpkins and corn for sale from the wagon. Joshua Hobart, Benjamin, and Johnny had hauled out chairs and tables from the church for the ladies, and

Lizzie spread out her hats on the table next to Mary's baked goods. She left room for the samplers at one end.

Mercy stood close by. "Now, don't let anybody buy my ABCs," she said. They all laughed. Mary told her to go find a hoop with Little Mary before all the big children took them. They watched the girls run off, ribbons flying behind them.

Patience sat at the end of the table and watched as Hannah and Sarah went with Jonathan to make their way through a maze of haystacks and cornstalks — built by Benjamin and Zeke. Caleb and his brother Joshua, followed by Mosh, hauled buckets of water for the apple bobbing.

She thought she felt a little dizzy but pushed the thought aside. When Joshua Hobart walked up with a big, thick rope and challenged the ladies to be a team against the men, she and Lizzie and Mary were all for it. The hats and pies had sold well, and it was time for fun. They sent Benjamin off to find Anna and Abbey before they lined up.

Mary was the shortest, so they put her in the middle, facing Zeke. The rest of the ladies took their spots according to height, and Patience was next to the last, with Abbey — the tallest — on the end. Benjamin was the tallest on the men's team. Patience couldn't help but think it would have been Jeremy if he'd been here.

Most of the children came to sit on the grass to watch the tug-of-war. They looked on in awe. The women pulled first and gained a little ground. Then the men pulled them back. The war was on. The children shouted, and it was lost on Patience who they cheered for. She pulled with all her might, and then all went black.

The next thing she knew, she was lying on the grass, and she could hear muffled voices as if everyone was talking to her. Then faces appeared as if they floated around her. Gradually, she could see the peering faces had bodies, and the first face she recognized was Joshua Hobart's. "Benjamin has gone to find Doctor Smith," she heard him say. She could hear Mary telling the children to stay back. Someone else said she needed fresh air. And then there was Lizzie with her elixir. Joshua helped her sit up, and Lizzie made her swallow.

All she could think to say was, "Who won?"

By the time the doctor arrived, they had figured out she was raging with fever. He asked Lizzie to dampen some cloths in the apple-dunking water and drape them on her forehead. A couple of his patients had had a similar fever, and it seemed to spike and then go away, and he predicted hers would do the same. He advised bed rest until it ran its course.

She tried to stand up, but Barnabas told her not to, and he scooped her up to carry her home. Mary told Hannah and Sarah to watch the younger girls and followed Barnabas. She helped Patience undress and get into bed and then sat with her until she was sleepy. It wasn't long before she felt her eyes closing. Mary kissed her forehead and tucked the pretty quilt with pink embroidered rosebuds around her. She told her Lizzie would come to check in on her tonight. She would be back in the morning.

Patience tried to get up after Mary left, but her head pounded, and she realized it was best to lie still. Mosh jumped up beside her, as if to keep her there, and she tickled his fur with her fingers in return. Sleep came in snatches, and she would wake with troubled thoughts of Jeremy and ships and Harry.

She woke in the morning before first light and saw the mug of cold sage tea next to her Bible, and plate of dry biscuits that Lizzie must have left the night before. She was up and sitting in her chair in the parlor when Mary arrived.

"Why are you out of bed? Are you feeling better?"

"I am. Just a little light-headed, so I thought I would sit here before going into the kitchen."

"Tsk. You are not going into the kitchen. I shall bring you some hot tea and some toast. Do you feel up to marmalade, or does your stomach bother you?"

She nodded and gave a weak smile. "That sounds good."

Mary came out with a tray and set it on the table. She handed her a mug with a sprig of sage in the hot water. She took another mug from the tray and sat down opposite her. "Did you sleep all right?"

"I didn't think so until I saw the tray Lizzie left me upstairs and realized I didn't even hear her come in." She put her head back to rest on the chair.

Mary studied her. "I think you've been through much lately, and 'tis catching up with you. You need to rest."

"I may not have a choice. My legs feel weak."

"Then you need to be back up in bed, and before I leave I'm going to make sure you are." She shook her head. "Let me feel your forehead." She got up and put her hand on

Patience's face. "You don't feel hot. But it does mean you must rest. I'm glad classes are not in session, but even if they were, we would cancel them."

Patience watched as Mary broke the toast in two and handed her a piece. She took a small bite but found she wasn't hungry. "Do you think Jeremy shall ever come back?"

Mary's hazel-blue eyes flew open wide. "I — I'm surprised you ask. You haven't wanted to speak of him, Patience. What brings this on?" She took the mug from Patience's outstretched hand and set it on the table.

She wasn't certain if she wanted to tell her of the conversation with Harry. She put her head in her hands. "I don't know. I thought about him last night when I was trying to sleep. Or maybe I dreamt of him."

"I don't know how to answer your question. I hope he comes back. We love him very much and shall miss him. But he doesn't have *The Swallow,* he has an estate that needs him. And we do not even know what he found when he got back to Mowsley. But he does have a strong sense of duty to the estate. He might not come back." Her eyes misted as she spoke.

Patience was crying softly into her hands. Her shoulders shook. Mary patted her.

"There now, tell me why you are so upset."

"Did you know that Harry was going to ask him to sail *The Annabelle* for him? That one of those cabins was for Jeremy and me?"

"Harry never said that. Jeremy didn't either." She took a sip of her tea.

"Well, Jeremy didn't know. Harry told me that when I went out there last Monday. He showed me the two master cabins. He planned on asking Jeremy, but then he was called away."

Mary looked down at Mosh and then back up at Patience. "Would you have done that?"

"Oh no, I couldn't." She picked up a napkin from the tray and wiped her nose. "But that is just the thing. Harry wants me to sail with him, to England. He wants me to go to Jeremy."

A little gasp escaped from Mary. "Really? He'd sail the ship?"

"Yes, and I believe he could."

Mary stood and began to pace. "Then you must go. Do you not see?"

Patience drew her knees up and hugged them. She rested her cheek against them. "I can't. I'm too afraid. I cannot get on that ship." Why did no one seem to understand that? Was no one else afraid to sail? Or have a fear that kept them from doing something they'd dearly love to do? Was she the only one to face this?

Her dearest friend sat back down in front of her and leaned close. "I'm going to say this to you, Patience, because you need to hear this. I have held back because you made it clear to me you did not want to discuss Jeremy. But you brought him up." She stopped for less than a moment for a breath. "You belong with Jeremy. God put him into your life for a reason. We may not know why he's not here, but you need to go to him. You must be stronger than your fears because you have God with you every step of the way."

She stared at Mary, a sheet of tears covering her cheeks, her bottom lip trembling.

Mary stood and pulled her up. "Now, I'm putting you back to bed. You must think and pray on what I have said. Lizzie shall be over later to see you. I hope when she comes, you shall tell her what you must do."

She led her upstairs and tucked her in with Mosh at her side. She covered Patience's hand. "You know what is right, and you know you are strong. Do the right thing, dear. God will be with you."

Patience listened as Mary went down the stairs and let herself out. Fresh tears came, as she knew they would. Then her body gave way to either fever or exhaustion. Perhaps both.

When Lizzie came later that day, Patience woke and was surprised to see Joshua Hobart with her. Lizzie plumped her pillows and brought her some broth. When she finished it, Lizzie took the bowl back to the kitchen.

Joshua cleared his throat. "Are you feeling better than yesterday? You gave us quite a fright."

"I think I am. In some ways. But 'tis been a hard day for me."

"Is there anything I can do for you?"

She tried to smile. "You are such a good friend. But I don't think there is anything anyone can do for me."

A cup of tea sat on the table, and he handed it to her. She took a sip, and he set it back down. "I wanted to come speak to you because Mary shared with me what you told her about Harry's ship."

"She did?"

"Yes, she's very concerned for you, Patience. I am, too. I know you are in love with Jeremy. And I know how much Harry cares about him and you."

She pressed her fingers against her eyes. She couldn't cry. Not now. "I don't know what to do, Joshua. I pray, but I can't see the way. I could never get on a ship again. I'm too afraid."

He picked up her Bible from the table and opened it. "Patience, this is Isaiah, chapter 41, verse 13. Listen. 'For I the Lord thy God will hold thy right hand, saying unto thee, Fear not, I will help thee.' What a promise. He holds our hand so that we might not fear."

"I — I believe that, Joshua. Only, 'tis so hard to remember it."

He leaned close. "The important thing for you to remember, Patience, is to put God first and then follow where He leads your heart, in faith, knowing He holds your hand."

# 40

*October 30, 1665*

Mary and Lizzie came to Patience in the morning. Her fever was gone, and she'd dressed and wandered outside to look at her garden. She walked through the spent flowers. So many of her plants were withered from the heat. Only her fat roses clung to their petals, not willing to let them drop until the first frost. She saw her friends walking up the flagstone path, and she called Mosh to follow her through the back door to greet them.

They came bearing food, and the three ladies sat at the kitchen table, sharing a morning meal.

Mary brushed some crumbs from the table. "We shall not stay long. You look so much better today. I know you have much to think about. I only want to say, we love you and whatever you decide we shall support."

Lizzie wiped the plates off with a cloth. "We both feel that way. Patience, I heard what Joshua said last night." Her violet eyes were moist. "I just want to add . . . I just want to say, Jeremy is your heart. He always has been."

Patience rose from her chair and took Lizzie in her arms. "I know what you are trying to tell me. Harry says he's my North Star. Thank you so much. You too, Mary. You both are the truest of friends. I shall think on all of these things. I shall."

They went out the door, and she knew they were heavy of heart. She was, too. But she knew what she must do. She put on her cloak and called for Mosh. They went directly to the livery to rent a wagon. Mosh hopped in, and she waved to a worried-looking Mr. Timms as she clattered down the lane.

She clucked at Chester and urged him to a trot. She might as well *be* brave if she was going to *act* brave. It was a cold ride — the weather had changed overnight — and she was glad when she pulled into Winter Harbor. She looked out along the wharf. There sat Harry on his trunk, his back hunched. He looked so cold and alone. He didn't even hear her as she climbed down from the wagon. Mosh ran up to him and put his warm nose in his lap.

"Oh, ho. Who's this now?" He petted the dog, but his eyes darted to her. He stood. "I prayed ye would come back."

"Harry, I don't know what to do." She looked out at the choppy bay. "I don't know."

"Child, the difficult thing is not in knowing what ye are to do. The difficult thing is in doing it."

"I want to go with you. I want to sail with you. You said something to me the last time I was here. You said Jeremy is my North Star. And he is. I want to go to Jeremy."

Harry wrapped his thick arms around her and swung her around on his wooden leg before he put her back on her feet. "We will do that then. I'll take ye to Jeremy. My crew is eager to go. I'll provision the ship, and we will sail before Sunday." He stopped for a moment. "Does that give ye enough time?"

So many things flashed through her mind. Mary. Her little school. Her dear friends like Anna and Abbey. Lizzie's Hat Shop. Her parents, who were buried here. Her life in Southold ran before her. But she knew Lizzie was right. These were her friends, and they were like a family to her, but Jeremy was her heart. And Joshua was right, too. If she put God first, the rest would be easy.

She looked into Harry's merry blue eyes. "I think I can do that. But I must go now and start getting everything ready."

"And not have fried fish with Mrs. Sweeney? She'd not forgive ye." He took her elbow and propelled her to dinner.

As they sat and ate, Patience peppered him with questions. "How many trunks may I bring?" "What shall Mosh eat on the voyage?" "When shall we get there?"

To the last he said it was too early to begin asking that question — but he expected he'd hear it many times.

He helped her back into the wagon. "I thought ye'd not be driving this thing by yourself anymore."

Her laugh rippled on the wind. "And I thought I'd never be sailing again." Mosh sat like he wanted to stay. "Come on, Mosh. We shall be back. You're going to like this, boy." She clucked at Chester as Mosh hopped in.

At home, she decided she would pack her trunks, four to be exact, before she told Mary and Lizzie. She knew they were praying she would go, but still it would be hard for all three of them. They'd been founding sisters, after all. But she wouldn't be the first to go. Winnie had been their founding sister, too, and she had gone to her Heavenly home.

She packed her gowns and petticoats into the trunks, and her thoughts turned to Mowsley. She'd been born there and hadn't left until she was seventeen. She wondered how much it had changed. How much had she changed? And Jeremy? Was he changed by what he'd found when he returned? What might he be doing now, and would he be glad to see her? He might have believed what she'd said when he left. What would she do if he held her to it?

She went to bed and fell into a sound sleep. And when she woke up, she was renewed in mind and body. She washed her face and sang as she pulled her clothes on. She told Mosh that as soon as they ate, they'd be going visiting.

As she sat at her table, eating a bit of cheese, she began a list of very important things she must take care of before she left. First and foremost, she would give her house to Lizzie to expand the hat shop.

Her list led to reflection. Her little girls. They would be the hardest to say goodbye to, because they would not understand. She would miss them terribly. Suddenly the realization that she might never see them grow up tore at her. But they would write, because she had taught them their ABCs. She would tell them they must write.

And Mary, sweet Mary. She would take the precious recipes Mary had given her over the years, and she would strive to bake like Mary. Jeremy would like that. Of course he would. And she would remember Mary every time she baked an apple pie.

Joshua Hobart. He was an interesting man. He cared for her deeply, that she knew. But he was wise beyond his years. And he would go far as a preacher. He knew his calling, and he was true to it. And he'd taught her how to find hers. He was a blessing to her.

Mosh trotted happily beside her as she walked past the church to Mary's house. She'd brought her list. Mary opened her door before she even stepped up to it. Her heart seemed to swell, and she blinked away tears when she found Lizzie, Anna, and Abbey were there to hear her news.

Mary served lemonade and ginger cakes, and they all sat around the old oak table in the kitchen. There would be no sewing today. Only fond memories to recall and future plans to discuss.

"Lizzie, I want very much to give my

house to you. You would be able to expand the hat shop like you've been wanting to do."

Lizzie's eyes lit up. "That is so very generous of you. I do not know what to say, but thank you." Her silvery curls bobbed as she got up and hugged her.

Patience patted her. "No words are needed. I cannot tell you how good it does my heart to know my parents' house shall be well loved, and I cannot think of a better use for it." She looked at Mary. "And I shall be leaving certain things in the house that I should like to give to you and your daughters. I packed most of my linens and clothes in my trunks. And a few of the things Mother left me. But many of the dishes and kitchen things I'm leaving for you to decide who might want or need them."

The more she spoke, the easier it was, and she savored the pleasure of giving.

Mary got up and poured her more lemonade. "This is all very kind and generous of you, Patience. But I think you are getting ahead of yourself. Why couldn't you leave your house in Lizzie's care and she can expand her hat shop? But keep your things stored upstairs. We'd rather believe you and Jeremy shall return. And you shall want those things someday." She looked at Lizzie.

"Am I right, Lizzie?"

"Of course. Patience, don't be so hasty."

Mary nodded as she handed Patience a cup. "You know we shall miss you as teacher of our little girls."

"That is one of the hardest things for me to leave." An idea occurred to her, and she turned to Anna. "I've tried to think of someone who could take over, but no one comes to mind. But if I may leave with you all of my material and supplies, perhaps you could pursue someone to run the Dame School?"

Anna smiled. "Why, yes. I could do that."

"Then 'tis settled. I shall leave the house and my things in your care, Lizzie. I do like the idea that Jeremy and I shall come back. But truly, if that doesn't happen, they are yours and Mary's, and you can decide what to do with everything."

They ate their crisp cakes and reminisced about the early years. How difficult those days had been, but they, and their relationships, had emerged strong and of good cheer.

Mary at last asked the question she'd been expecting. Most likely it was on everyone's mind. "When do you leave? We could have a dinner in your honor after church services this Sunday."

"Harry is planning to leave on Saturday. I shall take my trunks out the day after tomorrow." She looked away from Mary's crestfallen face. She knew her friend loved to feed everybody for any occasion.

"I see." Mary suddenly brightened. "Could we all come to your house in the morning? I'll bring the girls. And you don't need to prepare anything for us — I'll bring the food."

Gladness spread over her like sunshine in winter. "Oh yes, that would be perfect. I hope everyone can come. I might even put your sons to work loading my trunks in the wagon. Mr. Timms said I could use it, and he shall not even charge a fee."

"Oh, they shall drive it out for you, Patience. No broken ankles before you leave."

They spent the rest of the day talking about the ship's cabin that would be hers for the voyage.

"Lizzie, you did a grand job of finishing the rooms. They are luxurious, and I shall feel like a queen."

Lizzie lowered her lashes in gratitude of the praise and beamed. "Thank you. They are fit for the queen of hearts, Harry says." She looked up. "Now I know he was talking about you." She rubbed Patience's hand

and smiled.

Her friends thankfully avoided the subject of the journey itself. They knew her fear of sailing across the ocean was still there, and though she was conquering it, they must not dwell on it.

But they loved to talk about Jeremy. She admitted to her friends she worried he might not want to see her, and they tried to put that notion to rest. But it was there. It was that tiny piece she'd tried to bury in her heart. It pricked her when she least expected it, and she wished she could take back those awful words she'd spoken. But she could not.

## 41

*November 6, 1665*
*London, England*

The dock on the Thames appeared much the same as the last time Jeremy had seen it. He surveyed the bustle of activity from the deck of *The Merrilee*. The London backdrop looked as he remembered it, as well, but he had no desire to venture in. A plague infected the city. His first concern was to secure a carriage to take him to Mowsley, and that could prove difficult with the number of people fleeing to the countryside. Most likely, he'd been informed, his attorney had left the city, as well.

The journey from Long Island had been almost pleasant. But a small squall had rolled through and set them off course. It was followed by a week with virtually no wind.

Jeremy had rolled up his sleeves and worked as hard as any of the crew, and he arrived in London with renewed vigor. Now, he said his farewell to Captain Leo Thornberger and expressed his gratitude for the excellent voyage.

Leo used his influence to arrange a coach to pick him up from the dock, which Jeremy appreciated. It was little more than a hackney carriage, but it was adequate to get him straightaway to Mowsley. The only stop would be at The Sugar Loaf to have a bite to eat and drink.

He slept much of the way, waking from time to time to pull back the blind and check the progress and scenery. An occasional oak reminded him England no longer had the thick, lush forests of New England. As the carriage hurried along the road, the stale, thick air of London was replaced with the earthy scent of freshly turned wheat fields. Sheep began to dot the landscape, and he knew he was almost home. He didn't have a clue what he would find there.

The hills of Mowsley rose in front of the carriage, and he was now wide awake and straining to see from his seat within the carriage. The terrain was bleak, but it was a bleak season. As they climbed, the winter drab made way to blackened ridges, charred by grass fires. His chest grew tight, and he swallowed as the damage to the village of Mowsley became apparent. Most of the houses and shops had suffered damage, some completely destroyed.

The carriage turned onto Dag Lane and bounced along until it stopped in front of the Horton house and mill. Or what was left of it. He climbed out. The driver took his trunk from the top of the coach and deposited it on the ground. Jeremy paid him seventy shillings for the journey. He watched the coachman depart, then turned back to the ruins of his estate.

He left the trunk and walked to what was left of the timber-framed house. It resembled more of a burned-out hulk than the manor house he'd grown up in. He walked up the flagstone path and in through the gaping hole that had once been a door. Most of the second story had collapsed over the stairs and hall. He heard a child's cry and moaning and made his way through the debris to the parlor.

Mill workers, many with families, sat or lay about, hunger etched on their faces. It felt like a stone lodged in his chest, so painful it was to look at them, helpless and living among the ashes. They were dressed in rags, most likely the same clothes they'd worn the day the fire raged through.

He left the house through the back door. The sight of the tiny cottages, scattered between the house and the mill, burnt to ash, renewed the pang in his chest. They'd served as wicks to the fires that had raced so easily through the wheat fields and pastures and up the line of buildings from one end of the estate to the other.

As he looked at the path of destruction, he was astounded the house had survived at all. The mill was but rubble.

He found a man hauling water up from the stream on the far side of the property. He was hunched over the bucket, his face gaunt. He grasped him by the shoulders. "I cannot tell you how glad I am to see you. I am Jeremy Horton. What is your name, man?"

He looked overcome and barely got out words. "Henry, sir." He set the bucket down.

"Henry, are you the only one strong enough to haul water? Are you doing everything yourself?"

"I am trying, sir. 'Tis been hard. So hard. Before the fire, a couple of the men died of the plague. I was certain we'd all be sick and die. But after the fire, no one has been ill. But now we starve, and 'tis hard to know which is worse. The mill is destroyed. I didn't know what to do. All the homes are gone, and I brought the people into the manor house. I am sorry for that, sir."

Jeremy looked around at the drifts of ash formed by the cold north wind. "Don't apologize. You have done what needed to be done. Winter is coming, and they needed shelter. It's not adequate in its condition. But it's only by the grace of God we have any place at all for them."

"We've been starving, Mr. Horton. The parish in Mowsley has tried to provide, but after the first couple of months, they just had no more."

"I saw the damage in Mowsley." He raked his fingers through his hair. "Then food is the most immediate concern. I sent word to my attorney to send my funds, but I'm told he most likely left the city due to the plague. I do have some means, though, and I'll need to ride into Saddington to see if I can purchase provisions there."

"Thank you, Mr. Horton. You are indeed an answer to prayer."

He hoisted the bucket. "I take it, if you are hauling water from the stream, the well was destroyed?"

"Aye."

"Do we have anyone who needs to see a doctor?"

"Most who were burned died. A few still

might if their burns don't get treatment. But mostly hunger is our worst problem right now."

"And the horses? A wagon? Do we have any of those things now? I haven't even looked for the barn."

Henry shook his head and tears came to the man's eyes. "The barn is gone. The livestock, too, except for a few horses that were down at the river when the fire came through. Old Nell is the only one you can ride."

All those years growing up here — playing in that barn as a youngster with Thomas and Barn, and later riding the estate with Father and his brothers. Burned to the ground. For a moment, no breath would enter his lungs. At long last, he sighed. "Very well. Thank goodness for the horses. The saddles, bridles? All gone?"

Henry nodded.

"I'll ride to Mowsley and see if I can get a wagon, then I'll go out to Saddington."

They trudged toward the house. "We are going to have to figure out a way to rebuild the cottages. That house won't provide enough shelter when the temperatures plunge." Before he left he asked Henry to build a fire in the kitchen hearth.

He found a man in Mowsley willing to

sell a wagon, but he paid a good penny for it. At last he was on the road to Saddington. Mowsley, though suffering from the fires and the loss of crops in the fields, suffered even more from the devastation at the Horton estate. He'd always known how much Mowsley depended on the Hortons, but the full impact had not hit him until that day.

At the Saddington markets, he found bolts of coat cloth, linsey-woolsey, and linen and asked the tailor to make a variety of clothing articles and sizes for the people at his estate. Some of the shopkeeper's discards would keep them clothed until he could pick up the new garments. He loaded the cart with bread, cheese, butter, salted meats, pippins, and currants. He bought a cow and tied her to the back of the wagon. He could not believe how much better he felt on the way back to the burned-out mill, having accomplished so much for his workers.

But with the satisfaction came the memory of what he'd left behind. How good it would be right now to have Patience by his side. Why did he not ask her one more time? Why did he let her tell him no? If he'd gone back to her that morning, would she have come with him? Because he'd had no choice whether he could stay or go. And he found it compelling that, so many years ago, Barnabas had gone to the New World, led by God, and now Jeremy was returning to England, once again most assuredly led by God. If Patience could see the destruction here, he knew she'd understand. She always cared so much for people in need. And those little girls in her school. She adored them and taught them and cared for them so very much. She would take these women and children in her arms in a heartbeat and have such compassion for them. He knew that.

He stopped the horse in front of the house and took an armload of food up the walk. He was not prepared for the children who stood and stared with empty eyes when he walked in. How accustomed he was to seeing the healthy, bouncing Horton children crowd around him and beg for treats. He set his packages on what was left of the kitchen table and bent down with a loaf of bread and handed out chunks like they were sweets.

He took inventory of the utensils and crockery that had survived. There wasn't a lot, but the kitchen was probably the least damaged by the fire.

He wasn't much of a cook, but he put torn bread and currants into a crock and poured in some fresh cow's milk to moisten the mixture. He put it into the fire and hoped it would make a pudding. He sliced some ham and put it on a platter with some of the cheese. A few of the women offered to help, but they looked so weak and ill he could not accept.

As the sun went down, he took a walk to view the ruins of the barn and other out-buildings. On the morrow, he would spend some time in Mowsley. He wanted to visit the graves of his parents, and while he was there, he would look at purchasing lumber and nails. He might have to go back to Saddington, but he hoped to put his money back into Mowsley as much as possible.

He pulled his leather jacket close against the cold, and after checking on the house, he continued on for Mowsley. He'd stay at the inn tonight and be back as soon as he finished his business in the morning. As he walked out into the cold air, he heard a laugh. Patience? He turned back to peer into the darkness. A young woman held her child and looked up with a smile. "Thank you," she said. "You've been most kind."

"Pray, forgive me. I thought I heard someone I knew. Good morrow to you." He nodded and walked on. Would it always be like that? Would he hear her in a laugh, see her in a smile? He needed to put her out of his mind. There was much to do here. Truly, lives to save. If God wanted him here, He needed to make his way possible, and that meant forgetting Patience. *Show me Thy way, Lord.*

## 42

*November 1, 1665*
*Southold*

Patience's house was filled with her friends. Everyone in the village stopped in at one time or another, and she was thankful she'd had her trunks packed before she ever told Mary or Lizzie. As Mary had promised, Patience's kitchen was laden with food. Meat pies, stews, and roasts. Corn swimming in cream, mashed pumpkin and carrots. Sweets of every kind. Mary and Barnabas had prepared it all.

She was the guest of honor at her own house until a buggy pulled up with someone she was not prepared to see today. Joshua Hobart walked up the flagstone path with Harry on his arm. She ran to the door. "You have made the last day in my house perfect, Harry." She hugged him and then turned to Joshua for a hug, tears threatening. "I was not going to cry today. And look what you've done. A farewell for me is not complete without a farewell for Harry. Thank you so much." It seemed she constantly thanked this man.

Reverend Youngs delivered a farewell speech to her that was much like a sermon and touched her heart deeply. He talked of the early days when his flock had come with him from England through Massachusetts, and he spoke of her parents and how much they had meant to him. He ended with a prayer and a blessing for her and told her she must give their regards to Jeremy.

Her young charges, in their Sunday clothes, gathered to sing her the songs they'd learned over the years, and then she gave in to fresh tears. Mercy wanted to sit in Patience's lap whenever she sat down and Little Mary hugged Mosh and asked if they could keep him.

"Mosh wants to come with me, little one," Patience told her. "He's never been to England."

Mercy wiggled in her lap. "May we come, too?"

She hugged her close. "Oh someday, I hope you do. I should like that very much."

At the end of the day, the ladies gathered close around Patience. Mary stood with something behind her back. "We have something to give you, Patience, as our farewell gift. We hope you still have room for it in one of the trunks you packed."

She brought it around in front of her and unfolded the quilt the ladies had made with all of their signatures on it. In one corner was a square that read "Southold 1640, M. H.," and in the opposite corner she saw a square that read "Mowsley 1665, L. F." In the very middle was the square where she'd written "Patience Horton." Twenty-five years she'd been in Southold. More years than she'd spent growing up in Mowsley.

Patience took the quilt, carefully, slowly brought it to her face, and breathed in the essence of all the women's work. "Oh, how I shall treasure this." She looked at each of the ladies present. "Thank you, each of you. The names on this quilt are held forever in time. A time when we came together to Southold to serve God with our husbands and fathers and were blessed with friendship in the end."

She spread out the quilt in the parlor, and they all admired their handiwork. "This is the best gift you could have given me." She hugged Mary and Lizzie and then each of the other women in turn. She opened one of her trunks and tucked the quilt in beside her pink-and-ivory wedding dress.

Caleb and his brother Joshua took Harry and her trunks out to Winter Harbor in the wagon. She hugged and cried until her arms ached and her cheeks chapped when all of her friends left to go home.

Mary and Lizzie stayed behind to clean her kitchen and finally said their own good-byes. They clung to one another, and finally Lizzie pulled back. "We have one more gift, Patience. They shan't take up much room. 'Tis something I gave to Mary when she first left England." She took a small stack of handkerchiefs out of a bag. They had a delicate design of purple and red flowers. Between each were dried sprigs of lavender.

Patience held them to her heart. "I remember these. Thank you. You are true friends."

They hugged each other over and over, never wanting to let go.

When her friends were gone, she climbed the stairs to her room, and after changing into her nightclothes, she slipped into the bed under the rosebud quilt. She would leave it behind for one of Mary's girls. The friendship quilt was already packed in one of her trunks. She fell asleep as soon as she closed her eyes and dreamt of the only person in the world who could pull her from this place of her heart.

■ ■ ■ ■

The last day in her house, it snowed. She followed Mosh out to the garden in her robe and twirled in delight, immune to the cold. Her roses, almost like fabric now, gathered the snowflakes in their petals. She picked one and brought it in with her, tucking it into the basket that held her handkerchiefs.

She climbed the stairs for the last time to dress for the day. She'd picked her green velvet dress and a Lizzie hat with a broad brim and satin sash to match it. Barnabas and Mary would be bringing the wagon, and she skipped down the stairs to watch for them. Mosh pushed past her as if he were more excited than she. But as she walked through the kitchen to the parlor, her excitement waned and turned to a melancholy she knew would only lift by getting on the ship.

She opened her front door wide to watch the snow fall. She laughed when, around the corner, Stargazer came jingling all the way, pulling the red sled. This day would always be a picture in her mind, Southold in December.

Lizzie, Abbey, and Anna were in the sled with Mary. Joshua Hobart sat in front with

Barnabas. Another wagon filled with Hortons and driven by Benjamin rode up behind.

She called with a laugh, "You are early, you know!" Mosh barked as he took a leap into the sled and the ladies all feigned fright.

"Get in," said Barnabas. "We are taking you down to see Hallock's Landing before you go. You cannot leave without a last look."

She ran to get her cloak and valise and scooped up the little apple tree Mary's girls had given her for Christmas. She took one look back as she walked down the flagstone and only hesitated a moment.

They all drove down to the landing, did a swoop without getting out, and then headed for Winter Harbor and the rest of her life. She looked back over her shoulder and watched the Landing until they rounded a bend. She remembered her father carrying her mother through the waves to the shore while she waited back in the shallop for him to come back and fetch her. She could remember her fear.

She shook her head and turned to face Mary. Mary's kind eyes, like turquoise pools, searched her own. "Don't worry, Patience. You shall be all right. God shall keep you in His arms, this I pray."

Stargazer stepped into a faster clip when they reached the main road to Winter Harbor, and soon they arrived at the dock. Her breath caught. Over the week, Harry had *The Annabelle* lowered into the bay. Her sails were unfurled. Harry stood on the deck. They were ready to go.

Joshua helped her down while Harry came down the plank to greet them all. Fresh tears were shed, and there was not a one who didn't have a tremble in their touch when they hugged her.

Mrs. Sweeney came out. "I know you haven't an appetite right now, dear, but I made you a bite to take with you. Share it with Harry for supper. His cook can start in on the morrow." She kissed Patience's cheek and hurried away.

Mary grabbed her and wrapped her in an embrace. She wept as she told Patience, "Try to bring Jeremy home to us. You both come home."

"Oh, Mary, I shall try. But I don't know what to expect when I get there. And perhaps I can do this once, but I don't believe I shall ever be able to do it again."

"But promise me, if he is willing, you shall be, too. I must know there is at least a chance."

Patience held her hands. "Then yes, there

is a chance. That much I shall say."

At last they could not delay any longer, and she took Harry's arm and walked up the plank with him. Her knees knocked under her petticoats, and her throat had all but closed. She could not speak, so she just prayed.

She stood on the aft gallery and waved to the Hortons, the Fannings, the Youngses, and Joshua Hobart and didn't stop until the thin purplish line of the shore receded into the horizon and all she saw was water. She closed her eyes and prayed for a safe voyage. But she prayed, too, for Jeremy. For she hoped he would welcome her when he saw her, but she feared he would not. And standing on the deck praying, she realized for the first time the fear of his rejection was greater than her fear of drowning at sea.

# 43

*December 1, 1665*
*Mowsley, England*

Jeremy stood back with Henry, arms folded, and assessed their handiwork. His funds from London had been slow to arrive due to the plague. But his banker had sent them, and now fifteen timber-framed cottages stood in a row. They backed up to the stream and were located near the mill Jeremy hoped to eventually restore.

He sent Henry off to Mowsley to buy bedding and a few supplies while he helped the families move from the manor. The men and women grew stronger each day with proper food to nourish them. And the children thrived.

It was difficult to decide which needed his attention more — his house or building a barn. He decided to move into the house now that he had his workers and their families in their own cottages. It didn't matter much to him the condition. But a barn would enable him to put some of his men back to work.

The barn was raised and livestock purchased in less than a week. He bought several more cows and two goats from Saddington, and soon the women were making cheese and butter. From Gumley he bought a herd of sheep and several swine. In Mowsley he found a spinning wheel for Rose Gibson, the widow of his overseer.

The estate was humming with activity, and he turned his attention to the house. He requested Rose stay in one of the rooms that suffered the least damage. She would run the house, such as it was, as he rebuilt.

Over the weeks since he'd arrived, he'd spent little time clearing the debris. It was a painful process, sorting through family heirlooms. Some were destroyed to such a degree he was not certain what they even were. Only that the object once was important to someone.

Other belongings he left for Rose to determine if they were worth a cleaning or repair. Progress was slow, but at long last, he and Henry and many of the mill workers began the restoration of the house. Henry made daily trips to Saddington for timber or brick.

They began with the kitchen and his living quarters. The rest of the rooms could be restored one at a time with his mill workers and their families finally settled. He'd spared no expense on the cottages and barn, and he would spare no expense on the house. He wanted it restored to what it had been when his parents had lived here. Rose brought in some of the ladies to help her with furnishing the rooms as construction was completed. The mill construction would not begin until early spring.

The impact of the loss of the mill was great on the surrounding villages. For the little grain that survived the fires, there was no mill to process it.

Still, when he rode old Nell around the property, he was thankful for what he saw. The people were resilient, and the estate was recovering. He put the horse back in her stall and walked up to the house. Inside, the smell of smoke, so different than the normal cooking odors, still permeated the air.

Rose was in the kitchen cooking. "Will you be hungry soon, Mr. Horton? I've fixed a proper supper."

He chuckled because he knew she was teasing him about his dish with bread and currants and milk. He'd thought he'd made a pudding, but they'd called it a sweet gruel. "Aye. I am ready whenever it is."

He went up the stairs to his room. The trunk he'd brought from Southold still sat in the corner. He'd looked inside only long enough to pull out a change of breeches and a couple of shirts. Mayhap he should unpack and get settled in this room. He got up and opened the lid again. He had a few neck cloths he'd need over the winter, an extra belt, and some books Barnabas had given him. At the bottom, where he'd stashed them, were Patience's ivory combs. He'd tried to put a wall up against his feelings for her, but her words to him still stung like she'd just flung them at him.

He sat back down, the combs clutched in his hands, his head bent down to rest on his arms. How different his life was now, changed in an instant when he was thrown into the ocean. And then again in a flash with the fire. But this was where God wanted him, and when he looked into the faces of the mill workers and their wives and children, he had no doubt this was where he needed to be.

If Patience could not see that, then he'd been wrong about her. And truly, it was best he had found that out before they'd married.

## 44

*December 4, 1665*
The Annabelle, *Atlantic Ocean*

If Patience had thought the voyage would be easy after all of the well-wishes of her friends, she found out how wrong she was by the second day. Harry had told her the weather would be rough, but she'd not imagined anything like the high seas they were sailing through. To use his terms, when the starboard came up until she thought the ship might tip, she now knew it would come down with a crash, and waves would send the ship portside up. They'd clearly left Long Island during the worst season.

He'd hired a pilot to guide the ship, and though he was still the captain, it gave her peace of mind and him the time to spend with her. The ship was well staffed, and the cook was excellent. She heard the ship's bell ring every half hour and found it comforted her as a reminder all was well.

The saving grace of it all, of course, was her beautiful cabin — and Mosh. In the early days, she couldn't venture out. She welcomed Harry when he joined her for meals, but she had no appetite. He often came to play his flute for her or to ask her to read to him, which she gladly did, as it took her mind off the rising storms. Mosh did not leave her side.

Several weeks had gone by, and she remained in her cabin. One evening, Harry knocked at her door. As she walked to the door, she noticed she was not swaying and grasping at furniture to stay upright. When she pulled the door open, Harry was grinning, his blue eyes bright.

"Ye have to come out on the deck tonight, child." He took her hand and pulled her along. Mosh wagged his tail and followed.

The sea was dark but calm. The sky was a canopy of navy blue with a thousand points of light. The shimmer and sparkle took her breath away. A silvery slice of moon hung in the sky like a dainty slipper. Harry pointed to the brightest star. "Do ye know what that is?" In his excitement he didn't wait for her answer. " 'Tis yer North Star. It will take ye home to Jeremy."

They stood there a long time, and Harry told her of celestial navigation and pointed out the dippers and Milky Way. "Did not Jeremy ever tell ye these things?"

"Oh, I remember he did long ago. He was teaching Joseph, Barnabas's oldest son, all about it because Joseph wanted to learn. I think I was so sick of the sea, I didn't care to learn much about it. Though I've always loved to gaze at the stars." She shivered in the cold.

"They are brilliant tonight, but it makes the air seem colder."

"It is cold. Do you think we are past the worst of the storms?"

"I think anything can happen, but expect more storms before we reach London. Now let me take ye to yer cabin, or we need to get yer cloak."

"Remember when we sat on your old trunk at the wharf? Freezing?"

HHis chuckle was soft. "Aye, I do."

"Did you bring it?"

He looked up at the stars, scattered like shattered ice. "I did, and methinks I should bring it out to the deck on the morrow, in case we can sit out and stare at the sky again."

"And I think that is an excellent idea."

The next afternoon, he not only had the trunk sitting on the deck, but his fishing gear, too. "I thought ye needed to be out of that cabin whilst we have calm weather." He held up a wooden handline. "I have one for ye." He showed her the cork and willow floats and taught her how to set the line. She thrilled at the pull when a fish bit, and she hauled three in before Harry had one. Of course, he helped her bring them in. Mosh ran back and forth with each one.

That night after dining on their fresh-caught fish, they sat on the trunk and watched the starry night sky. Harry told her old sea stories and asked her if Jeremy had ever shared his with her.

"Oh yes, and sometimes more than once." She giggled.

Another night, as they sat under the stars, she asked him what he thought he would do after they got to London. "You'll come with me to Mowsley, won't you, Harry?" She scratched Mosh's head on her lap.

"Ah, I would like to see Jeremy, so if ye'll have me, I will come. But after that, I think I'll take to the sea. I've lived on land, and I've sailed on the sea. I thought I couldn't anymore, but we've proved that wrong, now, haven't we? Methinks I'd rather die on the sea than be landlocked the rest of my life. I know 'tis something hard for ye to understand, hating the ocean like ye do."

She let the motion of the ship lull her as

she considered what he'd said. "I'm not so sure I hate it, Harry, at least not anymore. 'Tis funny, but it was so long ago that I thought I hated it. I must have. But it is different now. I'm not sure why, it just is."

Harry chuckled. "Ye cannot say it's because of the weather. And by the by, it changes tonight. Have you noticed the wind pick up?"

She shivered in her cloak. "I did. We are going to have a storm?"

"Aye. Ye will want to be in yer cabin anyway, and to be sure, that will be the best place for ye."

They sat until the clouds moved in and obscured the stars. A few splatters of rain pelted them before Patience hurried to her cabin with Mosh, and Harry went to find the pilot to confer with him.

When her brush and mirror began to slide from the desk, she grabbed them and tucked them beneath her pillow. She sat on the bed and clutched the covers whenever the ship swayed. Mosh jumped up and curled up next to her. It would only get worse, and she breathed deeply to calm her fears. She remembered Joshua's words — "Put God first" — and she pulled out her Bible and began to read in Psalms. Her racing heart slowed, and her breathing calmed.

She lay down and watched the lantern by her door. The flame was out, but it swung back and forth, and each swing seemed faster than the last. She heard a wave crash on the porthole and watched fat drops trickle down the black glass. The chair she used at the desk slid across the room and hit her trunk with such force a leg snapped.

Her heart throbbed, and her pulse beat in her temples. Mosh trembled next to her, and she hugged him tight. The rocking slowed for a time, and she scooted down in the bed and pulled the covers up. The storm seemed to subside, and she closed her eyes, still clutching her covers and her dog. The patter on the porthole was almost soothing. If she could but sleep, she would never know how close she might come to death. She thought of Mary and Lizzie and seeing Jeremy again. She forced herself to think happy thoughts, and she began to drift into sleep.

A thunderous crash shattered her slumber, and she sat bolt upright and screamed. Her shriek frightened Mosh so badly he jumped from the bed and tried to get under it, but to no avail. It sat on a wooden base. He was back up on the bed as quickly as he had gotten down.

Patience thought the ceiling was falling

down, but when she opened her eyes, the rafters appeared to be in place. But the next moment, it seemed like the bed was above the rafters, so far over was the ship. Almost tossed from the bed, she held on to the sides with every ounce of strength she could summon.

When the ship righted, water poured under her door, and she was certain the ship was sinking. Where was Harry? Why didn't he come and get her? The boat lurched again. It bucked and lurched over and over. It reminded her of a time she was in a wagon and the horse reared and the wagon tipped. She was going to be sick.

She forced herself to get out of the bed, and her legs shook so badly she could not walk. She sat down, and finally she crawled to the chamber pot and retched into the bowl. No sooner had she filled it than another lurch of the ship tossed it from her hands, and the contents flew to the other side of the room. Her wails could not be heard above the relentless roar of the waves.

Harry had told her to stay in the cabin, but she had to get out. The ship was going to sink, and she'd die right here in this cabin. She tore the top bedcover off and wrapped it around her. "Mosh, come." He whined and moved away from her. "Mosh, don't do that. You must stay with me. Come now." He got up, his tail between his legs, and trotted to her. He licked her face. "Don't. Follow me."

She still could not walk, so she scooted across the floor between the ship's rolls. When she got to the door, she pulled herself up. She pushed on the door. It didn't budge. She heaved against it with her shoulder, and still it didn't move. She turned her back to it and slid down. She wept as she hit the floor and put her head to her knees. Why wouldn't the door open? What was happening out there? She screamed Harry's name and listened. She screamed again. He didn't come. No one came.

She thought she heard voices. She held very still and quiet and listened. Mosh got up and wiggled to her, and she hushed him and made him sit while she strained to hear anything she could. All she heard was the incessant crashing of waves on the deck, followed by water streaming in under her door. It didn't seem to be filling her cabin, but she thought by the time night was done, she'd be swimming or drowned.

The little apple tree lay on its side and Mosh whined as she stretched to retrieve it. She hugged the tree and Mosh to herself and began to pray. She fell asleep against the door with Mosh sitting next to her, guarding her in a way, but really too afraid to do anything else. She opened her eyes when she heard a board moved from her door. She looked at the porthole while she waited for the door to be opened. It was gray, and rain still pattered, though gently.

When the cabin boy opened the door, she was horrified. Nothing outside her door had remained the same. She grabbed his arm. "What's happened? Where's Harry?"

"Everything is all right, miss. Captain Dunning is on the quarterdeck. We've had a bad storm. That is all, miss."

She was amazed he'd said, "That is all." What did that mean? She stepped out of the cabin and went to find Harry. She found him sitting on the trunk, drenched, in the same clothes as she'd last seen him in, and more haggard and dejected than the day she'd come to tell him she'd sail with him.

"Harry, what happened?"

He looked up at her, mist in his eyes. "I lost one of me best last night. Could have lost more. Could have lost ye."

Her eyes were wide. "What do you mean?"

"The storm. I told him to reef the sails — we needed to get them rolled in. He went up, but a furious gale snapped the foremast. He was thrown overboard. We did everything we could to save him, but we had a ship to save, too." He shook his head. "The mast fell across the mainsails."

"Oh no, Harry. I tried to get out of my cabin last night. I was terrified. I thought I was going to die in there. But the door was bolted. How did that happen?"

"I told the boy to do it. I knew you'd come out, and if ye did, ye would have died." He looked almost angry, if he weren't so sad.

"I was so upset. And Joshua Hobart told me I just needed to remember that God would hold my hand."

"And He did."

"I don't think so, Harry. I was frightened to death."

"Ah, child. He does not say things won't happen to ye, He just says He will be there, holding yer hand. And see — it worked. Yer safe."

"Are we?" She looked up at the broken mast. "What shall you do? How are we going to make it to London?"

"I have the ship's carpenter repairing the mast. And we have sails to replace the torn ones. We will make it, don't ye worry."

The ship swayed, and she grabbed onto Mosh. "What if the mast can't be fixed?"

He stood and took her arm. "Then we limp into port anyway. We'll make it, but I'd like ye back in your cabin. I thank ye for the brave front here, but I'd rather have ye safe in yer cabin than me fishing ye out of the sea."

She turned at her door and hugged him. "It was a bad night for us, Harry. But don't worry about me. I shall stay in my cabin."

She climbed back on her bed and took out paper and a quill.

Dear Lizzie and Mary,

I shan't go into details, for I do not wish to worry you, but you would never believe the storm we just went through. And Harry was wonderful. I think he saved the ship and us.

I miss you both terribly, and of course all of the girls. But know that I am all right and surviving. Harry thinks three more days at sea. That could be all the more I can take, or at least would wish to. Mosh feels the same way. The little apple tree is surviving and I shall plant it at Mowsley.

One thing I have learned: if I can convince Jeremy to come back to Southold, I know I could make the journey across the pond again. That in itself is a miracle.

Your devoted friend,<br>Patience

P.S. Just writing to you makes me feel better. God knew what He was doing when He gave me you as friends.

*The Annabelle* took seven more days to make it to the London port, and limp she did. Patience had been concerned when the foremast could not be fixed, but Harry forged ahead, using the main and mizzen sails to their fullest. They stood on the deck as they sailed up the Thames, astounded by the sight of the city, so blighted by disease. When they docked, word was sent aboard not to disembark due to the high risk of the plague. Her heart ached. The broken mast had added days to their journey. How could she possibly wait another day? And what would Jeremy say when he saw her?

# 45

*January 14, 1666*
*London to Mowsley*

The pink light of dawn bathed her face as Patience awoke. She lay for a moment in her bed, nestled in the covers, and tried to gain her bearings. The bed swayed. She shifted and looked toward the porthole. The ship. Last night she must have only dreamt she was in Mowsley.

She settled back into the pillow, scratching Mosh's ear. In Southold they had heard little about the plague in London. But the news they'd received on the ship yesterday was horrid. No one was allowed into the city. No one was allowed out. Thousands were dying, and the fear of the spread of the disease consumed those who were healthy.

They did not wish to go into the city. Surely they would be allowed to leave for Mowsley today.

There was a knock at the door. She climbed from bed and donned her robe. A cabin boy brought in a pitcher of fresh water for her basin. "Does this water come from the city?" she asked.

"No, miss. We have plenty in the ship's hold."

"Could you please tell Captain Dunning I shall come to call on him within the hour?"

The cabin boy said he would and closed the door on his way out.

She washed her face and put on her green velvet gown. She brushed her hair and pinned it and wished for the hundredth time she'd not given the combs back to Jeremy. She gathered her books and her clothing and packed her trunk. She'd be ready when they could leave the ship.

She and Mosh found Harry on the main deck. He motioned for her to sit on the trunk. "What is it, Harry? Shall we leave soon?"

He shook his head, his blue eyes serious. "The gentleman from the city council told me I might be issued a certificate, for a fee, and if we can obtain one, then we might be able to find a carriage to rent. If ye are rich enough, ye can leave."

"But we aren't even in the city! Can we not simply find a carriage and go?"

"He told me they are locking people in their houses even if just one of 'em are sick. And carts come down through the streets at night and the drivers call out, 'Bring me yer dead.' 'Tis grim, Patience, and people are afraid. I grew up in London, did I ever tell ye? But I have no desire to walk the streets again. I have the money to get us out. We are safe on the ship whilst we wait. I know how ye are about wanting to go to Jeremy. I'm sorry."

She put her hand on Harry's as she looked out over the filthy city. She'd remembered it from her youth as a busy, fascinating place to visit. Now she could smell its stench even from the ship. "I shall be all right, Harry. We made it through the storm, we shall make it through this. We need to pray, not just for our journey to Mowsley, but for the sick people of London."

"Aye, that's my girl. I've been prayin'."

Three days later, they were in a coach and on their way, Patience's four trunks and Harry's one lashed on top. Mosh lay at Patience's feet. She pulled back the blind and leaned out the window to catch every bit of the countryside, blur that it was. She looked up at the driver, his thickly trimmed cape flying behind him, and laughed. "Harry, he looks like one of the king's men up there, and this a royal coach."

Harry's eyes were bright again. "It cost a king's ransom — it should look like one of his."

They stopped at the Sugar Loaf Inn for supper. They ate little meat pies, and then they were on their way and kept a brisk pace through the night. Patience could not sleep, and it was not just the jostle of the coach. She could not quiet her mind about Jeremy. She had been adamant when he left that she would never think of him again. Was it fair now to come to him and expect he would still feel the same about her? Was he even still at Mowsley, or did he find such devastation, no hope of restoration, that he'd left? Or, even more fearsome, had the plague spread to Mowsley? Could he be sick or dead? Not knowing what she would find haunted her.

She listened to Harry's gentle snore and wondered how he could sleep. But she was so thankful he was here, for without him she would not have made this journey. She remembered to pray, and though sleep did not come, a peace settled over her like a quilt made with loving hands. No matter what she would find, God was with her. He would hold her hand. She had His promise.

In the first light, the hills of Mowsley

looked like purple folds of velvet. She could see them in the distance as she peered from between the blinds, and the sight made her stomach grow tense. It was an odd layering of emotion. Dread or hope — which was it? — of what she would find at the Horton estate, but also the excitement of seeing the village where she grew up. Would it be very different from what she remembered, like London? Or was it more that she'd enhanced the memories over the years? Sometimes when she'd talked about something she recalled from Mowsley, Lizzie would laugh and say, "Oh, 'twas not that way. You were too young to remember."

As the coach climbed the ridge and drew close to Mowsley, her thoughts continued to tumble, until at last Harry woke up.

"Look, we are coming into town," she told him. Mosh put his paws in her lap so he could look out. "Not you, silly dog."

Harry opened his blind and watched the town grow near, but before they reached the shops, the coach trailed down the road to the Horton estate. A light snow began to fall.

Her face was out the window, her knuckles white, as she gripped the sash. The road was long leading in, and she strained to see anyone, hoping she would find Jeremy standing as if waiting for her. She drew back as hulking black forms that once were trees and piles of ash where crops once stood in the fields came into view.

They pulled in front of the manor, and Harry took her hand as she stepped out. She stood with the little apple tree clutched in one arm and Mosh by her side as he helped the driver pull the trunks from the carriage and then paid him for his service. As the carriage pulled away, she took in the full measure of the fire's destruction. The contrast of a burnt rosebush with a single untouched rose still clinging brought tears to her eyes. Frost glistened like sugar in its dried petals.

She looked from the rose to the house and searched the front window for a form, a glimpse of dark blond hair or the familiar frame of Jeremy standing in the doorway. But when the door did open, it was a pretty young lady with dark hair who stood there with a friendly smile. She wore a simple dress and dried her hands on her apron as Patience and Harry approached.

Patience's knees went weak, and she looked at Harry to speak for them. Mosh wagged his tail.

Harry nodded to her and tipped his hat to the young woman. "Good morrow, miss.

This is Patience Terry, and I am Captain Dunning. We've come a long way from New England to seek Mr. Horton."

"Good morrow to you both. Please come in. I am Rose. Mr. Horton is here, but down at the barn this morning. Let me offer you something to drink and a bite to eat, and I shall send Henry to fetch him."

As she and Harry followed Rose to the kitchen, Patience peered into the blackened rooms. The smell of stale smoke and charred wood, mingled with the burnt odor of horsehair wadding, assailed her. She was heartened to see the kitchen with fresh flooring, walls, and carpentry.

Rose placed tall mugs and a plate of bread and cheese on the table and had Harry and Patience sit. She stepped out the back door and talked to a man who was digging. He set his shovel down and left. To find Jeremy, she presumed.

She was sick at heart and so afraid now of what Jeremy would have to say. Had he forced her out of his mind, determined to move on with his life? Food did not appeal to her. Harry's hand covered hers, and she looked into his eyes only to see they held the same fear.

She heard Jeremy before she saw him. He was running to the back door, and soon it was thrown wide. She stood, tears falling freely, a hand to her lips. His broad shoulders filled the doorway, and his tallness surprised her as it always did. His sleeves were rolled up, and he had sweat on his brow despite the coldness of the day. His green eyes held a question, but only for a moment, and then he closed the distance between them in seconds.

He pulled her to his chest and rocked her, his chin resting in her hair. "I don't believe my eyes. I thought I'd lost you forever."

"I have been so afraid. So afraid of losing you, so afraid of crossing that ocean. And I was so afraid that I had hurt you and I would never have the chance to tell you I am sorry and I love you."

"I am so glad you came. I've missed you, Patience." He held her back and turned to Harry. "I don't believe I'm seeing you either, old friend. You sailed *The Annabelle,* did you not?"

Harry came to life. "Aye, I did. And she came with me. She did well, Jeremy, Patience did."

Jeremy let go of her for a moment and put his hand out. "This is Rose, the caretaker of the house, and Henry is my foreman for the estate. I couldn't save it without them."

Her last doubt was assuaged and her joy

complete. He bent to kiss her waiting lips.

Mosh would not be ignored any longer. He woofed until Jeremy bent down to him. "Oh, Mosh, I should have known you'd come, too." He rubbed the top of the dog's head and then stood. Harry, Rose, and Henry had slipped away. "There is so much to do, Patience. The homes of the mill workers were all destroyed, and the barn too. But we rebuilt them. The house still requires much work, and I need to rebuild the mill. Mowsley has suffered too."

"Can you take me out to see the damage?"

"Yes, of course, I'd like to do that. And I'll take you in to see Mowsley, too."

He pulled her to him and kissed her once more. She couldn't leave his arms again, no matter where he might go.

"Are you all right?"

"Oh yes."

"Did you bring your wedding dress?"

"Oh yes."

"I have the matching combs for it. Patience, I've handled things badly in the past. I was so bent on finding out what I was meant to do after *The Swallow* sank, I didn't consider your feelings or how long you have waited, and I'm sorry for that. I've missed you greatly. But mayhap this was God's way of bringing us together on His terms. It seems we've each discovered something about ourselves and how to trust and depend on God."

"I do think, Jeremy, if you'd stayed in Southold, I'd never have gotten on Harry's ship. You would have, you and Harry would have sailed it, but me? No. I know I wouldn't have. I was so unhappy with you when you left, but standing here with you now, I am so grateful for your sense of duty."

He bent and kissed her, then whispered in her ear, "Will you marry me, Patience? If it cannot be today, then soon. Promise me it shall be soon."

Her heart beat fast, and she could not stand, so she let his strong arms hold her. "Oh yes, Jeremy, yes."

He held her hand and led her to the front porch. They stood looking at the burnt land that stretched before them. Jeremy put his arm around her. "It will take a lot of work."

"It will, but I'll be here, working right beside you."

He kissed her hand. "I like that thought. But first I want to hear all about you and Harry coming across on *The Annabelle.*"

"Very well, I shall tell you. But then I want to hear your stories, too — all of them, and thankfully we have the rest of our lives for that." Her laughter was like wind chimes on the sea. "Now kiss me, Captain Horton. Please kiss me."

# Epilogue

*July 15, 1680*
*Southold*

The summer wind blew her skirt as Mary stood by the grave of her sweet Barney. The heavy blue slate lay over him, with the words he'd written so many years ago etched into the rock. She wiped a tear as she remembered how he'd wished to bring the stone, with the epitaph engraved, with him on their voyage from England to the New World. Had he thought he'd not survive the journey and his name and memory would perish from the earth with him?

Jay and Ben had stood next to her while Caleb, Joshua, and Jonathan lowered their father's casket into the ground. Barney's longtime friend, Reverend John Youngs, had died several years before, so Reverend Joshua Hobart officiated. A hymn sung by their daughters, Hannah, Sarah, Mary, Mercy, and their adopted daughter, Abbey, gave much meaning to the ceremony, as Barney had loved to sing the old hymns in his deep baritone. It was a beautiful service, and now she needed time by herself, next to the husband who had been the love of her life.

She liked that bayberry grew profusely in the cemetery, giving off a sweet scent, and from his grave she could see the house he'd built for them across the road. It was the first timber-framed home built on the east end of Long Island. Their children had been born in that house.

He had been a baker, a founding father of Southold, a magistrate, a member of the General Court of New Haven and Hartford, and much loved by the people.

Two months before, he'd developed a cough that would not abate, and when chest pain and fatigue claimed all of his strength, he took to his bed. A man who was up before dawn to work every minute of the day after spending time in Scripture and prayer, he sensed his journey on this earth was drawing to a close. When he asked Mary to bring him paper and pen to write his last will and testament, she knew his call to his Heavenly home was near.

She loved that he was generous to their sons in the distribution of his vast property, and she was touched that he wanted his Bible to be left to their youngest son, Jonathan. He put much thought into that decision. He provided for their daughters, as well, and because Mercy and Christopher Youngs were just beginning their married life, he left her a feather bed and cooking pots.

That he appointed Mary executrix of his will pleased her greatly and was his final compliment to her business knowledge and abilities. He left her with the new house, his father's ivory-head walking stick, the musket he called Old Quart Pot, and the cask they'd hauled together from Mowsley — the one that Lizzie's children liked to call "Uncle Barney's Money Pot." They still believed he'd brought it filled with gold.

She'd sat by his side during the past few weeks, while his children and grandchildren gathered around him. Friends came from distant places — Dirk from the west end, high-ranking government officials from Massachusetts and Connecticut, and even friends as far away as Barbados. They reminisced about their journeys together and the changes they had witnessed in their lifetimes. The only ones missing were Jeremy and Patience. They were still at Mowsley, and though Mary missed them so, Barney reminded her that they would see them someday in Heaven. In God's own time. They had laid her sweet sister, Lizzie, and Lizzie's husband, Zeke, the year after.

In quiet moments when he slept, Mary sat close, afraid to leave him for even a moment, and ran her fingers over his hands as if she might forget his touch when he was gone. She caressed his cheek and watched his every breath. When he opened his eyes to look at her, she was ready with a smile. At times they talked of the days when he'd taught her to bake, and she told him she'd never make a crisp ginger cake like he did, of that she was certain. In his last few days, she helped him to his chair by the hearth, his white hair still thick, his mossy green eyes as bright as ever. He asked her forgiveness for those difficult early years. But what person goes through life without ever hurting another? He was a human being, after all. He had shown her many times over his love and devotion to her. She told him he'd been forgiven long ago. How she loved that man.

She hadn't wanted to let him go. Tears trickled as she traced the words carved into the blue slate with her finger. Barney had died on July 13 — his eightieth birthday. He'd left an empty place in her heart, but he'd also left a legacy for his children and all the generations to come.

# ACKNOWLEDGMENTS

Which hope we have, as an anchor of the soul, but sure and steadfast, and it entereth into that which is within the veil.
Hebrews 6:19 (1599 Geneva Bible)

I am so thankful for this moment to share with you those who have encouraged and supported me, making it possible for this book, the third in THE SOUTHOLD CHRONICLES series, to come to fruition.

I give humble thanks to God, the Creator of all and the Light of the world. With God, all things are possible.

Thank you to my sweet family who show their support over and over. Thank you to my children, their spouses, and my grandchildren for being patient while Grammy is writing! My mother is forever my inspiration for the Horton stories. Thank you, Mom! My father is the rock of our family and gives me much to aspire to. He reads my manuscripts, and his enthusiasm is an encouragement to me. Thank you, Dad, for always being there. I love you! My husband, Tom, is always there, too. To brainstorm, read, and bring food to the table when need be. Truly, he's my helpmate, my love, and my North Star. Thank you — I love you!

A big, big thank-you to my Revell family for their dedication, expertise, and hard work to bring my stories to publication. I cannot begin to say how much I enjoy knowing and working with my editor, Vicki Crumpton. She is a delight, and I appreciate her wise insight, and I'm so very thankful for her. A big thank-you to editor Barb Barnes and freelance editor Charlene Patterson, Michele Misiak, Lindsay Davis, Twila Bennett, Claudia Marsh, Erin Bartels, Lanette Haskins, Karen Steele, Cheryl Van Andel, and their staff. They all give their best to make my book its best!

A very special thank-you to Barbara Scott and Greg Johnson of the WordServe Literary Agency, for their belief in my story and their dedicated work in bringing the Southold Chronicles to publication. Also, I am forever grateful to literary agent Natasha Kern. Her advice was life changing. Thank you, Natasha!

Warm hugs and a big thank-you to author

Jane Kirkpatrick for her warm, gracious support and advice. I've long been your fan and I'm so honored to call you my friend. Warm hugs and thank-yous to friends and fellow writers Karen Barnett, Patricia Lee, and Tammy Bowers, who took time out of their own busy schedules to critique chapters for me! You three kept me on track!

Thank you to Melissa Andruski and Daniel McCarthy of the Southold Free Library. Dan also works at the Southold Historical Society. Their expertise and friendship mean much to me.

A warm thank-you to my readers — you have joined me on the journey of my heart! A special thank-you to my BookLits, a group of readers who encourage me, pray for me, and joyfully put a shout out for me! I love you all!

# A NOTE FROM THE AUTHOR

It was many years ago that I took my mom, Helen Jean Horton Worley, to Long Island to see the Horton Point Lighthouse, named after our ancestor, Barnabas Horton. And it took a few years to begin writing the stories that filled my thoughts after that journey, but Mary Horton would not let go of my heart. *To Follow Her Heart* concludes THE SOUTHOLD CHRONICLES series, but I cannot tell you how much I have enjoyed delving into the past and creating stories around the ancestors I've lived with in my dreams!

I've connected with many readers who are inspired by their ancestors' stories, and I hope my books encourage others to find their own roots. Robert Penn Warren said, "History cannot give us a program for the future, but it can give us a fuller understanding of ourselves, and of our common humanity, so that we can better face the future." And I love the Corrie Ten Boom quote, "Memories are the key not to the past, but to the future."

A few notes on names: while THE SOUTHOLD CHRONICLES series is based on my ninth great-grandparents' real lives, Patience Terry, my heroine in *To Follow Her Heart,* is completely fictitious. The Terrys are indeed a family that came to Long Island in the 1600s and were instrumental in the founding of Southold, but I created Patience in the first book completely from my imagination. She was a character who grew in my heart — and Jeremy's, too! Not much is known about what became of Jeremy Horton, but family lore would tell you *The Swallow* and all of her records sank, and Jeremy survived and made his way to Massachusetts. While I've not found documents that support this, it did fit my story well and keeps his memory alive, at least in the imagination! The many children of Mary and Barnabas are recorded here, and I've included Abbey as an adopted daughter, as some lore suggests. Harry, like Patience, is completely fictitious. The ship Harry builds with Jeremy is named after my own grandmother, Annabelle Horton.

In my research, I was privileged to walk (literally!) the same paths and roads that Mary and Barnabas Horton tread. I touched the oak cask the Hortons hauled from Old England and the same wooden beams that were hewn from the North Fork timber. When I discovered Barnabas was a baker, I spent a full day at the Alice Ross Hearth Studio in Smithtown, Long Island, preparing food and baking bread just as they did in the seventeenth century. I adored meeting Alice, and I share her passion.

I hope you have enjoyed reading this book as much as I enjoyed writing it!

# ABOUT THE AUTHOR

**Rebecca DeMarino** is the author of *A Place in His Heart* and *To Capture Her Heart,* books one and two of THE SOUTHOLD CHRONICLES, a historical romance series inspired by her ninth great-grandparents, Barnabas and Mary Horton, who sailed from England to the New World in the 1600s and were founding members of Southold, Long Island, New York. She lives in the Pacific Northwest with her husband, Tom. Learn more at www.rebeccademarino .com.